BOOK 2 IN THE PROPHECY SERIES

FUTURE TENSE

A Disillusioned Soldier and a Computer Geek Hold the fate of the World in Their Hands

MARK L. MILLS

ISBN: 978-1-948638-51-7

Published by

Fideli Publishing, Inc.
119 W. Morgan St.
Martinsville, IN 46151

www.FideliPublishing.com

PRINTED IN THE UNITED STATES OF AMERICA

*Dedicated to my beautiful wife Marla, who has stuck with
me through the good and bad times
and to my wonderful children
Tim, Jordan, Jeff, Juliana, Carlos, Jose, and Mariel.
I love you all.*

CHAPTER 1

"All in corner!" the big one yelled in gravel-throated, broken English while wildly waving his AK-47 in the air. The three students and their professor jerked their heads up from their computer screens, frozen in shock. With their horrified facial expressions, they looked like wax figures the sculptor had captured in a moment of terror.

"In corner now!" Fiery eyes burned through a slit in the scarves the two men wore around their heads as they herded Professor Barry Goldschien and his three petrified graduate assistants into a corner like cattle to the slaughter.

"What do you want?" Goldschien stuttered fearfully. He was a small, balding man with a gray beard and a bulbous nose that looked like he knew his way around a bottle and he wore thick, tri-focal specs that looked more like goggles than glasses.

"All copies!"

"Of what?" Dr. Goldschien cried, genuinely confused and terrified.

"You know! Ten seconds!" The tall one jabbed the old man in the stomach with the butt of his gun. Doubling over and belching out a painful groan, the professor suddenly realized he might, indeed, know.

"Ten seconds ... or kill everyone!"

"But, we don't know what you want!" Goldschien feigned ignorance, frantically trying to buy some time.

"Atni al barnamij aw etmoot!" (*Give us program or die!*) the big gunman yelled, apparently forgetting his English as he shoved one of the students over a table, knocking a computer monitor crashing to the floor.

Goldschien understood the word *program* and could guess the rest of it. Next to religion and computer science, his third favorite area of study was linguistics and even in this horrific chaos, he noticed that there was something off about the man's dialect. It sounded contrived, like it wasn't his native tongue, and it almost sounded like Arabic with a Russian accent. He also noted that he looked too big to be a local Arab. "What program?" he said.

"Religion."

Professor Goldschien's face went ashen. "Which religion program? We have many."

"All religions and predictions."

"But, what could you possibly want with the ... ?" The charade was over. He knew now that he was talking about the *Prophecy* program and he wondered how he found out that it might predict the future.

"Ashra. Tissa. Thamanya."

These words Professor Goldschien understood as *ten, nine, eight*.

"But...!"

"Sabba. Sitta." (*Seven. Six.*)

"Wait ... wait ... let's figure out a solution..."

"Khamsa. Arbaa. Thalatha." (*Five. Four. Three.*)

"I can't..."

"Ethnain." (*Two.*)

"O.K! O.K! I'll get it! It's in the safe," Goldschien said as he moved tentatively toward a closet door with a combination lock on it.

"Waqiff!" (*Stop!*) the big one yelled as he jumped toward the professor, "Now open," he said in near-perfect English.

Adjusting his glasses over his pink, plump nose, Goldschien pushed several buttons nervously, but the lock didn't open.

Grabbing graduate student Sarah Thompson by her coal-black hair and jerking her toward him as she screamed in agonizing fear, the big one yelled "Any tricks, I kill the whore!"

"All right!" the professor yelled with sweat pouring down his face like a waterfall, "I just hit the wrong numbers." He re-did the combination and got it right this time. There in the closet were several clusters of supercomputer servers with fiber channel cards.

The gunman went right for the control panel and clearly knew what he was looking for as he stabbed at the keyboard. "What is password?" he demanded and Goldschien gave it up promptly.

"Hathe al nihaya," (*This is it.*) he said to his partner, seemingly satisfied with what he saw on the monitor. Then he yelled, "No copies?"

"No."

Jerking Sarah's head down again while twisting her hair in a knot, he said, "If you lie, she dies!" He seemed to enjoy the pain he was inflicting on her.

"No, there are no copies ... for security!"

The masked man let go of Sarah's now mangled hair as she fell to the floor in whimpering sobs. He removed all the computer cards delicately and put them in his briefcase. Turning around quickly he nodded to his comrade and they both sprayed all the computers in the room with bullets shredding them into metal shards. The professor and his students quaked at the gunfire, but they began to breathe a slight sigh of relief, hoping that the men had gotten what they came for and might now leave. But the hope was premature as the big one said cooly, "Ektilhom kolhom" (*Kill them all.*) and they nonchalantly shot all four of them to death. The two then ran out the door screaming "Alla Akbar!" (*God is great!*).

The same nightmarish scene was being played out in three different locations across Jerusalem. It looked like anyone who ever had anything to do with Professor Goldschien's software program was being systematically murdered. The men who had killed him and his students rushed back to their own Jerusalem apartment and handed the computer cards to the group's western-educated computer specialist, Ali Masef. Masef arranged all the cards into his own RAID array chassis and began first looking for the names of everyone that had ever worked on the program to make sure they hadn't missed anyone. For security reasons the list was quite short. In fact, only nine people had ever seen the program and Ali now checked the names against the list his big colleague had given him.

"Shakla jameel," (*Looks good.*) he said as he poured over the names one-by-one. Then he got to the last name on the screen ... a tenth name that appeared nowhere else. "Edna Moshkila!" (*We've got trouble!*), he said excitedly, "Wahid esma Mark Jacobs" (*Someone named Mark Jacobs.*).

Viciously pounding his fist on the table, the big one shouted in flawless English, "How did we miss it?" His previous performance with Professor Goldschien and his students had been an act. He often feigned broken English to appear more threatening. He knew a rabid, ignorant terrorist seemed more dangerous than the Cambridge-educated man he was.

But before Ali could answer, his computer monitor rapidly started filling with random numbers and letters. "Fairous!" (*Virus!*) he shrieked at the top of his lungs, fingers hitting the keyboard at break-neck speed as he tried to stop the worm from spreading. The screen kept filling page after page with gibberish even as he tried every trick he knew to stop it.

"Turn it off!" screamed his boss.

"I can't!" was all Ali could answer with disconsolate resignation as he threw up his hands in despair. "It's destroyed!" he finally said, dejectedly in perfect English. He had gone to Princeton.

"What do you mean?"

"They put a self-destruct virus in the program that no one could detect and it wiped it out." With the big man seething and cursing up a storm, Ali suddenly remembered that he had printed out the tenth name and address. Ripping it from the printer, he waved it in his face.

* * *

"The way I figure it ... it's good job security," said Scott as they perched on a hot, dry desert ridge, looking across the brown landscape at a hamlet of faded gray, pockmarked buildings.

"How's that?" Chuck asked, thinking more about the scorching desert heat than anything else. It was 130 degrees of sweltering, blistering hot that pierces your flesh like tiny daggers, penatrating your muscles and permeating your being all the way down to your bone marrow.

"Remember when we were kids and we'd catch lightning bugs at night?" asked Scott in an uncharacteristically nostalgic tone.

"Didn't do a lotta' that in San Diego."

"Well, we did in Texas. Anyway, as soon as you filled yer' jar with 'em you'd look out in the field and see a million more ... just like these jihadis."

Chuck wasn't sure if he wanted that much job security, especially when it comes to fighting a war he was feeling increasingly doubtful and guilt-ridden about. He knew he had killed many people who didn't deserve it, including too many innocent civilians who were simply in the wrong place at the wrong time. *How many died in all the airstrikes I called in*, he wondered with a heavy heart. But he was also plagued by all the jihadists he had killed in combat and there had been many. *Did they really deserve to die*, he asked himself. His doubts about the war and his part in it were growing and he didn't like it.

"Collateral damage," his superiors called it, but he was having a hard time accepting that. He also knew that it was primarily about the oil. But what he didn't understand was why we needed Middle-Eastern oil when America was the world's biggest producer of crude oil. *Guess we're just too far in bed with the Middle-East to pull out*, he thought, *and especially with Saudi Arabia*. That bothered him a little, considering their abysmal record on human rights.

He briefly thought about their recent cold-blooded killing of a Saudi journalist who was critical of their crown prince and the American president's reluctance to condemn them for it. The Turks even gave the CIA an audio tape of Jamal Khashoggi's torture and murder and they concluded that the prince ordered the execution. *I guess money trumps morality every time*, he mused with pun intended. But he knew this line of thinking would get him nowhere and would actually distract him from his mission, so he switched his attention to the village ahead. "It's quiet," was all he said as he was a man of few words.

"Too quiet," said Scott with a sweet Texas twang dripping into his ear like thick, syrupy barbeque sauce.

"How long've ya' been waitin' to say that?" Chuck said with a slight, wry grin while eyeing the strangely empty street.

"About 10 years."

"Only 10?"

"Maybe 12."

"We'll go in on-foot," Chuck spoke softly into his radio. He knew that if they drove in, there could easily be a few deadly roadside bombs waiting for them. Besides, a convoy would tip off the guy they were looking for and he would most likely fade away into the tunnels running under the town.

Chuck was Lieutenant Charles Lansing and Scott was his second-in-command, Master Sergeant Scott Sampson. With chestnut tan skin from the desert sun, short blonde hair, sometimes-sparkling blue eyes, and a sculpted muscular physique on a six-foot-one, 180-pound frame, Chuck sometimes looked out-of-place in this brutal, unforgiving environment. He looked every inch the all-American boy and some of his men occasionally referred to him as Captain America, though never to his face. But lines of the worst life has to offer were beginning to form on his once angelic face and the sparkle was beginning to fade from his eyes.

His was a childhood born of tragedy. His mother died in a car accident when he was too young to remember and his father died a year later from cancer. He had a few vague, cloudy memories of his mother calling him Charlie and singing to him, but all he remembered of his father was that he was a police detective in Washington, D. C. and his name was Jack. He also didn't remember much about what happened to him after Jack died, other than that he was adopted by a single woman named Jan. She died two years later from a brain aneurysm. Young Charlie talked very little during these trying years and Jan often worried that he was depressed.

But, after a short stint in a foster home, he was adopted by Don and Claire Lansing and moved to San Diego. He remembered Don asking him if there was anything he wanted in his new life and he said, "I would like to be called Chuck." It was Chuck from then on. He suddenly had an instant family with a younger brother named Mike and, for the first time in a long time, he was able to look forward instead of back.

He was a young man with an old soul whose men looked at him as a grizzled, timeworn, and unpredictable warrior who was way beyond his years. Most of the time, he had a look of powerful serenity on his face. But lately, there was something in his sometimes-smoldering gaze that suggested he was either planning something in his head or getting ready to spontaneously jump into action. You could never tell which one it would be. Chuck was a born fighter who cared more about his men than he did about himself and he was the leader of this special forces' unit called the Mad Dogs.

Scott was a big, dark-haired Texan who loved everything western. Some nights he dreamed that he was a gunslinger riding the open range in the 1800's. His favorite author was famed western writer Louis L'Amour and his favorite song was Bon Jovi's *Wanted Dead or Alive*, which he often sang out-of-tune and at the top of his lungs, driving his comrades crazy. "I'm a cowboy," he would squeal, "On a steel horse I ride. I'm wanted ... dead or alive."

Here his open range was a scorching desert wasteland and his steel horse was an armored Humvee. He never missed an opportunity to tell you that Texas is the biggest and best state in the union, that Texas barbeque is the best on the planet, and that Texans are the toughest people in the world. He had the cocky look and swagger of an outlaw and the men sometimes called him Tex. He was also the best strategist around. When their superiors laid out a battle plan for them, they welcomed Scott's ideas because they were often better than their own. He seemed to always know how to get the maximum number of kills with the lowest risk to his men, no small feat in this high-casualty battle zone.

They approached from the east with the blazing sun beating down behind them. "Always have the sun at your back," Chuck told his men, "Then you can see them better than they can see you." An informant had ratted out an ISIS militant who was supposedly hiding out in the village and said he would have some valuable information. To the Mad Dogs, *informant* was a dirty word because many of them worked both sides of the street. They were often working for the enemy and would supply false information to lure U.S. soldiers into an ambush.

As they walked silently along the dirt path, Private Jim Hawkins softly asked one of his notoriously strange questions. "Ya' know when it's the worst time to have a heart attack?" he said, gazing blankly at the horizon. No one answered as they concentrated on the path ahead, looking for possible land-mines.

"Well, I'll tell ya' when. It's while yer' playin' Charades."

The Dogs who heard him had to think about it for a few seconds before they started to smile inwardly. Not getting a reaction, Hawkins asked another weird one with, "Have ya' ever farted so hard so hard it cracked your back?"

But the Dogs were too busy focusing on the trail and the village up ahead to humor him. They were a little worried as they thought about all the past bad intelligence they had gotten that had put them in real danger. Walking slowly by abandoned, bombed-out buildings, they methodically made their way toward the town center.

"Yeah, this could be our Alamo," murmured Scott in a low drawl.

"Let's focus on this place here and now so we don't get surprised," Chuck answered, "Heads on a swivel boys." Calling his men *boys*, when many of them were older than him, may have irritated some soldiers, but not these guys. They knew him to be a tough, battle-hardened warrior who was exceptionally smart and their best bet for survival. After two tours in Iraq and Afghanistan, he had more kills and had seen more death than most and they knew that if anyone could bring them back alive, it was him.

In fact, on many missions he told his men that their main job of the day was to survive. At the same time, he often wildly risked his own life while telling them to protect theirs. They followed his every order without question because he never asked them to do anything he wouldn't do himself. His seeming lack of fear combined with an incredibly strong survival instinct made him the ultimate fighting man and a dependable leader. They also trusted his instincts, although sometimes his actions were unorthodox and some thought a little crazy.

Hugging the gray, bullet-riddled buildings, the Mad Dogs moved cautiously down the street, their senses keenly aware of the quiet emptiness. "What's up," Chuck asked as Private Mike Sandstone fumbled with the big .50 caliber machine gun he was trying to carry.

"I'm good," answered Sandstone, finally getting it under control.

"I wouldn't go that far," said Hawkins, "Just let us know if you can't handle it all by yer' little self."

"Up yers' Hawkins," said Sandstone, never one to ask for help, "I'm tryin' to do a little multi-taskin' here."

And there it was, the response Jim had been hoping for. "Multi-tasking?" he said slyly, "The only multi-taskin' you ever do is scratchin' yer' ass with one hand and pickin' yer' nose with the other."

"Shove it fool."

"Oh, I'm sorry ... I meant scratchin' yer' ass with one hand and pickin' yer' nose with the same hand ... in that order."

"Just can't get enough a' yer' adolescent wit Hawkins."

"Okay I guess yer' real multi-taskin' is jerkin' off while you're lookin' at porn."

"Yer' a pig," said Sandstone.

"I wish," Hawkins shot back, "Did ya' know a pig's orgasm lasts up to 30 minutes."

Mike could only shake his head while the men around him contemplated what a thirty-minute orgasm would be like and if it was really true. It was, but their thoughts were interrupted by Scott bringing them back to reality.

"That'll do," he said with a slight chuckle, "Now pay attention to those windows up there."

Normally, they all liked Jim Hawkins' baiting their comrades with insults and then heaping abuse on them for their responses, but not today. They were becoming increasingly aware that they might be walking into an ambush. Suddenly, their deadly suspicions were confirmed as machine gun fire erupted from the second story of two abandoned buildings on the north side of the road joined by other shooting from the street-level windows on the south side.

"So much for the reliable informant!" yelled Scott, diving behind a crumbling wall as Chuck and the Dogs took refuge behind two burned out cars and a broken down, mud-brick building. They were following more of Chuck's advice to always scope out any cover *before* you get shot at.

"Yeah, it's an oxymoron like military intelligence," Hawkins yelled back as he dove for cover with heavy fire shredding the cracked asphalt around his feet. He was a lean, wiry, yet muscular man with arms too long for his body. He was also one of the best marksmen in the unit and a prodigious boxer and martial arts fighter. Most of all, however, he never missed a chance to make a sarcastic remark, even under fire.

But insults, sarcasm, and vulgar observations weren't Hawkins' only talents. He also swore that he could sing through his butt. Chuck remembered when Scott bet him a paycheck that he couldn't do it and that led to the rest of the Dogs betting in a gambling frenzy. Hawkins promptly farted, "Mary had a little lamb" and took everyone's money.

"That's too simple," Ron Jenkins had said, "You gotta' do a real song."

"Alright, but you gotta' back it up with some *real* cash."

"Okay. Then *we* come up with the song, not you."

"That should be worth about 10 to 1 odds … let's do it."

And so ensued a flurry of bets from the Dogs and other units on the base. Then came the scramble to think of a song too hard for anyone to fart. Several ideas came and went with Mike Sandstone coming up with the winning tune.

"*Wide Awake*," he yelled and they all agreed that the old Katie Perry hit would be a hard song to sing, let alone fart.

"Piece a' cake," said Hawkins as he proceeded to butt-belch a near perfect-pitched rendition of the song, sounding a little like an out-of-tune Fluggle Horn, and made a lot of money doing it. No one could prove it, but they suspected that he and Sandstone had secretly chosen the song beforehand. The fact remained, however, that Hawkins still successfully sang it through his butt. In any event, that was Jim Hawkins, always obsessed with flatulence and other bodily functions and an expert at degenerate insults.

But not today. With bullets whizzing around their heads, all he was doing with the oxymoron remark was stating a fact. Army Intelligence, AKA the CIA, had been giving them far too much bad information lately and putting all of their lives at increasing risk. They were sick of it.

"Let's face it," Hawkins said on more than one occasion, "These CIA clowns are whiter-than-white. What real information is any self-respecting Arab gonna' give to the great white satan anyway?"

He ignored the fact that some of the more reliable informants were Israeli Mossad spies who looked like Arabs and were able to infiltrate some of the lower-level terrorist groups. But that job had a short life expectancy and there weren't too many of them left. He did admit, though, that the Mossad agents were a tough bunch and they made the CIA look like boy scouts.

"Most of the spooks are dufuses," Hawkins said once, "They went to the ivy leaguers and don't know their ass from a hole in the ground. You know the kind. They go to a steakhouse and order a chef's salad."

"Yeah," said Scott, playing along, "One time I saw one of 'em eatin' French fries with a fork ... with a fork!"

"Probably didn't wanna' get grease on his trigger finger," chimed in Steve Chamberlain, one of the Dogs' snipers. He had a wry sense of humor and you could never tell if he was kidding or not.

"My point exactly," said Hawkins, not really having a point.

Chuck usually stayed out of these conversations because unbeknownst to his men, he had been thinking about joining the CIA when he finished his tour of duty. He had actually wanted to be an FBI agent since he was a boy. But ever since a CIA officer approached him about working for the agency after his military career, he had been giving it some serious thought.

There was no time to think about any of that now, however, as they were pinned down on the street with nowhere to go. They couldn't hit the snipers because the apartment windows had been blockaded with slits just big enough for their gun barrels. In the past, the snipers had shot from the roof, but now they were afraid of drones overhead.

Chuck would have called in a drone here, but he knew the nearest one was at least 30 minutes away and they couldn't wait that long. He also knew that eventually the snipers would pick them off one-by-one and then move in for the final kill.

Without warning, he suddenly started stripping off his clothes as his men gawked in disbelief.

Although they had gotten used to his sometimes-unpredictable behavior, this was going a little over the top. Even in the chaos they noticed his carved body with bulging muscles. Out-of-uniform he looked like he would be more at home paddling a surfboard than in a hot combat zone and that is exactly what he used to do as a kid growing up in San Diego. When he wasn't quarterbacking his high school football team or setting new records on the track team, he was surfing the blue Pacific.

"What the hell!" Scott shouted. But Chuck didn't hear him as he stripped down to his shorts and wrapped two nylon ropes around his neck.

"Here we go again," said Hawkins calmly.

Over the thunderous gunfire, Chuck shouted, "If I make it to the roof, shoot the propane tanks!"

"Whaa..." Scott began, but it was too late as he watched his underwear-clad lieutenant take off running with two grenades in each hand. "What propane tanks?" he turned around and screamed at his men. No one knew.

Stunned at the strange site of a near-naked man sprinting down the south side of the street, the shooters in the upper floors of the north side stopped shooting for a few seconds. It was just long enough to let Chuck build up his speed. When the shock wore off and they resumed their firing, he was moving too fast for them to hit him and he was too close to the buildings on the south side for the ground-level snipers to get a clear shot at him.

As he continued his mad dash with bullets zipping by and missing him by inches, he pinpointed the lower-level gun slots and tossed a grenade into each one. One-at-a-time, the explosions went off. By the time the upper level snipers realized what he was doing, Chuck was two-thirds of the way down the street. Miraculously, he made it to the end of the road just as the upstairs snipers began shooting again at the rest of the Dogs.

Meanwhile, Chuck found a stairway up to the roof of the north side buildings. *Bingo!* he said to himself as he found what he was looking for. Two propane tanks sat in a corner. Some locals used propane to cook and they sometimes stored the tanks on the roof. Taking the two ropes from around his neck, he swiftly strung each through the handles of the tanks. Then, he skillfully lowered each one over the side of the roof so that they hung in front of the two boarded up windows.

"Shoot the tanks!" Scott yelled as he suddenly realized what Chuck was talking about. The Dogs sprayed the propane tanks with bullets and they both exploded, incinerating the boards and hopefully everything and everyone inside.

Glad they weren't empty, Chuck breathed a short sigh of relief. His men knew they didn't have much time as they ran for the building and hurtled up the steps to the first apartment. Chuck suddenly appeared at the second apartment and with one quick motion, they kicked in both doors at the same time. What they saw stopped them cold. Two enemy soldiers lay dead on the floor with a third severely wounded, but that wasn't the horrifying part.

There were also three children lying dead on the floor with their bodies ripped to shreds from the explosion. One boy, at least what was left of him, looked to be about 12 years old and still cradled an AK-47 in his small hands. Staring at the small forms in disbelief Chuck caught a slight movement out of the corner of his eye. He turned quickly as the wounded man on the floor tried to raise his gun. A quick bullet to the head cut that move short, but he noticed something odd about the man. He walked over to him and tore off the scarf covering his head and face. Long black curls of hair tumbled down the dead jihadist's shoulders and he realized it wasn't a *him* at all. He had just killed a woman.

Stumbling into the next apartment, he saw that everyone there was dead, including two more children and another woman. "I guess they got their women and kids fightin' their battles now," Scott said, trying to lighten the mood in the dismal room. No one responded as they began somberly searching the bodies. Without a word, Private Juan Rodriguez handed Chuck his clothes. The incident made them all hate the enemy for involving women and children in their fight. Some of them believed that if women and children were fighting in the war, they deserved to die, but he wasn't so sure. *How hard could it be to convince oppressed women and orphaned children that we are the bad guys? Besides*, he thought, *these people wouldn't be lying here dead if we weren't here.*

Then Chuck remembered what his father, Don Lansing, had said about that in their last conversation while he was home on leave. "They don't have much choice," he said, "Because they don't have a military and they need all the help they can get. To them it's a holy war and when yer' fightin' for God, everyone's a soldier." At that moment, it dawned on him that while many people may have no choice, countries do. America's choice was whether or not to invade a sovereign nation and he was beginning to wonder if it had made the right decision. He also had to ask himself if these innocent deaths were worth the cause he thought he was fighting for.

Questioning the war was new to him and he didn't like it. As they drove back to the base, he thought about what his dad had told him and that made his growing doubts even worse. "We never should've gone into Iraq in the first place." he said, "But then, I guess I'd rather do the right thing for the wrong reasons than the wrong thing for the right reasons." Don was a hard-looking, muscular man with an incongruous beer belly and a sculpted face full of deep-chiseled lines, each with its own story to tell. And he had intense, X-Ray eyes that sometimes seemed to burn right through you.

"What wrong reasons?" Chuck had asked.

"The non-existent weapons of mass destruction for one," came the obvious answer, "But more than that ... to the Muslims, invading Iraq was just another crusade in a long line of crusades and another war on Islam."

"That was a long time ago."

"Yeah and they have a long memory. They had over 200 years of crusades from Europe killin' 'em and tryin' to convert 'em to Christianity. Before that, it was Napoleon and after that it was England. They're sick of foreigners tryin' to run their lives and re-create their governments. All they see is outsiders invading their sovereign nation and stealin' their oil ... and why wouldn't they, since that's exactly what we're doing."

"Don't ya' think a lot of 'em are grateful that we took down Saddam?" Chuck had asked.

"I'm sure the Shiites are since he oppressed them for so long, but many more Muslims still saw it as another crusade and can ya' blame 'em? They've been invaded so many times in so many crusades, that's the only way they *can* see it. We're involved right now in six Islamic countries and ya' know how many Muslim nations we've bombed, invaded, or occupied in the last 40 years?"

"No, but I have a feeling yer' gonna' tell me."

"Fourteen! Fourteen countries and along the way, we supported some of their scumbag dictators like the Shah of Iran. The Muslim reaction to all this was a rise in extreme Wahhabism and Salafism and the beginning of the extremists like Al Qaeda and ISIS."

"Spoken like a true history professor," Chuck said, which is what his father was, "So lemme' get this straight, *we* caused the rise of terrorism?"

"In a way. We gave new life to a weakened Al Qaeda and gave ISIS a big crop of new recruits."

"Oh please!" Chuck felt like he had just been kicked in the gut and had the wind knocked out of him. The idea that America inadvertently boosted Al Qaeda and recruited for ISIS stabbed his heart like a knife.

"Yeah, Al Qaeda was fadin' until we launched what Islamists see as another crusade," said Don casually, "When we came in with guns blazin' they picked up a lotta' support from other Muslims."

"Don't ya' think they'dve come in even if we weren't there?"

"Not if Saddam had anything to say about it. He didn't like 'em because he was secular and they're Islamic die-hards. But, more than that, he was afraid if he let 'em in, they would eventually overthrow *him*. Besides, the Iraqi people didn't particularly care for Al Qaeda either, but they liked us even less, especially since we invaded their sovereign country. Nothing brings opposing sides together like a common enemy." Don also taught Middle-Eastern Studies.

"Okay. The invasion may've strengthened Al Qaeda, but what about recruiting for ISIS?" Chuck said skeptically.

"Well, sacking all the Hussein loyalists, the entire military, and all the Iraqi policemen was a start. The quarter-million cops and soldiers we fired suddenly needed a home, and they found one ... with ISIS. Besides a paycheck, it offered them a way out of their miserable existence, not to mention a solution to the world's problems. Namely, they promised to bring back the Caliphate and rule by Sharia law. You know, that Islamic legal system that'll cleanse the world of evil western influences and the problems that go along with 'em."

"Ya' know ... hindsight is always 20/20 and ya' gotta' admit, it seemed like a good idea at the time ... gettin' rid of the old guard and startin' over from scratch."

"Maybe, but we didn't think it all the way through when we did it. At first, the *old guard* led daily protests asking for their jobs back, but we ignored them and then they got desperate. They may've been strange bedfellows, but these guys had to go with whoever would pay them and that was ISIS. Then, of course, it got even worse when the Maliki government went down and those guys turned up with ISIS too."

"Oh, come on. They joined ISIS for the jobs! You gotta' be kiddin' me."

"Well, I spose' it was a little dogma too. ISIS gave 'em a spiritual cause to believe in that was a lot bigger than themselves and a chance to do their divine duty and fight a holy war against the infidel. And let's face it, America is about as infidel as they come."

"So, now we *created* ISIS!"

"No, but we sure made it easy for 'em to recruit more guys and now ISIS and Al Qaeda are competing with each other for followers. What really hurt, though, was the firing of all of those government bureaucrats. There was no one left to run things like the power grid and the hydro-electric plants."

"Yeah, I remember that."

"Once we got rid of the bureaucrats, the police, and the soldiers, we didn't have much to take their place so, who'd we get? A buncha' criminals and extremists on the police force and in the military. The chaos gave ISIS an opening to move in and move in, they did. By 2014 they had seized about a third of Iraq."

"But one thing you didn't mention is that the police and army were Hussein's Sunnis. If we'dve kept 'em, they would've butchered the Shiites."

"Ya' mean like the Shias are doing to the Sunnis right now?"

"Yeah," Chuck had to admit, "They're takin' their revenge for all those years of Sunni oppression, aren't they."

"But, it didn't have to go like that if we'd just done our homework and paid a little more attention to history."

Here comes the history lesson, thought Chuck, but he simply said, "What history?"

"Like when Nelson Mandela became President of South Africa after Apartheid. He didn't fire a single white bureaucrat, policeman, or soldier and these were the people who had abused, exploited, and killed his people. But he knew if he did, there would be no working government and it would be anarchy, not to mention that it might start an Afrikaner rebellion."

"The fact remains that we took out an evil dictator."

"And re-kindled the war between the Sunnis and the Shiites. Don't get me wrong son, some guys do need killin', but maybe Hussein wasn't one of 'em. As bad as he was, he was the only one keepin' everybody in check. He was also Iran's number one enemy and takin' him out made it the most powerful country in the region. That's a big problem since it's a major sponsor of terrorism. That's why Bush Senior didn't go after Hussein in the first war, because of these kinds of unintended consequences."

Just then the truck hit a deep pothole in the road and snapped Chuck back to the present. He hadn't thought much about this conversation and he wished he could forget about it now because it brought a whole new crop of doubts flooding into his head. Then, he suddenly realized that the first few seeds of doubt were inadvertently planted by his father way back then and now they were beginning to sprout. He didn't like them and knew it was dangerous because it could make a soldier hesitate for that crucial second on the battlefield and might get people killed. Luckily, Jim Hawkins interrupted his gloomy contemplations with one of his bathroom witticisms.

"Don't ya' hate the public restrooms that have the really thin toilet paper?" he said to no one in particular.

"Ya' dumb bastard," countered Private Intan Hasanov, the only Indonesian-American in the group, "It's so you don't use too much paper."

"But that's the point. You always end up pulling more thin paper off the roll than if you could've unrolled a shorter, thicker strip."

Here we go, thought Chuck as he realized what Hawkins was up to. His silly questions often set his comrades up for a hazing.

"And besides," Hawkins added, "You get poop on your fingers."

"Big deal! Yer' lucky you got toilet paper at all. My mom wiped my ass with her foot in the village latrine." Hasanov knew he shouldn't have said it as soon as the words came out of his mouth.

"I thought I smelled somethin' funky last time I had her ankles around my ears," shot back Hawkins and there it was.

"Yer' dead Hawkins!" Hasanov jumped out of his seat and lunged at him.

"One of these days, I'm sure," was Jim's only response in an ultra-calm voice and not moving an inch.

Jumping in-between them, Chuck said simply, "Save it for the bad guys boys," and gently guided Hasanov back to his seat.

"Yes sir," he said as he sat down, "But, why in the hell would anyone take the time to think of this sick stuff?"

Chuck often wondered the same thing, but for now he was actually glad for the distraction from his disheartening thoughts. The new ideas were vexing and he wanted to quickly shove them out of his head. So, he grabbed onto the first thing that came into his mind, which was the strange folder full of papers he found hidden in his parents' garage when he was home on leave. He was checking some of his old teen-age hiding places when he found it behind a loose brick in the wall. It was labeled *Prophecy and Redemption* and the papers were full of philosophical writings about life and death.

Sifting through them, he found an old encrypted email that looked like it had been deciphered. It was about a new computer program someone was testing to see if it could predict future terrorist attacks and it was called *Prophecy*. Across the top of the email, someone had scribbled, "Is this the prophecy I've been waiting for?" The rest of the papers lived up to the other part of the title, *Redemption*, because they sounded like whoever wrote them was looking for some kind of absolution for past sins. He couldn't imagine why they would be hidden in his parents' garage, but found them interesting enough to photocopy and bring back to Iraq to read when he was bored. He called them *The Book* and one passage seemed particularly relevant right now.

What is a Man?

The measure of a man is not how much wealth or fame
he has. It's not about how many people like and respect him

or how many friends he has. The measure of a man's life lies in his service to humanity, fighting for what is right, and improving other peoples' lives. And if he has to kill a few bad guys to do it and it's for a good cause, so be it. The real measure of a man is if he leaves this world even slightly better off than he found it, especially if it takes a sacrifice on his part to do it. The more you sacrifice for others, the higher your reward later. If he does all that and worships his God in the process, he will be rewarded in the afterlife. Call it karma or whatever you want. But the one thing I do not want is for my life to mean nothing – for my existence to change nothing. Human nature and its resulting politics don't change much and it is true that the more things change, the more they remain the same. I can't do anything about that. All I ask is to make a little dent in life's fabric, a little change, a little improvement. Isn't that all anyone can ask? Instead of trying to change the world, I am going to try to leave my mark on a small part of it.

It was written on what appeared to be an old dirty placemat of some kind and Chuck couldn't quite make out the faded words in the lower right-hand corner. It looked like "Al-Haj Hussein," but he couldn't be sure. He also couldn't quite figure out whose handwriting was on the notes and he could barely make out some of the scribbling. The part about killing bad guys did bother him a bit because he was beginning to wonder exactly *who* the bad guys were. He also wondered how *bad* they actually were and how *good* the good guys were. For some reason, he couldn't shake the old song by 70's rocker Dave Mason that goes, *"There ain't no good guys. There ain't no bad guys. There's only you and me and we just disagree."*

But the weird writings weren't the only things in the folder and he now thought about one item in particular. It was an old ID card with a younger Don Lansing's picture on it. The name under the picture was worn and almost illegible, but it looked a little like *Don Forester*. Looking at it more closely, however, he realized the "o" in Don could be an "a." He wondered why his dad would have a fake ID, but didn't give it much thought after that.

* * *

"At least 8 dead in four separate shootings. All academics affiliated with the University of Jerusalem and one rabbi." The aging TV belched out its bad news. Like poison it wanted to purge from its system, the electronic vomit kept coming just as graduate student Mark Jacobs reached for his pot pipe. The report splashed around the tired old apartment in-between beer cans and computer equipment and froze his arm in mid-air. His mesmerized gaze fell on the television set and he felt like he was in a foggy trance. But suddenly a shrill ring pierced the spell like a pin popping a carnival balloon as he numbly fumbled for his phone. His mouth opened, but no sound came out.

"Did you see it?" his friend, Julie Beckman said breathlessly.

No answer.

"Did you see the news?" she screamed.

"Yeah," Mark said in a stunned whisper.

"What's going on?"

"I don't know. I just ... it just started."

"You have to leave right now! Pack some things and get out! I'll meet you at our place."

"Why?" he asked, stupefied.

"Think about it! You're next! Get out now!"

As the blood rushed to his head, Mark ran for his knapsack which held the computer cards containing Professor Goldschien's *Prophecy* program. He had secretly copied it to work on at home. Grabbing the bag, he headed for the door, but stopped dead in his tracks as he heard footsteps pounding up the creaking outer staircase. Frozen in time and feeling like he was under water, his head instinctively scanned the room and then locked onto the closet.

The building was old and one of the flat's previous tenants was a Jewish carpenter who had survived the Polish holocaust. Recalling the days of hiding from the Nazi's, he had installed a small hidden compartment behind a false closet wall and that's where Mark bolted. He loved gadgets and had programmed a remote-control device for all of his electronics, which he now grabbed on the run. He also snatched a glass containing a solvent he used to clean his small tools and shoved it in the microwave. He didn't know where that idea came from, maybe an old spy movie. Then, quickly jerking the pouch of computer cards from his knapsack and sticking it in his pants, he pulled the hidden door open and slid into a space just big enough for his slight frame. Crouching down on bended knees, he tried to pull the panel closed, but it wouldn't budge.

A sharp pang of fear shot through his body as he now heard men speaking in Arabic out in the hallway. He pulled again, but still the panel was stuck. His heart pounded furiously and the sweat oozed from his pores as the men began breaking down the apartment door. Finally, summoning up a strength he didn't know he had, he pulled on the trap door with every ounce of his being and it suddenly came unstuck with a squealing sound you can only get from wood scraping wood. It crashed closed with a loud thud at the same time his front door flew off its hinges. The next few excruciating seconds were agonizing while he worried that the men had heard the door slam shut. If they did, it would only be a matter of time before they found the compartment and he was a dead man. But they didn't.

After an hour of sitting in the same position, Mark started to feel a cramp in his leg and realized he couldn't endure the pain for very long. He knew he shouldn't do it, but the throbbing ache left him little choice. It was either move it slightly and risk the men outside hearing it or wait until the pain was so unbearable that it would probably move involuntarily and ensure that they would hear it. As he started to move, he suddenly remembered his meditation.

He hadn't done it in a long time and used to make fun of his college roommate Seth Olsen who was a big meditator. "Eim," Seth would softly chant trying to get into a deep, transcendent state to which Mark would ask "You're what?"

"Eim," Seth would say again and again.

"You're what?" he would say each time until Seth finally gave up.

He then drifted back to his roommate's obsession with totally worthless information like the discontinuities in movies. They are the scenes that the continuity director missed, like when a character is holding something in one scene and not in the next. But then, he seemed to recall that Seth had made a lot of money writing a book about all those movie screw-ups. He also wondered if his old roommate was a little obsessive-compulsive. But all that now had to take a back-seat to his more immediate problem of trying to meditate his pain away.

CHAPTER 2

"Take a couple of hours off lieutenant and then come to my office for another briefing," Captain Sam Johnson said as he met the Mad Dogs' truck.

"Yes, sir," Chuck said saluting, "Let's hit the mess men."

Two hours later, it started out like too many other briefings from the captain. "It's a routine mission," Johnson said, but his face belied little confidence in his own words. He could only tell him what Army Intelligence told him and hope that the information was good. This one involved the Dogs patrolling a neighborhood that was reported to be protecting some militants. But there had been so many neighborhoods that turned out to be completely devoid of jihadists that Chuck wondered about the validity of any of the intelligence they were getting.

But duty called and they began walking the neighborhood, looking right and left, anticipating death at every turn. They found nothing suspicious and began to relax with the feeling that it was another wild goose chase. Then, from nowhere, a shot rang out.

"Over there!" Luis Salgado yelled pointing to a small house at the end of the street.

Anxiously, but warily they advanced, alternately taking turns one-by-one. They were surprised that more shots didn't come out of the house, but did as their training had taught them and approached it as if they would come at any moment. As usual, Chuck reached the front door first and signaled that he would break it in.

1 ... 2 ... 3, he counted on three fingers and then broke in the door only to charge into a strange scene. There, in the living room, was what looked like an Iraqi family standing over a dead girl lying on the floor. Still holding a handgun, a man was standing over her looking despondent.

"Atnie al mosadas!" (*Give me the gun!*), Chuck knew that much Arabic as he held out his hand. The man handed him the pistol. "Get Tariq in here!" he yelled. The Dogs usually took Tariq Muhammad with them as their interpreter and sometimes found him to be just as crazy and courageous as they were. From what they could tell, his family had been killed by the jihadists and he had nothing to lose.

Tariq rushed into the modest house and immediately shouted to the family, "Matha hadath?" (*What happened?*).

A woman was crying in anguish in the corner while an older man spoke to Tariq in Arabic. He then translated the tragic story with a look of gloomy resignation on his face.

"ISIS kidnapped his daughter," he stopped and it seemed as if he was having a hard time finding the words.

"Yeah," Scott Sampson said, "And then what?"

"They said they would rape and kill her if her brother didn't quit the Iraqi police force and he did. This is her brother," he motioned toward the man who had just handed Chuck the gun. He also appeared to have a tear in his eye. The old man kept talking, but Tariq hesitated again.

"Get on with it," Chuck said, getting a little impatient.

"They let her go." Another hesitation.

The Dogs were getting a little confused. By this time, with the old man saying much more than Tariq was translating, the Dogs could tell their translator was holding something back. Not knowing if there were militants just around the corner, they were getting a little edgy. Finally, Scott blurted out, "There's no time for this shit Tariq, just spit it out."

"Okay, okay," said the reluctant translator, "This was an honor killing. The brother killed her because the kidnapping tarnished the family's honor. It is ... tradition."

The Dogs were silent while they tried to comprehend Tariq's words. "Did they rape her?" Chuck asked, trying to find some sense in the situation. Tariq asked the old man and got what looked like a defiant response.

"They don't know, but probably not," was all Tariq could say with downcast eyes.

"Well, then how did it hurt their honor?" Chuck couldn't help but ask.

"It doesn't matter," Tariq answered, "They had her and could have molested her. That hurts their honor and killing her is the only way to save it."

Still perplexed, Scott blurted, "What kinda' horse-shit is this?"

"It's been tribal tradition for thousands of years," Tariq answered sheepishly.

"You sound a little sympathetic," said Scott as Tariq silently stared at the floor.

"Well, ya' know where you'll find sympathy in this world don't ya," piped in Greg Hanson.

"Where's that?" Scott played along.

"In the dictionary between shit and syphilis."

Regardless of Hanson's crude joke, the whole incident brought on an epiphany for Chuck. These people had obviously been kidnapping each other for thousands of years, but killing their own children to save the family honor? *How in the hell can we teach them human rights, let alone democracy, when they have no concept of either?* Then he remembered his father making that very point not-so-long-ago, but in a much more sympathetic way. He looked down at the young girl lying on the floor with blood streaming out of her chest and thought about arresting her brother. But something told him it would be futile. "As nutty as it may be to us," he remembered his dad saying, "It's their thing and just because we don't understand it, doesn't make it wrong." That sounded a little liberal coming from a conservative like Don but then it hit him. *Maybe that's what 'The Book' meant when it said just because we don't agree with their customs doesn't mean they're wrong and we're right.*

Is Everyone Right?

With billions of planets out there, anyone who thinks earth is the only one with life on it is a moron. There are 21 other planets that we know of that could support human life and those are just the ones we know of. There are billions more that we don't know anything about. And if there is life out there, anyone who thinks ours is the only reality is a bigger moron. That's why I don't understand people who are soooo sure they're right on things like morality issues. Take abortion. I don't believe in it, but I'm not sure I'm right, like the pro-lifers are. How do they know it's not the norm on some distant planet? And if it is, how does that affect what's right and wrong on ours? What's clearly right in one world may be clearly wrong in another and vice versa. If one man's fantasy is another man's reality (the lucky bastard) and one's fact is another's myth, couldn't one man's right be another man's wrong? So how can the fundamentalist types be soooo positive they are right? Is it because they just feel it in their gut? Why should I trust their gut? Is it because the Bible tells them so? What about another world's Bible? Or is it because admitting they could be wrong might crack their whole simplistic, black and white world view and lead to more uncomfortable questions about the grey areas of life? Maybe what's true on earth is true universally. But with billions of other planets out there, I doubt it.

Could it be? Chuck thought, *Could abhorrent things like murder be crimes here and perfectly acceptable in another world?* But he knew that was too much for him to comprehend or even think about right now. He also decided then and there that the writings could not have come from his dad because he was too down-to-earth and conservative to have existential thoughts like that. "Let's get the hell outta' here," he barked disgustedly and the Dogs walked down the stairs in single file. Tariq Muhammad followed, looking dejected.

"Wait up," said Jim Hawkins, stopping abruptly as if he suddenly had a flash of insight, "What do astronauts do when they fart in their space suits?"

"Maybe not the time or place," said Chuck.

"Okay. But speaking of farts … did you guys know that I can tell what people had for lunch by smelling their farts." Now everyone stopped at the bottom of the stairs to hear this one.

"No one was speaking of farts," said Luis Salgado.

"Yeah, I was … didn't ya' hear me?" said Hawkins and he continued, "Anyway, when my mom was breast-feeding me she was on a steady diet of hot peppers and brew fed to her by my perverted daddy who had a fart-fetish. He would load her up on habaneros and beer and then get right down there where the air is rare and inhale the potent mixture's resulting vile, nauseating stench."

"Why in the hell would anyone do that and what on earth does that have to do with guessing what someone ate?" asked Bill Rollins, nicknamed Duckman because of his fascination with duct tape.

"Don't encourage him," said Scott, knowing what was coming.

"Glad you asked," said Hawkins, "I guess the answer to your first question is that it gave him major wood. As far as the second, I guess drinking all that gassy breast milk gave me my under-appreciated talent."

"Yer' a strange one," said Allen Jones as the group started walking again, "That's all I can say."

As they boarded their Humvees, Chuck thought about how this was bizarre even for Hawkins. But it did lighten the somber mood and gave him something to think about other than his doubts about the war. He was grateful for that as he reflected on Jim and the rest of his men. It was almost euphoric as he briefly reflected on the fact that each had been carefully hand-picked for their individual talents, but they all had one thing in common. They liked to kill and they were good at it.

All had excellent athletic ability but each had his own unique, special skill. Private Mike Sandstone had been a gymnast and was double-jointed to boot. He could get into places no one else could by contorting his body in mind-boggling ways. Ron Jenkins had a rare eye condition, which enabled him to see clearly in the dark like natural infra-red goggles. Greg Hanson threw knives with incredible, pin-point accuracy when they needed silent killing. He learned the skill from his father, a circus performer who threw knives at his mother while she was strapped to a revolving wheel. Greg could also cut a man's throat by throwing a playing card at his neck. Then there was Jim Hawkins, a crack-shot and a talented boxer who switched to martial arts and achieved a 5th degree black belt. By combining the two forms of combat, he became a veritable fighting machine. Finally, there was Abdul Hameed, the only Arab Muslim in the group. He was one of the best snipers in Iraq, he spoke five languages, including Farsi, and he was a self-made medic to boot. Yes, each had his own specialty and Chuck's was assassination of all kinds. He could kill a man 15 different ways and he had already used 9 of them.

"Come one ... come all," Ron Jenkins yelled like a carnival barker as they drove onto the base, "Stick yer' ass in Private Hawkins' face and fill his lungs with your flatulence." Many soldiers on the base disliked Jim for his weirdness and they undoubtedly relished the idea of ripping one in his face. It wasn't long before they were lined up around the Dogs' barracks, betting wildly that he couldn't do it. But he could and he did. He walked away semi-rich.

* * *

Cramped in his tiny cell, Mark Jacobs was exercising his own brand of psycho-philosophical contemplation, but for different reasons. He felt like an over-stuffed suitcase bursting at the seams as he tried to meditate his joint aches away. But it seemed like the harder he tried, the more his mind slipped out of his meditation and back to his pain and predicament. Still, he pressed on, trying to manipulate his brainwaves into a relaxed alpha-state that would hopefully bring him some tempo-rary relief. He knew he couldn't force it, but could only let his mind drift around freely while gently nudging it toward one all-encompassing train-of-thought that would completely absorb him and help him ignore his throbbing leg. Now he tried to focus back on the religious verses he had found when he was a graduate assistant doing research for Dr. Goldschien.

A wealthy patron gave Goldschien a huge grant to research the world's major religions to see if they held the secret to getting into Heaven or at least into some kind of after-life. For most of his life he had been a ruthless businessman, amass-ing an immense fortune and becoming one of the richest men in the world. At the age of 85, he had more money than he knew what to do with and was now looking for some type of redemption for his past sins. Approaching the end of his life, he wanted to know how to get to the great beyond and figured the world's major reli-gions might have the answer.

Many of the verses Mark dug up in his research fittingly involved money, materialism, and greed and his favorite was a Hindu passage from the Bhagavad Gita.

> *"Bound by a hundred shackles of hope, enslaved by their greed,*
> *they squander their time dishonestly piling up mountains of wealth.*
> *Bewildered by endless thinking, entangled in the net of delusion,*
> *addicted to desire, they plunge into the foulest of hells."*

He guessed that it was probably the *"foulest of hells"* that got to the old man. Then it occurred to him that he would probably prefer the other Bhagavad Gita passage, *"Abandoning all desires, acting without craving, free from all thoughts of 'I' and 'mine,' that man finds utter peace ... even at the moment of death he vanishes, into God's bliss."* He figured that was the kind of salvation the rich guy was looking for and that spending his massive wealth on the betterment of society would be his road to redemption and his admission price to Heaven. Silently reciting the words helped take Mark's mind off of his pain, but if he stopped even for a second, it felt like his leg was being seared with a hot branding iron. So, he continued his silent mantra, *"No one can buy immortality with money."* This one was from the Hindu Brihadaranyaka Upanishad.

But now he was running out of passages on greed and avarice and he could feel the burn returning. So, he let his mind drift slowly back to more practical matters. He thought about how his religious studies lead to Dr. Goldschien's revolutionary research project in the first place. He was the one who actually stumbled onto it one day when he was randomly feeding sequences of letters from the Bible into the computer. Most of the words that came out were either gibberish or from a dead, ancient language that was too old to be interpreted, but some referred to real historical events.

He showed Dr. Goldschien who showed his benefactor and it seemed like good research for him to fund. So, began the religious code project that produced the software program dubbed *Prophecy*, which searched the world's major holy books for coded messages. Using it on religious texts like the Qur'an, the Bible, the Torah, the Bhagavad Gida, the Upanishads, the Tao Te Ching and I-Ching, and the Dhammapada was an enormous undertaking.

Prophecy was a numerical program that analyzed every first, second, third, fourth, fifth, etc. letter in a text and made whole words out of them.

Although he wouldn't admit it, Dr. Goldschien believed they could be code word messages from some kind of higher being who had been waiting for the computer age to be deciphered. He also hypothesized that there must be a motivation behind the cryptic messages and that it might be to predict the future and save the world from self-destruction and extinction. But with no real evidence for this hypothesis, he couldn't share his ideas with his colleagues, knowing that he would be ostracized by the scientific community.

The program did describe some events that had already happened, like 9/11 and the invasion of Afghanistan and Iraq. It also hinted that the catastrophic effects of global warming were closer than anyone knew.

But there was more. A lot more. However, much of it was unintelligible. There were words like "*Sperry,*" "*Garhwahl,*" "*Irian,*" and "Argo" that no one understood.

All of a sudden, he heard the man outside get out of his chair and walk across the room. *Did I make a noise without knowing it*? He feared that his leg had involuntarily spasmed. Then he heard the gunman sit back down and he breathed a silent sigh of relief. But at the same time, he realized that this practical line of thinking was beginning to diminish his meditative state and he could feel the pulsating pain starting to return. *Back to basics*, he thought, and he let his mind drift back to more ethereal thoughts about some Biblical verses that had often perplexed him.

He had always been taught that there is only one God and he remembered verses like Isaiah Chapter 45, verses 4 and 6 that say, "*I am Jehovah, there is no other God*" and "*....all the world from east to west will know there is no other God. I am Jehovah and there is no one else. I alone am God.*" But then there were more ambiguous verses like Psalm 82:1 that said, "*God rises in the divine council, gives judgment in the midst of the gods.*" He had always wondered if "*God rises in the divine council*" could mean that there are other gods on that council. And if God "*gives judgment in the midst of gods*" does that also mean there are other gods? After all, Genesis 1:26 says, "*Then God said: 'Let us make man in our image, after our likeness.'*" Why say "*our?*" Why not say "*my*" if there is only one of him?

But there was no time to contemplate questions like these because just then he heard the gunman outside get up from his chair again and he once more froze with fear that he had been discovered.

* * *

Halfway between sleep and wakefulness was a state Chuck often enjoyed because it enabled him to think about his life without any distractions. Now his mind drifted back to his childhood days of dreaming about being an FBI agent investigating unsolvable crimes. He watched all the FBI TV shows of the time, imagining himself as the only agent who could crack the tough cases. More than one aptitude test showed that he had a natural talent for inductive reasoning and creative thinking. A battery of tests he took when he enlisted determined that he would be best qualified for military intelligence, but his commanding officers thought he would be better suited to combat.

But now, as he lay on his cot, his mind kept drifting back to his doubts about the war. Feeling these doubts was a new experience for him and he didn't know how to handle it. *It's sure as hell not in the Army manual,* he unconsciously mused to himself but his unintentional humor didn't make the qualms go away. On the one hand, he knew doubts were dangerous because they could hinder your performance on the battlefield and endanger you and your fellow soldiers. But on the other, he had always faced up to the truth in every situation, no matter how hard it was to accept. Looking for any way out of these unaccustomed misgivings, he drifted back to his younger days of surfing and playing football in San Diego.

Before moving to California, Don was a journalist. After serving in the military, he started out as a sort of hybrid reporter, covering crime in Washington, D.C. and writing about the wars in Iraq and Afghanistan. After that, he began reporting on U.S. foreign policy and specialized in getting classified information through the Freedom of Information Act. All the while, he was working on his Ph.D. in International Relations and ultimately ended up writing a syndicated investigative column on past failed U.S. foreign policies in the perspective of modern times. He travelled a lot, interviewing government leaders and historians in other countries and sometimes in war-torn nations.

But the job was getting old and when one of his former news buddies offered him a college job in San Diego, teaching both History and Middle-Eastern Studies, he went for it. He continued writing his column and travelling for interviews and the college shared his expenses with the newspaper, enjoying the notoriety it brought them. Chuck remembered how his adopted father used to say there were three good reasons to teach and they were June, July, and August. He also remembered how dad often seemed to break life down into lists of two or three things. "You never wanna' run out of two things," he once said, "Beer and toilet paper."

Don was never very big on fatherly advice, but the toilet paper reference reminded Chuck of the time he said, "Life is like a roll of toilet paper. The closer you get to the end, the faster it goes."

"What does that mean?" Chuck had asked.

"It means," his dad said, "That you shouldn't waste life's precious time."

That memory had stuck with Chuck all these years and he was really giving it some serious thought these days.

Mom was a slight woman with a cool demeanor and a soft gentility that belied a tough inner-character. Her easy, blue eyes were quick to flash when she was angry and she used them like a weapon, often fluctuating between a doe-eyed gaze and a sharp, steely stare. Claire Lansing was the vice-president of a small, start-up software company that looked promising and she had met Don at a conference on foreign policy in the digital age. After a whirlwind romance, they married and shortly after that, adopted Chuck and put him in the same bedroom as her son from a different marriage. His name was Mike and he instantly took to Chuck as the big brother he always wished he had. Chuck was a bit withdrawn and standoffish at first, but it wasn't long before he warmed up to the idea of a little brother who looked up to him.

Mother and son were very different, but she was his best friend and seemed to be the only person who truly understood him. The best thing they had in common was their deep love and respect for her husband and his father, although he could be a lot to handle at times. Don was extremely opinionated about many things and he wasn't shy about pontificating on his views. While Chuck was a man of few words, his dad was often one of too many. He didn't talk *to* you. He talked *at* you. It wasn't a conversation as much as it was a speech and Chuck often had to remind him that he wasn't sitting in his class taking notes on his lectures.

Don was currently in the middle of a mid-life, patriotic love/hate crisis. He loved his country but believed the current administration was uninformed, impulsive, and dangerous. Most people were surprised to learn that he was a republican because many of his viewpoints seemed neo-liberal. But that was dad, the very definition of enigmatic. Then Chuck's thoughts drifted to the last time he had stood in that kitchen and it wasn't a pleasant memory.

"Chuck, I need to talk to you about something," he remembered his mother saying as she sat down at the table, smiling up into the increasingly creased, war-weary face of her 6'2" son towering over her.

"Sure mom, what's up," he had said, instantly noticing from her casual, nonchalant demeanor that whatever was up must be something serious. Whenever she had bad news, she hid it behind a calm, serene, almost joyful smile.

"Firstly, I want you to know that it's really nothing to worry about."

Now he knew it was something serious and he braced himself for the worst because when someone says there's nothing to worry about, there is usually a lot to worry about. "What is it mom?"

Claire went on to explain that she had breast cancer and had a double mastectomy a few months earlier.

"Why didn't you tell me?" Chuck asked in an injured tone.

"We figured you had enough on your mind over there."

Struggling for something to say, Chuck asked, "How did dad take it?"

"Oh, you know him ... he said he always wanted a Playboy pin-up for a wife and now he's got one ... complete with the staples." Claire threw an easy laugh her son's way, but Chuck couldn't return it. Not only did the Playboy pin-up remark show his father's age, but he didn't like his way of dealing with tense situations by making crass jokes, especially when it came to his mother. "So, they're sure they got it all?" was all he could muster.

"That's what the doctors say. So, there's nothing to worry about."

But there was something to worry about because the cancer returned with a vengeance and she died six months later. He came home on emergency leave just in time to watch his father nearly drink himself into oblivion over her death. He loved her dearly and she was also his best friend. Day-after-day he sat in the living room not talking and drinking whisky straight out of the bottle. Chuck tried to talk to him but got nowhere. "Thanks for tryin' son," he would say, "But I'll have to deal with this in my own way and sorry I can't be more help to you." Chuck noticed that when he looked at you, even in his stupor, his penetrating stare burrowed deep into your soul. Finally, he had to go back to Iraq before either could help the other through it. But then he realized that no one could help his dad through anything.

Now snapping back to the present, he looked for something that could take his mind off of the depressing memory and settled on another anonymous writing from *The Book*. He was still trying to figure out who wrote it and at first, he thought it might be his dad. *Why else would it be in his garage?* But after reading a few of the writings like this one, he realized they didn't sound like his Catholic father at all.

We're All One

Islam and Christianity are not as different as people think. After all, they were started by Abraham's sons Isaac and Ishmael. Isaac was an early Jewish leader and Ishmael started Islam. The Prophet Mohammed called Jesus Christ God's "spirit and word." Another of his quotes goes, "Both in this world and in the Hereafter, I am the nearest of all people to Jesus, the son of Mary. The prophets are paternal brothers, their mothers are different, but their religion is one." There is a passage in the Qur'an that describes Islam's feelings about the revelations handed down to Allah, Moses, Jesus, Abraham and his sons, and the prophets. The passage is Surah 136 and it says Muslims believe in these holy messages and that they "make no distinction between any of them." That sounds to me like Islam and Christianity have more in common than not.

Does that mean I'm fighting against my own religion? he thought.

But that heavy question would have to wait as he saw, through blurry eyes, a young corporal with puffy lips bending over him and saying, "Sorry sir but Captain Johnson wants to see you for a mission briefing."

When they got to Johnson's office, the corporal said, "The captain is with someone right now sir, so please wait here." With that, he turned around and walked out of the door with no explanation.

Maybe he has to hit the latrine, Chuck figured as he sat down, his eyes drifting over the small room and resting on the door to the inner office. Just when he noticed that it was open a crack he heard Captain Johnson's deep, gravel-throated voice.

"We can't win this one can we," came the stoic monotone.

You gotta' be kidding me, Chuck thought. Johnson was a little eccentric but he was a hardened war veteran and the last person you would expect to hear that from. But then came the answer from another man in the room that was even more disturbing.

"Duh!" came the sarcasm, "We never could. But then, winning was never the plan."

* * *

Mark held his breath and his heart beat wildly as he heard the gunman outside walk around his apartment. *What is he looking for?* But then he heard the glorious sound of him sitting back down and he exhaled with liberating relief. Always an excitable Type A personality, he had tried booze to relax and found it to be ultimately depressing, at least to his extreme intellectual abilities. It was fine for a while, but over time he found that the more he drank, the easier it was to drink more. "The more I drink," he used to say, "The more I drink." Finally, intoxication was too easy for Mark. It was too comforting. It felt like an old friend or a comfortable old easy chair. But it also dulled his otherwise sharp senses and he concluded that wasting his mind was not his destiny. Finally, after trying all the other mind-altering substances, he reluctantly tried meditation and found it to be relaxing, but also numbing to his always-active brain. After a while he developed his own personal mindfulness and reached a pleasant medium between transcendental meditation and hedonistic self-indulgence. Eventually, however, he gave that up and went back to booze and occasional marijuana.

But back to now, he thought, *Everyone has his limits and I've certainly got mine ... you just have to go beyond them. Beyond the bounds of pain.* Recalling his old meditation techniques, he then began to slip down and down, deeper and deeper into the recesses of his mind.

"Entazir hona, lamma yijee eqtila." (*Stay here and wait. If he comes back, kill him.*) The voice was guttural and determined and Mark knew he was in for a long, excruciating ordeal. *Must go deeper*, he realized.

After two hours it became apparent that the gunman who stayed behind wasn't going anywhere. Hiding in the small compartment, Mark had managed to keep the throbbing pain from his cramped leg down with meditation. *But that crap only goes so far*, he thought. It now felt like someone was shooting a propane torch directly onto his thigh and the sweat was pouring off of him, drenching his clothes. *Don't know how much longer I can take this.* But he knew the second he moved an inch, the assassin outside would hear him. He fingered the pouch between his legs, sensing that it was what they were looking for and remembered what a Buddhist Monk had told him once in Thailand. *When basic meditation doesn't work, go to real, concrete thoughts.*

So now he began thinking about his graduate student friend Julie Beckman. She was studying religious theology at another Jerusalem university and they had met at a party. At first, she seemed a little boring and a little strange. But as he talked to her, he realized that she was simply not concerned with impressing anyone with her wit and humor. She had it and a lot of it, but she wouldn't be the life of the party or even popular because she didn't think it was worth the effort. But with coal-black hair that floated around her head in sensuous waves, she moved with an animated grace and Mark found her a very appealing combination of looks and brains.

He also enjoyed her many unique ideas like her belief that you could tell people by the food they eat. "There's fish people and there's beef people," she used to say, "and I can spot 'em every time." Her theory was that people who eat fish are generally calm and less aggressive or hostile than people who eat red meat. She believed that fish people lived healthier and longer lives than beef people and science had proven her right to a certain extent.

But thinking about Julie carried Mark only so far and now he needed something new to focus on. He floated from subject-to-subject and finally decided on the pouch between his legs. He reflected back on how, as Dr. Goldschien's most promising graduate student, he had been the first one to identify several key words in the code the professor had given him. He remembered when Goldschien first told him about his theory of the secret language of all the major religious texts that could only be decoded by clusters of servers connected via fiber channel cards that use distributed parallel processing. When he explained that he wanted his help in developing software that would read the code and possibly predict the future, Mark thought he was a crazy old man. But he liked the professor and thought it might be fun to work on such a weird project. Besides, he needed the graduate assistant salary.

After months of intense work, Mark was more surprised than anyone that he actually developed the *Prophecy* program and that it worked. But he never got the chance to see it through to its full potential because Dr. Goldschien had to kick him off the project when he was caught hacking into the Israel Defense Department's computer system.

"I was just looking for the plans for their nukes," he had said innocently. But Israelis are quite sensitive about the nuclear issue and he had to go.

"It's out of my hands," Goldschien had said solemnly, "I wish things were different." What he didn't know was that Mark had made copies of *Prophecy* to play with at home, although it worked much slower there.

A stabbing pain now pierced his meditation back on those events and jolted him to more current theories about why these men wanted the program. All kinds of conspiracy theories ran through his mind, but the main one told him that it must contain something about them they don't want anyone to know. Considering the brutal murders they had just committed, he realized he absolutely could not let them have it. Besides, he knew they would kill him as soon as they got their hands on it and it might be the only thing that could keep him alive. Now it was a race between his pain and the man outside. *Who will give in first?* He knew it would be him. *Never really had a big pain threshold.*

Patience was never Mark's strong suit and he was getting more anxious by the second in his cramped little hiding place. He felt electrified with the hot currents of pain shooting up his leg growing exponentially. But he knew that if he moved, the madman outside would hear him and he was dead. So, he did the only thing he could do and went back to his mindfulness. What seemed to work best was mentally reciting religious passages he had memorized. He put his photographic memory to work and forced his thoughts back to some of the early Biblical verses he had found in his research that dealt with greed and materialism.

In the Bible, one-third of Jesus Christ's parables and preaching's were about giving up one's possessions and wealth and following him. But the one their billionaire benefactor wasn't particularly fond of was the well-known line in the Book of Matthew, *"It's easier for a camel to go through the eye of a needle, than for a rich man to enter into the kingdom of God."*

He had worked hard for his money and he wasn't about to simply give it all away because of one passage in one religious book. He hoped there was another, less drastic way to gain redemption and get into Heaven and he hoped *Prophecy* would find it. If not and if most or all of the world's greatest religions agreed with Matthew, so be it. And that's why he gave the University of Jerusalem $30 million to find out.

After two years of extremely complex power-processing on super-computers, Professor Goldschien and his team came up with the *Prophecy* program that gave them much more than they bargained for. Namely, the ability to find secretly coded messages in the world's holy books and maybe to predict the future.

But all these thoughts left Mark's mind as fast as they had come when he heard the gunman again get out of his chair. It was a terrifying sound and he again held his breath.

CHAPTER 3

As he sat in Captain Johnson's outer office, Chuck didn't know what to do. He knew he shouldn't listen to the conversation, but he didn't want to interrupt Johnson and his guest to tell them he was there. And he was afraid that if he got up and shut the door, they would know that he heard them.

Did the corporal tell him I'm here, he wondered. But then he realized that it wouldn't matter if he did or not. After weighing some quick pros and cons, he decided to stay put and ride it out. *Just following orders*, he thought, *and hey ... the corporal was the one who left the door open, not me.*

"What the hell is the plan?" he heard Captain Johnson ask incredulously.

"What little plan there is ... or was, my friend," the weary voice came back over the sound of ice cubes clinking in a glass, "is to slow down the clock and maybe prevent the crazies from taking over the whole damn place. Oh, and of course, to secure our oil supply."

"Never any intention of winning the war 'ay?" Johnson asked incredulously. Chuck remembered that his commanding officer was a man of few words who often let others do most of the talking.

"*The* war? *The* war? There is no *the* war. There are several wars that have been going on here for centuries and they're mostly tribal and religious. We're just referees and not very good ones at that. Hell, six wars are goin' on right now. But, with Iraq, we missed our best chance to end the insurgency before it started."

"What chance was that?"

"When we first went in, the generals saw a window of opportunity to wipe out the Fedayeen militants or, at least, do them some serious damage. But we let it slip away and the jihadists got too strong and we've spent every waking day since digging ourselves out."

"How's that?" Johnson asked.

"Well, the ground troops and generals told the SecDef right from the beginning that the Fedayeen would have to be dealt with and he ignored them. I think he was simply hoping for the best. Of course, the biggest mistake was to disband Hussein's military. They were mostly Sunni Baathists and they simply looted the weapons arsenals we didn't protect and faded back into the civilian population in the process. I mean, the military was a big part of the Iraqi people and they would've gone along with whoever was in power. After all, they're used to that in this part of the world."

"Maybe, but you're not givin' 'em much credit."

"Well, I'm not givin' us much credit either. Once again, in our glorious cowboy tradition, we charged in half-cocked, not understanding their culture and history and not really caring about either. No wonder they hate us."

"Even after we saved 'em from a tyrant and gave 'em democracy?"

"That's what the media tells us, but that's not how they see it. We always make the same mistake of thinking that everyone wants to be like us, but they don't. These people don't need or want what we have to offer and besides, you can't *give* anyone democracy, especially if they don't really understand it. They have to decide they want it and then get to it in their own time and in their own way. You can't *give* it to them and expect 'em to understand it and implement it instantaneously."

"Ya' think they preferred Hussein?"

"Nah ... but to them, we're just another colonial power invading their country and this is just another crusade to convert them to Christianity."

"Oh yeah ... the war on Islam that we've heard so much about. But, ya' know ... none of the soldiers I know consider this a religious war."

"Well, that's because none of the soldiers you know look beyond the barrel of their gun. You know how it is ... a soldier has to believe he's fightin' the good fight against the bad guys or he can't do his job."

"True. Ours is not to reason why and all that jazz."

"Yeah, but the Arabs do see all this as just another war against Islam. Not to mention stealing their oil."

"Well, there is that. But I still have a war to fight."

"I know man ... and so do I. I'm just not sure it's the right war. I mean Hussein really was a bad guy who killed thousands and the Iraqis may be better off without him. But we actually helped him do it by supporting him during eight years of the Iran-Iraq war. Hell, we gave 'em the chemical weapons we were afraid he'd use on us. It just goes to show that yer' friend one day might be yer' enemy the next. So, you're right. You never know who the bad guy actually is. Anyway, there're a lotta' brutal dictators out there and we can't take 'em all on. The only reason we don't take on the others is that they don't have any oil."

"Yeah, yeah, the oil! Always the oil ... but isn't gettin' ridda' one better than none?"

"That's one way to look at it, but at what cost? Is it worth 100,000 lives? 500,000? In the end, more Iraqis will probably die post-invasion than would've died under Saddam. We should've gotten out as soon as we got him and left 'em to sort things out on their own."

"Oh yeah, then it'd be civil war with ISIS killing everyone."

"Not everyone, just the Shia. But, that's inevitable anyway. The longer we stay, the longer the jihad goes on and, believe me, it'll go on a long time."

"What makes you say that?"

"Well, it's already become our longest war. Historically the shorter insurgencies go on for seven to ten years and the longer ones, more than thirty."

"Since when did you become the historian?"

"Since I've watched too many of these conflicts go south. But I mean, we can't be the whole world's police force can we? Besides, what makes us so sure we know what's better for other countries than they do themselves?"

"Well, it's pretty obvious that they can't run their own governments."

"Why? Because they have so much civil strife ... kinda' like us in our early days?"

"No, because they can't seem to handle a free country where their people have human rights."

"You mean a democracy, don't you? But just because they don't buy our brand of democracy doesn't make them wrong. Maybe some of 'em are supposed to have something other than a democratic government and it's part of their normal development. But we go in there and try to force our idea of democracy on them. Maybe we're interfering with their natural evolution."

"Well, I don't know if I'd call genocide evolutionary."

"There is that. The Arab dictators have been pretty brutal haven't they."

"Yeah and they've convinced a lotta' Arabs that democracy is anti-Islam so they can keep their power."

"True. But, again, what gives us the right to invade a sovereign country and tell 'em what to do?"

"How about the fact that the Muslims messed everything up."

"Not all Muslims. Most of 'em are okay and believe it or not, Islam is really a pretty cool religion. It's just the extremists who've hijacked it to fit their own agenda. The Qur'an actually tells Muslims that in war, they should only fight military targets, not innocent civilians. It also says a person can't be a martyr by choice ... only God can make him a martyr. It really all goes back to their history of tribalism and religious extremism. The Sunnis and Shiites have been fightin' since Mohammed's grandson was beheaded in 680. Ya' think they're gonna' stop now because we tell 'em to?"

"Then it really is a holy war to them?"

"Sorta'. I mean they don't kill themselves for fun. Many of 'em really believe they're fightin' for Allah. The rest of 'em are just Sunni thugs who want their power back."

"But let's face it … any way you look at it, we're on the right side. If I didn't believe that, I wouldn't be here," Captain Johnson said as Chuck heard ice cubes roll around in a glass.

"Yeah, we are. But we wouldn't have to be on any side if we hadn't invaded in the first place. Of course, we believed all that B.S. about weapons of mass destruction. Everyone knew Saddam didn't have 'em and we should've known he wasn't working with Al Qaeda."

"Apparently everyone but congress and the president I guess."

"Yup. When we drove the Taliban out of Afghanistan we should've left that crap-hole just like we shoulda' left Iraq when we got Hussein," he said, again clinking his ice cubes together, "It was Afghanistan that attacked us, not Iraq. Even the president's chief military advisor warned him against going in there."

"I do remember him saying if we break it, we own it."

"I think it was if you break it, you buy it and we did both. Now we can't pull out, even if we wanted to."

"Yeah, cause now we have to fight Al Qaeda *and* ISIS."

"And I hear Bin Laden's son is running Al Qaeda from Iran."

"Yupper … you heard right."

At this point Chuck was hanging on every word and he knew that he had already heard too much. He vaguely remembered hearing talk like this from his father a long time ago. But this was his own commanding officer and someone who was clearly well-informed talking about the futility of the war.

After several whiskies, the conversation continued but with louder voices, which meant Chuck could hear it even better.

"What about all the schools and hospitals we built and all the money we handed out?" asked Johnson.

"Ya' mean the schools and hospitals that were paid for but never built or never finished or the ones that were built with shoddy materials and poor workmanship? And the money! So much freakin' money down a rathole!" Johnson's anonymous guest said loudly, slamming his fist on a table.

"Calm down before you have a stroke," said Johnson, "You always get this way when you drink my expensive whiskey."

"Which is illegal here ya' know ... but I guess not for the ruling class."

"I don't see ya' turnin' it down, ya' lush. Besides, the base is technically U.S. territory, so I'm not breakin' the law."

"Fair enough. But the money was obscene. When we first took over, they hauled in 360 tons of cash on pallets. On pallets! 12 billion dollars in all, mostly in 100 dollar bills. We handed it out like candy to keep the government services going and didn't keep much account of it, so we really don't know where most of it went. All anyone had to do was write a fake name down in a notebook along with how they planned to spend it and that was it. No verification, no record-keeping, no real accounting."

"But in our defense, there was no organized system for payment, no post office, no banks, no way to pay anyone officially."

"That's 'cause we fired 'em all!"

"Well, it wasn't like it was our money anyway. A lot of it came from the oil-for-food deal."

"True, but it was still money that was supposed to rebuild Iraq and it was mostly stolen and misspent instead. Let's face it, they saw us comin' and took full advantage of it. It's a way of life over here and we fell for it hook-line-and-sinker."

"I'll probably regret asking this, but how much money do ya' think we lost?"

"Well, the State Department admits to losing about 6 billion dollars so it's probably more like four times that. For one thing, we know there were about 70,000 shadow civil servants on the payroll who never existed, but that's not even close to the worst of it."

"There's more?"

"A lot more. We're afraid that a lotta' the money went to Iraqi government ministries who're tied to the militias."

"So?" Captain Johnson resisted the inevitable conclusion.

"Don't ya' get it? We're worried that the money went to those militias and ultimately to ISIS and Al Qaeda to buy the guns that are killin' us."

"My army is givin' money to the enemy?"

"You act like this is the first time you've heard about it, but yeah, that's it in a nutshell."

"So, I'm paying people to kill me and my men." Chuck could almost feel Captain Johnson staring at the floor.

"Afraid so."

"This all makes it hard to figure out who our friends are and who are our enemies."

"Don't kid yourself. We have no friends here, just people trying to survive by supporting whoever is in power or whoever is paying the bills at the moment. They're loyal to whoever pays 'em ... as long as the payments keep comin'. But five minutes after they shake your hand, they're secretly supporting your enemy and you know what? I don't blame 'em."

"You don't?"

"Nope. Like I said, we're the invaders and they're fightin' back the only way they know how."

"Ya' mean like blowing themselves up in a crowded mall?"

"Yea, it sucks. But without an army, they believe that terrorism is their only weapon against the giant military powers."

Where have I heard that before? Chuck mused.

"That's a piss-poor excuse for killin' innocent women and children."

"Yeah, but it's their excuse. And tell 'em that when our bombs are killin' *their* women and children."

"That's collateral damage and you know it!"

"What's the difference ... they're still dead. To them, it's the same thing. Besides, they believe that no one is innocent."

"Yeah, I never got that."

"They argue that since we live in a democracy and we vote for our government leaders, we're *all* responsible for what those leaders do."

"That's pretty simplistic thinking don't ya' think? Besides, millions of Americans don't even vote."

"And doesn't not voting make them responsible as well?"

"O. K. Then they think that all Americans are responsible for all of our sins of aggression because they live there?"

"Well, technically speaking, when we elect our leaders, aren't we responsible for what they do? Especially, if we keep electing them and don't vote them out of office?

"Just a necessary side-effect of democracy."

"Yeah, tell them that when they're watching their family and friends get killed. But, they don't think much of democracy in the first place and we make it easy for 'em to believe that all Americans, including women and children, are the enemy."

"By doing what?"

"Well, for one thing, when we handed Iraq over to the Shia we ended up empowering the Shiite militias to retaliate against the Sunnis for years of oppression and they're butchering them as we speak. Kinda' hard to get around that one."

"Okay then, why do they kill their own Muslims?"

"It's partially tribalism, but really it's that any Muslim who doesn't side with them is their enemy."

Just then the skinny corporal with the big lips returned and immediately noticed the door ajar. Looking from the door to Chuck and back again, he suddenly realized his grave mistake and turned red in the face. Walking over to the door, he carefully and silently slid it shut, apparently unnoticed by the captain and his unknown guest. Not knowing what else to do, he sat down at his desk and acted like he was sorting through some papers.

"Does the captain know I'm here?" Chuck asked innocently, desperately trying to mentally digest all that he had just heard. In spite of his recent misgivings, he had always generally considered his mission a righteous one. But, for the last 20 minutes he had been introduced to many new doubts about that and he knew he was going to have to sort through a lot of painful questions he had tried to avoid before.

"Yes," the corporal lied, "But I'll remind him." Self-consciously pushing the intercom button, he said quietly, "Sir, Lieutenant Lansing is here for his briefing."

After a few seconds of silence, they both heard a door at the other end of Captain Johnson's inner-office open and close and then the intercom crackle to life with, "Send him in."

When Chuck entered the office, Johnson looked at him and said, "Get an earful lieutenant?" He was a stocky man whose puffed-out jowls contradicted his ski slope nose.

"I couldn't hardly help it sir," was Chuck's reply.

"Yeah, I'm gonna' have to get a new corporal. Anyway, don't give it too much thought soldier. It's above our pay grades and, besides, it can be dangerous."

Chuck knew immediately what he meant. If a soldier starts to have uncertainties about his mission, it can hamper his fighting ability. Nevertheless, he couldn't seem to push his mounting doubts about the war out of his mind and the conversation he had just over-heard brought them on stronger-than-ever.

"By the way," Johnson said out-of-the-blue, "How's yer' dad?"

He thought it was a little odd that Captain Johnson would ask about his father because they didn't know each other and, as far as he knew, they had never met. But he dismissed it as one of the captain's many eccentricities and answered, "He's fine."

"Good ... good. Now forget everything you just heard and let's get down to business."

Chuck knew he couldn't forget the conversation and he also knew that he was going to have to do something to bury his growing qualms and uncertainties if he was to do the job he was sent there to do. But now he had to ask himself if that job was right or wrong and that reminded him of something he had read in *The Book*.

Right and Wrong

It's not all that complicated. In our gut, we all know what's right and what's wrong, but life's grey areas can mix up the two. Does the end justify the means or is that just a cliché? Life is often too complicated for us to make the right choices. My own belief is that if it hurts good people, it's wrong. But hurting bad people to save good people is probably right, especially if it saves innocent lives. Enjoying the hurting, however, is probably wrong. It's all relative. It's not up to God to make us do what's right. It's up to us and us alone. We have to make those tough choices and if we search way down into our very being and try to ignore all the relativistic reasoning and rhetoric, we can figure out what is right and what is wrong. The problem is that it is often harder to do what's right than it is to do what's wrong.

After the mission briefing, Chuck thought about this passage as he left Johnson's office and realized that it did sound a little like his father. *But it can't be*, he thought. He couldn't help but ask the question, *am I hurting bad people to save good people or am I hurting the good people in the process?* Then it hit him that this writing related to something his father had said about doing the right thing for the wrong reasons or vice-versa. *Am I killing the right bad guys for the wrong reasons or the wrong bad guys for the right reasons? But more than that, do I enjoy it?* Part of him said yes, but he couldn't quite accept that. All he knew right now was that this kind of thinking could get him and his men killed.

* * *

Mark breathed a sweaty sigh of relief as he heard the gunman again sit back down outside his sweltering little cell. Knowing he had to stay completely still, he forced himself into a deep meditation on something he knew well from his research with *Prophecy*. It was the eastern religious passages about greed inhibiting one's spiritual development. Some of them are known for their renunciation of all material possessions and Mark now silently chanted one Buddhist verse from the Dham-mapada, "*The fool laughs at generosity. The miser cannot enter Heaven.*"

But meditations like this were not working as well as they had been and the pain from his leg cramp crept back to the surface of his brain. *Deeper*, he thought as he recalled another teaching of Buddha. *I renounce all my possessions without stint ... By means of this gift and its fruit may all beings in this very life be at their ease and may they one day enter Nirvana!*" But Buddha wasn't the only prophet who preached against greed. Mark now meditated on the soft words of the Tao Te Ching, "*Many loves entail great costs, many riches entail heavy losses ... no crime is more grievous than the desire for gain!*"

Now he was running out of the eastern religions so he drifted over to the land of Islam and the Qur'an, which says, "*Whoever desires the gain of the hereafter, he will give him more of that again; and whoever desires the gain of this world, we give him of it, and in the hereafter he has no portion.*" But the Qur'an wasn't always so charitable with verses like, "*Woe to every slanderer, defamer, who amasses wealth and considers it a provision (against mishap); Nay! He shall most certainly be hurled into the crushing disaster.*" Then there was this one. "*His wealth and what he earns will not avail him. He shall soon burn in fire that flames.*"

Unfortunately, the word "*burn*" brought Mark's present burning sensation in his leg to the forefront of his mind. So, swiftly, but gently, he drifted back to his meditations and back to the Bible. Back to James' "*Let the brother of low degree rejoice in that he is exalted: But the rich, in that he is made low: because as the flower of the grass he shall pass away.*" Then the Old Testament, the Torah, with Proverbs' "*Riches profit not in the day of wrath: but righteousness delivereth from death.*" And then there was Job's "*He hath swallowed down riches and he shall vomit them up again: God shall cast them out of his belly.*" And finally, even the Apocrypha, the books that were left out of the Bible, with Hermas' "*Beware, ye that glory in your riches, lest perhaps they groan who are in want, and their sighing come up unto God, and ye be shut out with your goods without the gate of the tower.*"

But, meditation only goes so far and as he sweat through his self-imposed internment in his tiny cell, Mark realized it was time for a more proactive approach. His clothes slid against his skin like wet paste as he fingered the remote control in his pocket and hesitated. *What've I got to lose.* He pushed the button and half-expected something to happen instantaneously. Of course, he knew nothing would and he waited. And waited. And waited. It got to the point that he almost forgot what he was waiting for. But 2 minutes later he remembered, as he heard the man outside get up from his chair again.

He must hear it, he thought as the floor creaked with the gunman's footsteps toward the kitchen. The steps suddenly stopped and Mark estimated that he must be standing in the adjoining dining room. *Not too fast.* There was no sound for what seemed like an eternity and then more footsteps. The assassin now seemed to be walking slowly around the kitchen trying to determine where the soft buzzing sound was coming from. Then he turned and found it, but not quite fast enough.

The explosion sounded like a dynamite blast and anyone in the area who heard it probably thought it was another suicide bombing. It blew the gunman back thirty feet into the air and instantly started Mark's apartment on fire. *Time to move!* But he couldn't. His legs were so cramped they were almost paralyzed. Unconsciously, he pushed the door panel open hard and was hit with a blast of hot air coming from the fire that was fast incinerating his apartment. *Well, at least my arms are working.* But his joy at that revelation didn't last long as he realized they were half-frozen from crouching too long. He also knew that if he didn't do something and do it fast, he would burn to death or die of smoke inhalation or both.

With one last burst of adrenaline, he stuffed the pouch of computer cards in his pants and raised his stiff, numb legs out of the compartment with his cramped arms. Then with a strength he didn't know he had, he clumsily dragged himself across the floor like a double amputee who lost his wheel chair, trying to avoid breathing in the toxic smoke. But that was a little difficult with the intense exertion he was putting his body through. *Kinda' like running the hundred-yard dash with your mouth and nose stuffed full of cotton,* he mused in a panic.

The flames licked his clothes and stabbed at his skin and he was glad his shirt was soaked with sweat as he turned blue and felt like he was about to explode. Almost to the end of the living room, he was just about to open his mouth and suck in some air when he reached the front door that the gunmen had set back in place after breaking it in. Throwing himself against it, it easily gave way and he went crashing through into the stairwell. But the air rushing in through the opening now ignited the pent-up combustion inside and a firestorm of flames and scorching heat blasted out as if from the gates of hell, searing his skin and sending him tumbling down the stairs. As he hit the bottom step he rolled to his feet into the foyer looking like a drunken stuntman. With blistering flesh and aching muscles, he stumbled out onto the sidewalk, tripping over a smoking hulk. Glancing down, he noticed it was the charred body of the gunman who had been blasted out of his apartment window. For many years to come, he would have a hard time getting that smell of burning flesh out of his nostrils.

It was only then that he wondered if putting the can of solvent in the microwave and turning it on with his remote control had been such a wise move. In the past, he had put popcorn in the microwave before a girl came over to watch a movie and then turned it on from the couch, making fresh popcorn for himself and his date. *Worked every time,* he thought, *but never thought I'd use it like this.* He had never planned on killing anyone, but he rationalized that it was him or the gunman.

His shirt had been partially burned off and as he ran and stumbled down the sidewalk with arms and legs flailing out in all directions, he made quite a site. You don't get rid of a two-hour cramp in a couple of minutes and several times his legs gave out and he sprawled on the pavement. Kids were watching and laughing while their mothers tried to scurry them away.

A testament to how commonplace explosions had become in Jerusalem, he noticed several bystanders simply looking on in disgust as they moved back from the fire. But he noticed something else too. A look of approval and even joy on some of the faces. He could even swear he saw two Arab-looking guys giving each other a high-five. Now here came the fire trucks with their sirens blaring. *Hope they can save my place. But now, where do I go? Oh yeah, the park. But will Julie still be there?* Looking around and behind him as he stumbled down the street in an awkward run, he didn't see anyone following him. But he didn't look the one place he should have: up.

CHAPTER 4

It sounded like heavy line zipping through a deep-sea fishing reel as Chuck repelled down the metal threaded nylon cord into the pitch-black darkness of his next mission. He hit the ground running and as the helicopter quietly moved on to its next drop, it sounded more like a room fan than a chopper. He smiled inwardly at the thought of the conspiracy buffs' belief that these black helicopters were part of a secret United Nations army trying to take over the world.

One-by-one, the Mad Dogs dropped into the black abyss and ran to their assigned positions in the Syrian city of Raqqa. Their coal-black uniforms made them virtually invisible as they faded into the shadowy landscape of bombed-out buildings to await the arrival of ISIS soldiers trying to hold onto their last bit of territory.

Raqqa was the first city ISIS took over before crossing the border into Iraq and capturing the city of Mosul and beyond. After those victories, it declared the establishment of an Islamic caliphate based in Raqqa that would rule over the 10 million people in the areas it controlled and all Sunni Muslims around the world.

After nine months of fighting, allied forces had taken back Mosul and were gradually forcing ISIS to give back much of its captured territory. The defeats were a big knockback to its dreams of an Islamic empire and losing the capital of its newly-founded kingdom would be the final blow.

Once a city of 200,000, Raqqa was now all but deserted after its citizens fled the ISIS takeover and the U.S.-led military coalition's massive airstrikes that followed. More than 5000 bombs, missiles, and shells left a moonscape of smashed buildings and dead bodies, most of them with their flesh eaten away by wild dogs.

After some skirmishes with the Syrian Democratic Forces, an alliance of Syrian militias, ISIS had retreated to the inner city and suburbs of Raqqa where they did what they usually do, split up and hide out in many different houses and underground tunnels. Thrust and retreat in short burst attacks was their signature strategy and they didn't have to kill very many enemy soldiers to consider an attack a win. Because they were outgunned and outmanned, even killing one or two or a handful of their enemies was a victory for them and it often made it onto the Internet.

But this time there was a big piece of the puzzle they didn't know about and that was that the SDF and allied forces were actually driving and maneuvering them like a herd of cattle. Using methodical firing patterns, they were wedging them into a narrow escape route and herding them toward the streets that fed into the neighborhood where the Mad Dogs waited in ambush.

They operated under radio silence so that the enemy wouldn't know they were there. Besides, American soldiers were supposed to be acting in more of an advisory role, not aggressively fighting on the front lines in Syria and the last thing they wanted was for the news media to get wind of it. "We're not here," they often joked, and then came the inevitable, "But if we *were* here, we would only be advisors."

Once the last bit of human cargo was unloaded, the black helicopter quietly slipped off into the sweltering darkness. *I had to choose this position didn't I*, thought Chuck as he settled into the disgustingly foul sewage ditch made even worse by the 120-degree heat. He chose it because of its panoramic view of the area, but now he was having second thoughts as the fetid fumes of human waste, decay, and rotting food filled his nostrils. "*Oh well,* he realized, *too late now* and he covered himself with camouflage netting that blended in well with the sandy brown ditch. He knew he needed a distraction to make him forget about the putrid smells of the ditch and he got one when Jim Hawkins interrupted radio silence with, "Why do men's bikes have a cross bar?"

Chuck clicked his radio as a warning to stay off the radio while smiling inwardly. Then it was down to the dirty business of ignoring the rancid odor. He did what he was trained to do and tried to focus his attention on something else. Coming up with nothing, he ran over in his mind the contents of his 75-pound backpack. It was mostly full of ammunition for his modified M-4 Carbine rifle but also had a few hand grenades and other goodies in it. The gun had a 100-bullet replaceable magazine and a rocket launcher. With a customized silencer it was quiet. But more importantly, the muzzle flash suppressor kept it from making a flash when it fired, making it hard for the enemy to see your position at night. Without a suppressor all they had to do was look for a flash and shoot at it. The infra-red scope enabled Chuck to see 100 yards in the dark and the shells easily punched through most plaster walls. His infrared goggles had a flip-down telescopic lens, through which he could now see some of his men run up to the rooftops with their M-1 .50 caliber machine guns. With these they could shoot the enemy in a 180-degree area around them. *I just hope the bad guys don't have these goggles too*, he worried.

But he didn't have time to give that much thought because at that moment an emaciated dog with its ribs sticking out jumped over the ridge of the ditch and stopped just short of his camouflage, staring at him. *Does he see me or just smell me?* was Chuck's silent question. *If he just smells me, he may only bark a bit and move on. But if he sees me, he'll bark his fool head off and we're all sunk.*

He was suddenly glad he had chosen the sewage ditch because the stench might cover up his own scent and the malnourished canine's eyesight might not be good enough to see him under the camouflage. He was also thankful that there were no street lights on this road. Knife in hand, Chuck was already planning exactly how he would slit the dog's throat. But then things suddenly got much worse.

A young Arab boy ran over the ridge and down into the ditch yelling and laughing and stopped just a few feet from him. *Uh Oh!* he thought, *this can't be good.* A barking dog revealing his position would be bad enough, but a live human being could blow the whole operation and probably get everyone killed. Without moving a muscle, he readied himself to pounce on the boy and knock him out. Then he would kill the dog.

The boy laughingly scolded the scrawny dog, probably for running away, and rubbed what was left of his fur. Then in an instant they were both gone. All Chuck could see through his camo netting was the back of the boy jumping over the ridge of the other side of the ditch. *Thank you, Lord,* he silently whispered in his inner voice as he finally exhaled, *that kid must have one hell of an immune system if this is his playground.*

Once the boy disappeared into the haze, he tried to settle his mind on thoughts that would carry him through the long wait he knew was coming. Just then, without knowing why, a passage from *The Book* popped into his head.

One God

I like the old analogy that God is at the top of a mountain and there are hundreds of paths up to the top. Each path takes a different route, but all reach the same point. I think all religions worship the same God, they just don't know it. The Jewish, Christian, and Islamic Gods all came from the God of Abraham. Is it too much of a stretch to believe that the Gods of all religions are the same God? Hindu Scripture says, "In whatever way men approach me, even so do I go to them." Doesn't this mean that God approaches different cultures of people in the form each will understand, but he's really the same God? It makes sense that God would appear to different groups in different ways and appeal to different people through different belief systems. In a pragmatic way, Islam works best for Muslims, Christianity works best for the west, and so on. I think God allowed all cultures to put their own stamp on him to better understand their own faith, but that all religions are basically the same. That's why I say we worship many gods, but they are all the same supreme being.

Now I'm fighting my own God, he thought forlornly. This one sounded a little too existential for dad, but it did sound about right for his old friend Tom Griffin. He had been raised a strict Catholic but at the age of 13 he developed a big interest in two things: martial arts and other religions like Buddhism and Baha'i, two belief systems that recognize the validity of all religions. By the age of 16 he had earned a brown belt in Karate but still he remained a Christian. Chuck always wondered how he seemed to reconcile his Christian faith with eastern religion. To explain it, Tom once told him about the lost years of Jesus Christ between his childhood and the beginning of his ministry. He said he believed those 18 years were largely spent in the far and middle-east, in India, and maybe Tibet, where he learned the elements of Buddhism, Hinduism, Islam, and Judaism and combined them to make the new Christianity.

According to Tom, some ancient Tibetan texts talk about a Saint Issa who traveled from Palestine to India and spent 6 years studying the Vedas and the Upanishads with Brahmin Priests. Then to the Himalayas where he mastered the teachings of Buddha, to Iran, then called Persia, supposedly to study Islam, and onto Egypt where he learned the secrets of the pyramids. Finally, it was back to Palestine at the age of 29. Tom theorized that Saint Issa was actually Jesus Christ.

"There are a lot of similarities between the religions," he argued, "and they do preach a lot of the same stuff."

"How so?" Chuck had asked.

"Well, for one thing, Jesus says 'do unto others what you would have others do unto you' and Buddha says 'with pure thoughts and fullness of love I will do toward others what I do for myself.'"

Wanting some ammunition of his own, Chuck remembered looking up a Bible verse, "What about John 3:36," he said, "It says 'Whoever believes in the Son has eternal life, but whoever disobeys the Son will not see life, but the wrath of God remains upon him.' Not exactly pluralistic is it."

"Maybe the Son is the Son of Islam, Hinduism, Buddhism, Judaism, or whatever 'ism' you want," was Tom's simple comeback, "Or maybe religious texts aren't supposed to be taken literally."

At least he said 'maybe,' Chuck thought as he remembered how open minded his friend was.

Then he remembered how Tom's beliefs irritated his father. Don Lansing was a strong Catholic, although Chuck wondered how strong, since he usually attended Sunday Mass pretty hung-over. The worst was one morning when he was so dehydrated, he snuck a drink out of the holy water. He admitted that all religions are basically the same, but he felt a person should choose one or the other. "You can't just make up your own religion," he would say, "Your friend is not exactly Martin Luther." He also called Karate a *pussy* sport that wouldn't stand up to a good old-fashion, beat-down and he sometimes referred to Tom as "kung fool."

The writing sounded a lot like his old friend, but *why would Tom hide something in my parents' garage?* Then again, this one didn't sound like Don either.

* * *

There it is! Mark almost shouted as he ran down the street. He had now regained most of his coordination and was overjoyed to see the park he knew so well. *Please say she's still here,* he desperately prayed. The air was dry and flat and the incongruous green foliage smacked of a small desert oasis. He hoped she was there. While he was running, he thought he heard a helicopter overhead a few times, but this wasn't unusual in the suicide bomber-ridden West Bank.

"Mark!" he heard from back in the trees. Instantly, he headed for the spot where they had spent so many romantic nights. They embraced with not so much as a word and held onto each other as if for dear life. "I've been worried sick ... what took you so long?" Julie said.

"You wouldn't believe it," Mark answered, "What in the hell's goin' on?"

"I have no idea ... except that it's gotta' have something to do with that nutball program you're working on."

"Ya' mean this," Mark said as he pulled the pouch of computer cards out of his pants.

Suddenly, there were gunmen everywhere. They came out of the bushes, the trees, and even the nearby park ranger building. He had been followed, probably by a silent helicopter. "It's the Mossad," Julie screamed, "It must be." She was hopeful, knowing the Mossad probably wouldn't kill them.

But it wasn't the Mossad. It was the same men who killed the other professors and students and they soon came to that terrifying conclusion. The idea that they were both now about to die started to fight its way into their consciousness and each looked to the other for guidance. Mark, feeling they had nothing to lose, yelled "Run," and they did. They ran like they had never run before. They ran so fast, it was as if they sprouted wings.

The gunmen opened fire in a blazing fusillade of bullets that no one could escape. But upon hearing the shots, Mark and Julie, knowing the area intimately, instinctively dove behind a retaining wall they had made love at several times. This was familiar territory to them, but not to the killers. Unfortunately, it only bought them about a minute's worth of time while the enemy regrouped and came after them.

"Give it to them," Julie screamed.

"They'll kill us!" Mark said in a surprisingly calm voice. "It's the only thing keeping us alive," he said as he realized that they might, just might, realize that in their gunfire they would probably hit the pouch and destroy the cards. *But maybe that's what they want*, he thought. It was a calculated risk and even he didn't know where his reasoning, not to mention his courage, came from. He stood up, holding the pouch in the air and shouted, "You want these! Shoot 'em!"

The guns stopped and there was an eerie stillness. The air was hot and dry, there was no breeze, and there wasn't a sound to be heard. It was if the whole world had gone silent for these few seconds. Then, "Give us package and you live."

"You let the girl run away safe, I'll lay it right here and then I go away." Mark had no idea where his confidence and bravado were coming from, but he rather liked the feeling.

After some muffled discussion he heard, "Nohno mowafiqoon," and then quickly, "We agree," in a thick, angry accent. But then, all the voices he had heard that day were angry. Turning to Julie he calmly said in a voice he had never known before, "Go ... run as fast as you can straight to the airport and get the hell out of this nightmare. I'll hook up with you later."

"But..."

"No time for buts," he said in a voice he still didn't recognize but was beginning to feel comfortable with. He grabbed her and kissed her hard, as if they were in an old movie, and yelled "Run!" She did and never looked back.

They shot her dead in her tracks and tried to shoot Mark, but he was too quick for them. Diving into the bushes behind the wall, he had no idea what he hoped to accomplish, but it seemed to be the only option he had. Lying there with the gunmen converging on him, he prayed for divine intervention and he got it. Suddenly, the whole area erupted into one giant cannonade of gunfire. But these gunshots sounded different, almost as if they were from different guns. He hunkered down in the fetal position and hoped it would all end. It did, in another eerie silence that also sounded different. But he was in no mood to find out why as he ran faster than the 5.10 hundred yard dash he ran as a track star in high school. He ran for his life now, the *Prophecy* computer cards intact.

* * *

It was the waiting. The Dogs knew that getting in position early while it was dark meant some agonizing hours of waiting. Combat soldiers will tell you that the worst part of their job, and something they do far too much of, is waiting. It was often *hurry up and wait* and it could be nerve-wracking. Waiting for orders. Waiting between missions. Waiting for the next patrol. Waiting for an IED to blow you to bits or a sniper you'll never see shoot you in the head from 500 yards away. But Chuck had the patience of a fisherman. Maybe it was from his long days surfing the Pacific, waiting for the perfect wave. Maybe it was from his high school football days, waiting for that perfect pass opportunity. But whatever it was, he would now need it as he perched in this Syrian stinkhole waiting for the bloodbath that was sure to come.

"You feel like you're on the crapper," Jim Hawkins had said once, "Like you're waiting for that last little turd to drop. You wanna' squeeze it out but you know if you do, you'll smash it into your butt-crack and have a dirty butthole. So, you sit there trying to force your cheeks to relax so it can drop on its own and you can have a clean wipe."

Chuck didn't know if that was a good analogy or not, but today it was a particularly excruciating kind of waiting because they had to stay very still for many hours so that the locals wouldn't see them and report them to the enemy. They knew that SDF forces would tell them when and where the ISIS soldiers were coming, but that didn't make the hours of staying hidden and immobile any easier.

They were all taught how to put their minds in a sort of removed, disconnected state or semi-trance to endure the waiting, but at the same time stay vigilant and focused on their mission. The base psychologist showed them some small mental tricks to let their minds wonder between random thoughts without getting distracted by any one particular notion and to remain fully aware of everything around them at the same time.

Chuck's thoughts travelled back to his father's advice that a person can think *too much* and the thoughts can get in the way of one's instincts. "Every operation needs good planning," he would say, "But when the bullets start flying, even the best plans often go out the window and you have nothing but your instincts ... you just have to know how to recognize them."

"How do I do that?" Chuck had asked, wondering when his dad had ever seen any bullets flying.

"You'll have to figure that one out for yourself. Some people use deep meditation, some daydream, some pray, some just sit quietly. But you won't always have that luxury, so you'll have to learn to tap into your own instinct in your own way."

Chuck had spent the last few years doing just that and had developed the instincts of a great warrior and leader. But, just as planning is no substitute for good instinct, instinct without good planning won't do it either. He knew you needed both. Then he remembered that his dad said not to worry too much because for him, that instinct came naturally. He wondered if it really did.

To pass the time patiently, Chuck had always been able to occupy his mind with mundane thoughts that didn't distract him from his surroundings. But lately, whenever he had too much time on his hands, his mind was taking him places he didn't want to go. Doubts about the war were randomly creeping into his head and every soldier knows how dangerous those doubts can be. If you don't believe in the war you're fighting, it can chip away at your incentive and motivation to be the fighting machine you need to be to survive and help others survive. Fleeting questions like *should we be here? Are we making things worse? Do these people even want us here? Do they consider this just another Crusade and a war on Islam?* And then the big one: *Did we create ISIS?* These are the questions that are dangerous for any soldier to ask and they all knew it.

Knowing he had to push the misgivings out of his mind, Chuck again shifted his thoughts back to the men around him. They were a crazy bunch, but very skilled soldiers, each with his own deadly specialty. The big Texan, Master Sergeant Scott Sampson liked to tell anyone who would listen that everything was bigger in Texas and after seeing him in the shower, his comrades were beginning to wonder if it was true. One thing Chuck knew for sure was that Scott was a tough warrior and, at the same time a tactical genius, and someone you wanted to have your back.

Chuck's reflections then floated to Lance Corporal Skip Bailey. He was from the hills of Tennessee and they called him Penpal because he wrote so many letters home. He also kept a journal and wrote in it religiously. He never said much, but when he did talk, everyone listened. It wasn't that what he said was so profound, it was just that he talked so little, the other men wanted to hear whatever he had to say. Many of them often wondered what he was writing in that little green notebook of his.

Then there was Will Daniels, the one they called JFK. Private Daniels saw conspiracies behind everything from the CIA killing President John F. Kennedy to the oil companies murdering the guy who invented the 100 mile-a-gallon carburetor to a faked moon landing. Most of the Dogs thought he was a little crazy, but they liked to hear him espouse his conspiracy theories.

But thinking about his men was a little too distracting and it was only a matter of time before he drifted back to *The Book*.

No Such Thing as Time

Albert Einstein said, *"The distinction between past, present, and future is only an illusion, however persistent."* In other words, there is no such thing as time. It exists only in the mind. We made it up to satisfy our neurotic need to measure our lives in increments and keep track of how long we have to live so we can count it down in days, months, and years. Time doesn't pass or go fast or slow because it doesn't exist, except in our minds. We created it and now it runs our lives. You can't enjoy each moment of life and live in the present if you are constantly looking at the clock. If you do, you're like a dog on a leash and time is your leash. You're not its master, it is yours. It doesn't serve you, you serve it. You have to meet its timetable, it doesn't have to meet yours. It makes you worry about what you already missed and what you might miss in the future. If there is no time, all things are happening at the same time and at different times simultaneously. If that is true, I write these words now, I wrote them 10,000 years ago, and I write them 10,000 years from now, all at the same time. Krishna says *"there never was a time we didn't exist and there will never be a time we don't exist."* Does that mean we are actually living and dying at the same time; that there is no time and space and as we live, we die? Damned if I know. Then there is the more mainstream religious way of looking at time. In the Old Testament Rabbi Elijah Solomon writes, *"All that was is and will be unto the end of time."* In the New Testament Psalm 90:4 says *"For a thousand years in your sight are as yesterday."* Does this mean that all time exists at the same moment and that there are no time and space limitations? All I know is that there is no such thing as time as we know it.

Now this can't be dad, he said to himself, as he knew that neither of his parents were existentially philosophical. In truth, it sounded a little like his best friend in high school, Tom Griffin. *But why in the world would Tom's journal be in our garage?* He remembered how Tom believed in time-travel, saying that time was fluid and flexible. He was convinced that a strong enough gravitational pull, like that in black holes, could make time bend back on itself meaning travelling back into the past. And he liked to quote T.S. Eliot's famous line, *"time present and time past are both perhaps present in time future, and time future contained in time past."*

But, whoever wrote this *Book* entry, Chuck disagreed with it. He liked the chronological orderliness of time and believed that without it, life would be pure chaos. *Besides*, he thought, *living for the moment is okay if you live in fantasy land, but not in the real world*, and living in the real world he was. Then he remembered being surprised one day back in high school when he came home to find Tom and his dad discussing time and existence. After Tom left, Don told him his friend was a freaked-out hippie, but he had the vague suspicion that the two agreed on more than his father would ever admit.

No way could it be Tom's journal, he thought as he was snapped back to the present by a slightly nasal voice over the radio saying, "What ever happened to the B battery? We've got the double A and triple A, the C and *D*, but where's the B?" It was Private Jim Hawkins again with one of his strange observations. Chuck clicked his radio three times, signaling for silence. Hawkins often irritated him, but sometimes, like now, his bizarre remarks helped pass the arduous time and relieve the mounting tension. The rest of the men simply smiled inwardly, grateful for the distraction.

Hawkins was a crack-shot marksman who grew up on a ranch in Montana. A natural born killer and the best shot in the Army, he had saved many soldiers' lives along the way, which was why he was often forgiven for breaking protocols. He usually said whatever came to his mind, even if it went against orders. As usual, the rest of the Dogs simply ignored his odd question.

His musings about his men now spoiled, Chuck latched onto the first random thought that came to his mind, his high school football days and particularly his friend and favorite wide receiver Tom Griffin. Everyone called him Buddha because of his deep interest in Buddhism and other eastern religions, which he simply called *spiritualism*.

Back in those days Tom divided most of his time between surfing, football, meditation, and Martial Arts. Chuck asked him many times to surf with him, knowing how dangerous it can be to surf alone. But he always answered that he had to do it alone to avoid any distractions from his oneness with the ocean. What worried Chuck was that Tom regularly surfed the most hazardous areas with the most treacherous rocks and reefs. But you couldn't talk him out of it because they had the best waves. Possibly because of his transcendental ability to focus and concentrate, he was never injured in a surfing accident.

As far as football was concerned, the team had a unique offense with Tom sometimes playing wide receiver, sometimes tight end, and sometimes even running back. But whatever position he played, Chuck knew that if he got the ball within three yards of him, he would catch it. It was like he had human radar. Without looking, he seemed to know the second the ball left his quarterback's hands and exactly when and where he had to turn around to pluck it out of the air. But many times, he didn't turn around at all and the ball simply dropped over his shoulder into his outstretched arms so that he didn't miss a stride. It was as if he deliberately regulated his running speed to get himself to the exact spot at the precise moment the ball would drop out of mid-air. How he knew the exact millisecond Chuck let go of the ball was beyond him, since the timing of every play was different, but he was glad that he did. It gave him a lot of self-confidence in his throwing arm and allowed him to take chances with his passes that he couldn't take with any other receiver.

"How the hell do ya' do that?" Chuck asked him once as he stepped out of the shower, drying his long hair that stretched down to the middle of his back.

"Do what?" asked Tom, "Take a shower?"

"No, ya' dunce. How dya' know just when the ball's coming."

"Oh that," Tom said, wearied by the question, "I become one with the ball."

"Sounds like a loada' crap."

"Not buying it, huh," Tom said, "How 'bout this? It's the cosmic connection I have with my quarterback."

"More bullshit."

Finally, feeling Chuck's frustration, he said, "Okay as crazy as it sounds, this is the real story. Everything and everyone in the universe is made up of molecules and molecules are always moving in a constant state of flux."

"Oh man, here it comes," Chuck said like he had heard it all before.

Ignoring the slam, Tom continued, "No, I'm serious. All molecules vibrate. I vibrate at one speed and rhythm, you vibrate at another, and the football vibrates at still another. Through meditation I have learned to identify the ball's vibration pattern and I can feel it getting closer to me. The vibration gets more intense as it gets closer and it reaches a crescendo when it's right over my shoulder. I turn around and most of the time, it's there."

"Kinda' like a pigskin orgasm, huh?"

"I said crescendo, not climax."

"Is that why you sit out on the field sometimes staring at the ball? Are ya' trying to get a feel for its vibrations?" Chuck said a little incredulously.

"Maybe," Tom answered.

Staring at his friend for a good 60 seconds, Chuck didn't know whether he was pulling his leg or not. But then he decided that even Tom wouldn't make this one up. "I'll go with practicing the same pass 15 times a day."

"Could be that too," laughed Tom, "Or it could be that I hear you say '*turn*' when the ball is almost there."

Chuck was stunned. Watching Tom running down the field, he often whispered '*turn*' when the ball reached him. "How in the hell do you know that," he said, "I never told you I say that."

"Maybe a lineman told me," Tom said with a roguish grin.

"No way," Chuck replied with growing wonder, "I always say it under my breath."

"Well then, I guess we're back to that cosmic connection with my quarterback."

"Ya' mean you read my mind?"

"I mean maybe I actually do hear you ... in my mind."

Again, Chuck couldn't tell whether his friend was kidding or serious and had long ago stopped trying to figure him out. But whatever it was, he knew Tom played with the grace and precision of a ballerina and often seemed to be almost in a trance, like he was in his own little world. He was just happy that his friend made him look like a great quarterback.

Surprisingly, while receiving the most passing yards of any player in school history, Tom sometimes disparaged the very game he excelled at and warned of the uselessness of competition. "We're all connected parts of the same organism," he would say in the rare moments he actually spoke, "Why do we need to be better than each other? Does your right arm need to be better than your left? Should your feet have to compete with each other or should they work together to achieve the best outcome? Why not just do our own personal best and not worry about competing with others?" He didn't really care one way or another if the team won or lost its games. He only wanted to perform to the best of his own abilities.

But feeling he owed more to his own spiritual growth than to Chuck and the team, Tom decided not to go out for football in his senior year. He wanted to concentrate on his eclectic faith and martial arts training instead. But Chuck could be persuasive and after appealing to his sense of an organic, cosmic link between the two of them, he relented. Chuck suspected, however, that he did it for their friendship more than any supernatural connection. He just couldn't say it. The team went to state that last year, thanks in large part to the Lansing/Griffin combination.

Shortly after graduation, Tom suddenly disappeared with no explanation and no good-bye and this was just the kind of mystery that titillated his curiosity and made him want to be an FBI sleuth. Upon further investigation, he found that Tom apparently wanted to make a clean break from everything and start from scratch in another land. All his parents could tell Chuck was that he had gone to a school in China to study Buddhism and martial arts. When he tried to look up the school on the Internet he found nothing. So, he went to an old Chinese man in San Diego who Tom introduced him to once and asked him about it. At first, he was reluctant to say anything but then he asked, "You the football player?"

"Yeah," Chuck answered, "I was Tom's quarterback in high school."

"What did he say about catching the football?"

Chuck thought this question was a little strange but figured he had nothing to lose by answering, "He said he felt its rhythms and vibrations and knew exactly when to turn around and catch it."

"Sounds like his loada' B.S.," the old man said laughing, "All I can tell you is that he badgered me for information on a mythical school in China that teaches Buddhism, mysticism, and intensive martial arts. The rumor is that they go all the way up to a tenth degree black-belt."

"Tenth?" Chuck said as he wondered about the old man's sanity, "The highest I've ever heard of is 7th."

"The ancient stories say they actually go higher than 7, but only a few have them."

"Do they get weapons training at this mythical school?"

"Yes," the old man said, "With everything from swords to knives to nun chucks to escrima sticks to Chinese throwing stars."

"But is it real? Is it a real school?"

"Some people think it is, but I think it's just a legend," the old man said with a twinkle in his eye and Chuck could swear he saw him wink.

But real or not, Tom's mother told him that after seven years in Asia, he was now working for a humanitarian aid organization in Washington, D.C. His nostalgia was cut short, however, as Private Hawkins interrupted his and everyone else's thoughts with another physiological witticism.

"Hey guys," came the nasal voice, "Is there anything sweeter than trying to pinch a pimple for days and then it finally pops? It's like an acne orgasm." As usual, it was a Jim Hawkins quip about a bodily function and this one reminded some of the Dogs of just how young they were. Two still had acne. Once again, Chuck clicked his radio three times.

The radio was silent for close to 45 minutes until it made 4 distinct beeps. Each beep represented 15 minutes and that was a message from the SDF that their prey was about an hour out. Chuck then sent the men his own code of 4 beeps to make sure they understood the timeline. The waiting was almost over.

CHAPTER 5

A half-hour later the radio beeped twice meaning the Dogs' target was now 30 minutes away. Chuck relayed the beeps to his men and waited. 20 minutes later it came, the long-awaited voice over his radio's scrambled frequency. The frequency to his men was deliberately unscrambled. "Hold," it crackled, "ETA zero-niner," meaning nine minutes to action, not enough time for the enemy to figure out their plan or locate their position and certainly not enough time to stop the ambush. But it did give the men just enough time to move their arms and legs slightly to work out the kinks and cramps before they had to jump into action. The waiting was almost over.

SDF troops were now marching in from the other side of the neighborhood, pounding artillery as they went, and soon the enemy would be running right toward the Dogs. At least the ones that hadn't left town or slipped back into the Raqqa population. Chuck knew they would be back after the fighting died down to resume their hit-and-run guerrilla attacks. But, *at least we'll get these guys*, he thought.

"Home to Dogs," his earpiece crackled to life again, this time for the real thing. He responded by pushing a silent button on his belt twice.

"Fifteen-degrees north," the voice said. Three drones hovered over the buildings in front of them sending infra-red, real-time pictures of the ISIS positions back to the mobile command post. The post added satellite and blue print overlays of the streets and alleyways they walked and the buildings they were hiding in and sent them to a tiny screen in each man's helmet so they could see exactly where their foes were hunkering down. Without the drones it would be nearly impossible to see the enemy duck down narrow streets, creep around alleys, pad across rooftops, and head toward them. Of course, it didn't help that anyone who had stayed in the city welcomed the militants into their homes as they fled. They were afraid not to.

They were funny-looking things, these drones, and they were very popular. The Air Force had its MQ-9 Reaper and Predator, which looked like an upside-down airplane. The Army had its Raven, Shadow, Hunter, and I-Gnat, and the Marines had their Pioneer and Dragon Eyes. All total, about six or seven hundred of them were flying the unfriendly skies of Iraq and it was getting congested. Many of them were piloted by satellite from 7000 miles away at Nellis Air Force Base, 30 minutes outside of Las Vegas. It was like a giant video game, except that there was a two-second delay in the control of the aircraft.

They didn't only track enemy troop movements and fire missiles at the jihadists, however. To bury roadside bombs, the militants often burned gasoline on the asphalt to soften it up and then put the explosives beneath it, and it was the surveillance drones that came in handy here. Their heat sensors could detect the hot spots and warn nearby troops. Some bombs were activated by a radio frequency and sometimes an Air Force plane would fly over and flood the area with multiple radio signals, setting off the bombs.

"Sixty seconds," the radio voice pulled Chuck into the impending battle and he relayed the message to his men. They didn't know exactly what was about to hit them, but they knew it was big and that all hell was about to break loose. At least 60 ragtag enemy soldiers were running toward their position firing backward at an invisible enemy. Explosions could be heard in the background, but the real action was about to begin right here.

"Hold," Chuck radioed to his men. Ten seconds later it was a simple, quiet "Go."

The .50 caliber machine guns erupted from the rooftops like it was the fourth of July as Chuck and his men methodically picked off the moving targets one at a time with rapid, but precision fire. The enemy couldn't figure out who was shooting at them or from where. They kept running in total confusion. They thought they were running away from the action, not right into it.

"Ayna hom?" (*Where are they?*) a voice screamed from their ranks.

No answer.

"Ana la arahom!" (*I don't see them!*) someone else yelled.

Now the enemy was darting back and forth, trying to figure out how to escape the cascade of gunfire raining down from above and below. The only problem was that the more they ran, the more they died. They would have been better off hunkering down behind some cover until they could figure out where the unseen enemy was. Now there were only 10 of them left. Chuck finished off three and his men took the rest. Then total quiet. Even the big guns stopped.

Eerie, he thought.

"Second wave. 30 seconds," the radio voice said.

"Nobody move," Chuck said into his mouthpiece. Everyone froze in position and waited. They followed their lieutenant's orders without question because they knew he was always right. It was like he had an instinct for what the enemy would do. They all remembered once when he said he could smell an approaching enemy.

"How can you distinguish any smells in this stink-hole," Corporal Luis Salgado said.

"I grew up on a farm," was all Chuck would joke.

While they stood like statues, Jim Hawkins piped up with one of his strange questions, "Ya' ever pick your nose or rub yer' eyes with drain cleaner or battery acid on your fingers?" This made some of the Dogs snicker, thinking about the times when they did pick their nose or rub their eyes after putting drain cleaner in a sink or oiling their gun or cleaning crystallized sulfuric acid off of their car battery. None of the substances had any place in one's nose or eyes. Funny, what you think about when you're at death's door. As distracting as it could be, however, many of them felt empowered by Hawkins' casual attitude toward death and danger. Not fearing either, seemed to embolden them to conquer both. This nonchalance possessed them entirely and made them fearless soldiers. Soldiers who would survive.

And here came the enemy. Other fighters had joined the second wave and now at least 40 of them were bearing down on the Mad Dogs. Not exactly a scene from *Lawrence of Arabia*, turbaned men with scarves over their faces and carrying AK-47s came running into the Dogs' unexpected trap.

"Light 'em up," Chuck said coolly to his rooftop gunners and the .50 cals ripped through the militants like a hot knife through butter. They started dropping like flies, but they were quick studies and this group was a little smarter than the first, as they ran for cover. Chuck knew this was their best chance for a maximum kill and said simply, "What, you wanna' live forever? Advance." As if in an old western movie, each man walked slowly forward, firing and killing each fighter as he ran for protection. They could see the soldiers who were relatively close through their infrared goggles, an advantage the enemy didn't have, and with short bursts of fire, they hit their marks. For those farther away and harder to see, several drones hovering overhead focused an infrared laser beam on them and the Mad Dogs shot at the light.

"Grenades," he said, like he was ordering lunch at a diner, and they started firing their laser guided grenades at the fighters who managed to dive behind cover, blowing it all apart. The grenades looked like giant bullets and were guided by a software program. The computer figures the distance to the target and adjusts the force of the launch and how long it will take to explode. But they couldn't get to all of them and seeing that they were about to become sitting ducks, Chuck yelled, "Fall back!" The last man on the line, Sergeant Bill Rollins, hesitated only a second and that's all it took for a jihadist sharp-shooter to get a bead on him from a nearby apartment building. With a lucky shot, his head exploded like a ripe melon and at the same moment Chuck saw two of his men on the left flank go down. Instantly two other Dogs ran to them and helped them up. *Thank you Kevlar.* Uniformly they all dropped back as the rooftop machine guns covered their retreat.

Then, suddenly, a deafening silence. It was a standoff and time for the machine gunners to run as they had undoubtedly been spotted. As they beat their retreat down the stairs to the building's basement, all that was left was the distant sound of muffled helicopter blades chopping the air.

"15 degrees southeast," Chuck said into his radio and the dim sound suddenly shifted, just barely.

Ten seconds later it was, "Spray 50 degrees," like he was telling someone to water the garden.

Then it was nothing but ear-splitting, thunderous explosions as the silent helicopters suddenly made a lot of noise strafing the area. The Apache Longbows were kill machines armed with a .30 caliber machine gun and eight Hellfire missiles under each wing. The Blackhawks' two 7.62 mm machine guns hanging out of both doors sprayed everything in sight and the Cobra's turreted cannon peppered the area with 20 mm bullets while it fired its TOW and Sidewinder missiles at specific targets. Some of the older choppers carried four pods with 20 missiles each and the missile heads contained hundreds of darts that pierced anything and everything in their path. If you were on the ground, you were dead. Chuck's geographical instructions were critical because he didn't want them shooting his own men. But to make sure, he had moved the Dogs back about 30 yards to watch the carnage and to shoot anyone who somehow managed to escape.

The sound was deafening as the militants took overwhelming fire, just barely able to shoot back, but with no precision. The walls around them disintegrated until they realized they had nowhere to hide. In ultimate desperation, the ones who survived the onslaught fled. Unfortunate for them, they ran right into the death fire of the Mad Dogs and it was soon close to being over. The helicopters slipped silently back into the sky and the shooting died down.

"Hold," Chuck calmly told his men, and they knew there may be yet a third phalanx coming.

* * *

Blindly running through smacking branches and searing long grass, Mark suddenly realized that he had probably eluded whoever was chasing him. Then he painfully realized that he left the only woman he had ever loved behind to die.

Why didn't I ever tell her? The guilt was almost unbearable as he screamed "Julie!" But being the logical scientist he was, he also realized the massive gunfire was far behind and he wondered why. Then it hit him.

They were shooting at each other, not at him, which means there were now two forces in play. Either one force was protecting him against the other or, more likely, both wanted *Prophecy* and were willing to kill each other and him to get it. He wasn't naïve enough to think that anyone came to his rescue out of any altruistic motives. Both definitely wanted it and that made him wonder just exactly what it was that he had. But for now, it was run or die so he bolted through the trees and bushes with wild abandon. But, just as he crossed a deserted street, a sleek, black Chrysler convertible screeched to a stop right in front of him with its door open. "Get in!" the driver yelled. Looking back over his shoulder, Mark saw two approaching gunmen not far behind. He dove in head-first and the car sped away as fast as it had come.

"Stay down!" the driver said as he swerved around a corner. Crumpled upside down in the passenger seat, Mark looked like a broken store mannequin. Then they both heard it. Helicopter blades slicing the air overhead. The driver pulled an Uzi out of his jacket and started firing up at the chopper. Machine gun bullets ripped through the car's body and Mark would never forget the sound they made whizzing by his head, pulverizing and shredding the Chrysler. They barely missed him, but not the driver. Blood was shooting out of his neck and his head looked like a smashed pumpkin. Trying to upright himself, Mark couldn't dwell on the grisly scene for long as the car swerved into the curb. Miraculously, that bumped it back onto the road and suddenly the sun disappeared.

Finally working himself right side up, he saw that they had entered a tunnel. He also noticed that the driver's gun was resting on his leg, which was pressing slightly down on the accelerator pedal and the car started scraping the side of the burrow wall. Instinctively, he turned the ignition key off, grabbed the gun, and lifted the bloody leg off of the pedal. The convertible slowed down just enough for him to jump out right before it exited the tunnel and slowly collided with a light pole. Crouching and rolling on the pavement, he stood up to see the helicopter hovering over the tunnel entrance. Nothing to do but run back into the tunnel and he did. But then a new fear gripped him and he felt like he was being strangled as he saw a second helicopter approaching the entrance. *Who are these guys!* But no time to ponder that one. Then he prayed. He prayed for a door, a window, anything he could escape through. And there it was! A door in the tunnel wall.

It was almost as if God was giving him a doorway to Heaven. But as he grabbed the knob, his joy was short-lived as he discovered that it was *locked*! His head shot back and forth just in time to see black-clad men descending from both helicopters on ropes. Then it hit him. He still held the ultimate lock-pick. *The gun!* The first few shots sent the Uzi flying in all directions. All directions except at the door knob. But Mark was a fast-learner and gripping it tightly, he pumped more bullets into the knob, knocking it completely off the door. Crashing through it, he heard the distant sound of gunfire and bullets riddled the walls around him. His head immediately crashed into an overhead pipe as he realized he was entering a small sewer tunnel. Head ringing, he ducked down and blindly hurled himself through the pitch-black corridor as fast as he could. Twisting and turning through numerous curves and banging and bruising his body every step of the way, he finally came to a shaft of light shooting down from above. Shining through slits in a manhole cover, it threw shards of golden luminance into the tunnel revealing a ladder to the top. It was the most beautiful thing he had ever seen.

With renewed vigor, he climbed to the top and pushed on the cover. Locked in place by a padlock, it didn't budge even a centimeter. Panic gripped him as he heard voices coming down the passageway. Instinctively, he shot his remaining bullets at the lock and blew it apart. Throwing the gun down, he pushed upward, but still no movement. Then he saw it. A floor jack. Jumping down from the ladder, he moved the jack under the cover and feverishly pumped its handle. It moved the heavy iron plate just enough to make a small opening. The voices were only a few yards away now and he heard one say, "There he is!" Bullets whizzed by his head as he defied gravity and flew up the ladder. He squeezed his slim frame through the opening and out onto a busy street just as a pickup truck came barreling down on him. Instinctively hitting the concrete and rolling out of the way, he rolled right into the path of an oncoming Volvo. With quick reflexes the driver swerved around him and he jumped to his feet to see a miracle.

Fifty feet away, the bus was closing its door and getting ready to pull out. Heart pounding and head splitting, he sprinted forward and beat on the bus door with his fists. Surprisingly, the driver opened it for him. He got to his seat just in time to look out of the back-window and see the first head poke out of the manhole. Fortunately, his assailants weren't as skinny as he was. He turned to the inside of the bus as the other passengers stared at his scorched and torn clothes and scraped, bleeding body. Finally, he took a breath. *Who are these guys?*

* * *

The Dogs held. They held. And they held some more. No one said a word and they held. The sweat was pouring off of them by the gallon and they held. No one moved and each went into his own customized stoic mindset that enabled him to endure the exhausting tension, tormenting heat, and mind-numbing scene of death and destruction before them. It was like an extremely painful and torturous state of suspended animation that one simply accepts as the life of a desert soldier.

"He acts like he has all the time in the world," Ron Jenkins whispered to Greg Hanson.

"He knows exactly how much time he has," answered Hanson, "And that's how much time we have."

Private Hanson was mostly right, but for the wrong reason. Chuck knew something that some of the Dogs only suspected, that they were bait. Bait for a latent group of militants who had undoubtedly been monitoring the entire battle, waiting for the helicopters to leave so they could come in and attack the special forces unit that did much of the killing. They knew that this unit often stayed behind for mop-up operations and that there was sometimes a small window of opportunity to attack them before the helicopters came back and picked them up. A victory over such a unit, even with high casualties, would be a big public relations victory for them and would probably increase their recruitment.

The ISIS soldiers believed the ultra-organized nature of the American Military made it predictable while their own erratic nature made them unpredictable and they were often right. But they hadn't figured on the reverse being true when it came to Lieutenant Chuck Lansing and Sergeant Scott Sampson who had planned this bait and switch operation.

Chuck's radio crackled to life. "They're not buying it," a voice said, "Holding at 50 yards out."

"Retreat for pick-up!" Chuck uncharacteristically shouted into his radio, figuring that ISIS was now listening in on his radio traffic. The Mad Dogs instantly realized what was going on and began a slow, orderly retreat.

"Gotta' give 'em time to get to the party," Jenkins said to Hanson, trying to make up for his earlier criticism of their leader. The Dogs then spread out and began to move back.

After just a few steps Chuck got another message over his radio. "Sixty on the move southwest," the radio voice said, meaning the infrared cameras spotted about sixty militants moving into the area from the southwest. The Dogs continued their slow retreat and Chuck thought he could hear a slight chop, chop of a silent helicopter blade off in the distance. What he didn't hear was the Reapers silently hovering nearby waiting to launch the next explosive conflagration.

"That's far enough," Chuck told his men over the radio, "Extraction in five minutes." Again, he figured someone was listening in.

He was right and through their infrared goggles, the Dogs could see enemy soldiers pouring out from behind the buildings into the street from all directions. The only problem was that they were heading right for them and the attack helicopters and drones were nowhere in sight. Chuck didn't need to say "hold" over the radio because the men knew what they had to do. At that moment, they were nothing more than bait and they were fine with that. Nonetheless, it was difficult watching a bunch of hostiles coming at you and doing nothing as they all sweated bullets. Inescapably, they worried that something had gone wrong with the attack forces. *Maybe a sandstorm*, Chuck thought. Sometimes a sandstorm would come up out of nowhere and envelope everything in its path. He remembered once seeing a wall of sand blowing toward him, giving him only a few seconds to find cover.

But patience and discipline paid off as when the militants began firing at them, the Apaches, Cobras, Blackhawks, and Reapers swooped in like hungry vultures, shooting anything and everything in the area. Unavoidably, that included the Mad Dogs and they knew it. Wasting no time, Chuck yelled, "Retreat!" But he didn't really have to say it as the Dogs knew what was coming and beat the bricks as fast as their stiff legs could carry them. Just as Chuck started to hit his dead-run, a slight movement caught the corner of his eye and sent a message to his brain that he should take notice.

It was a little girl covered with dirt and dust standing in a doorway of some long-forgotten public building and holding a tattered doll that had seen better days. Instinctively, he bolted over to her, swept her up into his arms, and ran away from the now fierce firefight, all in one swift motion. As he ran off into the volcanic night, he stepped on a broken sign that had fallen to the ground and for a split-second he thought he recognized the words printed on it. *Al-Haj something*, he thought fleetingly. But his adrenaline wouldn't allow him the luxury of thinking about that long enough to make a mental connection and he ran on, losing any short-term memory of the episode.

Unfortunately, he had lagged behind his men for a few seconds, which was long enough for the big missiles to strike and the concussion threw him and his new passenger rolling in the dirt. Tucking his body around the girl, he rolled right back up to his feet, placing her gingerly on the ground and motioning for her to stay still. He then noticed that his men were in the firing position to shoot anyone who might miraculously make it out of the kill zone alive and realized he and the girl were in the way. Again, in one hasty motion, he pulled her down and, laying on top of her, aimed his M-4 Carbine at the battle. But, the girl had other ideas and started squirming frantically. He tried to keep her down, but noticed that some militants did indeed make it out of the fray and he could not keep her contained with one hand and fire with the other. Something had to give and it was the girl. She wriggled out from under him and just stood there watching Chuck try to sniper-shoot the escaping ISIS soldiers. He looked back at her for one second and was surprised to see a calm and serene look on her face. The look said that this wasn't the first time she had seen a firefight like this. And for another brief second, he realized how much voluminous information one single facial expression can communicate. But, now he had to snap back to the reality of keeping his men alive and returned to picking off the fleeing soldiers one-by-one.

Between finishing off the stragglers with his expert marksmanship and looking back for the girl, Chuck was approaching exhaustion. He looked for her fervently, but she was gone. She had faded back into the routinely-violent fabric of life in Raqqa. It was undoubtedly the only life she knew and somehow, he felt like she would be all right. *They're survivors.*

"Let's go," Chuck said calmly and he and his men returned to the area one last time, heading straight to the machine gunners' basement positions.

Trying to put the girl out of his mind, his thoughts were now totally honed in on the exact location of his machine gunners who had given them so much cover. "Jim! Buck!" his men yelled. Then, faintly, they heard "Over here!" And there they were, two grimy, gritty, filthy soldiers digging themselves out of the rubble. The same scene repeated itself in the basement across the street, although with a little more difficulty as that building had been accidentally hit by a missile.

Doing a radio headcount, they all realized they had lost two men. "Bill and Duckman didn't make it," Scott said quietly and they all froze in their tracks for what seemed like an eternity. It hit Chuck in the pit of his soul and he felt responsible for his comrades' deaths. *I should've retreated sooner. Why do I always have to push it to the last possible moment?* Now Bill Rollins and Allen Jones were dead. What didn't occur to him was that overall, pushing the envelope had probably saved more lives than it lost.

Bill Rollins was the comedian in the outfit and often sent the Dogs into fits of laughter. Then there was Allen Jones, affectionately called Duckman. *What a character,* Chuck thought as he remembered fondly how he got his name. Allen always carried a roll of duct tape with him and said it was the best thing ever invented, next to Velcro, Super Glue, Viagra, and the birth control pill. The Dogs made fun of him for the duct tape until it saved their lives a few times.

But now Chuck was forced back to the present as they tallied up the enemy casualties. They had killed almost 130 ISIS soldiers, which was unusual since they normally attack in very small groups making it hard to kill them in large numbers. This was the single largest battle so far and they had lost only two men. But for that reason, Chuck still considered the mission a failure. The moral question was, of course, *is it worth it?* But the practical question was *is 130 enough?* Or were they producing more than 100 terrorists for every one killed as the man who sent them into Iraq had said? Yes, even some military leaders worried that we were producing more terrorists than we could kill. He hung his head in doubt and knew that for the sake of the rest of his men he had to recover quickly. All they could do now was board the awaiting helicopters. The grieving would have to wait.

As they rode the helicopters back to their base in stony silence, they all thought about their fallen comrades. Normally they would look forward to hot showers to wash the smell of gun powder, sweat, and in Chuck's case, sewage from their bodies. But the worst was the smell of burning flesh from the scorched bodies they left behind. It often took days to get that one out of their nostrils. Not today however. Today it was the hollow feeling of losing a family member. As their leader, Chuck felt like he was to blame and asked himself over and over what he could have done to prevent their deaths. *Could I have planned better? Should I have positioned them better?*

As if he read his mind, Scott Sampson, who had made the plan with him, said, "Don't go there chief ... it was a good plan and there's nothing else we could do."

Statistically speaking, losing two men and killing 130 of the enemy was a pretty good ratio. But he felt that losing even one man was too many. *And for what?* he pondered, *Besides, who is the enemy anyway?* But what was really tormenting him was the tragic face of that little girl. Was he really fighting for her protection and freedom or was he helping to destroy both? Now he braced himself for what he knew was coming next. Lately, when he had thoughts like these, a pounding headache came along with them and now one was coming on fast. He wondered if someone or something was trying to tell him something.

* * *

On the run, ragged, burned, and bloody, Mark sweltered in his bus seat in a panicked daze. Going over the last few hours in his mind, he could scarcely believe what had happened. His head was throbbing and he was bleeding on the seat. Just as he was starting to feel like he could breathe a sigh of relief, he looked out of the back window to see a horrifying sight. A black Cadillac was fiercely passing cars right and left and gaining on the bus. *Who are these guys?* he asked himself again. With no time to contemplate that question, he jumped out of his seat and ran to the front of the bus.

"Turn right!" he yelled.

"Sit down sir." The driver responded.

Seeing no choice, Mark pulled part of the pouch out of his pants and screamed, "I've got a bomb. Turn right or I'll blow us all to hell!" Every Israeli understood bombs and the driver did as he was told. Just as the lumbering bus turned the corner Mark pulled the exit lever and opened the door while yelling, "Keep driving!" Then, like a hobo jumping off a freight train, he aimed his body forward, leaped out of the door, and hit the ground running. He ran for the nearest building, bolted through the first door he came to, and ran up the stairway in front of him. It was an old broken-down apartment building and luckily the security door was unlocked.

Still scared of the mad bomber, the bus driver kept driving with the Cadillac right behind him. The car then passed him and skidded to a stop in front of the lumbering vehicle, forcing it to a stop. Two men dressed in black jumped out of the Caddie and climbed aboard the bus whose door was still hanging open. Methodically they walked down the aisle slowly waving their guns back and forth looking for Mark. "Where is he?" one turned and asked the driver in a heavy accent.

"He got off back there," he said motioning behind them.

Quickly sizing up the situation, the two gunmen bounded off the bus and yelled to their comrades. "Cover the street. He jumped off back there." The four men tried every door on the street and they were all locked. Then they came to the apartment building door and threw it open.

Meanwhile Mark was huffing and puffing up the stairs until he frantically reached the rooftop door. *Locked! The front door is open and the roof is locked. Why not!* he thought as he frantically looked around for something he could use to break the door down. And there it was, a fire extinguisher hanging on the wall. He quickly grabbed it and started pounding the doorknob. It broke off on the fifth hit and he flew through the door out onto the roof. Swiftly sprinting across the rooftop, he saw that his only possible escape route was to the building next door, which was at least a 6-foot jump. Recalling his high school long jump days, he ran back toward the door to get a run for literally the leap of a lifetime. Hearing his pursuers running up the stairs behind him pumped him up with adrenaline and once again he ran faster than he had ever run in his life. He reached the edge of the roof just as the four men burst through the door behind him. The first thing they saw was him flying through the air, pumping his arms and legs as he went. He hit the other roof running and rolling as the four gunmen ran toward him firing.

With bullets whizzing by his head, he ducked behind a large roof air conditioner and then worked his way around to the new rooftop door. *Locked!* Not surprised, but very scared, he peeked around the corner to see the men on the roof he had just come from maneuvering a long board across the space between the two buildings. *Oh crap!* He ran to the opposite edge to see if he could jump to the next building. *Nope.* It was at least ten feet and he wasn't that good. Desperately he scanned the roof for anything that he could use to break the doorknob on this door. *Nothing!* Poking his head around the air conditioner, he saw one of the men crawling across the board as the other three held it in place. He was almost ready to surrender and give them the cards, hoping for mercy, when he saw it.

CHAPTER 6

I t was dark in the Mad Dog's barracks. Dark with depression over their lost comrades. Though he didn't feel like it, Chuck knew it was time for some heavy grieving and even heavier drinking and that meant a visit to Captain Johnson.

"Request permission to go to Pancake sir," he said to the captain.

Johnson looked at him long and hard and Chuck almost thought he noticed some empathy on his stony, emotionless face. "You deserve it son and I'll clear your schedule for the next 48 hours," he said, "Just be careful."

Pancake was the name they had given a village outside of Baghdad that had been flattened by bombs in the first Iraqi war and left with one building standing. The Dogs had turned it into a getaway complete with a refrigerator full of beer. They used it to decompress after some of their more brutal missions and the brass looked the other way. Captain Johnson sometimes even sent patrols by the abandoned village to guard against anyone who might get a little too curious about them. They also had trip wires all around the building that would set off alarms if anyone other than the patrols came close.

They sat on old, musty chairs with moldy stuffing coming out of them while they drank beer and listened to rock-and-roll music. They had pirated what little electricity was left in the area. Occasionally, some of them brought Iraqi prostitutes there, but they didn't want to make a habit of it for fear that informants would reveal their location to the wrong people. It seemed like the more grueling the fight, the more they needed Pancake, and the Raqqa fight was an especially tough one. But, while they all tried to drink a lot after big battles like this one, the combination of sleep deprivation and sheer exhaustion usually limited them to a few beers each and a wearied sleep for all.

Now the mood was somber as the Dogs tried to drown their grief in a sea of alcohol as fast as possible. Scott always said you have to drink fast so you get drunk before you get tired. He now broke the silence with, "Here's to Bill, the funniest mother I ever knew," and they all took a long hard pull on their beers.

"What great impressions," said Juan Rodriguez.

"Yeah," said Chuck, "Everyone from the president on down."

"And here's to Duckman," said Mike Sandstone raising his glass, "The guy who saved our asses more than once with that damned duct tape of his."

"Here. Here," they all chanted as they reflected on the time they were pinned down by the enemy in an Iraqi village with no way out. Duckman crawled onto a nearby school bus. He ripped off the big inside mirror that bus drivers use to watch their little passengers and duct-taped it to the bus ceiling behind the driver's seat. Then he broke the side mirror off and held it up to that mirror, which reflected the front windshield. That way he could crouch down, looking backward into the rearview mirror reflecting the big mirror and see out of the windshield without exposing himself to enemy fire.

"Remember what he said when he stole that bus?" said Ron Jenkins, barely able to hold in his laughter.

"Yeah," said Scott guffawing and spitting out a mouthful of beer, "Attention passengers. The bus will pick you up at the end of the alley in 10 seconds."

"He sounded like a freakin' tour guide," said Luis Salgado.

Chuck remembered how casual Duckman had sounded on the radio as if he was announcing departures and arrivals at the bus station. Guiding it by the mirrors, he gunned the bus down the alley in first gear. This was no small feat considering he had to steer with one hand and hold the mirror and shift gears with the other while working the clutch and accelerator with his feet. The big hulk went careening down the narrow street, knocking over streetcarts, scraping the alley walls as it went, and taking on heavy enemy fire.

Grinding the gears to a halt, he opened the door and yelled, "All aboard." The dogs scrambled onto the bus and hit the floor as ISIS militants pummeled it with bullets that ripped easily though its thin metal, turning it into Swiss cheese. Jerking down the road in a drunken swerve, they felt a powerful blast as a Law Rocket blew off the top half of the bus. "Air conditioning!" Duckman yelled as he finally sat upright and managed to drive in a straight line of escape. Everyone dove into fits of laughter at that memory and then the room went dead-quiet as abruptly as it had erupted in raucous laughter. Again, they settled back into their silent grief.

At that moment, Jim Hawkins returned from the latrine and stopped short. With his head bowed and a weird look on his face, even for him, he looked up and said, "I just took such a huge dump that my pants fit better."

No response.

"Okay then," Jim said, "On a more practical note, have you ever noticed how obsessed people are with their shit? They always gotta' look at what they just put in the pot. What do they think they're gonna' see? Is it gonna' jump out and say thank you for givin' me life?"

"You probably look at yours," said a slightly homo-phobic Greg Hanson, "To see if there's any blood in it from yer' last butt-ramming."

Now it was on. It started out as a soft, short chuckle, then slowly grew into a communal snort, and finally ended up in another giant group-fit of hysterical laughter. Hawkins had gotten what he wanted, but when the laughter died, another somber silence settled over the men as they descended back down into their grief on their way to some booze-soaked, mind-numbing relief.

After a few songs went by, Private Rick Steadman tried to lighten the mood. "Speaking of bizarre shit," he said, "I just heard a weird story about an aid convoy that got ambushed somewhere in Syria from a guy who just got back from there."

"What was bizarre about it?" asked Chuck, welcoming the distraction.

"Well ... he said snipers picked off the guys guardin' the convoy one-by-one and then came down from the hills to kidnap the aid workers and steal the supplies."

"Yeah," said Scott, "What's new about that?"

"I'm gettin' to that. So about 16 or 17 bad guys come down and surround the lead trucks. Some more soldiers pop up and the shootin' starts. When it was over, all of the good guys were dead but only about five of the bad guys."

"So, what happened to the rest of 'em," said Ron Jenkins, now getting a little enthralled with the story.

"That's the weird part. He claims that then some crazy civilian in a white robe jumped on top of one of the trucks and threw knives at the enemy, killing about half of 'em."

"And the other half?" Now Mike Sandstone was getting interested.

"That's the unbelievable part. After he killed five of 'em with his knives, he did a flip off the truck with a sword in one hand and Chinese throwing stars in the other. The guy claims that as he ran at them, he hit the first three with the stars right in the neck and cut two others down with his sword."

"What about the last two?" asked John Boland, mentally adding up the casualties.

"Apparently, he stuck one guy with his sword and disarmed the last guy all in a couple a' seconds."

"Why didn't they just shoot him?" asked Ben Jackson.

"I know how it sounds," said Steadman, "And I asked the same thing. All he said was that the fools were so stunned at first that they hesitated and by the time they started shooting, the crazy ninja was moving so fast and bobbing and weaving so much that they couldn't hit him."

"So, what happened to the last bad guy?" asked Scott.

"That's where it gets even better. He said he told that guy to run back to his friends and warn them that the same thing would happen to them if they ever attacked another aid convoy."

"Sounds like a loada' horse-shit to me," said Hawkins.

"Probably is," said Steadman, "But it's just what this guy said."

Soldiers often heard tales of heroic acts by other soldiers that were probably exaggerated or flat-out lies. But, this was the first one they had heard about a super-human civilian.

"I'd like to meet this crazy ninja ... if he exists," Chuck said as he surveyed his engrossed men.

"That's a big if," said Scott laughingly, "Sounds to me like a Bruce Lee wannabe. But if he does exist, putting you two together might cause a nuclear explosion and get us all killed in the process. No offense."

"None taken," said Chuck with a slight grin that he had to work at as he noticed Corporal Skip Bailey scribbling in his journal. "Are ya' gettin' all this down Penpal?" he said.

"Huh?" said Bailey looking up from his notebook red-faced.

"Are ya' writin' a novel from Steadman's fairy tale?"

Regaining his composure and with a serious tone, Skip said simply, "Actually I'm writing about whether these assholes really appreciate what we're doing over here or just want us to go home."

"Where'd that come from Corporal?" said Chuck surprised. But, not really wanting an answer, he recovered with, "Well, if they don't, maybe God does."

"Maybe, but I'd like to hear it from them once in a while. It'd make me feel like I'm doing the right thing."

"Ours is not to reason why ... "

"Yeah ... yeah ... I know, but sometimes it's hard not to."

"That doesn't rhyme," Chuck said, "Besides, my ole' pappy used to say if you want people to thank you for fightin' their fight or doin' the right thing, yer' on the wrong planet."

"Apparently, your old man was right, but it's a little cynical don't ya' think?"

"Maybe, but it's thinkin' like that gets you nowhere and might get ya' killed." What Chuck didn't say was that his own doubts were growing daily and he couldn't stop wondering if his dad was right; that they never should have invaded Iraq in the first place. Then a casual comment hit him like a ton of bricks.

"Ya' know," Mike Sandstone said, "The reasons we got into this thing in the first place don't really matter. What does matter is that these guys we're killin' are really bad guys."

That's it! How simple. That's why I'm here, to kill bad guys!

"Yeah," said Ben Jackson, "But they don't think they're the bad guys. They think they're fightin' for their country and their God." This was another idea soldiers didn't want to dwell too much on.

What was it dad said? Chuck thought, *Oh yea,* "*What would you do if another country invaded the U.S.?*" He remembered answering, "*Fight, of course.*"

Scott Sampson usually kept quiet during discussions like this, but now he simply said, "All I know is that they're like cockroaches. The more ya' kill, the more come out of the woodwork."

They thought about that one for a while. All had the same thought at one time or another and the question was could they ever kill enough of them.

"The hell with that," Scott said, raising his beer can, "To Duckman and Bill." They all followed suit and once again toasted their fallen comrades.

"Duckman and Bill," they said in unison and Chuck thought he noticed a few sloshed-but-tough tears. Then they all settled back into a semi-drunken meditation, each with his own demons. Most reflected on their lost friends. But some of their thoughts drifted to that ever-nagging doubt about whether or not their country was really looking out for them.

They had all heard about too many young soldiers with PTSD, Gulf War Syndrome, neurological abnormalities, kidney stones, lymphoma, and other forms of cancer. Some had their prostates removed because of prostate cancer and the worst were the recently married ones whose surgeries made them impotent. The rumor was that it was from breathing the smoke from the burn pits where they burned everything, including toxic materials, or from the radiation emitted from depleted uranium shells left all around the Iraqi desert. 315 tons of depleted uranium dust to be exact with radiation that lasts for about four-and-a-half billion years.

In 1991 the U.S. and its allies blasted Iraqi vehicles with armor-piercing shells made of depleted uranium on the "Highway of Death," 11 miles north of Kuwait. The Dogs couldn't help but notice the tanks, armored personnel carriers, and other military vehicles still sitting there in the desert, rusting and emitting radiation. Depleted uranium is super tough material and makes for great weapons. Unfortunately, the shell holes are 1000 times more radioactive than normal background radiation and the areas around the vehicles are about 100 times more. Some scientists say it is a veritable toxic wasteland.

But the bigger problem is that when a depleted uranium round hits its target, as much as 70 percent of it can burn up on impact, creating a firestorm of ceramic-depleted uranium oxide particles. The residue is an extremely fine ceramic uranium dust that can be spread by wind, inhaled and absorbed into the human body, and soaked up by plants and animals, becoming part of the food chain. Once lodged in the soil, it can pollute the ground water and there was strong evidence of skyrocketing birth defects among the Iraqis who live in the area. Though an army manual told the soldiers there was nothing to worry about, they wondered.

Just when he thought he could drift off to sleep, Chuck's satellite phone rang. "Roger," he said and then turned to his men, "R-and-R goes on, but I gotta' go to another briefing," he said. Half-expecting something like this, he had nursed only one beer during the night.

"Let's go" Chuck motioned to Scott and Junior Sergeant Joe Gercek. Joe was originally from Turkey and had long ago converted from Islam to Catholicism. "From one extremist religion to another," Jim Hawkins sometimes chided him. The three of them jumped in their Humvee and drove off into the ominous, murky night.

* * *

Mark's mind went soaring back to his high school track days as he stared at the steel cable hanging from the construction crane poking it's towering arm over the edge of the roof. Quickly gauging the distance from the crane to the next roof, he calculated that if he ran fast enough, he could swing on the cable to the roof, but there would be almost no room for error. With no time for more exact calculations, he headed for the cable and heard, "Hatha howa!" (There he is!), as he ran.

Now running at an increasing speed with bullets zipping by his head, he grabbed onto the cable and sprinted full-bore in a semi-circle around the roof. When he reached the edge, he launched himself into mid-air and swung in an arc, kicking his legs all the way. He flew through the air feet first and twisted his upper body forward as he went, just like he used to do in the long jump in high school. Finally, he crash-landed onto the edge of the next roof in a violent collision, barely clutching its precipice with his bleeding hands and arms and held on for dear life. His heart now pumping wildly, he heaved himself up over the edge with gunshots still ringing in his ears.

Running for cover, he glanced back at the men still shooting at him, amazed that he hadn't been hit. But as he ducked behind the rooftop air conditioner, he realized that he was a moving target and too far away for their handguns. There was, however, one troubling thing he noticed in his furtive glance. There were now only two men on the other roof.

That means the other two went down to the street to the apartment building I'm on! Of course, this roof door was also locked and quickly looking around, he saw that there was no fire extinguisher and, alas, no crane. The next building was too far away for a long jump and now, drained of all ideas for escape, he was again about to give up. *End of the line!* It seemed that things couldn't get much worse as he stood there numb and helpless. Then he heard it.

It was a chop, chop, chopping sound like a sword hacking through thin air, and it was coming from above. Slowly raising his head to the sky, he looked directly into the sun, but there was something in the way. *A helicopter. More bad guys!* He bolted to the far side of the building but that made him an easy target for the gunmen. Darting back the other way, he suddenly froze as he realized that he would be in the helicopter's gun sights. *What the hell?* he thought as he looked up and saw what looked like a rope ladder come tumbling out of the chopper. Fully expecting another gunman to climb down it, he began to run, but to where, he didn't know. The helicopter followed him with the ladder trailing a few feet behind him. Then a strange thing happened that made him stop abruptly. The two men on the other roof began firing upward. *Why would they shoot at their own people?* There was only one answer. *They aren't their people.*

As Mark stopped with a jolt, the ladder passed him by and was now dangling just beyond the edge of the roof. He knew he had only one chance. *Wish I would've worked harder in track.* Summoning up every scrap of energy he had left, he ran at breakneck speed for the ladder, knowing that this was it. He was most likely looking at three possible scenarios. First, if he missed the ladder, he would undoubtedly fall to his death on the street below. Second, if he caught the ladder and managed to climb up into the helicopter, the men flying it may well be the bad guys and it wouldn't be long till he was ... you guessed it ... dead. Of course, the third option was the preferable one. In it, he makes it into the chopper and the guys inside are the good guys.

The helicopter stayed still as the pilot realized that if he tried to move the ladder closer to Mark, it would make it harder, not easier, for him to grab onto. As the wind swooshed by his head, he heard the two missing men burst out of the rooftop door and start shooting. Knowing he had only one chance, it was do or die as he left his feet and leaped off the edge of the roof into thin air. His flight suddenly seemed to shift into low gear and everything went into slow-motion. He felt like he was running underwater and seconds seemed like hours. *I'm not gonna' make it!* But he did. Hitting the ladder in mid-air and at full speed, he grabbed onto one rung with his left arm and wrapped his right arm around the rope. All four gunmen now fired at him and he could once again hear the bullets whizzing by his head. But then, he felt the chopper moving away and heard its reverberations fading into the wind.

Now wrapping his left arm around the other rope, he hung limp as a wet rag as he flew over the streets and rooftops of Jerusalem. *Finally, a break,* he thought as he looked up and wondered who these guys were. Once again, however, there was no time to ponder the question because he suddenly slipped downward and jerked to an abrupt halt. *What the...?* Then another slip and then another. Looking up, he saw that some of the bullets had struck the rope ladder and one of the ropes above him was unraveling.

"Climb!" a voice shouted from the helicopter and he did. Realizing his only hope was to climb above the frayed rope, he reached for the crooked ladder steps and pulled himself up inches at a time as the rope continued to unravel. The problem was that the harder he pulled on the ladder, the more the rope came undone. Just when he thought things couldn't get any worse, they did. With horror, he noticed that the other rope was starting to unweave too. *They couldn't hit me, but they hit both ropes!* Then it all got even worse as a computer card began poking its way out of his pants. *After all this, they come out now!* Letting go of the rope with his left hand, he poked it back in, feeling it dig into his thigh while holding all his weight with his right.

He then desperately grabbed back onto the rope and looked up at the chopper with a pain and trepidation that must have struck the man who told him to climb the ladder because he yelled, "He's not gonna' make it! Go down!" Just then, the frayed rope slipped again and with a fierce jerk, came completely apart, leaving Mark flying crookedly through the air. Now with his life literally hanging by a thread and the one remaining rope peeling away, he thought it was all over. He had always heard that at a time like this, your life passes before your eyes. But all that was passing before his was a blur of streets and buildings as he flew through the air.

Figuring Mark's only hope was to get him down to the ground before the last strand broke, the chopper pilot started a quick descent. But then came the power lines and he had to go back up. Slowly, the chopper descended to the nearest flat rooftop, but not quite slow enough as the last strand split in two and Mark fell eight feet to the hot asphalt roof in one swoop. He hit hard, but instinctively rolled to his feet unaware of his swelling cuts and bruises and the growing pains in his body.

Running blind with no idea of where he was going, his eyes suddenly focused on the chute used for sliding construction trash down to the street. *Must be remodeling,* he thought as he bolted for the opening. Just like the huge water park he had frequented as a kid in New York's Adirondack Mountains, he threw himself into the downward tunnel feet-first and slid all the way down, landing in a dumpster. Climbing unsteadily out of the trash bin, he staggered and then ran as fast as his bruised legs could carry him. Realizing the helicopter was watching him and not completely sure who was flying it, he raced for what looked like a wooded park. Ducking under the nearest trees for cover, he could hear the blades cutting the air like a knife chopping vegetables. *Now what?* Fervently, he looked from left to right and back to front. He knew the chopper would see his exit from the small patch of woods, no matter which way he went. That meant that instead of east, west, north, or south, he had to go up or down. Up was definitely out and that left down.

Remembering the sewer tunnel from before, he began looking all around the ground with quaking fear. Then, he suddenly realized that the tunnels only ran under the streets, not the adjoining land. There would be no tunnel here and that made him stop once again and stand there numbly, not knowing what to do. Things looked bleak and he saw no way out. *I'm not a spy*, he thought, *what in the hell am I doing here anyway?*

He was about to give up all hope when a loud, thunderous growl came blasting out of the woods wrecking the quiet solitude of his defeat. *Now what!* he mouthed a silent scream and braced for the worst.

CHAPTER 7

N*o rest for the weary,* Chuck mused as he walked into Captain Johnson's outer-office for another mission briefing. He was more-than-surprised when Johnson yelled, "Come on in son, yer' gonna' have a visitor."

"Yes sir," Chuck saluted, wondering who it could be.

"Don't ya' wanna' know who's comin'?"

"Yes sir."

"Do ya' remember a guy named Tom Griffin?"

"What ... why?" Chuck was stunned at the news.

"Well, it seems Mr. Griffin was runnin' an aid convoy over in Syria and wants to stop by here on his way home to see his old buddy. He'll be here in a couple of days and we're putting him up for a night."

"Yes sir," was all Chuck could say, thinking it was strange to have a visitor and even stranger that the Army would give him accommodations.

"Now let's get down to the briefing," Johnson said, matter-of-factly.

Chuck listened intently as he described the upcoming mission, but on the walk back to his barracks he thought about his high school football days and how much fun it was when he hit his long-haired friend, Tom Griffin, with a long pass. He didn't know what to think of his favorite receiver back then. He knew that he was a better athlete than he was and that he reached that level by very different means. He also knew that Tom was his friend, which placed him in a very small group. Chuck was a loner who kept mostly to himself, but popular nonetheless. Everyone wanted to be his friend. He just didn't particularly care about being theirs. A psychologist might say he had been abandoned so many times, that he avoided getting close to anyone.

Not your typical jock, Tom had a big interest in eastern religions and mysticism. After practice, he would sometimes sit out on the field staring at a football for an hour or more and before a game, he often sat in a room by himself in deep meditation. The rest of the team thought he was crazy or, at least, eccentric. But no one dared criticize him because he was their best receiver and their best hope for making the playoffs. He never celebrated a miraculous touchdown catch with his teammates. Instead, he would calmly walk back to the sidelines, sometimes making the sign of the cross.

Contrary to Tom's new age spiritualism, Chuck was practical and somewhat uncomplicated. "It's a war," he told his teammates back in high school, "And we've got better strategy. Now if we're tougher than they are, we win." His coach called him a natural-born warrior and an instinctive leader because he got every last ounce of effort and energy out of his players. They trusted him more than they trusted themselves and played their hearts out for him. He was also one of the few quarterbacks in the conference who often blocked for his running backs.

Reminiscing about Tom made Chuck remember one of the longer entries in *The Book*.

Find the Child

Ever wonder why we seemed to have more transcendental experiences when we were children? It's because our adult brains are too jumbled up with life's complexities to see beyond this existence. If you want to figure out what life is about, you need to find your inner-child. Becoming the child you once were will restructure your neuro-pathways and turn your brain into a receiver of the thought waves of other souls around the universe and of the messages from the collective universe itself. That's the only way you can figure out what is beyond this earthly plain. But no matter, because thinking like a child again has the added benefit of making you happier. Just when you think you have everything and everyone figured out, you don't. When you're young, everything is new to you and that makes life interesting and exciting. By the time you're middle-aged you think you're too old to have a sense of wonder and things don't appear so new and inspiring. You think you've seen it all, but actually you haven't. Your mind has gotten tired and you've gotten too mentally lazy to look for the newness that is there. You've been conditioned to believe the novelty of life wears off and that as you get older you get wiser. But older doesn't necessarily mean wiser. Instead of gaining wisdom about life, you begin to ignore all the little variations and subtle distinctions in humanity that make everything and everyone different. You settle instead for a generalized view of life and take on the belief that there's nothing new under the sun; that there's nothing exciting left in life. It's easier that way because you don't have to think as hard. Besides, your ego makes you think you've figured out all the nuances of existence. But you're kidding yourself because like the human genome code, the code of the human spirit is too broad to crack by pure intellect and logic. It takes the mind's eye and imagination of a child. You have to devolve and recapture that child's wonderment, that awe of life. You have to once again look at things through the freshness of a child's eyes, but your maturity and egocentrism won't let you do it. It's not until you realize that there is nothing so beautiful as the uniqueness of the human spirit that you can learn to appreciate the many nuances in the human condition. Then, and only then, will you regain your interest in life and in living. I just wish I could follow my own advice.

Definitely not dad, Chuck thought as he walked into the barracks, *but who could go back to their childhood in this hellhole anyway?*

"Attention!" Scott said as he saw him come in.

"At ease men," Chuck said, "Time for another fun and exciting mission."

* * *

At first Mark didn't recognize the thundering growl that sounded like the roar of an angry beast. But soon it was undeniable as it grew louder and louder until it became the screaming howl of a speeding motorcycle. It came to a screeching halt three feet from where he stood and the helmeted driver yelled, "Get on!" He jumped on the back with no hesitation. *What've I got to lose?* The bike sped away through the trees and under their cover made a sharp, rubber-peeling U-turn. Jumping a curb and flying four feet in the air, it emerged from the woods out onto the street. The helicopter followed and started firing on them. *So much for these guys being on the right side.*

Running every stop sign and stoplight, the Kawasaki did all it could, but it wasn't enough as an eighteen-wheel semi-truck backed out of an alley right in front of it. The driver's instantaneous plan must have been to slide underneath the trailer and straighten back up on the other side, but it didn't quite work out the way it does in the movies. The bike slid all right, but it overcompensated on the recovery and flipped too far the other way. It crashed into a loading dock throwing Mark into the air. Miraculously, he landed smack-dab in the middle of a big dumpster, the trash and cardboard breaking his fall. Checking himself for serious injury and not believing he had only cuts and bruises, he climbed out of the trash bin and ran to the motorcyclist who had saved his life. He looked like a bloody pretzel. Mark looked up at the Kawasaki lying on its side with its back tire spinning freely and made a quick decision. A veteran of crotch rockets in his youth, he grabbed onto the handlebars. Pulling in the clutch, he yanked the bike up and jumped on it, speeding away in an instant and pulling a wobbly wheelie all the way. *Nice bike,* he thought, impressed with its power. Then he noticed the bent handlebars and looked up to see the chopper still following him. Revving the motor up past its safe RPM range while twisting, turning, and leaning into corners with his knee two inches off the pavement was difficult with the crooked handlebars and he didn't know if he could hold it.

But then another marvel happened as he glanced up to see an Israeli Police helicopter flying close to the chopper that was pursuing him. *Maybe they finally ran out of airspace,* he hoped, realizing he was running out of miracles, especially for a Jewish boy from Queens. He juiced it up to 90 miles-an-hour and zipped away as the Israeli helicopter led the other chopper away.

Still not satisfied that he was in the clear, Mark drove that cycle like it was the last thing he would ever do in his life. Then, with a sigh of relief, he subconsciously slowed down at a stoplight. "Now what?" he half-mumbled.

"How about getting in this car and saving your life," came a voice from inside the black limousine as it pulled up alongside him.

Mark mouthed a silent "Whaa?" as he stared silently at the man's face framed in the smoked glass window.

"Well, how 'bout it? Do ya' wanna' live?"

Mark briefly toyed with the idea of a sarcastic answer like, "No, I'd rather die," and then getting out of there full-throttle. But something told him he was going to need some help sometime and he thought this might be the time. "Yeah, I wouldn't mind living," he decided to say and the long car pulled over to the side of the road.

"Well," the man said moving out of the shadows, "That's the right answer and if you get in, you'll get to do some truly meaningful work."

Jumping into the back seat, Mark asked, "Whatdya' want from me?"

"I think you know," the man said as he put a hood over his head, "The cards in your pants could very well hold the key to the world's future."

"Only the world?" said Mark, finally getting in his sarcasm, "Just one question ... was the helicopter yours?"

"No," was all the voice said and then, "We just shot the rope."

"Pardon me for asking, but what if the rope had broken?"

"We would've just picked up the cards. But we were reasonably sure you'd get to a roof before then."

"Great," Mark said casually as he realized that there were now at least two and probably three factions after him and his cards. *Who are these guys?* he thought.

"I know what you're thinking," said the man in the back seat moving his face forward out of the dimness, "You can relax ... we really are the good guys. We work for the Americans and the Israelis are helping."

Mark couldn't believe it. He expected someone sleek and debonair who looked like he just stepped out of a James Bond movie. But this guy was a pudgy, balding man with soft, putty-like features and thin shocks of red hair hanging down the sides of his head. He wore thick glasses and looked more like a frumpy old college professor than a spy.

Sensing Mark's reaction, the man held out his hand and said, "I'm John Smith and I'm glad to finally meet you. Consider me a partner in our mission to save the world."

Right, John Smith. Couldn't we be a little more creative? Figuring he was a spy, he said, "CIA or Mossad?"

"How about free-lancer?"

"How about mercenary," Mark answered shaking his outstretched hand, "But a little melodramatic aren't we?"

"Maybe, but there's only one way to find out. We're taking you to the most advanced computer system in the world to complete your research on Prophecy."

That peaked Mark's interest but at the same time, he blanched at Smith knowing the name of his program. "What do you think it'll tell you?"

"Hopefully, lottsa' things, but mainly about future terrorist attacks. One thing we would like to know now, though, is who else is after it and why."

"Who do you think they are?"

"We're not really sure. The guys that turned your apartment building into an ash tray looked like Arabs, but they may be East European, Russian, or even Chechen."

"Oh, those guys," Mark said stunned at the news that his whole building had burned down. He worried about the fate of his neighbors. *I started the fire,* he thought. "Why do you think they want it?" he asked, slightly recovering his composure.

"That's what we'd like to know. Whatever the reason, with these guys it can't be good."

That confirmed Mark's earlier suspicion. *Prophecy may contain something about a terrorist plot!* They drove on and he mulled that one over. One thought led to another in a progression of logic and then it hit him. *They've been hacking into Dr. Goldschien's computer and probably mine too. So much for academic freedom, not to mention, privacy!*

"Now let's go see your new office," John Smith said as he pulled something out from under his seat, "I hope you don't mind wearing this hood, but you're better off not knowing where we're going."

"Sure," Mark said as everything went dark under the hood, "Why not go the full spy thing."

"We prefer the word patriot," said Smith, "Spy sounds so overly-dramatic.

* * *

Accept My Loving Religion or I'll Kill You

What really stymies me is all the wars (including Iraq) that have been fought over religion and how many millions of people have been killed in the name of God. The Crusades, of course, resulted in a multitude of Muslim and Christian deaths and the Spanish Inquisition burned many non-Catholics at the stake. How duplicitous when so many religions purportedly worship a loving God.

This short passage from *The Book* seemed especially key to Chuck as he and his men silently crept down an alley near the Al Hasan Mosque while a larger force prepared to attack the building from the front. An informant had told them that a major ISIS leader was hiding there along with a big cache of weapons. Satellite surveillance showed an unusual amount of activity there and Intelligence believed the mosque might be a front for ISIS. Infra-red satellite pictures also revealed a large underground cistern beneath the mosque and now the Mad Dogs were looking for its hidden entrance. For $50,000, an Iraqi spy had given them the location of the entrance, which was covered with wood and bricks.

"Silencers on," Chuck said calmly into his radio as they moved slowly down the alleyway following the directions of a GPS satellite locator. "Here it is," Chuck said, coming to an abrupt stop in front of a pile of rubble. Several men started pulling the old bricks and boards from the pile and it wasn't long before they uncovered a brick wall. They studied it for a few seconds, trying to determine the best way to dismantle it, when Chuck picked up a long two-by-four board and hit the wall hard.

"Ya' ever wonder why a two-by-four doesn't really measure two inches by four inches?" came Jim Hawkins' voice over the radio. Once again, no one paid any attention and the wall caved in like cardboard. They all realized at the same time that it was fake and they battered it with their gun butts, ripping the remaining pieces out by hand. There below was a steel ladder leading down into a dark cavern.

"Ever wonder why gas prices end in nine-tenths of a cent?" said Hawkins as they started climbing down the ladder. This time it was a particularly relevant question considering the part of the world they were in, but nonetheless, no one paid any attention.

As always, Chuck went first, motioning for Scott to come next. The rest of the men silently followed, bracing themselves for the unexpected. As they descended into the black hole, they could hear the first volleys of artillery being fired outside at the mosque. The fire was more of a diversion and for show and intimidation than anything else because the troops didn't want to damage the mosque too badly. If they did, pictures of the *sacred ground* being attacked would find their way around the world the next day and not do much for America's already tarnished image. Chuck reached the bottom and it smelled musty and moist, something he wasn't used to in this dry, desert country. Peering through his infrared goggles, he picked his way carefully and slowly through the darkness as Scott whispered in his ear, "Smells like bad meat or good cheese."

Then, up ahead, a sudden movement. They had expected guards to be posted at the entrance and they weren't disappointed. Chuck also expected them to be wearing their own infrared goggles and again, he was right. But their goggles were old and not as advanced as theirs. Before the guards could get off a shot, he threw a flash grenade at them and all his men instantly pushed a button on their goggles, lowering a protective screen over their eyes. The flash, made even more intense by the jihadists' light-sensitive goggles, blinded them, and at the same time allowed Chuck and his men to see in the dark. The blast paralyzed the militants just long enough for the Dogs to pepper them with silenced bullets.

"Move," Chuck said, knowing they had to get to the next flank of guards. Four abreast, they all ran forward into the void, stepping over the bodies with their laser sights projecting red dots all over the cave walls in an eerie light show. Then, a slight rustle up ahead.

"Hit it!" Chuck yelled as he and the men in his line dropped to their knees and fired. It was like an updated civil war skirmish as the line of men behind them fired over the stooped men's heads and the men behind them stood on tip-toe and fired over theirs. It took four seconds to kill the five guards and now Chuck and his men could see a light up ahead. At the same time, he could hear artillery outside starting to pound the neighborhood. They came to what looked like the bottom of a spiral staircase and carefully began picking their way up the steps while removing their goggles.

Climbing up out of the darkness, the Dogs found themselves in a ground floor main room and breathed a sigh of relief that it wasn't guarded. Either none of the insurgents above had heard the shooting down below or they were all called away to fight the attacking troops. Using hand signs, Chuck motioned for pairs of them to split off in different directions and the hunt was on. Scott followed him down a hallway and they could hear the increasing artillery fire outside. They also heard voices from rooms ahead and above yelling, "Areed rosas" (*Reload.*), "Sawob naho al mabani" (*Aim for the buildings.*), "Anthor lil helicoptarat" (*Look for the helicopters.*), and "Jeeb al sarookh" (*Get the missile.*). It was this last one that concerned Chuck the most. He expected them to have rocket propelled grenades, but he suddenly realized they could have Stingers.

"Take out the rooms," he said softly, "We'll hit the roof." He figured if they had RPG's they would be on the roof.

Atheists are Stupid

To the atheists who say you can't prove God exists, I say you can't prove he doesn't. If you ever wanted evidence of God's existence, ask yourself who else could have produced something as complex as the human being? Even many scientists say human DNA is too complex to have been created by accident from some primordial soup and evolved by natural selection. Call it intelligent design or whatever you want, but it was clearly no accident. What could have produced human beings other than something far superior to them?

Chuck didn't know why this writing from *The Book* popped into his head as he stealthily approached the rooms inside the mosque. He smiled inwardly when he thought back to his mother's strong Christian faith. But there was no time for reflection on that now as more artillery fire erupted. Using the gunfire as cover, Scott Sampson surprised the ISIS fighters in the first few rooms on the right while Chuck cleaned out the ones on the left. Hearing the shooting, militants started flooding out of the rooms ahead into the hallway, but like a well-oiled machine, Scott and Chuck made short work of them. They both threw grenades into the rooms to make sure they got everyone. They then ran up the staircase at the end of the hall, skipping the second floor as Chuck said into his radio, "Team 2 hit the second floor. Team 3 the roof."

The sun was just starting to show its golden lip over the horizon when Chuck and Scott poked their heads out of the rooftop door. Luckily the jihadists were looking out over the walls at the approaching troops and not back toward them. Chuck went left and Scott went right, both spraying everything that moved. They dropped like flies when all of a sudden, Scott caught a glint of something to his right. He wheeled around to see an enemy soldier turning a rocket propelled grenade launcher directly at his lieutenant. "R.P.G.!" he screamed and started shooting. But a building spire was blocking his shot and the soldier fired. Luckily the warning came in time and Chuck hit the rooftop rolling as the grenade whizzed over his head with a "ssshhh" and disintegrated a big brick column on the other side of the roof.

Meanwhile, Scott maneuvered himself into a position where he easily picked off the militant who fired the R.P.G. and several others coming up behind him. But he hadn't noticed one behind him and the bullets hit his Kevlar vest knocking him to the roof-floor. Chuck jumped to his feet and nailed the shooter. He ran over to help Scott just as Team 3 burst through the doorway at the other end of the roof and they now had most of the jihadists in a vice. With Chuck standing up and Scott shooting from the prone position, the crossfire killed everyone in sight and the noise brought the other Dogs to the roof. Fortunately, after killing everyone they found on the lower floors, Team 2 had now made its way to the roof where they finished the job in a three-way shootout.

"Yeah baby, whatdya' think a' me now?" Scott yelled as he unfurled the Iraqi flag and began waving it at his fellow soldiers on the ground below. It was the *all clear* signal that they could enter the mosque safely. And they did, shooting several stragglers trying to escape. As the troops moved in, the Mad Dogs worked their way from the top floor down, going room-to-room searching for the ISIS leader. What they found instead was a room in the basement, next to the cistern, with maps on the walls, advanced computer equipment on the desks, and sophisticated radio equipment spread all over the tables. "Must be headquarters," Scott said as he noticed a cigarette still burning in an ashtray.

"Heads up," Chuck said, "They might still be here." Scanning the scene carefully from left to right, like reading a book, Chuck took in every miniscule detail of the room. He picked up the cigarette and held it next to the cistern wall. The smoke drifted toward the bricks and he shouted, "Grenades at the wall!" as they all jumped back. Everyone ran back to the opposite end of the room and took cover as four men tossed their grenades and then took cover themselves. The wall blew into pieces and when the smoke and dust cleared, they fired several more grenades through the gaping hole and took cover. Carefully picking their way through the jagged cavity, the scene stunned all of them. It was a large dormitory, about a football field long, and there were dead bodies along the other side of the destroyed wall. At the other end of the huge room they saw people running away and shot everyone they could. The remaining grenade launchers got most of them and for the rest, Chuck radioed the helicopters outside to get them as they emerged.

The Dogs inspected the bodies but no ISIS. "The same guy who told us about the entrance probably warned him," Chuck said nonchalantly, knowing that the ISIS leader probably escaped hoping the Americans would destroy the mosque, turning public opinion against them. But he hadn't planned on the Dogs, who were now inspecting every inch of the giant underground room.

"Look over here," one of them said and they all peered through a hole in the far wall made by the grenades. It led to another large room and they used sledge hammers to knock the rest of the bricks out. Stepping through first, as he always did, Chuck could hardly see through the smoke. But when it cleared, the sight before him was unsettling. Ahead of him were rows and rows of weapons and box after box of ammunition. Picking their way along, they found a treasure trove of both American-made M-4s and Russian-made AK-47s, large machine guns, grenade launchers, at least 50 boxes of grenades, 100 Chinese-made rifles, and most troubling, several Stinger Missile Launchers. The military said any Stingers left over from the war in Afghanistan should be expired and obsolete by now, but every soldier wondered if that was true. Then, at the end of the long room came the most disturbing site. It was a door leading into yet another room, but that wasn't the mortifying part. The sign on the door was every soldier's nightmare. It was a skull and crossbones and could mean only one thing.

* * *

"Dr. Weiss, I would like you to meet Mark Jacobs," said John Smith as he pulled the hood off Mark's head. Standing in front of Mark with his hand outstretched was a short, balding man in a lab coat.

"Very glad to meet you at last," said Dr. Weiss, "You must be tired after your ordeal, so let's get you settled and rested up a bit before we show you around. What can I get you?"

"Some food would be nice. Oh, and if you're gonna' hood me again, would you mind washing the hood first?" Both men laughed as they led him to his room.

"How 'bout some tea," asked Dr. Weiss, carrying in a tray.

"Sounds good," said Mark, "Now what is it you want me to do here?"

"Surely you've guessed by now. We want you to program your copy of Prophecy to make some specific predictions and tell us what the bad guys are up to."

"How do I know you're not the bad guys?"

"Do we look like terrorists?"

"I don't know. What do terrorists look like these days?"

"Well, do we look like the guys who burned your apartment down and tried to kill you."

"Good point," said Mark with a wry look on his face, "But I'm not sure they were terrorists ... and for the record, I burned my own apartment down."

"To escape, I presume. How resourceful of you and that resourcefulness is what we need. Besides, I think you'll like how we've improved your program. We've taken it one step further and you will be impressed."

"One step further," Mark said with increasing curiosity, "You mean you have a copy?"

"Unfortunately, yes. We've been working with our own poorly pirated copy, but it hasn't been going too well."

"Glitches?"

"I'm afraid so. Unlike yours, ours had to be made in too much of a hurry and it doesn't work as well as your copy, which you so kindly brought us in your pants."

"How do you know that?"

"One of life's little mysteries, better left unsaid."

"Well, now that you have my copy," Mark said, still a little dumbfounded, "What do ya' need me for?"

"Because you know the program better than anyone else still living."

That brought the dismal memory of Mark's dead friends and colleagues and the men who killed them to mind and he said, "How did these guys, whoever they are, find out about Prophecy?"

"Probably the same way we did," Weiss answered with a shoulder shrug.

"Which is better left unsaid?"

"Right."

"So, what kinds of predictions of the future did your research turn up?

"Not so much predictions of the future as confirmations of the past."

"Huh?"

"You know how Prophecy works. You analyze sequential letters and feed it words. Then, if you get lucky, it finds related words and gives you a message. For instance, we fed in '*Hitler*' and got '*evil*' and '*Jews killed*.' We fed in '*9/11*' and got '*Trade Center*' and '*Saudi terrorists*.' You get the picture."

"No predictions?"

"Well at first we thought we had a doozy. When we fed in '*nuclear*' and '*bomb*' and we got back words like '*plutonium*' and '*cancer*' and '*satellite*.'

"And?"

"And, then we researched everything that has ever been written that contained those words."

"Kinda' like Google on steroids?"

"Yes ... kind of like that," said Weiss in a condescending tone, "For a while we thought maybe *Prophecy* might be predicting something to do with a nuclear bomb that might pollute the environment with radiation and spread cancer all over the place."

"How's that?"

"We also found the number 238."

"So?"

"It followed plutonium."

"Plutonium 238 ... the nuclear battery?"

"That's the one. It's a great power source for things like spaceships that go where sunlight is too dim to energize their solar cells or for satellites because they last for years. In fact, the word is that they want to use it to power a spacecraft to Pluto. Unfortunately, it's also hundreds of times more radioactive than the plutonium used in nuclear bombs, hot to the touch for decades, and a speck of it can cause cancer."

"Hence, the cancer."

"Right ... and in 1964 a rocket malfunction destroyed a navigation satellite powered by Plutonium 238 and spread radioactivity around the earth. The U.S. has been importing it from Russia since the Cold War with the agreement that neither of us will use it for military purposes. But now they want to use it for things like spy satellites to spy on terrorists and there are even rumors they want to use it to power space weapons. Whatever the case, the Russians are ramping up their production of 238 and they'll likely produce over 300 pounds of it over the next 30 years. That'll leave about 50,000 drums of radioactive waste to add to the already huge stockpile of waste they don't know what to do with. And that's a pretty tempting target for terrorists don't ya' think?"

"Yeah, but that's decades from now. What about the immediate threat?"

"Right. As I said, that's what we thought at first. We actually kind of relaxed when we realized that if Prophecy was predicting something that would happen 30 years from now, the danger wasn't so imminent. But then the extremists came after you and we knew there must be more to it."

"And you want me to find it."

"Yes. But first I need to ask you if your *unofficial* research turned up anything remotely related to a terrorist plot."

Mark looked Dr. Weiss up one end and down the other and decided if he couldn't trust him, he couldn't trust anyone. So, he told him his secret. "I did find phrases like '*mass death*' in correlation with words like '*nuclear*' and '*accident*.'

Dr. Weiss looked sober and concerned as he thought that one over for a few seconds. "A nuclear accident is certainly a possibility," he said, "But I think we're looking more for a premeditated plot."

"So, I shouldn't pursue this?"

"Not for now. But come with me if you would." Dr. Weiss gestured toward a door on the other side of the room. When Mark entered the room, he was stunned by what he saw. Before him was the largest collection of rack-mount servers in a RAID array chassis that he had ever seen. "Meet the Great OZ," Weiss said proudly.

"Clusters of servers connected via fiber channel cards I presume," said Mark in wonder.

"You got it. We use state-of-the art parallel processing and they're loaded with all the original texts. All they need is your cards."

"Original!" Mark blurted out, astonished that they had the original religious texts in their original languages.

"Yes ... remember this is the ancient Holy Land. We've got a lot of things the rest of the world doesn't even know about."

"Works for me," said Mark, trying to mentally digest the Doctor's remark, "But why so big? Why do you need such a huge system for simple text analysis?"

"That's where we've taken it one step further and mainly it's for the context. Knowledge without context is worthless."

"Come again?"

"The religious books by themselves do us no good. We need to find out how they fit into the overall context of every conceivable event or issue or series of events or issues that are related or unrelated and look at how they interconnect or don't interconnect."

"And that takes a lot of storage space and massive ram."

"You got that right."

"One more question," said Mark, "You work for the U.S. and Israel. The guys who were after me might've been terrorists. Who was in the chopper?"

"We actually don't know," answered Dr. Weiss, "But we're looking into it. We're really quite concerned."

"Not half as concerned as I am."

Dr. Weiss looked at him long and hard and after a long and awkward silence said, "That's probably true and that's why it's in your best interest, as well as ours, to find out what their ultimate plan is ... if there is one."

"To keep them from killing me?"

"Among other things ... and maybe to keep them from killing many others."

CHAPTER 8

"Clear the area!" Chuck shouted and his men instantly obeyed. "Call for Decon," he yelled, referring to the Decontamination Unit that investigated chemical weapons sites.

"Nerve gas?" Scott Sampson yelled at Chuck as they ran back toward the cistern.

"Or worse!" he answered.

"Looked kinda' old," said Sampson hopefully as their flashlights steered them through the blackness.

"Not that old," Chuck answered ominously, "Besides everything's old here."

"Whatever it is, we paid for it," chimed in Will Daniels, A.K.A. JFK, as he caught up with them at the entrance to the cistern.

"Oh boy, here we go," said Scott knowing what was coming, "Let's get it over with Daniels."

"Just sayin' ... we gave Hussein the makings for chemical weapons when we backed him against Iran," he said, almost out-of-breath, "And a lot of the guns probably came from us too. Kinda' like when we supplied Bin Laden with guns to fight the Russians and then he turned 'em on us. But most of 'em ... well ... where do ya' think Hussein's billions of dollars went?"

They continued their near-blind run through the dark, dank cavern as Chuck thought about the ridiculous irony of ISIS using their own weapons against them and started wondering just how smart his country's shifting alliances had been. But there was no time to ponder all that as they heard more gunfire outside and realized the mop-up operation was underway.

"Stop," Chuck said easily as they all came to an abrupt halt, knowing he meant that they should wait until the shooting slowed or stopped. It was a short battle with scattered skirmishes here and there. They didn't catch the man they were looking for, but they did find a huge cache of weapons, killed a lot of militants, and captured a good number of prisoners.

In spite of the big success, as they walked out of the basement, Chuck's mind drifted toward the men he had lost over the last year. Their faces haunted him and were forever imprinted on his brain like the brand burned into a cow's hide. Before Bill and Duckman, there was Bob Higgins and Hank Dempsey, two men he had lost a month earlier when their Humvee was blown off the road. Higgins' body was so gnarled and twisted, it looked as if his bones were trying to escape through his skin like the monster trying to break through Sigourney Weaver's stomach in the 1979 movie *Alien*. He then shuddered at the thought of George Bachman and John Wilson who had both been shot to pieces a year earlier when they couldn't find enough cover. He had been forced to call in "Spookie."

That dredged up the firefight to end all firefights in the mountains of Afghanistan as his unit was pinned down on all sides. It was sure death. He had only one option and that was to radio for *Big Spookie*, a low-flying airplane whose left side was nothing but big guns. It flew in a circle around the designated area and shot everything in sight. It was a last resort effort and if you were there, you grabbed any cover you could find and hoped it was enough. For George and John, it wasn't.

The memories of his lost soldiers burned in his soul and he felt as dark as the hot Iraqi sun was bright as he thought about the letters he would now have to write to his dead comrades' families. *Is all this really worth the price?* He was starting to feel more and more like his dad, that the U.S. had no business in another country's affairs and that it would get too many people killed in the end.

"What the hell!" said Ron Jenkins, stopping to look at a large paper taped to the wall, "Look at this."

"Lemme' see that," said Scott as the Dogs crowded around the poster, "Tariq, come here a second."

Trying to elbow his way through the cluster, Tariq finally stared at the poster in disbelief.

"What's it say?" asked Scott.

The picture was of Chuck standing beside Scott, Ron, and Steve Chamberlain with captions under them.

"Under Lieutenant Lansing's picture it says '*$20,000 for the head of this man.*' Under Scott, Ron, and Sniper Steve it says '*$5000 for one of his men.*'" Tariq struggled with the words. But there's another caption under that says, '*These men are killers of muslims.*'

"Lieutenant, you should see this," Scott said, summoning Chuck.

He looked long and hard at the photos on the poster and then said with a grin, "Is that all we're worth? Let's frame it and hang it up at Pancake. It needs some décor anyway."

Scott took the poster down and handed it to Chuck while the Dogs looked on with stunned expressions. This was the first time they had ever seen a wanted poster in Iraq and they each slowly started to wonder if ISIS was targeting them and their leader. While Chuck acted like it was no big deal, he started to ponder the same thing as he remembered all the times he felt like he was being watched. But more importantly, he silently asked himself, *am I a killer of Muslims?*

They walked toward the approaching hazmat trucks where they would be decontaminated in case they were exposed to any toxic chemicals and saw that the decontamination team's helicopter was landing nearby. *I wonder just how old that lab is*, Chuck thought. While other rescue helicopters landed all around them, they scanned the 360-degree area of their retreat. Finally, they could all take a collective breath, but not for long.

All of a sudden, a full barrage of mortar and machine gunfire broke out from the apartment buildings across the street and the Dogs were forced to dive for cover. Just as Chuck dove behind a broken-down brick wall, one of the hazmat trucks blew up in a burst of flames. With no air support this time, they were forced to pelt the building with their own grenades, shooting them through every window facing the street. Maneuvering around to the rear of the building, more troops did the same on the other side, adding a tank and a couple of .50 caliber machine guns to the assault. Although he knew it wasn't the time or place for reflection on *The Book*, the title of one writing seemed appropriate for the situation.

No One Gets Out of Here Alive

Sir Thomas Browne said "Life is a small parenthesis in eternity." I say life is a grain of sand on an endless beach. It is a very brief stop on the way to the hereafter and a preparation for eternity. It is also a test. If you pass, you go onto a happy eternal life (some call it Heaven). If you fail, you go onto a sad, maybe even horrible eternal life (some call it hell). And death is just another form of life, a different kind of existence. We're all afraid of it because it's unknown, but it's not until we embrace it with all its mystery that we are truly free. Fear death and death will find you. Embrace it and you will learn how to live with it. You can't truly live until you no longer fear the end of your earthly life. Besides, if you live a good life, seek the truth, fight for what's right, and worship your God, what have you got to fear? As Seneca said, "The whole of life is nothing but a preparation for death."

Seneca! You gotta' be kiddin' me! thought Chuck, snapping back to reality. The only person he had ever heard mention Lucius Annaeus Seneca was his well-read high school friend Tom Griffin. Tom loved the Spanish writers and their preoccupation with death and he always wondered why. Seneca, a playwright and the first well-known Spanish intellectual, became a Christian. At the top of his fame in Rome, the insane Emperor Nero ordered him to commit suicide and he did, unflinchingly. Then there was Garcia Lorca who wrote lovingly and morbidly about the ultimate dance with death: bullfighting. Chuck remembered that Tom had actually taken some bullfighting lessons while studying in Spain and was considering becoming a Toreador. But again, *why would Tom's journal be hidden in our garage?*

He couldn't remember the exact moment he went from being master soldier to super soldier. But he was pretty sure it was right after reading this writing. Its message was that it is dangerous to be too concerned about your own life and death because it makes you vulnerable. He also knew that if he wanted his men to be fearless soldiers, he had to set the example as the most fearless of all.

Hurdling back to the present, Chuck led the Dogs' rush into the apartment building where all the gunfire had been coming from. The artillery had relentlessly decimated the building, allowing them to break down the apartment doors one-by-one searching for militants. In one apartment he noticed a dead woman lying on the floor with a rifle across her chest. She was about eight months pregnant. In another, an older woman came running at them screaming in tears, "Qatalt ahli!" (*You killed my family*!). She then fell to her knees in uncontrollable sobs and began tearing at her clothes. It was at that moment that Chuck began to seriously doubt whether these people were better off under Saddam Hussein or the U.S. occupation. Whether or not this woman's family shot at them in the battle seemed irrelevant. It was her family and he had helped kill them. *Does losing your whole family justify freedom from oppression?*

After searching the entire apartment building, Chuck and his men walked out into the searing sun and smoldering street back to the remaining hazmat trucks. Out of the corner of his eye he thought he caught the glint of something shiny off in the distance. Through the whirlpool of emotions in his head and the whirring chopper blades smacking the air above, he again felt something else. Something strange. Like someone was watching them. *Maybe they're watching me,* he thought.

* * *

Using some of the most advanced super computers in the world, Mark began his painstaking research into the world's major religious books in the heavily-guarded compound. Using standard research techniques, he started out general and then went to specific. He began with words like *"crisis"* and *"disaster"* and *"attack"* in many different languages and dialects. He then planned to work toward a more focused search for any sign of a terrorist threat. It was painstaking, code-breaking work, complicated by the fact that each book was in its own original language and required massive and meticulous translations. Then the code had to be broken, but there were codes within codes. Some of the inner codes were simply groups of consonants from different languages with no vowels whatsoever. Additionally, some words were actually anagrams made up of letters from other words. It was incredibly complicated research, but it was the project of a lifetime and he knew it.

Working 10 hours straight with coffee and pastries as fuel, he fed the general words into the computer, which contained all the original religious texts like The Bible, The Apocrypha, The Qur'an, Bhagavad Gita, The Upanishads, The Torah, Dhammapada, The Vedas, and Tao Te Ching. He was ultimately looking for more specific results like *"terrorism"* or *"terrorist attack,"* but he knew he would have to sift through hundreds-of-thousands of words to get there. It was a mammoth task made even more difficult by having to use all the different languages like Arabic, Hebrew, Indian, and Chinese and the different dialects in each. It was also hard to know which words to use in the first place because many of our present-day languages didn't exist when the original religious texts were written.

The first phase turned up hundreds of crisis and disaster-related phrases like *"mass death"* and *"loss of life."* After analyzing each one, he found predictions of past terrorist mass-murders like the Mumbai massacre, the Lockerbie bombing, and even 9/11, but no future attacks. Then he got many natural disasters that had already occurred like the giant earthquake in Pakistan that killed 87,000 people and the big one in Iran that killed 26,000. And there was the Tsunami that devastated Indonesia. But then he stumbled onto the words *"earth"* and *"heat"* and *"ice"* and he knew instantly that it must mean global warming.

Looking up several recent news stories on climate change, he discovered that the catastrophic effects of global warming, like major droughts, cataclysmic storms, severe heat waves, and other weather extremes, were probably coming a lot sooner than anyone had predicted. But the biggest threat of all was rising sea-levels. According to the most recent information he found, Antarctic glaciers and ice shelves are melting faster than scientists realized because of an influx of warm ocean water due to a warming earth. The fast-melting ice will cause sea-levels to rise a lot faster in the next few decades than earlier predicted and that will most likely cause catastrophic flooding, threaten drinking water supplies, and devastate ecological systems for both humans and animals. In fact, the Antarctic is losing six times as much ice as it was four decades ago.

But that was not what he was looking for. So he narrowed his focus and got several strange words that were foreign, yet vaguely familiar. Words like *"Sperry,"* *"Irian,"* *"Garhwal,"* and *"Argo."* He sensed a hazy recognition of some of them, but he couldn't quite put his thumb on it. It was a puzzle and his natural inquisitiveness was now running at full speed. *What else can I do*, he pondered.

Then he came across hundreds of words like *"eruption,"* *"death,"* *"devastation,"* and *"volcano."* After programming thousands of word combinations into several languages, he started getting numerous hits on the term *"super volcano."* Although he knew this wasn't what he was looking for, his curiosity got the better of him and the search was on. He found that the Mt. St. Helens volcanic eruption, while dramatic, was actually quite small compared to a super volcano. It destroyed 60 kilometers of forest while a super volcano would be at least 1000 times its size and cover whole areas like England or the state of Connecticut. Furthermore, scientists estimate that there are as many as 40 super volcanoes around the globe and the odds say at least one is waiting to happen.

The earth's crust is only 25 miles deep and under it is a turgid turmoil of intensely hot molten lava under extreme pressure and looking for a way out. 74,000 years ago, it found one in a super eruption in Sumatra called Toba. Scientists say its ash blocked out the sun, killing all plant life, and wiping out 90% of the life on earth.

One of the possible super volcanoes is located smack dab in the middle of the major U. S. tourist attraction, Yellowstone National Park in Wyoming. Under Yellowstone lies a big lake of boiling lava and experts say the area experiences a super eruption about once every 600,000 years. It has now been over 630,000 years since the last big one. That explosive disgorgement buried what is now Rapid City, South Dakota, which is 400 miles away, under a mountain of ash.

If it would erupt today, it would incinerate everything within a 100-mile radius and send a cloud of poisonous ash across the prairie at high speeds. It would take less than 30 minutes to cover all of Wyoming and cross into South Dakota. In Rapid City, the ash would be over eight feet deep and clog all the vehicles' engines, ruling out any type of rescues. Almost immediately, anyone outside would be suffocated by the toxic sulfuric ash, which mixes with the fluids in the lungs and forms a cement. A wet cement that you drown in.

Within a week it would immobilize the entire country with 2/3 of it covered in ash. The ash would wash into the rivers making a muck and clogging the drinking water systems. There would be massive flooding in the Midwest. Trucks couldn't drive and planes couldn't fly so there would be no way to deliver food and supplies and many people would starve to death. But it gets much worse.

Within weeks, temperatures would start to plummet as the sulfuric gas clouds spread around the earth. Skies would become overcast, which would cut down on solar radiation, and it could put earth into another ice age. Mark recalled the Bible's prediction of increased natural disasters like earthquakes and then remembered that Israel lies on top of one of the most earthquake-prone areas on Earth. He wondered if Mount St. Helens in Washington state and Mount Pinatubo in the Philippines were examples of the prophecy coming true and if the really big one would hit his Holy Land second-home. He certainly hoped not.

But this speculation along with the strange new words he had found would have to wait because the computer was now beeping with a hit on one of the words he had programmed in earlier. It was programmed to set off an alarm when it found a keyword in three or more of the texts that related to the words "*terrorist attack*" and it was now doing just that.

As Chuck walked to the mess tent to meet his old friend Tom Griffin, his mind wondered back to a passage from *The Book* that sounded like him.

God is Us

Who or what is God? I think he is all life. We are him and he is us. All of life makes up God and God makes up all of life. And if we are God and he is us, God must be the universe and it must be him. But what is the universe? Just like multi-trillions of drops of water make up a river, countless atomic particles make up all of this world. And they're all the same. In fact, the heavy metals and other elements in our bodies are the same materials as in the stars, which makes us physically the same as the universe. If God is the universe and is in all of us, then we must all be the universe and it is us. Even as a self-professed agnostic, Einstein said, *"I believe in Spinoza's God who reveals himself in the harmony of all being,"* which suggests to me that we're all part of this infinite body of energy called the universe. If you want a visualization of this, imagine a little ball of light rising up from every living thing in the world. Each ball is that being's energy and as they rise up, they all combine into one big bright light that is God. Is this what is meant by the

Christian belief that God is in all of us? And conversely, does that mean that all of us are in God? Can we then say God is us and we are God? But who are we? Are we infinite and ever-lasting? Baruch Spinoza wrote in Ethica, *"I mean a being absolutely infinite-that is, a substance consisting in infinite attributes of which each expresses eternal and infinite essentiality."* I wonder if existence is a constant line of energy stretching from the big bang to the end of time and we are all bumps on that line and manifestations of that energy. And remember, energy can't be destroyed. All this suggests to me that life doesn't end, it just changes. Whatever makes us who we are, lives on beyond the death of our physical, corporal bodies. Call it Heaven, Nirvana, or whatever, I think when our bodies die, we become part of the overall energy of the universe.

As for this cosmic scribbling, Chuck disagreed with the writer, whoever he was. He believed God was some kind of concrete entity and he liked organized religion where things are more defined and not so obscure or nebulous. He also didn't see the need to look at life or death in existential terms. He felt that trying to figure out what life is all about is futile and a waste of time. To Chuck, it was very simple. There were good guys and bad guys and his job was to kill the bad guys. Like his dad always said, some bad guys are so bad that they need to be killed to protect the rest of society. The only problem was that, lately he wasn't as sure about that as he always had been and he was less sure who the bad guys really were.

"Ya' coulda' picked a better vacation spot," Chuck said as he walked into the mess tent.

"Yeah, Syria was much better," Tom said nonchalantly, looking up from his cup of coffee, "At least they had better coffee." They took a few seconds to look each other up and down and then broke into a spontaneous bear hug that neither could resist.

"Got a haircut, I see," Chuck said as he loosened his grip, slightly self-conscious of the uncharacteristic embrace.

"Got 'em all cut," Tom said, "It works better with the suits I deal with."

Chuck sat down and looked at his 6' 1" old friend with blonde hair slightly hanging over his ears. Like Chuck, he looked a little like he would be more at home floating on a surfboard than in an office.

"I've been sittin' for three days," Tom said, "Can we take a walk."

"No argument here." Chuck didn't really feel like walking but how can you say no to an old friend?

As they walked around the compound, they talked about Tom's job and what brought him there and when that wore itself out, they reminisced about their high school days and some of their old friends, although there weren't many. But like most old friends who hadn't seen each other in a long time, the reminiscences only went so far and the conversation began to drag. Not wanting to waste their reunion in an awkward silence, Chuck went back to Tom's job.

"So, what're you up to with your NGO," he said resignedly.

"All kinds of things," Tom answered, 'But mainly we arrange for humanitarian aid wherever it's needed most."

"Including combat zones?"

"Especially combat zones ... Syria and Sudan being the worst."

"Yeah, I hear Assad and the Russians are blowing up aid convoys."

"That's the rumor," Tom said.

"What're ya' doin' when you're not runnin' convoys?"

"Well, remember the old line that it's better to teach a man how to fish than to give him a fish?"

"Yeah."

"That's my latest project but instead of fishing, it's farming. The plan is to give small farmers in Africa a smart phone and what we call a backpack farm with everything you need to farm 3 or 4 acres."

"The backpack I get, but a smart phone?"

"It will give them the instructions for farming."

"And how much would that cost?"

"That's the beauty of it," Tom said with growing excitement, "About $10 a month will be enough to feed a farmer's family with a little left over for other expenses and that's quite a feat for Africa. But, enough about me. What're you up to? Still fightin' the good fight?"

"I'm not sure how *good* the fight is, but yea, I'm still fightin' it."

"Whatdya' mean?"

"You know how it is," Chuck said, wondering if he really wanted to talk about his doubts with Tom, "Fighting for people that hate your guts."

Tom hesitated as he wasn't sure if he wanted to talk about it either. "I guess, but can you blame 'em? To them it's just another crusade by a foreign country killing their kids."

"Man, you sound like dad!"

"How is the old man?"

"He hasn't really been the same since mom died and he's as mean as ever. But you guys probably share the same opinions about the war."

"I 'spose and I know it's a lot more complicated than the crusade thing. Part of it is probably also the madrasas."

"Ya' mean those Islamic schools?"

"Yeah, it doesn't help that they take in homeless kids and teach 'em to hate America."

"Not to mention blame us for all their problems."

"But it wouldn't have to be this way. How about if we took the money we're spending on the war and gave it to these Muslim countries to build public schools that would actually give their kids a more objective education? It could still be Islamic, but it wouldn't have to be so anti-American. Wouldn't that get at the root of the problem and slow down the production of new terrorists? I mean, wouldn't it be kinda' hard to hate the hand that feeds you?"

"I suppose, but some of the hard-core Arab countries would never take the help because it would show the world that they can't take care of their own people. Besides, they wouldn't want to alienate their different Islamic factions."

"Good point. And I 'spose even if they did take it, the corrupt governments would steal it and they'd keep hating us. I guess it's a little unrealistic."

Chuck was a little surprised at this admission, but continued, "But, isn't it kind of a moot point anyway? I heard that there aren't all that many of those schools anyway. Like in Pakistan, I heard that only 2% of the kids are actually in them."

"Yeah, I read that too," Tom said, "But 2% is a lot in a population of 200 million and it's probably more than enough for a steady supply of future suicide bombers who come from the poorest of the poor."

"Well, maybe we should just give 'em more money to help with the poverty."

"That would be nice, but like you said, the corrupt governments would just keep it. It is an economic inequality problem though. A lot of poverty could be wiped out if we put an infinitesimal tax on all bank and stock transactions in the world."

"How infinitesimal?"

"Just one-half of one-tenth of one-percent would raise $100 billion."

"Wow!"

"Wow is right, but it would probably be too much to ask of the world's billionaires.

"What about the richest countries in the world sharing some of their wealth?"

"Yeah, if they put in just one-half of one-percent of their respective budgets each year it would go a long way toward fighting poverty. It would sure be a better way to spend their money than some of the ways they spend it today."

"But don't they already do that with foreign aid?"

"Only America, but even we don't give other countries enough when you compare it to the money we spend on wars." Tom was on a roll and now unrelentingly spitting out numbers in a flurry like a human calculator. "The U.S. spends $500 billion a year on our military but only two-billion dollars a year on foreign aid for Africa where 8 million people die each year from poverty and one-fourth of the kids are undernourished."

"That's 'cuz they don't have any oil."

"Some parts do ... like Nigeria, but that money goes to the dictators, not the people, and the oil companies have ruined those areas anyway."

"Yeah, always the oil isn't it, but let's get back to the real world. Isn't the first obligation of any country to defend its borders?" Chuck asked like the loyal soldier he was.

"Yes, but isn't $500 billion to kill people going a bit far when it could actually save lives?"

"Maybe, but who really knows how much it takes to defend our country? Besides, if we don't defend ourselves, nothing else makes any difference."

"Spoken like a true patriot. But the problem is that more crimes have been committed against our own people in the name of national defense than I can count."

"Okay. I'll give you that. But I still say if you short-change national defense you may be left with nothing to defend."

Ignoring the point, Tom went on, "Our main goal should be to save lives, not take them."

"Isn't that what we're doing by fighting ISIS?"

"Sorta," Tom answered, "But not nearly as many as we could have saved with more money for ... say ... public health programs. Besides, who says we didn't create the problem in the first place?"

Oh man, Chuck thought, *I know what's coming.* "Ya' mean, how we created the very enemy we're fighting," he said resignedly, "Namely ISIS? I think I've heard that one before."

"You said it brother, not me. But maybe if we hadn't done that, we would be saving the lives of the very people we're now killing."

"That's a little above my pay grade old friend," Chuck said, not giving away his recent doubts, "But what about these health programs?"

"Well, for one, you could prevent malaria for just seven dollars a person."

"How's that?"

"Seven dollars would buy a net treated with insecticide that goes over a child's bed and lasts for five years. Two kids under a net would be seventy cents a year per kid."

"Wow!"

"Wow is right."

"You sound like you've rehearsed all this."

"I had to ... for my fund-raising speeches."

"You ... fund-raising?"

"Hey ... saving the world ain't cheap and the rich folks won't listen if I don't spout off the numbers."

"How 'bout the big powers-that-be? Do they listen?"

"Sorry to say ... they don't. But I have to keep tryin'. ... what choice do I have?"

Chuck thought about that and realized that because of his beliefs and principles, his friend had no choice. *But, I do,* he suddenly realized and that epiphany vaguely occupied his mind for the rest of what was turning into a long and arduous conversation that was bringing on one of his throbbing headaches.

"But it gets better," said Tom, "Ya' know what the biggest health problem in the third world is?"

"No clean water?"

"You got it. Seven-hundred-and-fifty-million people on this planet have no access to clean water and in the next decade two-thirds of the world will be fighting a daily struggle to get it. And that's another project we're working on."

"What is it?"

"Believe it or not, it's a simple pipe that goes into the dirt with a fan at the top that pushes air below-ground. A chamber in the pipe cools it and water particles collect in a reservoir."

"Man, that doesn't sound like a lot of water."

"It's not ... right now. But it's still evolving and in time, one unit might put out up to 11 gallons of potable water a day and if there were thousands of 'em, that's a lotta' water and the best part is that it's cheap and easy."

"That's cool, but it sounds like you'd need millions, not thousands of them to have a big impact here."

"That's true but it's gotta' start somewhere and it also won't work everywhere. It works best in areas where you have significant moisture in the air and soil."

"So not very well here, huh?"

"No, mainly in semi-arid areas and probably not much there either. But there is a more temporary measure we could take and it's really cheap."

"What's that?" Chuck asked, grateful for a possible answer instead of another difficult question.

"It's a simple straw with carbon filters and a bacteria-killing resin and a little iodine inside. People can use it to drink out of mud puddles and it could prevent about 6,000 deaths a day. It filters out 99 percent of the waterborne bacteria and parasites and it lasts for a year.

"Wow!" Chuck said again, "But what about the rest of the germs?"

"Viruses can still get through and so can arsenic, but it prevents cholera, typhoid, dysentery, salmonella and a bunch of other rotten diseases. It would probably cost less than three bucks to make and people could wear it on a string around their necks. But the rich countries of the world aren't interested and no one in the poor countries even knows about stuff like this because they're not in the information age ... it's more like the stone-age. I mean for a measly million bucks a year we could hook up most of these African villages to the internet where they could get all kinds of health information over their cell phones."

"What about the people who don't have 'em?"

"These days, most Africans do have 'em ever since they made 'em cheap enough and people can buy minutes and even seconds of time on them. Remember, many of the third-world countries bypassed land-lines and went straight to cell phones."

"Still, not everyone has one, right?"

"True, but those who don't will use their friend's phone. That's how it works in the third world."

"Okay, but don't they still need electricity to charge the phones."

"Two words for ya'. Solar power. It's come down in price so much that even poor countries can now afford it."

"What about no internet?"

"Ever heard of satellites? There's a lot of 'em up there doin' nothing."

Tom was more animated than Chuck remembered him and his mind was approaching exhaustion from the bombardment of woeful and pessimistic information he was getting from his old friend. He desperately wanted to change the subject.

"Enough shop talk," he said, "There's something I've always wanted to ask you about our football days."

"Shoot."

"Not exactly the word to use around here," Chuck joked, "But remember how you always knew exactly when to turn around to catch the ball?"

"Oh yeah," said Tom laughing.

"And remember telling me that you felt the vibration and rhythm of the ball as it came toward you?"

"Yup."

"Was that true or a buncha' your cosmic B.S.?"

"Back then I did believe it. But now ... after thinking about it a little, I think that was the best explanation I could come up with at the time."

"And now?"

"Well, I still don't really know how I did it, but I have a theory."

"What is it?"

"The only thing I can think of now is that our brainwaves were linked in some way. I think brainwaves are like radio frequencies. If two radios are tuned to the same frequency, they can communicate. If two brains are on the same wavelength, I think they can also communicate."

"So, our brains were communicating when I threw the ball?"

"In a sense. You always had a razor-sharp focus and when you threw the ball, your brainwaves were completely focused on it and it alone. I think our brainwaves were somehow on the same frequency and I was unconsciously receiving the message that you had just released the ball. Then, I must've instinctively ticked off the time it would take for it to get to me and intuitively turned my head or reached out and let it drop into my hands."

Chuck stared at his friend for several seconds and then said, "That sounds about as wacky as the vibration theory."

"It does, doesn't it," Tom said, again laughing, "But who knows? One of 'em might be right ... or neither of 'em."

They both laughed hard as they realized they would never know how it had worked. They just knew it did. What Tom didn't say was that he believed all his deep meditation somehow made his mind more receptive to Chuck's brain waves when they connected with a pass. *Maybe later*, he thought.

"But one thing I do believe is that we're all psychically connected in some way and all our actions or inactions affect other people." The conversation went on into the night reminiscing about some of their most memorable games and catching up on some of their old friends. But their tongues were tired and eventually they ran out of things to talk about. While he hated to admit it, Chuck was glad that the visit was about over because his head was pounding worse than it did when he was under fire with explosions going on all around him.

He walked Tom back to his tent slightly regretting not telling him about his doubts about the war and a bit thankful that Tom didn't bring it up. "Here we are

Tom. It was so great to see you again. I guess we've both been through a lot since high school."

"Yeah," Tom said, instinctively knowing that Chuck was thinking about how different their lives had turned out, "We may seem pretty different from each other, but I'm bettin' we're more alike than you might imagine."

The two old friends stared at each other for a full 30 seconds with Chuck briefly pondering how his old peacenik friend could be anything like him and he wondered what he meant by that. They embraced in a spontaneous hug that surprised both of them as neither was very physically affectionate and Chuck said a little nervously, "Well, let's do this again, but next time under better circumstances."

"That would be good. Why don't ya' give me a buzz next time you get to Washington and we'll have some laughs. Maybe the conversation will even be a little lighter next time."

"Good idea."

"Bye Chuck. Now don't go gettin' yourself killed over here. You've got a lot of good left to do in this world."

Again, Chuck wondered what he meant by that, but dismissed the thought as he turned and walked back to his barracks to gulp down his usual handful of aspirins. His growing doubts about the war had been giving him bad headaches and the heavy conversation he had just finished made it worse.

CHAPTER 9

Typing commands fast and furiously, Mark yelled, "Talk to me baby," at the supercomputer. And it did, spitting out the words *"rogue state," "Korea," "Russia," "atomic,"* and *"waste."* "This has gotta' be it!" He was amazed that he may have stumbled onto the answer so quickly. Now diving in head first, he began running several programs simultaneously to see what other clues he could find in the holy books.

While the processors whirred on, he walked over to the desktop computer and did a Google search using the three words as key words. What he found made him even more anxious.

Because the number of nuclear-armed countries has risen from five to nine since the 1970's, the possibility of nuclear material falling into the hands of terrorists has increased right along with it. North Korea has been selling nuclear technology to other countries. Pakistan is developing small, portable tactical nuclear weapons that can be used on the battlefield, even as its domestic extremist threat grows. And Russia is a treasure-trove of unregulated nuclear material.

Because the old Soviet Union was such a closed society, it didn't have adequate security for its stockpiles of nuclear waste. They didn't think they needed it and, at the time, didn't think anyone would bother to steal it. There were no radiation detectors for the nuclear dump employees to walk through when they left work and no surveillance cameras to watch them go. In other words, workers could easily smuggle out a softball-size chunk of nuclear material in their lunchboxes. The scary thing is that it takes only a small piece of highly enriched uranium to make a nuclear bomb. Now much of it was unaccounted for and one Georgian official claimed there was enough uranium missing to make thousands of nuclear warheads.

But making the bomb is the easy part. Getting the enriched uranium is the challenge. Unfortunately, there is a lot of it around and not only in Russia. Pakistan's lead nuclear scientist sold huge amounts of nuclear material to Iran and

North Korea and uranium enrichment centrifuges to other countries in a black-market network. They're still out there. The big question is did he sell any of it to Al Qaeda and did it ultimately make its way to ISIS? Mark read that the CIA believes the Pakistani scientist had at least met with terrorists.

The big fear is over ISIS's call for attacks against the West. Security agencies are afraid that they will use a dirty bomb containing a small amount of radioactive material that is relatively easy to obtain. A dirty bomb in a suitcase could contaminate several city blocks and potentially much more if the wind spreads the fallout. Neighborhoods, subways, or airports might have to be sealed off and the cleanup would be so expensive that the economic effects could be devastating.

The scary part is that ISIS may already have nuclear materials. When they took over Mosul in 2014 they stole about 40 kilograms of uranium compounds from a university. It was low-grade uranium and probably not harmful, but it does show that they may be interested in dirty bombs.

Another example of ISIS's interest in radioactive ingredients occurred in Europe when Belgium announced that a suspected terrorist had been watching a Belgian nuclear official who had access to nuclear materials. Belgium's nuclear safety agency even said there was concrete evidence that terrorists were planning to do something that involved one of their nuclear reactors.

But Russia is still the main worry. During the turmoil that followed the breakup of the Soviet Union, radioactive material was often stolen from lightly guarded nuclear reactors. Police found shipments of it going through European cities like Prague and Munich and believe that large quantities of it are still out there and waiting for a buyer who will pay the highest price. The area that worries authorities the most is Abkhazia, a notoriously corrupt dictatorship in Georgia, with links to Iran. With no recognized borders, the region makes a good transit station for smugglers and there is some evidence that nuclear materials have been smuggled through there. More recently, when Russia invaded Ukraine, it destroyed 29 radiation detectors that monitored the movement of radioactive material along the Russian-Ukrainian border, which could make smuggling there easier. Intelligence analysts surmised that the Russians might have done that so they wouldn't get caught trafficking in nuclear material.

Now Mark's eyes widened in amazement at what he read. Russian officials admit they know for sure that the Russian Mafia and quite possibly one terrorist group have cased their nuclear sites. But again, Russia may be the smallest threat. Under the Atoms for Peace Program, America sent nuclear materials to countries around the world in return for them letting the U.S. inspect some 17-billion tons of nuclear ingredients at their nuclear facilities.

But dirty bombs are only the most likely part of the story. While a full-scale nuclear weapon is unlikely, if terrorists get their hands on enough highly-enriched uranium, they could theoretically make a full-scale nuclear bomb. North Korea already has more than 12 nuclear warheads and has reportedly developed missiles to carry them all the way to the U.S. West Coast. Intelligence experts are also worried that they may share their technology with terrorists.

The really frightening part is that it doesn't take a Manhattan project to make a nuclear bomb. You can find the directions on the Internet. It can be as simple as a shell made of highly enriched uranium metal fired into a tube also made of highly enriched uranium metal to create the critical mass you need for a nuclear explosion. The firing mechanism fires off a shower of neutrons at just the right moment when the two pieces come together. A terrorist group with a physicist and a good machine shop could make it if they had the highly enriched uranium.

Because traffic on the high seas is largely unregulated and because there are too many shipping containers for the U.S. Customs Agency to search, it wouldn't be that hard to smuggle a nuclear bomb into the New York or San Francisco Harbor in the hull of a ship. There could easily be hundreds of thousands of casualties. Just when Mark thought things couldn't get any more intriguing or depressing, the alarm went off as he got another hit. This time the word "*Mayak*" and the numerals *7, 1, 2, 1*, and *8* came up. "*Mayak*" he discovered right away was a collection of 231 solid radioactive waste sites in the town of Ozersk, Russia. *But what are the numbers?*

Further research showed that a number of countries paid Kazakhstan to take in their nuclear waste. In fact, 270 million tons of low-dose waste are stored in five locations around the country. But the storage facilities must not be very good because Kazakhstan has a radiation-caused cancer rate 5 times the norm. The country is on its third generation living with the waste dumps and most families have relatives who have cancer or who have died from it. But, while disturbing, none of this had any relevance to what Mark was looking for, so he went back to the strange numbers.

He ran every sequence of numerals possible and got nothing. Then, thinking it might be a numerical code, he matched each number up with each letter in the alphabet. Still nothing. He tried everything he could think of but still nothing. Frustrated, he glanced at his watch to see how long he had been working on this one and noticed its luminous date. *That's it!* He had been analyzing each numeral as a single, stand-alone digit when the last four were actually two pairs of digits. *It's a date!* Looking more closely at the numbers, he suddenly realized the date was July 12, the next day. His face went ashen-white as he screamed for Dr. Weiss.

* * *

It was pitch dark when Chuck walked into the Mad Dogs' barracks. He stripped down to his skivvies and laid down to try to sleep. But the harder he tried, the more difficult it became. His thoughts involuntarily drifted back to his conversation with his old friend and the renewed doubts it brought with it. In particular, he pondered what Tom had said about spending so much money killing people in wars instead of saving and improving lives. As usual, he had a cosmic take on things when he said that all people are psychically connected and everything we do affects everyone else. It vaguely reminded him of one of *The Book's* entries, he just couldn't remember which one. He saw figuring that out as an opportunity to take his mind off of his ever-growing uncertainties and he knew he wouldn't be able to sleep until he did. Using his miniature flashlight, he pulled *The Book* out of his backpack and scanned the pages until he found it.

Everything is Connected

I think there is a single force moving within all of us. There is an energy that unites us all and we are all transcendentally connected with everyone's molecules intertwined with everyone else's. I think everything in the universe is made up of imperceptible strings that vibrate at different resonances. Somehow all these strings are linked together and that's why every action has a reaction and everything you do affects something or someone else. The world has an overall rhythm. Everyone and everything has its own sub-rhythm and they all culminate into one giant, collective tempo or rhythm of life. But, there are positive and negative rhythms. When people do the right things, they put out positive energy and their specific sub-rhythms are in tune with all of life's other rhythms, producing good results. When people do the wrong things, they put out negative energy and their sub-rhythms are out of sync with all the other rhythms of life, producing bad results. In musical terms, it's like when each guitarist and a keyboardist play their own individual melodies, but all fit together with the drummer's basic beat and with the overall rhythm and tempo of the song. Musicians will tell you, by the way, that it is often the note or the rhythm you don't play (call that the non-rhythm) that makes the music. What does this mean? That all things are connected and moving together in rhythms, sub-rhythms, and non-rhythms and everything you do has a negative or positive effect on everything else.

This one definitely sounded like one of Tom's existential theories, but again, Chuck didn't believe he wrote it. While he didn't know who wrote *The Book*, one thing he did know was that this entry was making him sleepy. So, he put away and started to drift off to sleep.

Because of the intense heat, several of the men slept in the nude and Greg Hanson was one of them. Unfortunately for him, he often slept on his stomach. Several minutes into Chuck's attempt at sleep, a naked Jim Hawkins snuck up to Hanson's cot and in one deft move, squirted shaving cream all over his butt and crotch, laid on top of him, and then quickly jumped off, turning on a dim overhead light in the process. Through groggy eyes, all Greg Hanson could see was a naked man he had seen earlier in a skirt and blouse jumping off of him leaving a slimy white substance on his crotch and rear.

"Was it good for you Greggy?" Jim whined in his best falsetto voice.

"Yer' dead!" Hanson screamed as he bounded out of his bed and tore after Hawkins, screaming every obscenity known to man and a few that aren't. The rest of the Dogs woke up trying to focus their blurry eyes on this surrealistic sight of two naked men running around the barracks in the dark. It was ludicrous and hilarious at the same time as Hawkins artfully dodged Hanson's grabs, but suddenly tripped over a foot locker. A victim of his own momentum, Hanson crashed into him and both men tumbled to the floor in a collage of flailing, naked arms and legs. Seeing the shaving cream on Greg's buttocks, the Dogs instantly grasped what had happened and began laughing themselves into a frenzy. The spasms of raucous laughter came hard and fast and exploded into convulsions of hilarity. It was almost as if they had been holding back a year's worth of laughter for this very moment.

Finally, just as Hanson landed his first real punch, Chuck pulled himself out of his own hysterical stupor and laughingly said, "Yer' a cutie Jim and Greg, you oughta' be grateful for the action. Now let's kiss and make up. Uh, let me rephrase that. Let's save this one for the ring. Right now, we need the sleep."

Both men instantly stopped in mid-action with Chuck's first few words. That's how it was with the Mad Dogs. No matter what they were doing at the time, when their lieutenant spoke, they stopped and listened. This blind obedience had saved their lives on more than one occasion. As for *the ring*, whenever any of the Dogs had a real dispute, they settled it in the boxing ring with the entire platoon betting on the fight.

”Yer' mine," Hanson said as they went back to bed.

"That's all I ever wanted," squeaked Jim in his flamboyant, falsetto voice while blowing him a kiss and prancing back to his bed. The truth was that everyone, including Greg Hanson, knew that Jim was the unit's best boxer and no one could touch him. His unusually long arms gave him a longer reach than most boxers and he had grown up with five brothers who pummeled him daily. He also realized at a young age that in order to be heard above the fray, let alone get himself out of fights, he had to be a comedian. He had his entire family in stitches from the age of nine with his peculiar sense of humor. Of course, it didn't always work and many times he went too far with his strange observations. In fact, his school counselor recommended psychological therapy for him. To this suggestion Jim responded with, "Don't you know that most psychologists go into psychology because they're nuts themselves and they're trying to figure out their own mental illness?" He got the therapy anyway and when the therapist asked him what he liked to do he said, "I like to sit on my hand until it goes to sleep and then whack off. I call it the erotic stranger." After that, the therapist cut their sessions short and eventually ended them altogether.

But right now, in this 120-degree Iraqi inferno with its own brand of insanity, everyone knew the laugh was over and they tried to settle back down into their cots. Strangely enough, the absurd two-man show had loosened them up and relieved some of their collective mounting tension. For the first time in a long time, they got an unusually good night's sleep. Jim Hawkins had done it again.

The next morning a messenger came into the barracks with the unexpected news that Chuck was being given an unscheduled leave. The Dogs' mission had been canceled and he was told to take the next transport out. The only problem was that he didn't know if he wanted it. But that didn't really matter because he had no choice and he knew it.

* * *

It was July 13 and 22 hours after Mark discovered a planned Russian sale of uranium to terrorists. He worked all night to pin down the where and when of the transaction but finally passed out from exhaustion. 10 hours later he awoke to the smell of eggs, coffee, and croissants.

"Thought you were never gonna' wake up," said Dr. Weiss jokingly.

"I'm not," Mark responded groggily. But he got up anyway and wolfed down the breakfast the servant had laid out for him on a tray next to his bed. He throated the omelet and croissants in one big gulp, washing it all down with ice cold orange juice and steaming hot coffee.

"Ready to go back to work?" Dr. Weiss asked with a slight tinge of a German accent. He had lived and worked all over the world and probably lost most of it in the process. Mark looked at him quizzically.

"What happened in Russia?" he asked a bit surprised and still a little groggy.

"You'll be happy to know that Russian agents apprehended several mafia people in the middle of selling uranium to terrorists. The Russians say it looks like the terrorists were tied to ISIS and were planning on making a nuclear bomb. It turns out they've been watching these guys for some time and when they got our information they raided their home right in the middle of the deal. They also found ocean charts and maps of New York in the terrorists' house and think they were planning on blowing up the New York Harbor."

"Not bad for a day's work!" Mark clapped his hands together in satisfaction. But he noticed Dr. Weiss was not celebrating. "What?"

"An early victory like this makes me nervous ... it's like it can only go down from here."

"Ah c'mon Doc, it's still a win isn't it?"

"Yes, but not entirely. Our analysts don't think this was the big doomsday attack. They think the terrorists might not even have been able to pull it off and they think the big one is still out there."

Mark's jaw dropped along with his excitement as he suddenly realized that his work was far from over. "Are ya' sure?" he asked in a low monotone.

"No, I'm not, but I'm not the one who matters. The people we work for are and that's all there is now. One very good thing came out of this though. They now believe a little more in *Prophecy* and have committed many of their resources to helping you in your research."

"You mean they didn't before?"

"They had their doubts. These are hard-core skeptics who suspect everyone and everything of some conspiracy or another and they only trust hard evidence. That's why it took the Russian affair to make them believers, and some of 'em still aren't."

"So ... I guess that means back to the old drawing board, huh?"

"I'm afraid so. Are you ready?"

"Ya' know ... I actually am," Mark said as he leaped from his bed and headed for the bathroom, now almost eager to get on with his research.

"Let's hope we find the answers in time," Dr. Weiss said with a practiced calm, but Mark thought he noticed some inner anxiety in his voice.

Walking down the hall to the computer center, he noticed the ornate furnishings of the big mansion. There were marble lions' heads on the door frames and gold trim around the windows. Glancing through one window he caught site of a man in green fatigues walking by carrying a gun. Looking around further, he saw several other armed men patrolling the area around the grounds. They looked like Israelis, but it was hard to tell. *Probably Mossad.* The thought of being guarded by the world's most elite spies comforted him a little, but also made him even more apprehensive over the fact that he was important enough for their protection in the first place. He remembered Dr. Goldschien saying once that the Mossad made the CIA look like Boy Scouts. *I wonder who owns this place.*

But Mark was now more interested in his research than in who was picking up the tab and at this point, he was simply glad to be alive. Practically skipping into the computer lab, he picked up where he had left off with words like "*crisis,*" "*disaster,*" "*flood,*" and "*drown.*" He got thousands of hits and had to sort through them carefully, looking for the one that would signal a terrorist plot.

Five days later he had gotten nothing. He came across a lot of false leads like "*murder*" and "*infants,*" which he took to mean abortion. Reflecting on the Biblical Commandment that says, "Thou shalt not murder," he really wondered if it was referring to modern day abortion. Like many men, he had always put off making any definite decision on his views of abortion. He guessed he was more pro-life than anything. But then he got his girlfriend pregnant and wondered if he was really pro-choice. *Thank goodness she was.*

Whatever his belief, his research turned up some startling facts that made him wonder if abortion might just be a modern-day plague. Facts like nearly a billion abortions have been performed around the world, which, depending on how you look at it, means almost one billion babies have been killed. Abortion is legal in 61% of the world, but that means only 54 countries. It is illegal in 97 countries. Still, there are about 46 million abortions conducted each year on the planet. The numbers go on and on and Mark hadn't considered the moral issue for years, but now he suddenly realized the core of his beliefs. *When conception does or does not begin is a distraction from the real issue, which is whether the baby's life is taken inside or outside of the womb. It is still taken. It is still a life denied. Either way, isn't it murder?*

He was well aware of the pro-choice argument that if abortion is illegal many women will die in backroom abortions and isn't that a form of murder? But they are two different issues. One is a morality question and the other is a practical consideration. Women dying in backroom abortions is tragic, but it has nothing to do with whether or not abortion is murder. You can't argue that abortion should be legal so that women don't die in backrooms if it is indeed murder. One has nothing to do with the other. Mark went on to reason that with millions of barren parents on a waiting list to adopt, what's wrong with having the baby and putting it up for adoption? He also couldn't understand how anyone could be both anti-abortion and pro-capital punishment since both take lives. But he finally realized that this couldn't be the terrorist threat he was looking for and was a distraction from his real project.

"Why do you think we had such a big success early on and have gotten nothing since?" he asked Dr. Weiss.

"Well, it might've been random chance or maybe we were using the wrong key words ... or..."

"Or what?"

"Or ... it might've been part of a divine plan."

"Whatdya' mean?" asked Mark, sensing Dr. Weiss's reluctance to explain.

"Maybe we got the hit because the Russians were about to sell their nukes to the terrorists and if we didn't stop 'em now, who knows what might've happened."

"Maybe, but I think I'll go with random chance."

"That works too, but if it was part of a divine plan, that means more big revelations may be coming."

Mark was about to answer that conjecture when they both heard a strange noise. It was a sort of cracking sound like someone was popping the air bubbles in packing plastic. It was then followed by a faint tapping noise that sounded like it was coming from one of the boarded-up windows. Mark was curious because he had been told that the house was acoustically insulated so that people outside couldn't hear anything inside and vice versa. Walking over to the window, Dr. Weiss peered through a paper-thin crack at the edge of the sill and couldn't believe his eyes. Right outside the window a shoot-out was going on between his guards and several men with scarves wrapped around their heads. Looking down, he saw what was making the tapping sound. One of the guards lay at the foot of the window, shot in the chest, and he had been tapping at the window to warn anyone inside the house.

Dr. Weiss yelled, "Follow me!"

Realizing the danger, Mark followed without question as Weiss led him down a long corridor. Stopping at the end of the hallway, the doctor pulled a painting away from the wall and pushed a button behind it. A hidden panel opened and he yelled "Come on!"

As the gunshots got closer and they heard footsteps running toward them, Mark again followed the instructions without question and ran past him and down the stairs behind the hidden compartment. As soon as he cleared the first four stairs he heard a gunshot behind him and a scream. Fervently glancing backward, he saw the panel closing. All he had time to assume was that Dr. Weiss had been shot and somehow managed to push the button and close the door before he fell. *I just hope those guys can't open it back up,* he thought as he jumped the last few stairs and wound up in a long dark tunnel with cast iron pipes running everywhere.

CHAPTER 10

A streak of lightening split the sky as Chuck gazed out of the rain-stained window of his boyhood home in San Diego. Rain had been rare here lately, but not as rare as in the Persian Gulf, where he had spent the last couple of years. When it did rain there, the raindrops coalesced with sand and dirt to look like mud falling from the murky sky. *Dirty rain*, the soldiers called it. Mixed emotions and conflicting sensations competed for space in his brain on his last day of leave as he waited for his father to return and take him to the airport.

It had been a week of a parade of relatives lining up to talk to him and he was glad it was over. The home and neighborhood he grew up in never looked quite the same after being away for so long and now he sat at the kitchen table he had sat at so many times as a boy. As he let his mind wander, the vague seeds of doubt about the wars in Iraq and Afghanistan drearily returned. He was still unaccustomed to these kinds of misgivings and knew that they can be dangerous if they get out-of-control. They can hinder a soldier's battlefield mission and put his comrades in danger.

At that moment, his gloomy thoughts were interrupted as Don pulled into the driveway honking his horn. Rush hour and a rain-slicked freeway made it a long drive to the airport. When it rains in Southern California, oil and other car fluids rise up to the road surface and make traffic move even slower than usual. Nevertheless, after too many years of drought, Californians welcomed the rain like an old friend they hadn't seen in a long time.

When father and son ran out of small talk the conversation dragged. Chuck wanted to talk about anything except his mother, thinking that if he ignored it, the lingering pain might go away. Grabbing onto the thought nearest the surface of his brain, he reflected upon his growing doubts about the war and subconsciously hoped his dad might say something to quell them. They had avoided the subject for a long time. But with nothing else to talk about, he figured it was time to end their moratorium on discussing what was now the longest war in America's history.

"Whatdya' think of the president saying we beat ISIS?" he asked.

After a few seconds of stunned silence Don said, "Ya' really wanna' talk about this now boy ... when yer' goin' back?"

"Don't call me boy."

"Oh right, I forgot how much you hate that."

"About as much as you like bein' called old man. So whatdya' think of it?"

"Not much."

"Why not?" Chuck braced himself for a long-winded diatribe that never came.

"Because we didn't beat 'em. Sure we drove 'em back to their last holdouts in the Middle Euphrates River Valley, but they'll be back, especially after we pull out of Syria."

"Yeah, I'm not sure if that's such a good idea. Doesn't it leave the door open for Assad and his Russian buddies?"

"Yea, without us there, he'll run wild and Russia will help him do it. And that's not to mention Iran and Turkey. Plus, pulling out now is like hanging out a 'welcome back' sign for the jihadists."

"How so?"

"It's one giant step backwards to 2016 when we didn't have boots on the ground in Syria. Back then, we had no human intelligence to tell us where ISIS was. Since we sent in those troops, we've known where they are and we went after them at every turn. Now we won't know dick and, like I said, they'll be back."

"Yeah and it seems like a waste of the last three years training the Syrians to fight ISIS and backing the Arabs and the Kurds against them, doesn't it?"

"Yup, especially since we haven't trained nearly enough of 'em ... and, of course, then it's back to the poor Kurds. Turkey is already setting up troops to attack them once we're gone."

"What do ya' think the Kurds'll do?"

"I hate to say it, but they'll probably have to make a deal with the Assad regime to protect themselves after they've been fightin' 'em for years. It's the weird, shifting alliances over there and just one more stalemate in a long line of stalemates."

"Stalemates?"

"You know. They make advances ... we push back ... they pull back. We dig in ... we pull out and they come back. They fight each other. They make deals with their former enemies. Then it starts all over again in a never-ending feedback loop with no winners and no losers."

"Oh, I don't know about that. We've won a few."

"Yeah, but our concept of winning is a little different than theirs."

"How so?"

"Well, whenever we do win a round, we hear back here at home about the big victory over there. But the Muslims look at it like David and Goliath and they're David. So, even when they lose a battle, they win because they're fighting the big, powerful Goliath."

Chuck thought about that one and said dreamily, "So it goes on-and-on with no end in sight?" He suddenly realized that the endless futility of the war was vaguely what he had been thinking in the back of his mind, but he couldn't quite put it into words. Sometimes you don't realize you believe something until you hear someone else say it.

"Yup ... stalemate. Our fearless leaders think you can shoot your way out of an insurgency but you can't. Our basic strategy has always been to kill more of them than they do of us, but that doesn't work in the Middle-East because the more of 'em we kill, the more come back at us."

"Yeah, my sergeant says they're like cockroaches. For every one you see, there are ten more hidin' in the dark."

"Well, that's not exactly accurate. They're not really hiding in the dark and when we kill one, we're actually recruiting ten more."

"What?"

"Yeah, when they see us kill their fellow Islamists, they sign-up for the holy war. It's like pushing in on a balloon."

"Come again?"

"When you push one side in, the other side bulges out. Anyway, killin' more of them than they do of us doesn't work and never has."

"Then, what can we do?" Chuck felt like a fish going for the bait, but he couldn't stop himself.

"Buy our way out, I suppose."

"Like when we paid the Sons of Iraq to fight ISIS?"

"Yup ... and it worked pretty well for a while because they knew the territory and the enemy. But then our greed got the best of us. We stopped the payments and expected the new Iraqi president to take over."

"Yeah, I guess we forgot Maliki is Shiite and there was no way he was gonna' pay a buncha' Sunnis anything."

"We didn't forget ... we just didn't wanna' pay anymore. The upshot was that they couldn't feed their families and they needed a new payin' gig."

"Enter the jihadists?"

"Yup. Al Qaeda and ISIS. That was the only game in town and their only option."

"You sound almost sympathetic."

"No, just realistic about our military strategy ... or lack of it. Even the generals know there'll be no military victory in the Gulf."

"How 'bout Syria?"

"No way ... not with Russia backing crazy Assad."

"Afghanistan?"

"None there either. But see ... we never should've gone to war with the Taliban in the first place."

Chuck was stunned. "Ya' gotta' be kiddin' me. They hid Bin Laden!"

"Yeah, but we never really knew for sure if they knew about 9/11 before he did it. They probably did, or maybe they just turned a blind-eye to it, but we don't know for sure."

"I think it was pretty obvious that they did know."

"Maybe, but it's a moot point because practically speaking, they're the big kahuna in Afghanistan. They're well-financed by the dope trade and they have safe refuge next door in Pakistan. How're ya' gonna' beat all that?"

"But they're evil sons-a-bitches."

"True enough and some guys just need killin' but not all of 'em. They're not *all* bad guys and many are true Islamic believers. But, whoever they are, we shouldn't be wholesale killing everyone on the other side. Instead, we need to pin-point more individual bad guys with surgical precision. Unfortunately, governments don't do that very well. It takes smaller, elite fighting units."

"Like the Dogs?"

"Yup, but without all the stupid rules of engagement."

"I hear that. So, what do we do with the Taliban?"

"I hate to say it, but the only way outta' this one is a negotiated peace with them."

"Well, word is that we're already meeting with 'em."

"Yea, it looks that way. But with these guys, it could take years ... if ever. Remember ... they have a world of patience."

"I'm beginning to see that."

"So, whatdya' get?"

"Stalemate."

"That's what they call it."

"Then, I spose' it's just a question of who blinks first."

"Oh, it's not a question. We will. The Islamists are never gonna' give up because they're fightin' a holy war for their God and we're fightin' for oil. That makes them a lot more determined and a lot more patient than we are. Like I said, even if we drive ISIS out, they'll be back."

The conversation had gone in several unexpected directions and hadn't done much to dispel his doubts about the war. In fact, it had made them worse and now the atmosphere in the car was tense and still. Lost in brooding thought, Don went pensively silent as he stared at the rain-soaked traffic jam in front of them. His face was chiseled full of deep lines, each with its own story to tell. It was the calloused look of a hard-lived life, which Chuck never really understood because his life hadn't been that hard. He, on the other hand, had seen more than his share of blood and death and had the physical and mental scars to prove it. He remembered Don saying once, "It's not the age, it's the mileage." *What mileage?* he thought.

Then, he remembered the drinking. His dad had always been a heavy drinker, but more so in the last few years since Chuck had enlisted and especially since his mother died. To Don, drinking had always been like a sport and he was a star athlete. He didn't just *drink* his expensive, imported beer. He made love to it, gently caressing and fondling the glass like a woman's breast. Sometimes he even played with it like it was a child's plush toy. But these days, Chuck could tell that it was less a sport to him than it was a release from his pain.

* * *

Looking back up the stairwell Mark didn't see any light, which hopefully meant that the killers couldn't re-open the secret door. He started feeling his way down the dark tunnel step-by-step until he bumped into a large iron pipe junction box with what looked like a spring-loaded, cast iron cover. He started to feel his way around the pipes when he heard voices at the other end of the tunnel. *Oh great! Now I'm surrounded!* Then he heard the voices again and he was sure that one was speaking English. "I'll go in ... guard the door," the voice said. Mark thought it almost sounded like a New York accent and he briefly mused about the fact that New York City had its own special city accent, like Boston and Philadelphia.

Shaking that thought out of his head, he quickly and quietly ducked back behind the junction box. Then, he couldn't say why, even later when reflecting on the experience, but he pulled the junction's cover open as far back as it would go and waited silently. Here came the footsteps and he thought he could see a form coming toward him holding a flashlight. *Just a little closer,* he thought. *Just a little more,* as the footsteps and light got closer and closer. *It's now or never.* Mark let go of the heavy metal door and its tightly-wound spring sent it crashing into the figure with a bone-crushing thud, sending him flying backwards onto the filthy tunnel floor. He was knocked-out-cold with his short, stubby machine gun still strapped around his arm. Mark instinctively tore the Uzi from his hands, grabbed the flashlight, and scurried down the tunnel with no idea of what was ahead. All he knew was that he had nowhere else to go.

After walking about three city blocks, he could barely make out a thin shaft of light streaming down from above and slightly illuminating what looked like the end of the tunnel. He switched off the flashlight and froze as a voice said, "Jim" in good old American-style English. Knowing that he had to answer, pretending to be Jim, he scraped his gun butt on the concrete to mask his voice and said in a low macho voice, "Yeah, get out now. I'll cover you." Hoping against hope that the killer would think he really was Jim and run away, he had no idea what to do next. So, he just stood silently while there was no sign of the man at the end of the tunnel going anywhere. Anticipating what was to come, Mark quickly darted behind a group of pipes just as a flurry of bullets came whizzing by his head. *I guess he knows I'm not Jim.*

When the gunshots stopped, Mark reached his gun around the pipes aiming it at the end of the tunnel and pulled the trigger. He remembered from his last go-round with an Uzi to hold on tight to brace for the violent kickback. He emptied the gun's magazine and then waited, realizing *I either got him or I didn't.* After that less-than-profound epiphany, a strange and almost-uncanny calm came over him. *I'm either dead or I'm not.* With that fatalistic thought in mind, he stood there for what seemed like an eternity with his anxiety returning. Then, all of a sudden, he heard the most beautiful voice he had ever heard in his life.

"Mr. Jacobs," it said, "You can come out now. We got 'em all and we have a car waiting for you."

Mark vibrated down the rest of the tunnel like an electric shaver shaving a stubbled chin. A large African-American man awaited him at the other end and offered his hand to help him up the ladder. He took it gratefully. "Nice shootin' Tex," the man with the beautiful voice said as they climbed up and out into the too-bright sunlight. He had been down in the pitch-black tunnel so long that the light blinded him as he climbed into the back seat of the waiting car. It was only then that he took his first deep breath of the day.

"Did Dr. Weiss make it?" Mark asked his rescuer in a trembling voice as the Saab cruised down the highway. He was almost afraid of the answer. The large man simply shook his head. It was the answer he dreaded.

Mark's next question was predictable. "Who are you?" he asked.

"Call me Bill," the large man said.

"Who're you with?" came the next obvious question. Mark still wasn't quite sure who the good guys and bad guys were.

"We're with the U.S. Government and we'll be protecting you during your research."

CIA. Actually, Mark was relieved that it was his own government that saved him for a change and he didn't want to push it.

"Who were those guys?"

Shifting uncomfortably in his seat, Bill said, "I wish we knew."

"They sure as heck weren't Arabs!"

Bill was a bit startled that Mark knew this and said simply, "No they weren't."

Mark sat back in his seat to ponder that one. "So now I've got Arab terrorists and one ... maybe two ... other groups after me," he said shaking his head, "How lucky can I get."

"Actually," said Bill, "We're not sure if the first group *was* Arab."

"Well, they sure looked and sounded like it!"

"Yeah, that might've been a ruse ... we don't know. It could've been the Russians or some rogue organization, but somehow, some other groups found out about your research and tried to capitalize on it."

Man, this just gets weirder and weirder, Mark thought in shocked disbelief.

It was getting dark as the car drove through the gates of the long, winding driveway of yet another mansion. The driver must have called ahead because the gate opened just as they arrived. They drove around to the back of the palatial villa and into a large garage whose door closed behind them. Mark started to get out, but Bill grabbed his arm and said, "Wait just a minute." He understood why as the whole car started moving downward. It was parked on an elevator that lowered it down two stories to an underground fortress. *Man, I think I spent enough time underground today.*

"You'll be safe here," Bill said, "A lot safer than at the other place." Mark thought he said it with a bit of a sneer, and almost wondered if the last house was owned by another intelligence agency, say the Israeli Mossad, and this one was run by the Americans. *So, I guess that makes this one safer.* He was getting more confused by the minute. Bill then led him into a small apartment and said, "This is where you'll be staying. Now come with me and I'll show you your computers."

"Do ya' think I could shower up first? That tunnel was pretty dirty."

"Sorry, but it's imperative that you get right to work. Apparently, some new intel says the attack may come sooner than we anticipated." Then, as if he had a second thought, Bill stopped him in the hallway and handed him a tiny cell phone. "You're safe here," he said, "But if anything should happen, call the number programmed into this phone."

Mark dumbly stuck the telephone in his pocket and stumbled after him. Along the way, he couldn't help but notice the conspicuous absence of any guards. Sensing his concern, Bill said calmly, "They're here ... you just can't see them. The last place had too many of 'em walking around in plain sight and that made you too visible." They entered a massive computer lab that was even bigger than the last one. It had several server clusters that he had never seen before and he said wryly, "I take it these aren't out on the market yet."

"I'm afraid not. And they probably never will be. But they should do your work a whole lot faster than the last ones."

Mark couldn't resist. "Well then, why didn't you just bring me here in the first place?"

"It's a long story, but basically the bad guys got to you before we did. And then there's the territorial issues and, you know, the politics."

Mark *didn't* know and at this point he didn't care. What he really wanted badly was to crawl into a nice, soft bed and sleep the last 12 hours away. But that was not to be and he figured he might as well get down to business. He started out with the words he had found at the last lab. He hoped "*Sperry*", "*Garhwal*", "*Irian*", and "*Argo*" would guide him to something big. Maybe they were just weird enough words to do that.

CHAPTER 11

"So, what's the answer oh wise one?" Chuck broke the strained silence, vainly hoping that a little sarcasm might help dispel some of his growing doubts as he and his father continued their drive to the airport.

"Damned if I know. What I do know is that we never should've invaded Iraq in the first place. But like I've said before, I'd rather do the right thing for the wrong reasons than the wrong thing for the right reasons."

"Come again?" said Chuck, vaguely remembering him saying that.

"If we're lucky, we did the right thing for the wrong reasons. The only problem is that we got some unintended consequences in the process."

"Whatdya' mean?"

"You have to go way back to the beginning when all this idiocy started. Back to right after 9/11, when the president said Hussein had weapons of mass destruction and that he might share them with Al Qaeda. Those were the wrong reasons ... and neither was true."

"So, he didn't have 'em ... we didn't know that at the time."

"Well, Bush was told that but he didn't want to believe it."

"So, he lied."

"I'm afraid so. Then again, he's not the first president to lie to get us into a war."

"Yeah, there were no weapons, but how do ya' know Hussein wouldnt've joined with Al Qaeda?"

"Because they didn't like each other. He would probably rather chew on tin foil than hook up with them because he was secular and they were extreme Islamists. Besides, he was afraid that if he threw in with them, they'd get a foothold in Iraq and eventually try to take over. But the kicker is we should've known that going in."

"How could we know?"

"For one thing, the CIA said there was probably no connection between them."

"Well, that's good enough for me. We both know the spooks are never wrong."

"Yuck it up laughing boy, but right or wrong, that's not what our president wanted to believe, so the Pentagon told him what he wanted to hear. A team from DOD reported that there was a real danger that Hussein would share his supposed WMD with Al Qaeda and the administration latched onto that as the big reason to invade Iraq. The only problem was that the team was headed up by two boneheads with no intelligence experience. They just told him what he wanted to hear."

"But, in the end, we did end up taking down a rotten dictator and an oppressive regime," Chuck said.

"Yes, but at what cost?"

"A lot of lives I guess," Chuck said dreamily staring out of the window, "But haven't things changed? It's not exactly like the old cold war days is it? I mean this is a whole different kind of enemy."

"You got that right, but the old rules of war still apply and the first rule is know your enemy. We don't even know who this enemy is because we were too arrogant to find out before we went in."

"We know they're killers."

"Yeah, killers with a cause. They believe, or say they believe, that they're doing God's work and that makes them a very dangerous adversary."

"Maybe you're right. Maybe we shoulda' thought about that before we went in."

"Maybe's right. That's the problem. The sad reality is that it's always the guys who never served in combat who make these decisions and start the wars."

"The SecDef at the time was a Navy Pilot." Chuck also knew his military history.

"Who never saw any combat. Then there was Vice President Cheney who got five deferments during Vietnam."

"Ya' mean like our current president?"

"Well, at least Trump's were sorta' medical."

"Ya' mean his bone spurs? Didn't his doctor tell the draft board that he had spurs without actually examining him?"

"Yeah, there is that. That doctor actually used to brag about writing him a phony letter."

"And, of course, there's his National Security Advisor."

"Yeah, there's another giant war-hawk who never served."

"Kind of a maniac, isn't he."

"Well, at least Trump never made millions off a war like Cheney."

"Not yet anyway. But he's sure made a lot of money off everything else."

"Ya' mean like foreign dignitaries staying at his expensive hotels? Good point. But when Cheney left office, he became CEO of the military's main contractor and invading Iraq made his company trillions of dollars. A shady little conflict of interest, don't ya' think?"

"Maybe." Chuck did remember, but he also remembered that his father could be a bit of a conspiracy buff and he preferred to believe that it wasn't all that corrupt and calculated.

"And, of course," Don went on, "There's our old commander-in-chief, who served in the National Guard at home and never even finished that. Ya' can't really know what war is 'till you shoot a man face-to-face or stick a knife in his ribs and gut him like a pig. It changes you forever and makes war the absolute last resort."

"Sounds like a line from a movie ... but ya' know," Chuck said, "I remember you talking like that once when I was a kid and I thought then, *how would you know*? Do you remember that?"

"Not really, but then we forget more than we remember."

Thinking this was a dodge, Chuck said, "Well, I ask because you never saw any action like that in Afghanistan ... did you?"

Casting him a quick glance with a wry smile Don said simply, "You're right. I worked in support, but I knew a lotta' guys who did."

"Sorry dad, I didn't mean to..."

"Yes you did and that's okay. I was probably plowed when I said that."

Suddenly another memory popped into Chuck's head as he remembered hearing his dad on the phone one time when he was about 11 or 12 years old. It was foggy, but he distinctly remembered him saying, "I've already died once in my life and I think that's enough don't you?" He couldn't hear the voice at the other end of the phone, but then he heard Don say, "Yeah, Dan Forester is dead and gone. Let's leave him that way."

He hadn't thought about that in a long time and now he instantly remembered the ID he had found in his parents' garage that said "Dan Forester" and started to wonder if that was his father's alias. *But why?* he wondered.

Sensing his thoughts, Don said, "Ya' know what the whole thing stems from in Iraq?"

"No, what?"

"The fact that it's not a real country."

"Whatdya' mean?" Chuck regretted the question as soon as it came out of his mouth, knowing he was now in for an incessantly long and boring history lesson.

"The imperialists drew artificial borders back in the colonial days before those areas were nation-states, so they've never felt any sense of nationalism or loyalty to their country. That region had been part of the Ottoman Empire when the Piquot/Sykes Agreement carved it up for the Brits and France."

"The Piquot what and whose-it?" Chuck feigned ignorance, knowing that his father was enjoying this.

"The Piquot/Sykes Agreement. The one where Winston Churchill and Gertrude Bell stuck three very different provinces together and called it Iraq."

"Oh, *that* Piquot/Sykes Agreement."

"Yeah, that one," Don said with a slight smile sneaking onto his stony, wooden face, "But because it wasn't a real country, the people felt no sense of nationalism and their loyalties were to their tribes, clans, and religions, not to their made-up country. Americans feel like Americans, but Iraqis don't really feel like Iraqis. Anyway, we were naïve enough to think that creating these artificial boundaries would make everyone live together in peace and harmony after centuries of killing each other."

"So, how should they've done it back then?"

"Well, for one thing, if we'd done a little research we might've discovered how fiercely independent these people are and realized that they never got along in the past and weren't likely to get along in the future just because we tell 'em to. More of our arrogance." Don was getting on a roll now.

"And then?"

"And then, separate them by their tribes and religions and give each one its own province. You split the country three ways between Sunnis, Kurds, and Shiites. They swap cities and villages and we pay for it."

"You're talking about moving them out of their ancestral homes and that would never work because they're so important to them," Chuck came back, "Besides, there are deep divisions within the Sunnis and Shiites themselves and even some in the Kurds. How are the rival factions gonna' get along when their own people can't get along with each other?"

"Okay so we don't move 'em that far and we separate them more by sheer geography. We could even move some of their major cultural and religious sites with them, brick-by-brick if we have to. The Kurds get the north, the Shiites get the south, and the Sunnis get the territories in between."

"They wouldn't go for that because they think those sites and the land they sit on are holy to them. Besides, what about Baghdad?"

"It's already kinda' divided by the Tigris River. The Shiites on the east and the Sunnis on the west. We could just leave it that way."

"I still don't think they would all move."

"Then we go to Plan B. We set up twenty or so semi-autonomous regions under a central government in Baghdad and give 'em three posts in an Iraqi congress.

Kinda' like we did in Afghanistan with the warlords. I mean we have fifty states, why can't they have a few?"

"But, they already set up a congress that's supposed to represent different regions," Chuck said with a hint of friendly condescension in his voice.

"Yeah, but they didn't include the militias and tribes who were left with little choice but to join the jihadists. Besides, the government is largely Shiite so they didn't give the Sunnis much oil and that didn't go over real big with them."

"Okay, but back to this three-way split. If we'd done that, wouldn't Iran have moved in and taken over?"

"Not totally. Iranian Shiites will only be able to take over the south where the Iraqi Shiites already are. The Kurds'll keep the north and the Sunnis will keep their lands."

"That all sounds great ... on paper. But I doubt it would work."

"You're probably right. Besides, the real problem for the Kurds is Assad."

"How so?"

"They're fightin' terrorists and takin' over territory in the east while he's fightin' 'em in the west and consolidating his control there. Whatdya' think happens when he makes good on his vow to take the whole country back?"

"A new war?"

"You got it. I can't see any other option, especially since Assad won't be able to resist taking over the big oil fields under Kurdish control. And the Kurds are worried that once ISIS is out, the U.S. will pull out its support."

"Wouldn't be the first time would it?"

"Not so much. We've abandoned them before and it looks like we might do it again."

"But why would the president pull out all of a sudden like that?"

"Because the president of Turkey asked him to, and he couldn't wait to put it out in a tweet. You know he thinks he knows more than his military advisors so he never consulted them and went straight to the public."

"Well, we do need them as an ally and I 'spose Trump doesn't wanna' piss 'em off."

"Yeah, but in our fight against ISIS we've been supportin' the other Kurds that they consider their enemy."

"Ya' mean the PKK?"

"Yup. They've been fightin' a separatist war for 30 years and our support for them hasn't been too popular with the Turks. But, of course, Syria isn't the Kurds' only problem and Turkey isn't their only enemy."

"Ya' mean Iraq?"

"Yup. We've been allied with both sides in the fight between Baghdad and the Kurdistan administration in the north and you gotta' wonder how that's gonna' turn out."

"Sounds like a quagmire."

"It's worse than a quagmire. Add Trump's confrontational stance with Assad's big ally, Iran, and we might end up startin' a bigger proxy war over there that no one can win."

"Stalemate?"

"Exactly."

"I suppose ... but there doesn't seem to be any real solution to any of this does there?"

"Sure looks that way. Certainly, no country or government has the answer because there is too much greed and politics always gettin' in the way."

"Greed?"

"Yeah, when oil was discovered way back when, everything else took a back seat to profit."

"Always about the oil isn't it."

"Always has been. Why do ya' think we invaded Iraq in the first place?"

"Don't tell me, let me guess. To take their oil?"

"Yup, to ensure a steady supply of oil."

"Well, if governments can't do it, what choice do we have?"

"The only choice you and I have is to work at solving small parts of big overall problems by working independently and unfettered by big government and the bigger politics that go along with it."

"Been readin' *Soldier of Fortune,* have we?"

"I like to call it *Mercenary Monthly.*"

"There is no such thing."

"I'm speaking purely theoretical," Don said with a wry smile, "Purely theoretical."

"So, yer' not goin' mercenary on me?"

"Not any time soon my boy."

Chuck bristled. "I haven't been a boy for 15 years," he said, "But you're still an old man."

"That I am and I'm gettin' older by the minute."

"Too bad yer' not gettin' wiser along with it." Chuck didn't like insulting his father, but he liked being called boy even less, "But then again, neither am I."

"You're too young to be wise," Don said laughingly, "But I feel like I've learned the same lessons over and over in my life. I just keep forgettin' 'em."

"Well ,I'm glad we got that outta' the way," said Chuck as they pulled up in front of the airport.

"Look ... I hope I'm wrong. I hope we get lucky and things actually settle down over there."

"Me too," Chuck said as they looked at each other and laughed half-heartedly with gloomy resignation. Don pulled Chuck's duffle bag and brief case out of the trunk and uncharacteristically, they hugged each other for several seconds.

"I love you son," Don choked the words out, "And I'm ... I'm very proud of you."

"Love you too dad," Chuck said as he picked up his bag and walked away trying to remember the last time his father had said those words to him. Turning around as he entered the terminal, he saw Don staring after him with a pained look on his face. Walking through security with a heavy heart, thoughts of his mother's death and his father's pragmatic views on the war competed for the dark space in his brain. His dad won and as he boarded the plane, the tiny doubts about his mission slowly began slithering their way back into his consciousness and he knew he would have to push them back out before they grew too big to ignore.

As the plane took off, he desperately wanted to think about something else, anything else. He tried to let his mind drift aimlessly, but it kept coming back to his doubts about the war. He tried blanking his mind into a meditative state, but that didn't work either. Because it was constantly bombarded by an information overload, Chuck's generation believed that a blank mind was a bad thing. Many people completely missed the mental and physical benefits of quiet meditation and believe you have to be constantly thinking to make any headway in life. Combine this with all of life's problems being solved in a thirty-minute TV show or the instant gratification of a video game and you get a whole generation who can't conceive of a tranquil, thought-free mind.

As he stared out at the cottony clouds sailing by, he knew he needed a distraction from his depressing thoughts, but what? Then it hit him. Reaching down into his brief case, he pulled out one of the many strange writings from *The Book*.

A World of Corporate Shills

We live in a media myth of shadows dancing on the wall of a modern Plato's cave. Not a real world with real problems and realities, but a fictional world, which the media tells us is real life. It's all about what they want to sell us, not about what they should tell us, and we are all more than willing to buy. My mother put it best when she said jokingly, "It must be true, it was in the newspaper." We have been conditioned to believe that if it is in the paper, online, or on TV, it must be true. In fact, we are all suckers for that huge media machine. It's not the real world. It's the world corporate America wants us to believe. It's not that capitalism is wrong, it isn't. But it is out-of-control and the result is this media fantasy world we live in. A fantasy world fueled by vendors who want to sell us all sorts of things and who convince us that we must have them or our lives are incomplete.

He had no idea who the writer was, but this one sounded a little like his father. He seemed to hate journalism, which was odd since that's what he taught and where he spent his professional career. Chuck felt like he grew up in two different worlds. The world he saw and the world his father told him about. His mother refused to sit in the same room with him while he watched a TV newscast because he literally threw things at the television set. "Blow-dried buttheads," he called them. "Broadcast journalism! What an oxymoron." He complained that it was hard to teach journalism these days because of the sorry state it was in. Apparently, *in his day*, journalists considered it their job to be society's watchdog and to catch our leaders in lies and wrongdoing. "Now people don't seem to care about any of that, so neither do the journalists," he often said.

But these days it was hard to tell what Don Lansing was thinking. He kept mostly to himself and Chuck remembered him saying that there are two things a man does alone; gamble and exercise. One time, after a pint of whisky, he said a man also kills alone because it is such a personal thing. But Chuck simply marked that one up to drunkenness. He did gamble occasionally and kept himself in good physical condition. But he never mentioned the other thing he always did alone; drink. Chuck sometimes felt that instead of him guzzling booze from the bottle, it was sucking the very life out of him. Criticizing the government was one of his favorite past times now and Chuck had told him more than once that instead of griping, he should go out and do something about it. He usually got a sort of ironic stare in return.

Overall, he considered his dad kind of a Walter Mitty type who lived cathartically through the exciting lives of others. But there was that time he heard his mother talking on the phone, telling a friend that Don had always had a sort of death wish. Eavesdropping, he heard her say that when they were in Pamplona, Spain she couldn't talk him out of running with the bulls and that he had waited until the last possible moment to jump down off the fence and run barely in front of their deadly horns. This didn't jive with his image of his father and he had buried it in his subconscious. But now, for some reason, it came back to him as he drifted off to sleep to the soft drone of the plane's engines.

* * *

"Louis." "Nopd." "Ayles." It was all a quandary. Even with his recent discoveries, the unexplained little details drove Mark crazy. Taking a break from his tedium, he walked into the next room where CNN was broadcasting a documentary on the recent increase in major hurricanes caused by global warming. Going from natural disaster to natural disaster, they were now showing video of Hurricane Katrina that hit the U.S. Gulf Coast in 2005. Lost in thought, he stared at the TV screen blankly, watching scenes of trees bending in the high winds and thousands of destroyed houses. Then he saw it. It took a few seconds for it to sink in, but when it did, it pierced his brain like a dart popping a carnival balloon. There, in front of his eyes was a New Orleans Police Car with the letters NOPD on the side. *"Nopd" is the New Orleans Police Department and "Louis" has got to be Louisiana. It's for King Louis!* He hadn't gotten it before because not all the letters in NOPD were capitalized making him think it was some random word from an ancient, unknown language. Besides, he and most of the world had long ago forgotten about the hurricane as it became just one of many natural disasters in a growing line of global calamities. In an explosive epiphany he realized that *Prophecy* had predicted Hurricanes Katrina and Rita that devastated New Orleans, killing almost a thousand people.

Jumping back on the computer he did more word and number searches and noticed the number *"60"* and the terms *"1 foot up"* and *"2 feet down"* kept recurring. More research showed why. In the last 60 years New Orleans has sunk 2 feet while the ocean level in the Gulf of Mexico has risen 1 foot. He also found articles quoting some scientists as saying that in the next century, the ocean level will rise another 2 to 6 feet and flood the whole Gulf Coast. Right now, New Orleans is seven feet below sea level. *Why do they even build in a place like that? Surely once it's rebuilt it will flood again.*

Furthermore, he discovered that ocean temperatures have risen one-degree Fahrenheit over the last 30 to 50 years and this small increase has increased the number of hurricanes and their intensity. He found two studies that said in the past 35 years the number of Category 4 and 5 hurricanes worldwide has doubled while the wind speed and duration of all hurricanes has increased by 50%. The temperatures of the ocean currents in the Gulf of Mexico run deeper than most, which means stronger hurricanes are yet to come. On top of that, the Gulf's wetlands used to dampen the incoming storms' intensity and cause them to lose strength as they came inland. But now those wetlands have mostly been developed into housing projects and they don't dampen anything.

Presented with the scientific evidence and in the face of *Prophecy's* code, Mark was now forced to take global warming more seriously. *But what does this have to do with the future of mankind?* He mentally answered the question almost before he finished asking it. All future predictions are meaningless if it's going to be Noah's Ark all over again. *Why worry about a terrorist attack if the earth, or at least its coastlines, are going to be flooded into oblivion?* He knew, of course, that it all depended on the timing of these events.

Still, he couldn't help himself. Irresistibly, he researched the New Orleans Flood further and came up with some interesting key words like *"greed"* and *"corruption"* and terms like *"capitalist excess."* In researching hundreds of news articles related to these words, he found some interesting things, but none helped him in his ultimate quest. Then he found the words *"Holland"* and *"levy,"* and he knew instantly what was going on.

CHAPTER 12

"**I**know you just got back lieutenant," Captain Johnson said upon Chuck's return, "But since your last leave was cut short, I'm givin' your guys another 24-hour leave. You can join 'em at Pancake."

Chuck was stunned by the news. "Thank you, sir," was all he said with a slow salute.

"And son," Johnson said with a half-grin, "Don't relax too much." Chuck turned around and walked out the door with his own version of a semi-grin.

"JFK ... how 'bout another one of yer' lame-ass conspiracies," he heard Scott say as he entered Pancake. When Scott saw Chuck, he yelled, "Attention!" and they all sprang to their feet.

"At ease men," Chuck said, "I wanna' hear it too."

"Well, since you asked," said Will Daniels, ignoring the slight. He was glad to have a chance to share his theories with his buddies who usually didn't want to hear them. "This one's about Arab duplicitousness and American schizophrenia."

Oh, great, thought Chuck, *just what I need right now.* "Just be careful about the American part," he said. He was now worried that Scott had opened a door he would rather keep closed.

"Did ya' ever wonder why 15 of the 19 nine-eleven hijackers were from Saudi Arabia where Osama Bin Laden is from?" Daniels continued in his typical Socratic style, "And why the 9/11 Commission refused to release 28 pages of its report and redacted so much of it?"

"The only thing I ever wondered about," said Jim Hawkins, "is why the Battle Hymn of the Republic says '*mine* eyes have seen the glory of the coming of the lord' instead of *my* eyes?"

"Yes, yes, it's one of those profound mysteries of life and one so intensely important to all of humanity, that I'm surprised no one has answered that question yet," answered Daniels.

"That's what I thought," said Hawkins, half-serious.

"But, can we possibly leave that heavy philosophical conundrum for now and get back to my more frivolous question about the 9/11 report?"

"Don't tell me ... let me guess," chimed in Chuck, wanting to dilute the answer that he knew was coming, "It showed the Saudis might have supported the hijackers."

"Maybe ... but we don't really know because they censored their own report. But the Saudis are our best friends over here and there's a lot more to it than that."

"And how's that?" asked Scott.

"Well, the Saudi government is constantly trying to keep the Wahhabis happy by secretly supporting the terrorists."

"The Wah-whoees?" interrupted Mike Sandstone.

"The Wahhabis. Their major religion is Wahhabism, that radical brand of Islam that says it's okay to kill infidels like us and Muslims who commit sins. And it's okay to overthrow your rulers if they're corrupt, which the royal family is ... in spades. But, as I was saying, they can't afford to keep them too happy or they'll piss us off. So, they support them and fight against them at the same time. That's where the duplicitousness comes in."

"Dupli-what?" said Skip Bailey, AKA Penpal.

"For you less educated people," said Will in a voice full of condescension, "That means saying one thing and doing the opposite. No offense."

"Offense taken ... ya' snob. Why don't ya' just say they're liars?" Bailey said in his slow, syrupy southern drawl.

"Because duplicitousness is a more accurate word ya' hillbilly. Anyway, the Saudis have spent about 70 billion dollars trying to spread their Sunni version of Wahhabism around the world."

"So what?" said Chuck, "Where's the conspiracy?"

"Well, for years they've funneled billions of dollars to terrorist groups through their big charity organization, the Saudi High Commission. The Saudi king was its president and one of its biggest offices was in Bosnia-Herzegovina which gave them a foothold in Europe. Two weeks after 9/11, NATO troops raided their office and found floor plans for European and American military buildings, instructions for making fake State Department badges, and before-and-after pictures of the World Trade Center. What does that tell ya'?" A look of fear suddenly spread across Will's face as he realized he was now bordering on insubordination.

Throwing him a composed look of warning, Chuck answered his question. "That they must have been planning attacks in Europe and the U.S.?"

"That's what a lot of people thought," Will said apologetically, "Unfortunately, no one did anything about it and the Saudis continued their strong alliance with America like nothing ever happened. This was about as duplicitous as you can get."

"Okay, I'll bite," said Chuck doubtfully, "If the Saudis secretly support guys like ISIS, why are they fightin' 'em now?"

"More duplicitousness. It's all for show. They wanna' show their western allies that they're on their side in the fight against terrorism. But they've got 7000 princes and a lot of them, along with the Wahhabis, agree with the extremists. They just can't show it. If they did, they would lose their U.S. and western world support."

"Okay," said Chuck, "So where does the schizophrenia come in?"

"It's us and our addiction to Middle-Eastern oil, which is the reason they are our big buddy. Big oil owns congress and the White House and it does supply millions of jobs. They've convinced a lot of people that renewable energy is unrealistic and too expensive, even though it has gotten very affordable."

"How affordable?"

"Well, since 2009 the cost of solar panels has dropped by 87% and wind turbine prices have come down by 67%."

"Where do you get this stuff?" Chuck asked, genuinely wanting to know.

"It's all online if you know where to look."

"Yeah, well," said Hawkins, "I heard that 99% of the people who use percentages are full of shit."

"Thank you for that profound wisdom from the peanut gallery," Daniels said, "But how about this for some actual facts and figures. You do know that oil and coal pollute our air and water and kill millions of people in the process, right?"

"Duh," was all Jim could muster.

"Great comeback. But I'll bet you didn't know that the damage to people's health costs more each year than the cost of the electricity fossil fuels generate."

"That's a little hard to believe," said Chuck.

"I know it is," answered Will, "But even if it isn't true, can you imagine what would've happened if we would've poured two-trillion dollars into alternative energy research instead of into Iraq? We wouldn't need their oil, we probably wouldn't be fighting this war right now, and thousands of Americans and Iraqis wouldn't be dying."

"Whoa' there cowboy," said Chuck, "If we get rid of the oil companies, we're gonna' lose a lotta' jobs."

"I'm not saying get rid of 'em. I'm saying change them. But do it *gradually* ... and get us off our dependence on Middle-Eastern oil."

"And how exactly do we do that?"

"By continuing to drill for more oil and natural gas in the U.S. while gradually converting to renewable energy. The oil companies will take over the renewable industry anyway and can re-train their employees to work in it. Right now, the wars we fight over Middle-Eastern oil are short-term solutions to long-term problems and both countries are guilty of it. Hell, even though Saudi Arabia is gonna' run out of oil in 50 years, they haven't drilled any new oil wells in the last twenty. They haven't developed new industries like they should've and may end up going backward and turning back into a tribal sandbox. I doubt they can live off their investments in the west forever."

"But I heard they're looking at developing giant solar panel farms in their deserts and will sell the electricity to surrounding countries."

"That they are, my friend, but it is in the very preliminary planning stages and there is a lot of opposition to it."

"But, right now, the royal family is still our best bet for keeping the oil flowing our way ... right?"

"Right and the American oil companies are so far in bed with 'em, there's no getting out. Besides, like you said, they've got the oil so we love 'em because the alternative is their Wahhabi extremists who might shut it off. The Saud family must've made a deal with them so they could control the oil and politics and let them control the religion. The family is actually Wahhabi, but just out of convenience. Their real religion is money and power. So, they walk a fine line because they're part of an extremist religion that both protects them and could destroy them. They need Wahhabism to validate their rule, but constantly have to placate them by looking the other way when some of their members support terrorists like Bin Laden while cozying up to the Americans in public. The Saudis even gave the Taliban millions of dollars. But here's the irony. It's also the Saud family that keeps the Wahhabis in check. If it weren't for them, the whole country would've probably gone totally extremist a long time ago and that wouldnt've been good for our oil supply. We like the royals and the way they keep the oil comin' and the prices down."

"Where does ISIS come in?" asked Chuck in a weary voice.

"Oh, some more extremist Saudis undoubtedly support ISIS in some ways, but they don't want them to do too much damage to the West because it's bad for business. The Saudis have a lot of money invested in the U.S. so what's bad for us is bad for them."

"So, it's not just the oil business, huh?" said Chuck, hoping to steer the conversation away from oil, which he was sick of hearing about.

"No, but it started there and oil continues to be the driving force behind our cozy relationship. It's actually always been about the oil on both sides. An army runs on oil and we need theirs to stay in business. "

"So once again," said Chuck with resignation, "It's all about the oil. We start wars with countries like Iraq over oil. Isn't that argument getting' a little tired? What about terrorism?"

"Well, we can't very well let a guy like Saddam control the second biggest oil deposits in the world can we? But it's more complicated than that. The root of it all is really the military-industrial complex mentality," referring to President Dwight D. Eisenhower's famous warning about industry and the military getting in bed together, and war becoming a self-serving business for both of them. It was a warning that most ignored at the time.

"But don't they need each other?" asked Juan Rodriguez.

"That's the point. They need each other and they need wars to justify their existence ... not to mention their outrageous profits. But they also believe it's good for America and that it's the military-industrial complex that keeps our economy going. It's endemic in our thinking and it's why so many countries hate us for interfering in their affairs. But we think we know what's best for them better than they do themselves and we subscribe to the old Roman philosophy that *it doesn't matter if they love us as long as they fear us.*"

"This sounds a lot like your other bogus conspiracy theories," said Scott Sampson with a skeptical tone, "Do you have proof for any of this or are ya' just shootin' yer' mouth off?"

"The proof is right in front of our faces if we would just look at it. Before the first war, the Assistant Secretary of Defense even wrote papers saying it didn't matter what other countries thought of us and that we were justified in launching a pre-emptive strike to protect ourselves, especially when it came to oil-producing countries. They didn't even try to hide it. When a reporter asked the SecDef how we were gonna' pay for the first Iraqi war he came right out and said "With their oil." So, we steal their oil to pay for our invasion of their country. What possible right do we have to take a country's resources in the first place ... especially when we're using them to attack them? How can that possibly be justified?"

"Okay, okay. We get your point," Chuck said, realizing this line of reasoning was getting dangerous, "But what's wrong with making war against the bad guys and benefitting our economy at the same time? How about that for an existential question?"

"Well, for one thing," Will said, "it doesn't always benefit our economy. In fact, sometimes it sends it into a recession from all the excessive spending. It really only benefits the very rich."

"You might have a point there. But what about fighting against the bad guys?"

Daniels knew he was on shaky ground with this one and thought about the question long and hard before answering, "With all due respect sir, sometimes we use the bad guys as an excuse for war without knowing who they really are or what they're fighting for. I hate to say it, but one man's terrorist can be another man's freedom fighter."

This tired old adage brought howls of laughter from the men and Chuck wanted to quickly change the subject to something a little less incendiary. "Alright, remember, the first amendment gives us all the right to express our opinions ... no matter how idiotic they may be. Now let's get back to the economy Will."

Throwing Chuck a grateful glance, Daniels continued, "Well, for every soldier there are millions of people whose jobs depend on war. But it has become all too political. When congress buys a new weapon, the arms maker immediately floods key congressional districts with money for its production."

"For example?" said Scott.

"The B-2 Bomber was a good one. Pieces of it were made in literally every state in the union, so if anyone ever tried to phase it out they would hear howls from all the districts' congressional representatives. It's the same old military-industrial complex that needs to feed itself. Oh, and don't forget that we're the world's number one arms dealer, which may give us another incentive to keep things riled up around the world."

"That's quite a mouthful," said Chuck.

"Well, in the end, it's all about the money."

"Everything's about the money," Jim Hawkins chimed in, tired of someone else having the floor, "Let's face it, life is like a shit sandwich. The more bread you have, the less shit you have to eat."

"Thank you for that profound toilet wisdom Jim," Will said, snubbing the old joke.

"No, I mean it," Hawkins said, "Even the government has put an actuarial value on human life."

"What the hell are ya' talking about Hawkins?" said Daniels, not wanting to give up his soapbox, "You should stick to yer' juvenile wisdom."

"Okay. How 'bout this for wisdom," Jim said, "Ya' ever wonder why yer' car beeps when the people in the front seat don't put on their seat belts but there's no beep for people sittin' in the back?"

"Never did, but why don't you tell us," said Chuck, grateful for the change of subject.

"Because it would cost the auto industry $325 million a year to put in a back seat beep."

"So?" said an annoyed Will Daniels.

"So," said Hawkins, "That $325 million would save 44 lives a year. 325 divided by 44 is 7.4 million, meaning the value of each life that would be saved is $7.4 million."

"Again, so?"

"So, the Department of Transportation values each life at $6.4 million, a difference of $1 million a life. So, if the car companies put seat belts in the back, they would lose $44 million a year on paper. So, no beeps in back."

Everyone in the room was a little dumbfounded by Hawkins' revelation as they had grown accustomed to his crude, and usually uneducated, remarks. But he wasn't finished.

"Yeah," he said, "Most government agencies put a monetary value on human life. The EPA's is $10 million and the FDA says it's $7.9 million."

"So, what's a soldier's life worth?" piped up Skip Bailey.

"Not much," answered Hawkins, "Probably less than his life insurance."

It was a sobering thought that their lives were worth less than the average person. But then, soldiers have always known that they were expendable.

The silence of the room was broken only by Chuck saying, "Thanks for that depressing information, Jim."

"Yeah, this is getting us nowhere," said Scott, "Let's listen to some tunes." And they did, for the rest of the night until they drifted off into an exhausted slumber.

But with the doubts now hanging over his head, Chuck couldn't sleep and spent most of the night trying to sort out Will Daniels' conspiratorial ideas. Politically, Will was a liberal and Chuck knew that liberals were famous for their conspiracy theories while conservatives either discounted them or considered some of them to be acceptable. Then he remembered *The Book*. In light of the recent elections of a conservative American president and a republican senate, one particularly relevant passage stood out in his mind.

> *Conservatives are not necessarily stupid, but most stupid people are conservatives* — John Stuart Mill

This would suggest that conservatives are stupid, which would mean that liberals are smart or smarter. But I don't think conservatives are stupid as much as they are plain stubborn and unrelenting, which seems to be working for them in recent elections. Conservatives often see life in terms of black-and-white with no shades of gray in-between. Liberals, on the other hand, don't see enough black-and-white and see too many gray areas everywhere. But many voters prefer black-and-white over gray and that's what draws them to conservatism. They think life shouldn't be as complicated as liberals say it is and yearn for the "good old days" when life was simple with absolute rights and wrongs. Many also consider liberals to be intellectual elitists who over-complicate what should be simple issues in life. Liberals, on the other hand, say conservatives are narrow-minded and accuse them of pandering to voters by over-simplifying everything. But sometimes life really is black-and-white. Sometimes there really is an obvious right and wrong and that's where the conservatives shine. In essence, narrow-mindedness wins by being narrow-minded. Unfortunately, conservatives are also often satisfied with being only half-right and aren't too concerned about the other half. But one thing you can't deny is that conservatives are the better politicians and seem to read the electorate much better than liberals these days. Maybe they aren't so narrow-minded after all.

But there was no time for any political meanderings as Chuck's phone rang and he instinctively knew he wouldn't be spending a relaxing night at Pancake. Knowing that this late at night it was unsafe to drive the roads in small groups, he looked from man-to-man to see who was the least intoxicated. "Scott, Brian, Joe, Dan, Steve, Abdul, Moreno," he said, "You're with me," and they left in two big Humvees.

* * *

More research confirmed what Mark suspected. The Dutch had built strong levies that would withstand the strongest floods. No politics, no corruption, just protection for the citizenry. On the other hand, in New Orleans and Louisiana in general, he found that corruption was rampant in the building trades and much of the money meant to build the strongest levies was skimmed off the top. Consequently, they got weak levies that broke under intense rain. Then, to make matters worse, while politicians shouted that the rebuilding of New Orleans should be done by local construction companies, most of the contracts were handed out on a no-bid basis to out-of-town companies who had been big political campaign contributors. *Sounds about right*, he thought.

After weeks of caffeine-inspired, non-stop research, he had the shakes. But he was still optimistic that the mysterious words "*Sperry,*" "*Garwahl,*" "*Irian,*" and "*Argo,*" would lead him somewhere. Then it all came crashing down on him in thundering disappointment. All at once, he discovered that "*Sperry*" is the name of a glacier in Montana's Glacier National Park that has shrunk from 800 to 300 acres since 1901. In fact, the sheer number of glaciers in the park has gone from 150 in 1910 to fewer than 30 today. Further disappointing was the revelation that "*Garwahl*" is an area of the giant Himalayan Mountains in India where glaciers are also melting fast. He found that researchers believe most of the central and eastern Himalayan glaciers could disappear in 30 years or so, helped along by raging forest fires caused by a severe heat wave and resulting drought.

"*Irian*" refers to the equatorial glaciers on the summit of Mount Jaya in Irian Jaya, Indonesia that are also disappearing fast. Additionally, experts say the ice on Africa's most famous mountain, Mount Kilimanjaro in Tanzania, shrank by 80% in the past century. But glaciers in the European Alps are also melting rapidly. From 1991 to 2004 twice as much glacial ice melted away in Europe than in the preceding 30 years. Then there is the huge ice field in the Patagonia region of South America between Chile and Argentina that is also thawing at an alarming rate. It looked to him like glaciers were melting all over the planet and much faster than anyone had predicted. In fact, scientists say that if they keep melting at their current rate, most of them could vanish by the year 2037.

But why do I care? Mark's question was answered almost immediately as he came across a scientific article that said accelerated global warming could produce major droughts and famine across the globe, which could push the death toll into the billions. Glaciers are the planet's largest source of fresh water after polar ice, which is also melting. 40% of the people in the world get their drinking water from glaciers, which eventually melt into streams and rivers. If they melt too fast there will be nothing left to feed those streams and rivers and we will run out of drinking water. Currently, the United Nations has identified 150 flash points where people and countries are likely to fight wars over water, which would result in mass death.

Going back to *Prophecy*, he found the words "*Swiss*" and "*floods*" and after a little digging, found that melting glaciers had caused severe flooding that recently devastated parts of Switzerland. *Another past prediction that doesn't do me any good,* he figured. But still nothing on "*Argo.*"

He also ran across some new words like "*Larsen*" and "*ice*" and numbers like "*720 billion*" and "*40.*" With that last number, he wondered if there was any correlation between the number "*40*" and the 40 days and nights it rained in the Biblical Noah's Ark story. But after running countless programs, he deduced that "*40*" applied to the fact that 40% of the Antarctic ice cap has melted in the last 40 years and that, currently, it is warming at twice the speed of the rest of the earth.

But things are just as bad at the other end of the planet. According to the National Center for Atmospheric Research, Arctic sea ice is melting three times faster than had earlier been estimated. In 2016, the Arctic sea ice reached its lowest level ever with each of the 16 months leading up to September of that year breaking the global average high temperature record. To put it in perspective, in the last two decades the Arctic has lost an area of ice roughly the size of Texas. In 2017, an iceberg the size of Delaware broke off of the Antarctic and another one weighing in at one-trillion tons broke off of Western Antarctica.

Scientists theorize that the earth might be experiencing feedback loops that feed on each other and speed up global warming in a vicious cycle. As ice melts, more ground is exposed. The ground absorbs more of the sun's heat, which melts more ice, and it starts all over again. Also, as the ice melts into the oceans, the sea water becomes dark and the dark water absorbs more of the sun's energy and heat, which melts even more ice.

As far as the future is concerned, Mark's research turned up some frightening predictions like if the entire Greenland ice sheet melted, it would raise global sea levels by 23 feet, swallowing up places like coastal Florida and Bangladesh. The Antarctic holds enough ice to raise ocean levels more than 215 feet, which would destroy a lot more than that. His head was now a whirlpool of numbers swirling around in a sea of confusing data. But science is numbers and numbers don't lie. Again, however, he wondered what the point was of worrying about a terrorist attack if the planet might soon be under water.

But then there were those mysterious words like "*Argo*" and if that weren't enough, a new word had cropped up. It was "*Ayles*" and he couldn't make sense of any of it. He knew his only hope was to keep doggedly searching. His mind also drifted back to his last computer lab and poor Dr. Weiss. *Who knows what life-changing discoveries he might've made had he lived.* Rumor had it that he was working on a revolutionary mathematical formula that might shed a little light on the origins of the universe. Supposedly, he had uncovered six numbers that were present at the moment of creation and that determined life and the shape of everything in it. He had also determined that 3 and 9 were important numbers and Mark recalled him quoting Nikola Tesla as saying, "If you knew the magnificence of the 3, 6, and 9 you would have a key to the universe." He had no idea what that meant, but he knew that Tesla was a brilliant man who was ahead of his time and that he was obsessed with this idea. Like many scientists, Dr. Weiss was very guarded about his work and unfortunately, it probably died with him.

But coming out of his melancholy, Mark realized that there was still that annoying "*Argo*" and "*Ayles.*" *What the heck are they?*

CHAPTER 13

Have to have bad to have good or
happiness is a warm, fluffy towel

We've become a pill-popping society who can't handle pain or any bad feelings. Feel pain? Take a pill. Not happy? Take a pill. We've forgotten that pain isn't always a bad thing and that it's actually a signal to our brains that something is wrong. Besides, enduring the pain instead of masking it makes you stronger. And then there is the anti-depressant generation. Feeling down? Take a pill. I'm not talking about people with screwed up brain chemicals. They need the anti-depressants and thank God for them. I'm talking about the everyday, down-in-the dumps blues that everyone gets. After all, we can't feel bad, can we? We can't allow depression to creep into our lives, can we? Have your kids got the adolescent doldrums or are they a little unfocused? Give them a pill. We think feeling sad is absolutely intolerable. Well, here's a news bulletin. Feeling bad is a natural part of life. It's not supposed to be covered up. When you feel down you should embrace it as a natural, innate slice of life, not run from it. You should actually be glad when you feel bad because it means that eventually you'll probably feel good. Somehow, we've lost sight of the fact that for there to be a good, there has to be a bad. In order to feel good, we have to feel bad sometimes.

More psycho-babble, thought Chuck as he drove back to the base in two Humvees with Scott, Joe Gercek, Dan Walker, Brian Malone, Luis Moreno, and Steve Chamberlain. Once again, he had to leave his men at Pancake for another last-minute mission briefing. But he had to admit that the part about pain not being such a bad thing sort of guided his life. He embraced pain and made it his friend and that made him a very good warrior.

"Whatdya' think the mission is?" asked Sergeant John Boland back at Pancake as the night wore on. The Mad Dogs were feeling the nervous exhaustion that comes from too many sleepless nights and a lot of killing.

"I don't know, but we'd better not make this a big one, just in case," answered Butch O'Shaughnessy, AKA Irish.

"Probably another suicide assignment that no one gives a shit about," threw in Mike Sandstone.

"Well that's a happy thought," said Ron Jenkins, wanting to shift the conversation to something less depressing. "JFK, how 'bout some more conspiracy B.S.?" What he didn't know was that Will saw Chuck's absence as an opportunity to get into some hard-core conspiracy theories.

"Glad you asked," he said and without hesitation, he launched into another tirade, "Guess where these guys got a lot of their guns."

"Where?" asked Jenkins

"Us for one. We supplied Hussein with weapons during the 8-year Iran-Iraq war and he had arsenals all over the place. When we invaded they were left unguarded, the insurgents cleaned 'em out, and now they're using 'em on us. But the neighbors are giving 'em guns too and I'm sure China and Russia are right in there pitching. As you've noticed, Russia's Kalashnikov is the most popular gun. The AK-47 accounts for about 80% of all the assault rifles in the world."

"What about our guns?"

"Not as good as the AK. It shoots 600 bullets a minute and will still be firing in sandy or wet conditions that'll jam ours."

"Oh, that's great ... the enemy has a better gun than me."

"Don't worry," Will said with a laugh, "His is a lot older too."

"So, we gave 'em the guns that're killin' us?" asked Juan Rodriguez.

"Afraid so," said Will, "But let's change the subject. Did ya' ever wonder why when they banned all flights after 9/11, they let a plane fly around the U. S. picking up Bin Laden's relatives and fly them back to Saudi Arabia? Don't ya' think the FBI might've liked to talk to them and ask if they'd heard from ole' Osama?"

"I always wondered about that," said Jim Hawkins.

"A lot of people did. The official word was that they were trying to protect the relatives from retaliation by angry Americans but at that time, Americans didn't know it was Osama. Again, that's where our schizophrenia about oil comes in."

"Whatdya' mean?" asked Rick Stedman, surprising everyone in the room because he normally didn't join in on conversations like this one.

"President Bush was an oil man and Saudi Arabia is the big oil producer," said Daniels, "So, he couldn't afford to piss 'em off. Hell, to show ya' how tight they were, one of his brothers has made his entire living off dealing with the Saudis. Besides they own about an eighth of our economy and that's just the part we know about. Lord only knows how many subsidiaries and umbrella corporations they've got their teeth into. Anyway, good old capitalistic greed did that."

"Hey that was our commander-in-chief," said Mike Sandstone half-joking. Then more seriously, "Besides, didn't he want to make Iraq a democracy ... and wouldn't that be a good thing?"

"No, I think it would be a *great* thing. I liked Bush's intentions, they were just unrealistic. It's hard to give people a democracy when they don't really understand what it is. Some of them believe democracy is anti-Islam and that man can't make his own rules to live by ... only Allah can do that."

At that point, the conversation began to lag and the Dogs were feeling their fatigue. One-by-one, on the couches, chairs, and beds strewn around the house, they drifted off to sleep. The last notes of Guns n' Roses' *Welcome to the Jungle* faded out as the last soldier drifted off to sleep.

Around midnight the call of nature stirred Private Jimmy Gable out of his foggy stupor. But as he started to get up, metal canisters came crashing through all the windows shooting out smoke in all directions. "Gas!" he screamed as he put a blanket over his face and frantically tried to wake the others. They started to stir, but it was too late as the gas filled everyone's lungs and knocked them out. Not even Jimmy could withstand its potency as he crumpled to the floor in a heap. It was special nerve gas that Saddam Hussein had developed and the weapons inspectors never knew about. It incapacitated, but didn't kill. Now kicking in the doors and windows, gas-masked men rushed in. They quickly slung the unconscious men over their shoulders and hauled them back out. As they emerged from the farmhouse, one of them thought he saw a figure running away from his truck. He fired his AK-47 at the dark form, but the bullets cut through thin air and he figured it was his imagination. They loaded the limp bodies into their two trucks and drove off into the dark, desolate, and always perilous Iraqi night.

* * *

Mark's further research found other words indicating that the earth is absorbing much more heat than it is giving off. *Duh. No kidding.* All this pointed to one thing and that was that the scientists and the environmentalists were right. We're polluting the atmosphere with greenhouse gases and deleting the ozone layer causing the earth and its oceans to warm up much faster than anyone thought. According to one 2018 study, over the last few decades, the world's oceans have soaked up 60% more heat than was earlier predicted.

The earth's climate does naturally warm up over time, but spreading cities and deforestation are speeding things up. The big problem, however, is the buildup of heat-trapping gases like carbon dioxide, methane, and water vapor. The U. N. says carbon dioxide or CO_2 alone has increased by 30% since industrialization took hold in the mid-19th century. According to one study conducted by 450 scientists from more than 60 countries, the amount of carbon dioxide in the atmosphere is now the highest it has been in 800,000 years. It's no wonder that 2015, 16, and 17 were the hottest years on record.

He remembered an old college professor who said people forget that when they fill their gas tanks with gasoline it all goes up into the atmosphere and every mile driven produces one more pound of CO_2. The average American alone shoots 24 tons of it into the air every year. That same professor said it's kind of like piling extra blankets on the planet and making global temperatures shoot up faster than at any other time in the past thousand years. And it's beginning to show. According to NASA, Greenland is now losing 53 cubic miles of ice per year. That's twice the amount it was losing ten years ago. NASA also says that since 1990 the planet has experienced 15 of the hottest years in recorded history.

Some estimates say the Arctic Polar Ice Cap is declining by at least 9% every decade. NOAA says that declining sea ice and rising arctic temperatures have become the new norm. Unbelievably, one expert says there might be no polar ice left by 2060. The fear is that the melting ice will ultimately raise ocean levels by more than their present one-inch-per-year. Scientists say if the sea level rises more than three feet, coastal areas and low-lying island nations could be underwater by the end of the century and some estimate that it will be a lot sooner than that, like in 20 years.

Some scholars say history shows us that climate shifts can happen very fast. One German Government report says the earth's temperature may rise enough for the West Antarctic Ice Sheet and the Greenland Ice Cap to gradually melt away, which would raise sea levels world-wide by up to 30 feet. This would submerge vast areas of land and, more importantly, big cities like London, New York, San Francisco, Miami, Bombay, Calcutta, Sydney, Shanghai, Lagos, and Tokyo, killing millions. Indonesia's environment minister warned that his country could lose 2,000 of its 18,000 islands to rising sea levels by 2030.

Studies also showed that global warming is heating up the oceans and releasing methane from the ocean floor at a much faster rate than previously thought. Permafrost that has been frozen for thousands of years is now thawing at an alarming rate and releasing methane and carbon dioxide into the air. Once in the atmosphere, they help trap heat on the planet in the greenhouse effect. The trapped heat thaws more permafrost and the vicious cycle starts all over again.

Methane, in particular, is a problem. In a snowball effect, when the methane is released it causes more temperature increases, which cause more ocean warming and that produces more methane gas. Scientists used to see methane plumes at the bottom of the ocean that were 10 meters wide, but now they find them a little over a half-mile in diameter.

But the methane isn't just coming out of the ocean. Global warming may also be causing dangerous methane gas to bubble out of the soil five times faster than previously thought. Scientists estimate that more than 8 million tons of methane is released into the atmosphere each year. *Okay, okay. I get it. The ocean is one giant cauldron of boiling stew and the earth is just one big baked potato. So, tell me something I don't know.*

His request was granted as he discovered that about 129,000 years ago warm weather melted a lot of ice and raised sea levels to 13 to 20 feet above what they are today. *No air pollution back then,* he thought. *Maybe it's just natural climate evolution.* Further research showed that several prominent scientists agreed with him and some actually argued that planet warming might not be such a bad thing. They argue that the earth naturally warms and cools over millions of years and they ask provocative questions like was life better when mile-thick ice-covered Chicago? Or was it worse when Greenland was so warm that Vikings farmed it?

Then he found an article that might explain these scientists' contrarian views. It said that the oil industry spent tens of millions of dollars on a disinformation campaign to cast doubt on the very existence of global warming and paid some scientists to argue that it doesn't exist. But then he remembered something that made that line of reasoning moot. Every day our cars and coal plants put 70 million tons of CO_2 up into the atmosphere. It holds in the sun's heat and causes global warming. While America holds less than 5% of the Earth's population, it produces 25% of its CO_2 emissions.

I understand the argument, Mark thought, *but are we actually destroying the environment?* Then he recalled a Biblical passage about God's return that made him wonder even more. Revelation 11:18 describes a council of elders saying that God would "destroy those who destroy the earth." Now he really began rethinking his casual attitude toward the environment.

* * *

As Chuck and his men bounced down the pothole-ridden Baghdad road on the way back to Pancake, he was anxious to tell his men what he had learned in the intelligence briefing. But when they arrived, they found the place empty except for six gas canisters lying on the floor. Chuck instantly grasped what had happened and woefully knew what was going to happen next. His men would be beheaded one-at-a-time on the Internet. *It's my fault! I should have known we were vulnerable here!*

But there wasn't time for remorse as someone came walking out of the shadows with his arms raised and shouted, "I'm a friend!" Chuck and his men raised their guns to see a vaguely familiar figure wearing the standard photographer's vest walking toward them. They didn't know his name but he looked like a news photographer they had seen taking pictures at several battles. He appeared to be in his early 50's and in good physical shape with a scrubby, salt-and-pepper beard and weathered eyes. His face had creases that looked like desert gullies with bushy, graying curls hanging unkempt off of his head and a swarthy complexion with leathery skin tanned by the desert sun.

"Jack Ryder, World News. I'm gonna' reach slowly for my press credentials." Still the Dogs kept their guns trained on him in a dead bead.

"Don't move!" Chuck grunted as he walked over to him and pulled the press pass out of his pocket. Looking back and forth from the pass to the man and eyeing him carefully, he said, "What the hell are ya' doin' out here?" He couldn't remember why, but for some reason, the name *Jack* sparked a warm feeling in him.

"Actually lieutenant, officially speaking, you're probably not supposed to be here either."

Fed up with more than he could take, Chuck sprang forward and hit him square in the stomach. The photographer doubled over from the punch but kept his feet. "Whether we're supposed to be here or not isn't any of your business dickhead," he said angrily, "Now tell me what yer' doing here or I'm gonna' let my boys get medieval on yer' ass."

"Don't shoot the messenger lieutenant," Ryder gasped, raising himself up, "I was watching you guys for a story on special forces I'm doing."

"Yer' out," Chuck said nonchalantly and began pushing him toward the Humvee, "And you're probably gonna' be arrested and sent home. You know the rules."

"I can tell you what happened here."

Chuck stopped with a jolt. "It's obvious what happened here," he said.

"But don't you wanna' know the dirty details from an eyewitness?"

"The details are probably that you stood by and watched my men get killed and didn't do a damn thing about it."

"Not killed. Kidnapped. And I may know where they took 'em."

Chuck looked at the photographer long and hard with his signature death stare. "Okay, tell us exactly what went on here and don't leave anything out."

Knowing Chuck was testing him, he said calmly, "Six of your men were drinkin' and fallin' asleep. I saw some guys dressed in black creep up to the house, but I couldn't do anything because there were eight of 'em and one of me, so I decided to see what they were up to. Then I saw one of 'em raise a weapon and I was about to yell to the house to warn them when they all shot gas cannisters through the windows. It was obvious they weren't gonna' kill 'em. They hauled 'em all to their trucks and drove off."

At that moment, Chuck thought he recognized the voice but he couldn't quite remember where he had heard it.

"So, you were about to yell out huh?" Private Dan Walker ran up and jammed a rifle butt in Ryder's gut and again he doubled over.

"I hope you guys don't make this a habit," Ryder spit out the half-joke with some blood sputum.

"He's got nothin'," Chuck grumbled as he started to haul him up to his feet and push him further toward the Humvee.

"Not necessarily," Ryder said in a tone that sounded like he was saving the best for last.

"What's that supposed to mean," Gunnery Sergeant Brian Malone asked.

Ryder looked at them all with a skeptic gaze and especially at Chuck before he answered. He seemed to be weighing giving them some deep, dark information or not. His normal poker face showed now that he had made his decision. "I may know *exactly* where they took them."

That was a bombshell and Chuck jumped on it with all fours. "And where might that *exactly* be?"

Jack pointed in the direction of Baghdad.

"Oh great," Chuck said sarcastically, "They're in the city of millions. Get his ass outta' here before I shoot him myself."

As the men moved toward him, Ryder piped up with, "Okay, okay. I do know their exact location."

"Well you must have one long lens to know that."

"I do ... sort of. It's a GPS satellite locator."

"What good does that do us ... unless ... "

"That's right. I managed to plant a homing device on one of the trucks and with any luck it will stay with the men, but not for long."

"What in the hell are ya' doin' with a homing device?"

"We're all issued them in case of kidnapping. We know no one will ever come and rescue us, but it makes us feel better knowing someone might know where we are."

It sounded like a flimsy story, but Chuck knew he couldn't afford to ignore it. "How did you attach it to the truck?" he asked, growing more suspicious by the second.

"With a magnet, of course," answered Ryder.

"And why would there be a magnet on the thing if it was supposed to be on your body?"

"Because I attached mine to my camera and found that kidnappers like to keep things like that, especially the expensive cameras."

"Sounds rehearsed," Chuck said, eyeing him warily. *Where have I heard that voice before*, he thought as he tried desperately to remember. He was suspicious, but he couldn't see a reason for Jack to make it all up. He was also desperate and knew he had few options. "Okay. Let's say you're tellin' the truth, though I doubt it. What if they separate our guys all over Baghdad?"

"They usually take all of 'em to one place first as a staging area and then split 'em up around town. That's why we gotta' move fast. They'll move by dawn."

"*We*? You surely don't mean *you*."

"Actually, yes I do. Here's the deal. You forget I was ever here and take me with you and I'll show you where your men are. What have you got to lose?"

"Don't think so. Why don't we just take the GPS from you and call it a day?"

"You could ... but I don't have it on me."

"Search him!" Chuck barked and his men instantly obeyed, roughing Ryder up more than was necessary.

"Nothing," Sergeant Malone said.

"Uh huh. What a surprise. Yer' up to somethin', I just don't know what and I don't have time to figure it out. So, you show us the locator and you go with us, but I still don't trust you and if you screw up once I'll kill ya' where ya' stand."

"Fair enough."

"Wait lieutenant," said Malone. "We can't take a civilian with us. If he gets killed we're screwed."

"Don't worry," Chuck answered back, "He's a hot dog and his bosses know he doesn't follow the rules. *When* he gets killed, they'll see that he's so far outside of his assignment they won't want to look into it too closely."

"But what if he lives and prints an article about us?"

"Well, then he'll be kicked out of Iraq and never work in a war zone again and I think he knows that." Chuck knew that if any journalist ever published a story about a special forces' covert mission, he would be in major career trouble and probably legal difficulty as well.

"Works for me," said Jack, "But I do need one more thing."

"What now?"

"A gun."

"Bullshit!" blurted Joe Gercek, "He'll shoot us or himself."

"Desert Storm vet. I can handle myself and besides, you need all the guns you can get."

In for a penny, Chuck thought. Besides, in spite of his strong doubts, he knew that every minute that passed was more time the kidnappers had to move his men far beyond his reach. He wanted to get official approval for a rescue mission, but knew it would take too long. "Get him one outta' the box," he said and the men started to grumble. "I know. I know," he said, "Yer' gonna' have to trust me on this one. I've got a feeling."

That seemed to mollify them as Chuck's instincts had paid off in the past. But they still wondered why he was so trusting of this photographer. And was he really a photographer anyway? They had their doubts.

Sensing their skepticism, Chuck said, "Like I said, if he gets outta' line I'll shoot him myself."

"We also need some Arab clothes," Jack said, unfazed by the threat.

"Also, in the box. Anything else? Shine yer' shoes maybe?"

Looking down at his boots, Ryder looked like he was considering the offer. "Maybe later," he said, "Now let's get dressed and go get yer' boys."

"How long've we got?" asked Chuck.

"Not long. They'll probably try to get your men to confess to America's war crimes on camera. They'll behead them on tape as soon as they can and post it on the Web."

"They'll never confess to anything," Scott Sampson said and the Dogs half-smiled knowingly.

"Good ... that might buy us some time."

"Or they'll just cut their heads off right then and there," said Scott with worry in his voice.

"They might ... but most likely they'll try to torture a confession out of 'em first."

"Get dressed and get the stuff," Chuck ordered. He wasn't about to follow orders from a news photographer, but right now it seemed like his only option if he wanted to get his men back. "Get it all," he said, "We can't use this place anymore." His men hustled to a hidden compartment under the building's floorboards. Pulling up a panel revealed all kinds of weapons they had accumulated over the last year, both theirs and the enemy's. They pulled out several long-range sniper rifles, a Stinger Missile Launcher, and a myriad of weapons of all shapes and sizes.

"Planning to start yer' own war?" Jack said.

"Ya' never know," Chuck answered, still trying to remember where he had heard that voice before, "Okay. Where's the GPS?"

"There's a little shed a quarter-mile down the road," said Jack, "It's there."

They drove to the shed and Jack jumped out. He ran into the shed and came out with something in his hand. "Here it is. Now let's find your guys."

The Dogs crowded around the GPS satellite locator and saw the blinking light that was their comrades.

"They're moving," Jack said, "It looks like they're heading right to one of their bases on the east end of town." This was no man's land. There was no Iraqi rule here. No U. S. rule. There was simply no rule whatsoever, except for the insurgents who had the locals scared to death.

How does he know where their bases are? Chuck wondered as his suspicions of this photographer grew.

"Give your drivers these coordinates and we'll take the two Hummers 100 feet apart."

"Why?" Chuck asked.

"Because if we come busting in there like John Wayne, their lookouts will see us and warn their compadres before we can reach your men. We have to look like regular patrols who don't know anything's up. I'll tell you when we pass the last lookout and we get off there."

"Won't they see us stop?"

"We're not gonna' stop."

"Sleds?"

"Sleds."

* * *

Mark was disappointed that all his research thus far revealed something everyone already knew. No terrorist attack and certainly no nuclear holocaust. Just global warming and a lot of air and water pollution. He had never been too troubled by environmental problems and thought that many of the environmentalists' concerns were alarmist with no real scientific basis. Still, the words "*Argo*" and "*Ayles*" kept popping up and he was hopeful, although searches for related words found nothing. It bugged him because buried somewhere deep in his memory "*Argo*" meant something. He just couldn't remember what. Finally, after multiple searches he came up with the word "*robot*" and it all suddenly fell into place.

He remembered reading about a big research project in which 1800 technology-packed robotic floats had been placed in seas all over the planet to measure their water temperatures. One of the scientists involved was named Jason and in an interview, he jokingly called his group of oceanographers the Argonauts after *Jason and the Argonauts* of Greek lore. Someone then unofficially dubbed the project "Argo." But because it wasn't the program's official name, Mark's research never turned it up.

In the Argo project, the robots regularly dive as much as a mile underwater. They take temperature readings and their measurements are supplemented by satellite gauging of ocean levels, which rise from both melting glaciers and the sea warming and expanding. The measurements determined that for every square meter of surface area, the planet is absorbing almost one watt more of the sun's energy than it is radiating back into space as heat.

Some scientists believe that global temperatures are shooting up faster than at any other time in the past thousand years. As evidence of rising oceans, they point to flooded rice fields in Bangladesh and the melting Antarctic ice caps. But global warming critics say that in the last 50 years the sea-level in Bangladesh has risen an infinitesimal seven-tenths of an inch, far too little for anyone to notice. For the Antarctic, they have no good answer.

Critics also say the earth has always warmed and cooled naturally and there is nothing to get alarmed about. When pinned down on the melting Sperry Glacier in Montana, they point to the National Climatic Data Center, which says summer temperatures over Western Montana show no warming trend whatsoever in the 20th century. Climate change scientists counter-argue that overall, five of the last six years were the warmest temperatures in recorded weather history. That's not to mention that the atmosphere's level of carbon dioxide is higher today than it has been in hundreds of thousands of years. The critics argue back that while all this occurred, the overall planet actually cooled. But scientists say you can't look at the earth as a whole, that you have to look at some of the coldest spots that have warmed dramatically and so the debate goes back-and-forth with no seeming end in sight. One thing that most scientists agree on, however, is that ice is melting, rivers are running dry, and coasts are eroding, all at an alarming rate. It was fast-becoming evident to Mark that it was all happening much faster than anyone had previously predicted and that worried many scientists. *Okay, but what about "Ayles"?*

CHAPTER 14

Go for It

With many things in life it's best to throw yourself into it 100% and not hold anything back instead of being careful, pensive, and tentative. If a race car driver sees smoke from an accident up ahead should he put on the breaks? No, because the drivers behind him will crash into him and possibly start a multi-car pile-up. Instead, he is supposed to accelerate through it. Just like when you're floating on your back. If you float tentatively, trying to keep your face out of the water at all costs, you won't float very well. You have to commit your body completely and arch your back as far as it will go, fully tilting your head into the water. With all that commitment, you'll float better. The lesson is that sometimes you have to be willing to lose something (like keeping your head out of the water) to keep it and sometimes you have to go all out and risk everything to achieve your goal.

Chuck thought he knew why he reflected on this entry from *The Book* as the two Humvees bounced down the bumpy desert road. It was probably because he was 100% all-in with this mission and there was no turning back. Snapping back to the present, he asked the alleged photographer Jack Ryder the question on everyone's mind.

"Why are you doing this?"

"The pictures," was all Jack said.

"Gotta' be more than that." Chuck looked straight into his ice-cold, expressionless eyes.

"Okay you got me," Ryder answered after a long pause of returning the stare, "Let's just say I owe an old friend a favor."

"What old friend," he asked, more confused.

"Not important. What is important is gettin' your guys out before they lose their heads."

"Couldn't agree with you more," Chuck said, not missing the double entendre. Then, more pensively, "But my superiors may have something to say about that. I imagine I'm looking at a court martial for an unauthorized mission if we make it back."

"First of all kid, that shouldn't even be a worry of yours," Jack said, "But second, I have a feeling they'll approve ... if we succeed."

"And if we don't? I guess it's a moot point. Anyway, my dad always said he'd rather ask for forgiveness than permission."

"Yer' dad's a wise man."

"You have no idea," Chuck said as he was beginning to agree more and more with his father's opinions on Iraq, although he had to keep them couched around his men.

"One more thing you should know before we go in," Jack said, suddenly turning serious.

"What now?"

"I'm pretty sure I heard one of 'em say '*he's* not here' when he ran out of the house ... and he seemed pretty pissed."

"So?"

"So ... they must've been lookin' for someone in particular and he wasn't there."

"And?"

"Wake up lieutenant," Jack grew impatient, "They wanted you."

"Why?" Chuck feigned ignorance.

"Because yer' the big John Wayne, swaggering American cowboy. You're the ultimate fighting man for the great satan my boy."

"Call me boy again and I'll drop ya' right here." Chuck never liked the word and he wasn't crazy about Jack's growing cockiness.

"Okay, lieutenant, calm down. Thing is, your unit has killed way more of their men than anyone else ... and you do it with such style. I mean if I wasn't in love with myself, you'd be my hero. Anyway, they hate your guts and taking you down would be a big victory ... all over the internet. But I get ya' kid. Whether ya' like it or not ... for you, killin' just comes natural."

That stung as Chuck began to contemplate his newly-bestowed hero status and the idea that he could be a natural-born killer. He never wanted to be a hero and he certainly never thought of himself as an instinctive murderer. *Is this what I've become?*

Sensing his feelings, Jack gave him some uncharacteristic counsel. "Kid, eventually your time and luck both run out," he said with a grimace and some sad resignation, "Then it's just pure instinct and that means kill."

Chuck didn't know whether to resent or appreciate the advice as the truck swerved to avoid hitting one of the many boxes on the garbage-strewn road, any one of which could contain an improvised bomb. If Jack was right, he realized the times when he thought he was being watched, he was. "So, I'm public enemy number one," he said after a long silence.

"Yup. A great honor isn't it?"

"You bet. What's the plan?"

"When we unload," Jack said turning toward Abdul Hameed and Joe Gercek, "These two will go in from the front where there's too many of 'em for a sniper to get. They'll fit in since they're Arabs."

"I'm not Arab you ignorant bastard! I'm Turkish," Gercek shot back.

"Arab ... Turk ... who cares? You look Arab and that's what might save your buddies."

With that in mind, Gercek shut his mouth, but Scott Sampson said bluntly, "Lieutenant ... you gonna' let this asshole call the shots?"

"Not crazy about it Sergeant, but right now it looks like our best shot."

"Hope you're right."

"Me too," Chuck said as they drove down the deserted road, "Me too." What bothered him was not Jack giving orders, but rather how he knew that there were too many people in the front for a sniper. *Please tell me he isn't a traitor and this isn't a trap to get the rest of us!*

"I never asked you," Chuck said to Jack, "What about our exit plan?"

"Taken care of."

"What does that mean exactly?"

"Let's just say our friends in the air will help us." Now Chuck knew he wasn't just a photographer. *Might be a traitor though.* As they drove along, he decided to keep an extra close eye on Ryder as they approached the coordinates.

"Slow and go," Jack whispered 30 minutes later. Over the radio, in his own quiet way, Chuck ordered his men to ready the sleds. They lowered what looked like a mechanic's roller bed with inflatable tires out of the back of the Humvees as they slowed to 20 miles an hour.

"Go," Chuck said and two men from each vehicle crawled onto the sleds. They looked like customized Soapbox Derby racers as they were then hydraulically lowered to the road. When they touched the pavement, the drivers slowed down again and the sleds disconnected and rolled to a stop. The trick was for the Humvee in back to swerve around the sled in front just slightly and not run over their own men. Two more sleds were lowered with one man on each and the process was repeated. The Humvees sped off into the night and the six of them rendezvoused in the pitch-black desert crouching around the GPS Satellite Locator. "There," Jack said as he pointed to the screen. He looked off into the moonless night with his telescopic, infrared goggles and said, "They're in that warehouse."

"What's the plan?" Chuck asked, almost starting to trust him.

"Gercek and Hameed go around the back and shoot two time-delay grenades behind the building next door for a diversion. Then they work their way around to the front and there'll be four or five guards at the entrance they'll have to take out ... quietly. Your best sniper sets up in the back to kill the rear guards.

"That would be Sniper Steve," Chuck said. Private Steven Chamberlain was the most accurate marksman in the unit and he took his craft very seriously. He told Chuck once that when he shoots at anything, he blocks out everything around him and visualizes the target in his mind. "It's just you and the target," he said, "with nothing in-between and in a sense, you become one with it. Then you gently squeeze the trigger, like you're softly massaging a girl's nipple." At the time Chuck thought it sounded a bit perverted. But *hey, whatever works,* and Steve was one of the best in the business.

"Good. Lieutenant, you follow Gercek and Hameed in the front and two of us will go in the back."

"What about transportation?"

"Who's yer' best car thief?"

"Moreno," they all said at once. Jose Moreno had spent his youth in New York City stealing cars.

"Private Moreno," Jack said, "You hot wire the trucks out front and that's what we leave in."

Chuck noticed how easy giving orders came to this photographer. *A little too easy,* he thought. "And our guys?" he asked.

"Kill anything that moves ... basically anyone who's not tied up. And I mean *anyone.* There'll be no time to be picky."

"You sound like you've been here before."

Jack slowly took on a sullen grimace and eyeing Chuck carefully said, "Yeah ... on assignment. Welcome to hell boys." Then he chuckled weirdly, "We're in their town now and if we get caught we're all gonna' be decapitated on the World Stage. But at least we'll get our 15 seconds of fame! Oh, and even if we are successful, we're probably not all gonna' make it."

Those words bothered Chuck. He knew it was true, but they certainly didn't sound like the words of a photographer and he almost detected a little excitement in Jack's voice. That made him wonder if he might be one of those cowboys who love danger and enjoy living on the edge, putting the lives of those around him at risk. He didn't like these reckless show-boaters, although he was sometimes accused of being one. They were always the ones to rush in first, even when they were outnumbered and outgunned. But in doing that, they sometimes got everyone around them killed.

Oddly enough, while they took the biggest risks, blindly charging in and putting themselves in harm's way before anyone else, they often survived while their comrades died. One theory was that the enemy was so shocked by their brazenness, they were stunned into inaction for the first few seconds, just long enough for the cowboy to get in the first shot. It was much like General George Patton in World War II when he would attack when everyone thought he would retreat. The only problem was that these kinds of unexpected attacks got a lot of soldiers killed. *Let's hope that's not Jack*, Chuck worried.

* * *

Just when he was beginning to feel bleak and hopeless about the world's future, Mark stumbled onto some slightly more optimistic words. Words like "*hydrogen*" and "*air*" and "*power*" and even the names of countries like "*Denmark*" and "*Iceland*." He wondered if this meant that the only way to stop the polar ice from melting and causing another Noah's flood was to start running the world on hydrogen instead of oil. Fuel cell technology involves shooting electrons through water and producing hydrogen for fuel. It doesn't pollute the atmosphere and the only by-product is water. He remembered, however, that hydrogen's critics say it still takes oil and gas to run the machines that produce it, meaning you're not really saving on fossil fuel use.

But *Prophecy* also had words like "*wind*" and "*sunflowers*," which challenged that criticism. Sunflowers produce a lot of hydrogen and they are very easy to grow. He found an article by one of the world's most eminent energy experts that said one million windmills in the U.S. alone could produce enough hydrogen to power the whole country. This would mean that wind, not fossil fuels, would produce the hydrogen. Certainly, there were enough open spaces on the Great Plains and in the west to build the windmills. And if there isn't, they can always put some up in the Gulf of Mexico off the Texas coast where there is plenty of wind. *Why couldn't this formula run the whole planet?* he wondered. Then he discovered that Denmark gets

20% of its power from wind and Iceland is converting much of its energy production to hydrogen produced by geothermal energy.

Then the computer spit out the words "*wave power*" and the term "^3He," which he knew was the designation for the isotope helium 3. He couldn't figure out how either one could be significant until he came across one theory that if you could somehow harness 1% of the world's ocean waves, it could power the whole planet. *But what the hell's the deal with helium?*

As much as he tried to steer his search to "*world devastation*" and "*world crisis*," Mark's research kept coming back to the same old stuff. Again, it was global warming and it looked like it was a lot closer than most people realized. In fact, some studies said we have a window of about ten years to do something about it or it will be too late. Even more frightening, Mark came across one report that said some harmful effects of global warming are not just coming, they're already here. All life springs from the ocean and according to this study all the oceans of the world are in trouble.

New NASA satellite data suggest that warming water temperatures are reducing the amount of food for marine life. One is phytoplankton, the grain of the earth's oceans. Some scientists theorize that global warming is reducing it, which could starve a number of ocean animals and upset the whole oceanic food chain. Scientists are concerned because many sea creatures are already being starved of oxygen by the increasing pollution being dumped into the oceans.

And then there are the algae blobs. Climate scientists say that the higher ocean temperatures produce more algae that contaminates food systems and can possibly hurt people who eat fish. From what Mark could tell, 2015 appeared to be a banner year for climate change discoveries and that year a giant bloom of algae was discovered along the West Coast of the United States. It began as a circular blob about 1000 miles long, a thousand miles wide, and 300 feet deep out in the Pacific Ocean. But it moved closer to shore and spread out along the West Coast. It was so big that fisheries from Southern California to British Columbia had to be closed. The bloom helped one species of toxic algae increase in record numbers and that species produces a neurotoxin called domoic acid. When shellfish and small fish like anchovies eat the algae, they can transmit the toxins to animals and the people who eat them.

Many scientists say that when the oceans go, so goes mankind. Climate change deniers claim, however, that the changes the oceans are going through are all natural phases of the earth's evolution. But by now, it was pretty common knowledge that the oil industry had been paying some hack scientists big money to say that global warming either doesn't exist or is simply natural evolution.

"How's it going?" Bill's question cut Mark's daydreaming short. "Found the apocalypse yet?"

"Not yet."

"Well, you know what we're looking for."

"I do and you'll be the first to know when I find it." The remark was sincere but hesitant because he still wasn't completely sure of who he was working for. Still, the thought lingered in the back of his mind that with *Prophecy*, maybe he could finish Dr. Weiss' work.

Who am I kiddin'? I'm no Weiss, he thought as the unexplained "*Ayles*" and "^3He" still tugged at his brain.

* * *

Chuck discretely headed for the front while Jack and Scott proceeded to the back. Knowing they had the most dangerous and crucial jobs in the mission, Joe Gercek and Abdul Hameed started out for the back of the building. If they were spotted, the operation would fail and everyone would die. Setting their guns up on their small tripods, they silently shot the time-delay grenades over to the next building and then slowly headed for the front, walking nonchalantly with their guns hidden under their robes. Moreno crawled to within 100 feet of the two trucks outside and Sniper Steve set up his infra-red scoped long-range rifle 75 yards from the back.

Rounding the front corner of the building but at a safe distance, Chuck heard four slight pops from Joe's and Abdul's silenced guns. In the shadowy darkness, he could see them dragging two bodies each around the front side of the building into the weeds. They were both big men with big, wide shoulders, and biceps you didn't want to mess with. Chuck also noticed that the two had borrowed the dead men's jackets and turbans, making them look like they were supposed to be there.

One minute, Chuck thought as he checked his watch. Motioning forward, the three stealthily crept into the warehouse, their senses on high alert. Chuck held up three fingers meaning the grenades' explosions were 30 seconds away and they each pressed themselves up against opposite walls. The seconds passed like hours.

Finally, *blam*! The 5-minute, time-delay grenades exploded right on-time. They waited. A rush of voices echoed toward them and through their infrared goggles they saw six jihadists leading their hand-cuffed men out of the building, each with a leash tied around his neck. Joe shot the two on the left and Abdul shot the two in the middle, leaving Chuck to take out the last two men on the right with precision shots.

"Where's Hawkins and Salgado?" Chuck yelled, suddenly realizing two of his men were missing.

"They took 'em away about ten minutes ago," said a groggy Skip Bailey.

Chuck instantly kicked each of the militants looking for signs of life. Seeing one man's eyes flutter open, he grabbed him by the arm and screamed in perfect Arabic, "Wain akhathohom?" (*Where did they take them?*).

The man closed his eyes and played dead. Chuck shouted "Golli aw amawtak!" (*Tell me or die!*)

He didn't move so Chuck casually shot him in his right leg. He jerked and screamed in pain. Pointing his gun at the man's groin Chuck screamed, "Al mara al jaya sawfa etfajrik!" (*The next one blows your balls off.*)

"Salif!" he squealed, still aching from the last shot.

"Wainah?" (*Where is it?*)

No answer.

"Wainah?" (*Where is it?*) Chuck's finger tightened on the trigger.

"Thlatheen kilo." (*Thirty kilometers.*). He pointed east.

Just then shots rang out from the back of the building as Jack Ryder and Scott Sampson killed the rear guard covering the kidnappers' escape. They met in the middle with their woozy men who were still recovering from the gas. Their reflexes were sluggish, but the one thing they did know was that their comrades had come for them and they had better follow their lead.

"Scott! Get the truck!" Chuck yelled as Scott Sampson immediately sprinted for the front door. The rest of them led their dazed men toward the back of the building and heard more shots as Sniper Steve killed insurgents trying to enter through the back door. Private Moreno already had both trucks running when Scott bolted out of the warehouse as ISIS soldiers ran toward them shooting. Fortunately, many of them were still rubbing the sleep from their eyes at this early hour and their aim was off.

Under heavy fire, Moreno and Sampson stayed low, ground the gears, and jerked the two rusty trucks around to the back of the warehouse. Sniper Steve came running up and they loaded everyone in a mass of crashing, crumpled bodies in the back and drove off into the darkness with four pick-up trucks on their tail shooting furiously. In the second truck, Jim Hawkins raised up with an angelic look on his face holding a Stinger missile launcher. Peering through the flip-up sight, he aimed at the first truck chasing them. He fired and sent it exploding into a rolling fireball. Luckily, the truck behind it smashed into the burning wreck, erupting into its own flaming carcass and sailing over the sand dunes lighting up the dark, lonely desert in its wake.

"BOGO!" said Hawkins as he made a make-believe gun out of his hand and raised it to his chin, blowing on the imaginary barrel, "Two for the price of one." That left two trucks, but there were also the lookouts to worry about. Scott and Moreno floored their vehicles to the limit, swerving them back and forth beyond their endurance, and the ISIS sharpshooters missed with every shot.

Unfortunately, the IED didn't. Using a cell phone from somewhere off in the darkness, someone triggered the improvised explosive device that had been planted in the road probably just hours earlier. It was a simple matter of dialing a number. Chuck's truck suddenly went airborne and flipped over throwing him and his men into the darkness. It bounced and crashed onto the unforgiving desert floor expelling the men that were left and sliding on its side like a toboggan on a snow-covered hill. Amazingly, it didn't explode into flames. But that's where the amazement stopped. Recovering from the crushing blow and with no air left in his lungs, Chuck struggled to his feet and took stock of his men. Two of them were obviously dead. Neither was thrown clear and one's head was crushed. Feeling intense pain himself, he realized he had either cracked or bruised his ribs. Both were intensely painful.

It wasn't logic and it wasn't instinct. It was pure animal rage as Chuck picked up the big .30 caliber machine gun and charged the enemy truck that was emptying out its soldiers. He gunned down everything and everyone in sight. Screaming in a sub-human screech, he blasted away with uncanny accuracy. It was as if he had a built-in laser guidance system steering his aim. "Into the truck!" he yelled as he finished off the driver and what was left of his men picked themselves and each other up and staggered toward the pickup. Scott took the wheel. But the last truck hadn't been standing still and now it came at them spewing machine gun fire with an inhuman fury.

"Paint 'em!" Jack shouted and, without knowing why, the soldiers aimed their laser sights at the truck behind them. With their own truck bouncing down the rough, pot-holed road, it was hard to keep the laser beams steadily trained on the truck but they held it just long enough to hear "locked on" over their radios.

Four seconds of an eternity later, the truck exploded in a frenzy of flames as its chassis went careening into the air in a blazing pyre. It lit up the night and the Mad Dogs cheered. *Definitely not a traitor,* Chuck thought as he realized that Jack had called in a drone strike. *Gotta' be CIA,* he figured. But the celebration was short-lived as their truck violently swerved off the road. All the dogs turned to see Scott collapsed at the wheel with blood spurting out of his neck. He had been hit with a lucky shot just before the insurgents' truck blew up and it looked bad. Unsteady as he was, Greg Hanson grabbed the steering wheel, pushing Scott's limp body out of the way, and steered the hulking rust bucket back onto the highway while Jose Moreno clamped his hands over the spurting wound. "Gimme' a rag!" he yelled, but Chuck already had the medical kit out and slapped a medicated bandage on it. Seeing his sergeant collapse made Joe Gercek realize he was also hit. In all the excitement, he didn't realize he had been shot in the arm. All had Kevlar bullet-proof vests on, but they didn't protect their head, arms, and legs. Gercek turned pale while Scott hung limply in his lieutenant's arms.

"Don't you die on me you son-of-a-bitch!" Chuck screamed, slapping him back to consciousness. Scott's eyes rolled back and forth in his head as he hacked up blood and for a second, they exchanged a terrified look.

"Don't talk about my ... my mother like that," he coughed between blood spits.

"Where to?" yelled Jack over the truck's muffler-less, screaming howl.

"Balad!" Chuck shouted breathlessly as his body began catching up with his adrenaline-soaked brain, "Radio in!" His head felt like the old truck engines they were revving up beyond their limits.

CHAPTER 15

Even though he knew he was supposed to be focusing on predicting terrorist attacks, the one thing Mark couldn't seem to shake was how much faster the Arctic Ice is melting than anyone had foreseen. Arctic temperatures are rising twice as fast as the global average and the ice up there is melting a lot faster than anyone predicted and could lead to rising sea levels around the world. A few years ago a chunk of Arctic sea ice the size of Mexico simply disappeared. In another analogy, some scientist figured out that the carbon dioxide emissions of a single transatlantic airline flight translate into a loss of 30 square feet of sea ice.

He didn't like these kinds of analogies and thought they pandered a bit too much to popular culture. But as he continued his research, he came across several studies that claimed global warming might be threatening a lot more than just the oceans. He found that some scientists believe it could cause catastrophic increases in various worldwide diseases as well. They say it causes floods and droughts which, in turn, appear to be causing epidemics in areas that are not prepared for the diseases they bring. Mosquitoes, ticks, and mice are surviving warmer winters and getting around more, bringing the diseases with them.

He read about one Canadian farmer who survived D-Day, but not a mosquito bite full of the West Nile Virus. The virus was not supposed to spread from the equator all the way north to Canada, but it did, and it hit a lot more than the farmer. It has infected more than 21,000 people and killed more than 800 in the U.S. and Canada alone.

But the epidemics didn't only spread from south to north. They also went straight up. As ice caps and glaciers melt, forests inch higher on the mountains and insects carry diseases from warmer lowlands farther up the slopes. In fact, one startling study says global warming has driven up temperatures in the Alps to their highest levels in 1300 years

Malaria is also climbing up the mountains and reaching populations in higher elevations in Africa and Latin America. Cholera is growing in warmer seas and

Dengue Fever and Lyme Disease are both moving north. Things are moving much faster than was predicted and, in his research, Mark found that diseases that were projected to hit in 2080 are happening about 70 years too early.

As a scientist, he knew he had to remain cautious and conservative about all this alarming information. But the most conservative findings he could come up with were from the World Health Organization, which has identified more than 30 new or resurgent diseases in the past three decades. Contextual research found that this is the sort of explosion that has not happened since the Industrial Revolution brought masses of people together in cities. In fact, the WHO believes even the modest increases in average temperatures that have occurred since the 1970's have begun to take a toll. It estimates that climate change is responsible for at least 150,000 extra deaths a year, a figure that will likely double by the year 2030.

More research found that thirteen of the twenty largest cities in the world happen to be located at sea level. That means that where people are most at risk from floods, so are hospitals and water treatment plants. As we saw in New Orleans, the health effects of losing those facilities persist long after the water has receded. To add insult to injury, he also read that while we're used to car emissions and industrial pollution hurting our air quality, the rising temperature by itself, increases the amount of ground-level ozone, which is a major component of smog.

Still no progress on the frustrating "*Ayles*" and "*^{3}He.*" But once again, global warming was not what he was looking for. Was it a big danger? Yes, but a long-term one and he was supposed to be looking for a more immediate threat of an impending terrorist attack. He knew he had to get down to business.

* * *

"One-niner Balad Medical, this is Dog 1. Coming your way with wounded. ETA 10 minutes," Jack Ryder yelled over the radio as the rickety truck screamed down the pockmarked Baghdad highway. Balad was an Air Force Hospital just north of Baghdad where they did about 400 surgeries a month. Squeezing their sergeant's neck to keep the blood from squirting out like a Roman fountain and with it, his life, the Dogs sped toward the gates of C Medical Unit. They screeched into the compound, all screaming "medic" at the top of their lungs. An emergency team was already there waiting with gurneys and they quickly rushed the wounded men into surgery. Chuck leaped off the truck and ran to a Humvee parked outside of the field hospital.

"What're ya' doin'?" Jose Moreno yelled.

"Goin' after Jim and Luis," he shouted as he started the Hummer and jerked it into a grinding gear.

Suddenly Greg Hanson jumped out in front of the Humvee and Chuck had to jam on the brakes. "Get outta' the way Private Hanson!" he bellowed as Jack Ryder and the rest of the Dogs came running up, all standing in front of the jeep. "Don't be stupid kid," Ryder said calmly, "You gotta' regroup and make a plan."

Pointing his rifle directly at him, Chuck said just as calmly, "Outta' the way Jack. You said it yourself ... if we wait, we lose 'em."

"I did say that, didn't I," Jack said with a smile slowly creeping across his face, "But if you go without a plan you die."

"Then I die," Chuck said with resignation, "But at least I'll have tried."

"Sorry kid, but you ain't goin' nowhere."

"Well I am," yelled Juan Rodriguez and with two long strides he leaped into the Humvee.

Swinging his gun around, Chuck said, "I'm not losing any more men Juan. Get out!"

But it was too late as it gave Hanson, Sandstone, and Moreno time to jump into the back. "Yer' all idiots," Jack yelled as he leaped onto Hanson's lap and said, "Let's go."

Looking at his men for a few seconds, the scowl began to leave Chuck's face as he yelled, "Okay, if yer' determined to die, grab some guns and let's go!"

The Dogs started to get out of the Hummer when Jack said, "Not so fast boys ... as soon as you're out of sight, he'll be gone." As the men settled back in their seats, Jack jumped out yelling, "This way!" and ran for a nearby building where he knew weapons were stored. With the Dogs following, he shot the lock off of the garage door and slid it open to reveal two big Army trucks fully loaded with guns and ammo. "Here's our ride," he said as he jumped behind the wheel of one and gunned its engine. "Follow me," he yelled as he stopped beside Chuck's Humvee.

"Where're we goin'? Chuck yelled back in amazement.

"You don't know?" Jack asked incredulously, "There's only one road to Salif. We go north and I'll signal when we hit it." And they were off into the breaking dawn.

* * *

"*Obesity*" and "*epidemic*" were two words Mark was surprised to find in his search for a terrorist threat. But nonetheless, there they were, along with words like "*plague*" and "*mass death*." Much to his disappointment, he found that world obesity rates have risen three-fold or more since 1980 and it is fast-becoming the number one cause of death on the planet. Globally, there are more than 1 billion overweight adults and at least 300 million of them are obese. In the U.S. alone, one out of three adults is obese and if things continue the way they are going, by

2030 it will be more than half. He discovered that obesity and overweight are the top causes of heart disease and pose a major risk for other cardiovascular diseases, chronic diseases like type 2 diabetes, hypertension and stroke, and some forms of cancer.

Current obesity levels range from below 5% in China, Japan, and some African nations (often because of famine), to over 75% in urban Samoa. But Mark found that even in relatively low-obesity countries like China, rates are almost 20% in some cities. In the U.S. nearly three-fourths of the men and 60% of American women are either obese or overweight and physical inactivity accounts for more than 300,000 premature deaths each year. "Sitting is the new smoking" is the current maxim, which is saying a lot since tobacco kills one-third to one-half of the people who smoke. In fact, cigarettes kill more than car accidents, homicides, suicides, AIDS, and drug abuse combined and there is one death every six seconds.

But the most worrisome trend he found was in child obesity. Kids are getting fat at an alarming rate with their adult lives cut short by many years. According to one Harvard study, 57% of them will be obese by the time they reach the age of 35. In the U.S. alone, the number of overweight children has doubled and the number of overweight adolescents has tripled since 1980, although recent numbers show a little improvement. People are simply not moving as much as they used to and they're eating more fattening foods. American children sit and watch TV instead of playing outside, schools have cut back or done away with physical education, many neighborhoods lack sidewalks for safe walking or bike paths for biking, household chores are assisted by labor-saving devices, the workplace has become increasingly automated, and kids eat too much fast food.

But the epidemic is certainly not confined to the developed countries and is actually increasing more dramatically in the developing world with nutrient-poor foods that have high levels of sugar and saturated fats. Mark found that recently developing countries had the highest number of diabetics. But his most disturbing discovery was that poor people are more likely to be obese than middle-class or wealthy people. Why? Simply because healthy, fresh foods like fruits and vegetables are more expensive than processed foods that contain high amounts of fat and sodium. In fact, there are 50% more obese adolescents in poor families than there are in middle-class or upper-income families. *As usual, the poor suffer at the hands of the rich.*

What's the solution? How about better nutrition education and more genetically engineered and cheaper crops of fruits and vegetables? *Maybe we could even genetically wire the brussell sprouts, broccoli, and cauliflower to taste better.* But once again, this wasn't Mark's problem and was not what he was looking for. What was his big problem and exactly what he was looking for was some kind of impending terrorist plot that would kill thousands and possibly millions of people and that, he hadn't done in a while. The dangers to society he was turning up certainly posed threats to our long-term survival, but that was the problem; they were long-term when his bosses were looking for short-term threats.

* * *

The Problem with Education

Everyone has something to say. Many just don't know how to say it. And many don't know how they feel until they express it verbally. But too many don't have the verbal skills to do that and we're left with millions of people who feel unfulfilled, not knowing how they feel about things because they can't put it into words. Consequently, there are millions of people who are incapable of forming an original, creative thought and who don't know their own feelings. Why? Because the educational system teaches them *what* to think, not *how* to think. It doesn't push their intellectual boundaries or teach them how to think critically and creatively. Ideally, kids don't need to know how to memorize. They need to be taught logic, reason, and how to think outside of the box. Then they need to learn how to coherently express their thoughts so that both they and their peers can understand them. But realistically, class rooms are too big and teachers' wages are too low for any of this to happen. Politicians will continue to hail the benefits of education while under-funding it and when the budget needs to be cut, it will always be the first to feel the ax.

This passage from the *The Book* drifted into Chuck's mind as they passed a new school on the way to Salif. He had to hand it to the reconstruction effort that built many new schools and he briefly wondered why the news media wasn't covering this rare good news. Then he recalled one of his father's few academic friends, a college philosophy professor, talking about the problem with the educational system. He was always a bit surprised at their friendship as this guy was existential and his dad was more real-world practical.

Listening in on one of their conversations once, he heard the philosophy professor say America needs to drastically increase its educational spending. His dad answered with the old conservative line that you don't solve a problem by throwing money at it. "You get what you pay for," his friend had said, "and if teachers' salaries go up you'll get better teachers." Of course, as a teacher, he was a little biased. But he did say the schools teach too much by rote and not enough critical and creative thinking. "They should teach you how to think," he used to say, "As well as what to think about." He was also long-winded, like this entry in *The Book,* and that made Chuck wonder if the journal was his. Then it hit him like a lightning bolt that his father sometimes talked about writing a book. Putting two and two together, he wondered, *maybe this guy gave dad his journal to use for a book.*

The sun broke over the barren, bleak landscape in a giant fireball turning land and sky into an immense, soft pastel red. Salif was a tiny village out in the middle of the desert where the kidnappers were hopefully holding Jim Hawkins and Luis Salgado. The Dogs knew they had to go in fast and quiet because if the militants saw them coming, they would likely kill their prisoners. Driving over the bumpy road, Chuck tried to concentrate on the strategy he was making up as he went along.

Jack turned the truck west onto the road to Salif and stopped abruptly. He quickly jumped out and placed a long-range motion detector on the side of the road. Without a word, he climbed back in and they were off again. Five miles later Jack pointed and said, "There it is." The fiery sun was beginning to splash scorching fingers of heat around the desert floor and shards of light were glaring off the few dirty windowpanes of Salif. "That shack," he said to Jose Moreno as he stopped again about five-hundred yards from the village. Moreno ran behind the hut with a big machine gun slung over one shoulder and the motion-detector receiver on the other. About a hundred yards from the village, the truck stopped again and the rest of the men piled out of the truck and Humvee, ducking low and running for Salif.

Normally Chuck would go in first, but sniffing the air and looking around furtively, something told him *not this time.* When they got to the village entrance he realized it was a perfect spot for an ambush. "Wait here," he said as he stepped out onto the pot-holed road and fired two silenced shots at the upper story of a building on the other side. All of a sudden, a barrage of machine gun fire rained down upon them and they all ducked behind what little cover they could find. They tried firing grenades at the enemy position, but the building was too well-fortified to penetrate and the gunners' openings were too small to get even a bullet through. They all knew that the ambushers could turn their guns on Hawkins and Salgado at any second now. They also knew that reinforcements could slip in from the unguarded side of the village at any moment and trap them in a vice.

The Dogs were trapped as Chuck desperately tried to figure out how to save them and Privates Hawkins and Salgado at the same time. But he knew that saving one might kill the others because as soon as the jihadists thought they were losing the battle outside, they would kill the two soldiers inside in their stronghold. It was a catch-22.

* * *

And then there was slavery. After inputting words like *"plague"* and *"social strife"* into *Prophecy* and sifting through thousands of hits, Mark came across the shocking phenomena of modern-day slavery. He knew this wasn't what he was looking for, but the subject was irresistible to him, especially since most of the religious texts, including the Bible, never specifically condemned slavery. And what he found was an astounding epidemic of global proportions. He discovered that according to the world's oldest human rights organization, Anti-Slavery International, there are currently over 20 million slaves around the world and the slave trade is thriving in at least 89 countries. And it's not limited to the third world. More than 80 women are being smuggled into Britain each week for the sex trade. They're even being smuggled into places like Minnesota with the promise of a green card and a good job. But when they get here, they find out that the "job" is actually prostitution and there is no green card.

And things are even worse in Africa where de-facto slavery is somewhat institutionalized. Although the slave trade was officially outlawed there in the early 1880's, forced labor continues in West and Central Africa today. An estimated 200,000 children from this area are sold into slavery each year. Many are sold as domestic servants, farm workers, and prostitutes to some of the wealthier, neighboring countries. North African Arabs often invade southern tribes, killing the men and enslaving the women and children. They consider it their traditional right to enslave southerners and to own them as personal property.

With the recent flood of African refugees fleeing war-torn countries, things have gotten even worse. Many of them sell everything they own to pay ruthless criminals to smuggle them into Europe. They pass through several countries with countries like Libya as their last way-station. But with the Libyan government crackdown on smuggling, many migrants are getting stuck there and are being housed in warehouses for long periods of time. The smugglers actually advertise them as excess merchandise and sell them at public auctions as laborers, gardeners, or housekeepers. But it isn't just Africa.

In many countries slavery is fueled by a rigid caste or class system. You are born into a class and you can never get out of it. The lower your caste, the higher are your chances of being forced into slavery. In India alone, children are kidnapped from their villages as young as five years old and between 200,000 and 300,000 of them are held captive in locked rooms and forced to sew clothes. In Haiti, children are forced into slavery cutting sugar cane. In Thailand, young girls are sold into prostitution. And in Mauritania it's all kinds of slavery.

There is also a lot of slavery in poor Asian countries and in Latin America, but there are more than 350,000 cases in the industrialized world. The State Department reports that some 50,000 women and children are trafficked every year for sex in the United States alone. And why? Because there is a lot of money to be made. The International Labor Organization (ILO) says slave labor generates over $30 billion in profits and that's no small change. Money is at the root of it all and there is a persistent rumor that the Chinese Triad runs much of it. The 500-year-old secretive criminal organization is said to be operating in 100 countries with half-a-million members, but many doubt that it even exists.

So, what do we do? Mark mumbled to himself. Then he read that the ILO recommends that wealthier countries should tighten up their labor and migration policies and look harder for cases of slavery. Others have suggested that America give foreign aid only to countries who pledge to stamp out slavery. But still others say that as long as greed and slavery are ingrained ways of life in many of these countries, there is no hope for change. And with that depressing realization, Mark knew he had spent too much time away from the real issue: a terrorist plot of mass death. So, he got back to work.

* * *

While the Dogs were pinned down with nowhere to run, Jose Moreno was on the lookout for ISIS soldiers who might be approaching from the south when he thought he saw something out of the corner of his eye. At first it was just a puff of dust off to the west, but then it grew into what looked like a truck driving across the desert. As it got closer, he could see that it was following a rough path that joined the main road. *Is it reinforcements?* He knew there was no way to know and remembered Chuck's rule *when in doubt, kill.* But he also knew Chuck didn't want him to kill innocent civilians, so he decided if the truck turned toward Salif he would shoot. If it didn't, he wouldn't.

It did and he jumped out from behind the shed and sprayed the truck with machine gun fire. It went careening off the road and rolled over sideways and end-over-end, bursting into flames. He realized he had hit the gas tank. Wanting to make sure there were no survivors, he ran up to the blazing hulk of steel and tried to make out the burning bodies inside. There were no guns that he could see, but some shovels had been thrown out of the back when the truck overturned. Then what he saw made him sick. His eyes came to rest on what was left of two of the bodies inside and they looked like young men. *Probably going to work*, he realized wincingly.

Back in the village, Chuck and the Dogs felt helpless as the one-sided battle continued, when all of a sudden Jack's voice came over the radio. "Cover me boys," he said calmly and coolly with a smile as he walked toward them with the Stinger Missile Launcher on his shoulder, "I always wanted to say that." They immediately began shooting at the snipers while Jack stepped around the corner out in the open, making himself a perfect target. Unhurriedly and methodically, he took careful aim as bullets shredded the broken asphalt around his feet. Unruffled, he adjusted the site and slowly squeezed the trigger. A big boom sent the missile dead-center at the small sniper opening and the building's façade buckled down onto the street, leaving the rooms inside exposed. The shot so inspired all the Dogs that, screaming like primitive warriors, they charged the building, killing anything and everything that might be left inside.

Hearing their war cries, Chuck ran up the stairs and kicked in the door of the nearest sniper den to find two militants dead on the floor, but no Hawkins and Salgado. His heart sank and at this moment he knew his life and death no longer held any meaning for him, but the lives of his men did. *It's like everything in my life has led up to this one moment.* Charging through a side door into the next room, he shot two escaping militants and greeted the rest of the Dogs coming in from the other side.

"How 'bout that photographer," Scott laughed almost tripping over the dead bodies lying around the room. Chuck thought one of them moved slightly, but had no time to notice as a voice came from the next room.

"Why do men have nipples?" came the familiar nasal sound from the other side of a wall that didn't quite reach the ceiling, "They don't serve any purpose." It was Jim Hawkins. Instantly, Jack and Scott kicked down the door and there he was, tied up and lying on his stomach in the corner of the room. He had been able to work some of the ropes loose enough to slither over to the wall and was looking through a small hole when they entered the other room.

"Too bad they didn't gag you," Scott said as they all laughed, "Where's Salgado?"

Now Private Hawkins got serious as they began to untie him. "Don't know. They took him about an hour ago."

"Shit!" Chuck rasped as he ran over to the body he thought he saw move. Slapping him hard over and over he yelled, "Wake up asshole!" He wanted to find out where Salgado had been taken, but the body lay limp. "Adrie enta aaish!" (*I know you're alive!*). His tirade was interrupted by Private Moreno's voice over the radio saying, "Enemy five miles." The motion-detector had detected several vehicles coming their way and they were undoubtedly filled with jihadists.

"Son, we gotta' go," Ryder said grabbing his arm. Chuck smacked him a hard-left hook almost knocking him to the floor and then resumed slapping the dead man. Wiping blood from his chin, Jack said, "Not bad kid, but we're not gonna' get anything outta' these mothers ... and the bad guys are comin'."

A strange and sad look came over Chuck's face and he knew he was right. "And there's gonna' be more than Moreno can handle," he finished.

Thinking he didn't want to lose any more men, Chuck said in an eerily calm voice, "Let's go." He didn't have to say it twice as everyone took off on a dead run for the trucks. But Chuck stayed behind for a little longer than Jack thought he should. When he finally came out running at full speed and jumped into his Humvee he asked him, "What took you so long?"

Without a word, Chuck opened his backpack to reveal five gas canisters he had found in the building. The same canisters used to gas his men back at Pancake. That seemed to satisfy Jack, for now. Burning rubber out of the village, they picked up Moreno who was now running toward them and then passed the truck he had destroyed.

"Take that path," Moreno said dispirited as he noticed Chuck's inquiring look. "Just kids," he said looking back at the smoldering wreck. They bounced down the trail and off into the morning heat.

CHAPTER 16

It was eye-scorching, skin-searing hot as Jasnine sat looking out at the heat waves rippling across the desert horizon like ocean swells. It was the kind of sizzling heat that is actually hotter in the shade, if you can find any, and makes you feel like your skin is melting. You can't really know what it's like unless you've been there and Jasnine Ahmed had been there many times. As an archeologist for a wealthy foundation in the U.S. she had been on many digs in deserts around the world. This time it was the ancient Sumerian site known as Um Al Agareb near Nasiriya in southern Iraq. Um Al Agareb means Mother of Scorpions.

She had coffee-colored, soft skin, liquid lips, and deep, penetrating eyes accompanied by a lithe, fluid figure with each part gracefully pouring into the next. Her glossy, lustrous hair was a flowing river streaming down her shoulders and she looked more like an exotic beauty queen than a scientist. But a scientist she was, though her beauty often made her look out-of-place in this mean and unforgiving wasteland. In contrast with the rough and rutted landscape, she was as lissome and svelte as a falling teardrop. *Maybe,* she reasoned, *this harsh land is partially responsible for the thousands of years of cruel behavior of its people.*

"Born in Baghdad, raised in Brooklyn," Jasnine liked to say. She had come to the United States with her parents shortly after her birth and remembered nothing of her homeland. Now she barely paid attention to the gunshots off in the distance. It wasn't an unusual sound for this area and it didn't distract her from contemplating her archeological mission to recover prehistoric artifacts from this ancient land.

Her mind wandered as she meticulously brushed the centuries off of the latest shard of broken pottery in the kind of oppressive heat that weighs you down and makes every movement a chore. She thought about how in civilized society your body naturally tries to keep from sweating to prevent body odor. But she was long past that now and was used to letting it flow freely until she was sopping wet. The sweat would then dry almost as soon as it came out of her pores and hers smelled sweet.

"Consider it an outdoor sauna brought to you by global warming," her friend and colleague Dr. Frank Tolliver had said when he told her about the dig. A dig in the middle of a hot, dry desert that was once a lush, green garden. The Garden of Eden, they hoped. And getting drenched and then dry didn't take long as she fastidiously dug, scraped, and dusted.

"Mother of Scorpions is kind of an odd name for the Garden of Eden isn't it Frank," she had said. Now she carefully picked and brushed her way around the once-colorful vase, thinking how hard it was to believe that this moonscape could have ever been a garden of anything. *But then again,* she thought as she scanned the brown and barren desert, *it wasn't always like this.* Some scientists speculate that after a very long dry spell, rains returned to the region in a period called the Neolithic Wet Phase and turned it from a desolate wasteland into a green and fertile paradise. There was much debate about when this may have occurred, but Jasnine believed it was about 6000 or 5000 B.C. Of course, there was also a lot of argument over *if* it actually occurred at all and, if it did, where exactly was the Biblical Garden of Eden?

One clue came from the Bible itself in the Book of Genesis 2:10-14 that says, *"A river flows out of Eden to water the garden, and from there it divides and becomes four branches."* Genesis says the first branch was called Pishon and the other three Gihon, Tigris, and Euphrates. These waterways suggest possible locations in Iraq, Iran, or Turkey. However, the Book of Ezekiel talks about Eden on a holy mountain, possibly in what is now Lebanon. But to make it even more perplexing, if the holy mountain is the Temple Mount in Jerusalem and Pishon, the original river, is the Jordan River, Eden could have been in what is now Israel. Or if the Gihon River is the Nile, as some believe, Eden may have been in North Africa.

Jasnine's money was on Iraq. Genesis was written from the Hebrew point-of-view, which often uses Israel as a starting point, and it says the Garden is "eastward." Consequently, many archeologists believe "eastward" means "east" of Israel. Of course, there is a lot of land east of Israel, but all of Jasnine's research pointed to Iraq.

Her favorite theory was that the Garden of Eden must have been somewhere at the head of the Persian Gulf at a time when the four rivers joined and flowed through an area that was then above the sea-level of the Gulf. Unfortunately, that would put it underwater now because of something called the Flandrian Transgression, which caused a sudden rise in sea level in 5000 to 4000 B.C. The theory says the Gulf began to fill with water and actually reached its modern-day level about 4000 B.C. swallowing Eden along the way. But it didn't stop there and some archeologists say it kept right on rising, moving upward into the southern regions of today's Iraq and Iran. Jasnine was one of those archeologists until Frank Tolliver showed her pictures of some bones found near Um Al Agareb by local scavengers.

"Dinosaur bones?" she said surprised, "That can't be."

"I know, but here they are and there's more."

"What?"

"Take a look at these satellite photos," Frank said, handing her the photographs he had gotten from the Pentagon.

The conditions were just right at the moment the pictures were taken to show an unusual pattern in the land. It was nothing of interest to the military, but a former student of Tolliver's found it quite intriguing. He was a CIA analyst and an amateur archeologist and he got permission to share the photos with Frank. After extensive computer enhancements, which showed what the land would have looked like at various stages of history, you could vaguely detect the outlines of what looked like dinosaur bones.

Looking up from the photos stunned, Jasnine mumbled slowly, "So if we date them at pre-Flandrian..." her voice wondering off.

"Sennott's crazy theory on steroids," Frank finished her sentence.

* * *

Roll with the Punches

Very few things turn out the way you expect them to. We all have this perfect life we think we will live and when things don't go as planned, we wonder what went wrong. The fact is that life seldom goes according to plan and if it does, it's often by accident. Things usually go wrong and one needs to adapt to it and roll with the punches. Often what you do proactively isn't as important as how you react to the inevitable and unpre-dictable difficulties and obstacles of life.

Chuck thought this writing from *The Book* certainly seemed appropriate for the current situation as the truck bounced down the pockmarked road. *Sounds a bit like the philosophy professor*, he mused, reminiscing about his father's old friend. He remembered that the professor had partially subscribed to the theory of chaos, the science of surprises that says no one can predict anything that will happen in the future. They were heading back to Balad Air Force Base with Jim Hawkins, but without Luis Salgado, and trying to figure out what they were going to tell their superiors.

"Nice job kid," Jack Ryder said jumping out of the still-moving truck as they pulled up to the base, "Remember ... I was never here."

"Right Jack ... thanks." Chuck had given up on complaining about Jack calling him *kid* as he watched the strange man disappear into the eerie Iraqi night, still wondering exactly who he was. Then it hit him like a flash of lightning. Jack was the voice he had heard in Captain Johnson's office. *So, Johnson is friends with a spook.* He then went straight to the hospital to check on his men. Joe Gercek got the million-dollar wound and was destined to be sent home. Still groggy from surgery, he opened his eyes to see his commanding officer sitting by his bedside, staring at the wall. "Not much on conversation, are we lieutenant."

No response. Just the stare.

"That's all right," Joe said in a weak voice, "It means a lot that yer' here. What about Sergeant Sampson?"

Chuck continued his blank, yet piercing gaze. The only close Army friend he had ever had, Scott Sampson, was unconscious and on a respirator after 4 hours of patch-up surgery. During the rescue chase he had taken one in the neck and another in the lower spine. One of the shots had caused severe nerve damage that only the most delicate of surgeries could fix. The Army doctor told Chuck that there were only three neuro-surgeons in the entire world who could do the procedure and, of course, none of them were in Iraq or in the military for that matter. It was pretty common knowledge that the best doctors didn't join the Army. His condition was too serious to move him so he would remain in the hospital's ICU unit until they could figure out what to do with him. Chuck couldn't stop himself from asking if it was all really worth it.

"Doesn't look good," was all he could say. Then, there was that other minor problem.

"I can't get you and your men outta' this one lieutenant," Special Forces Colonel Duke Abrams said when Chuck walked into his office. The Colonel was a combat veteran from Tennessee who had earned his stripes the hard way. Chuck had found him to be a straight shooter and an exceptional soldier and warrior. He was always the first to charge a position and, like Chuck, he never asked his men to do anything he wouldn't do. "Arab TV is already saying you killed women and children in your little raid and the brass is all over this one," he said in a stony voice.

Again, Chuck stared straight ahead.

"Besides, the State Department already thinks yer' a bunch a' renegades and there's this new Jag officer chomping at the bit to get his first big conviction. I'm afraid yer' all in for court martials."

Silence.

"Say somethin' lieutenant!"

But Chuck continued his blank stare at the wall. He honestly didn't care about any of this. It wasn't that he thought he was being railroaded, he knew he deserved punishment. It was just that he was losing his best friend after losing too many other men and *killing the bad guys* didn't justify it anymore. His father's arguments flooded his mind and he was now beginning to seriously doubt the validity of the war. On top of everything else, he was now a danger to his men and anyone around him because the militants were probably hunting him. And now he and the Dogs were going to be court-martialed for abandoning their post and running an unauthorized operation.

"You don't have to court-martial the men. They were following my orders," he said glumly.

"You know it and I know it, but they don't care and they're calling for all your heads. They want to make examples of ya'. I'm supposed to put you under house arrest lieutenant..." his voice trailed off.

Surprised, Chuck detected a *but* coming and he wasn't disappointed.

"But there may be an alternative ... if you're interested," the Colonel said.

"What kinda' suicide mission did ya' have in mind?"

"Not exactly a suicide mission, but one that requires some ... shall we say ... delicate discretion?" Colonel Abrams was a by-the-book Army officer and when he used words like *delicate* and *discretion*, it made Chuck more than curious.

The colonel was also a war hero early in the war. An Iraqi machine gun bunker had his unit pinned down while a Republican Guard division closed in from the rear, squeezing 20 American soldiers in a vice. Their sharp-shooter tried several times to shoot a hand-grenade through the bunker's thin opening but grenade launchers are not very precise and he missed each time. Seeing no way out for his men, Colonel Abrams rushed the bunker with hundreds of bullets barely missing him and one hitting his left arm. But that left his right arm free to lob a grenade through the slit in the concrete and three seconds later there was a compressed explosion.

He wasn't finished, however, as he ran to the bunker yelling to his astonished men, "Advance and stay low!" Opening the trap door, he jumped down through the small opening and throwing a bloody body aside, he manned the machine gun. Fortunately, the bodies of the three Iraqi soldiers inside had shielded the machine gun from the grenade's blast and it was more-or-less intact. Looking through the narrow opening, he saw that his well-disciplined men were crawling toward the bunker, following his orders to stay low. He also saw that the Republican Guard troop was advancing on them. "Hit the dirt!" he yelled and his men instantly flattened out on their bellies. Then shooting barely over their heads he machine-gunned down the entire enemy squad. One thing Chuck thought Colonel Abrams had was credibility. So, he listened.

"We've got reports that Iraqi police are helping ISIS run oil into Syria," the colonel said.

"Now there's a big shock." Chuck had heard rumors that about one-fifth of Iraq's daily oil production was being smuggled to neighboring countries. *Money will always triumph*, he remembered his dad saying. That meant thousands of trucks regularly hauling about 400,000 barrels of crude oil across the open desert and they needed police protection.

"Well, with the police involved, you can see why we don't want it to get out."

"So?"

"So, we want you and the Dogs and some other men to go in quietly and put an end to the operation. And we want you to bring the head of it in alive."

"And if we do?"

"We might see about quashing the investigation."

"Might?"

"O.K. ... Will."

"I'm not crazy about taking on new men," Chuck said, thinking it smelled a lot like a covert CIA operation with a hidden agenda.

"Ya' don't have much choice do ya'?" Colonel Abrams answered.

Chuck couldn't argue with that one, but what he heard next made him more suspicious.

"The leader of the smugglers is Omar Habibi," said Abrams, "And word is he's operatin' out of Rabiya. Now remember, these guys are like the Iraqi Mafia and there may be all kinds of illegal activities going on there. So, keep yer' eyes open for anything and everything."

"With all due respect sir, what does that mean?"

"It means *everything*! It could be anything from weapons to priceless artifacts stolen from the Baghdad Museum."

That sounded even more strange to Chuck as he thought, *Why would Abrams want guns and a bunch of artifacts?* "It's gotta' be heavily guarded," was all he could say.

"Yup. And problem is ya' can't see the guards. They're hidden as good as a raccoon with its eyes closed."

"So, how do we do it?"

"Satellite surveillance and you do your own recon."

"So, it is suicide."

"Not necessarily. Word is that they are so confident we'll never find them that sometimes they leave only a few guards protecting their perimeter. You just have to figure out when that is."

"Great."

"No one said it would be easy. But you'll have the latest satellite pictures and we'll launch a major assault on their oil smuggling operation while you come in under the radar from the rear."

Chuck weighed the risks to his men's lives against saving them from a court martial. He could ask them, but he knew their answer would be "Hell yeah." He also knew that things didn't sound right. This wasn't your usual mission and it sounded fishy that it would get him and his men out of all the serious trouble they were in. But most of all, he knew it all came down to whether or not he could trust the colonel. Like himself, he was a hardened combat veteran and seemed to be a solid patriot.

But still, Chuck thought, *it sounds funny.* "Okay" was all he said, "I'll do it. Let's see the pictures."

* * *

Jasnine sat and surveyed the barren desert landscape, pockmarked with holes local people had dug in search of ancient artifacts they could sell on the black market. She watched her assistant, Hanif, delicately work the small backhoe and glanced at the soldiers guarding the dig site from looters.

"It's impossible," she remembered telling Frank Tolliver when he showed her the pictures, "There shouldn't be dinosaur fossils there."

"Couldn't shmoudn't!" Frank said, "There they are."

And so began 11 months of intense research and computer photo-enhancement as well as trying to get permission to dig for fossils in war-torn Iraq. They tried to find the bones from the pictures, but the local who found them reportedly sold them, probably to ISIS. So, they would have to dig for more themselves and getting permission to do an archeological dig right now in the region was difficult.

If they really were prehistoric fossils, Jasnine figured they had to be several million years old. But she couldn't help but think about the discredited archeologist Dr. Jerome Sennott and his weird theory that dinosaurs lived at the same time as man and maybe even Adam and Eve. He even theorized that ancient writings about dragons were actually describing dinosaurs. That would mean that some dinosaur bones could be 6000 years old instead of millions of years.

To support his theory, Sennott often cited shaky evidence like dinosaur and human footprints found side-by-side in the Paluxy River bed near Glen Rose, Texas or ancient writings about dinosaurs and alleged cave drawings of dinosaurs and people together. Then there were the Acambaro figurines. Some 32,000 carved, dinosaur-like figures were found buried in Acambaro, Guanajuato, Mexico. Sennott argued that they were about 5000-6000 years old, which proves that the people who made them had seen dinosaurs. Unfortunately, their age couldn't be accurately determined and critics said their condition was too perfect for them to be that old. What no one could figure out was why there were so many of them.

Sennott hypothesized that a supreme being created man through evolution. In other words, God used six billion years of evolution to create mankind. Like evolutionists, he believed that life began in microscopic, amoebic form when lightning struck a pool of primordial soup at a time when all conditions were just right to produce a life-form. Much later, cold-blooded fish-like creatures came ashore as reptiles. They evolved into dinosaurs and eventually into warm-blooded mammals like apes. The apes, of course, evolved over billions of years into modern man, ala' Adam.

That, said Sennott, is where Genesis begins, after those billions of years of evolution. Or maybe, he postulated, God really did create the earth in six days but each day was simply a billion or so years long. Alas, there was no evidence in any ancient language that one day could equal one billion years. There was that passage in the Bible, 2nd Peter, Chapter 3, Verse 8 that says "... *To the Lord one day is as a thousand years, and a thousand years is as one day,*" but it referred to the end of the world not the beginning. Nonetheless, Sennott cited the verse as proof that in Biblical terms, six days may have been a lot longer than six 24-hour intervals. Most scientists discounted this idea as too much of an imaginative stretch with no scientific foundation.

In the end, Sennott answered his detractors by arguing that even if the six day/six-billion-year theory was wrong, a higher power still created man through evolution. God just explained it in the Genesis six-day account because that is the only story people of the time would understand.

Or maybe the men who wrote Genesis wrote it that way because they couldn't fathom billions of years of creation. Maybe there are no time and space limitations when it comes to God, which means it doesn't matter if it was a billion or a thousand because time is irrelevant. Maybe in His world one day *is* indeed one-billion or one-thousand years. Or maybe to God, a billion or a thousand years is *like* a day.

Of course, the creationists loved Sennott, but scientists thought he was a crackpot and Jasnine agreed with them. His theory had too many holes in it and the big one was something that Jasnine had always wanted to find as a lifelong career goal.

It was the blank spot in the evolutionary chain of events that many people refer to as the missing link.

According to the theory of evolution, all the stages of the evolutionary scale have some common characteristics and the stage that actually evolves into modern man should contain characteristics of both ape and man. Surprisingly, however, no fossil evidence of the ape-to-man evolutionary stage has ever been found and it appears to be missing entirely. Hence the missing link. It is the argument that many creationists use against the Theory of Evolution.

"Do ya' realize what this would mean?" Jasnine had asked Frank excitedly.

"I think so," Frank Tolliver answered, "But why don't you tell me anyway."

"If the missing link is in the Garden of Eden, it means Sennott may be partially right, he just didn't go far enough. It could mean that an asteroid really did destroy all the life on earth and interrupt the evolutionary chain-of-events at the point that prehistoric man would've morphed into modern man and maybe that modern man was Adam. It might have left the planet a desolate void for a billion years or so, but early man's DNA would've survived, possibly in an inert state. Then about 6000 or so years ago, something activated that DNA and made the jump from prehistoric man-ape to modern man and Adam was born."

"You're thinking of Eichstrand aren't you."

"A little bit," said Jasnine as she remembered Swiss Physicist Harold Eichstrand's theory that there could be as many as 11 spatial dimensions where our concepts of time and space don't exist. He postulated that with no earthly bonds of time and space, billions of years of evolution and the six days of Biblical creation may have happened at the same time, only in two different dimensions. Then the big asteroid hit and tore a hole in the space-time continuum, which separated them. They collapsed into each other at about the same time that Neanderthal Man was evolving in one and the Garden of Eden was being created in the other. Voila! Adam and Eve.

"Well you sound as crazy as both of them!"

"Probably, but think about it. The first words of Genesis go something like 'In the beginning, when God created the heavens and the earth, the earth was a formless wasteland and darkness covered the abyss, while a mighty wind swept over the waters.' What if the formless wasteland was what the asteroid left behind, complete with high, hot winds?"

"I thought you were an agnostic."

"I am, but it just sounds like too much of a coincidence. What else could cause a giant void like that?"

"I can't think of anything but a six-mile-wide meteor hitting the earth with the force of 10,000 nuclear bombs."

"That's right. It would kick up a hundred trillion tons of dirt and dust and make for one hell of a formless wasteland!" She had always been good with numbers and was now running out of breath from her excitement over the prospect of her very own beginning-of-life theory. "Besides," she caught her breath and went on, "We shouldn't let our earthbound perceptions keep us from thinking outside of the box. Maybe God did create humans by means of evolution and the asteroid interrupted the process. Then he finished the job using pre-asteroid DNA, which is why we have never found the missing link. What if this is it?"

CHAPTER 17

Back to the Future

We are brought up to believe that as time passes the world becomes more developed and civilized and humanity gets smarter and better. But that's because we are trained to look at history in chronological segments. If you look at the entire span of history instead of just isolated time periods within it, you find that it often not only repeats itself, but too often it takes one step forward and two steps back. Ethiopia was once that region's center of civilization. Now look at it. And the ancient Egyptians were said to be at one time, advanced beyond belief. But look at Egypt today. And then there's America. Just when we thought we had gotten by our racism we elect a president who takes us back to the dark ages and the racists and bigots come out of the woodwork. History really does repeat itself.

It was dusk and getting dark fast as the oversized jeep and two trucks bounced down the road, heading toward the northwestern border town of Rabiya. Maybe it was the ancient area they were in that made Chuck think of the historical writings in *The Book*. Or maybe he just needed to get away mentally. But whatever it was, the part about America made him realize that this writing was relatively recent.

With no time to consider this new revelation, he snapped back to reality and started looking at the six men Colonel Abrams had assigned to him with strong suspicion. They were soldiers all right, but they were just a little too slick to be dog soldiers like him and his men. They were also eerily quiet and two of them carried rifles with extra-large barrels that Chuck and his men had never seen before. *And why the two big trucks? What did they expect to find? Gotta' be CIA spooks.* But he knew he had no choice if he wanted to get his men out of a court martial.

The convoy left the road and drove out into the pitch-black desert night, stopping about 1000 yards from Rabiya. Through long-range, night-vision binoculars Chuck confirmed what he saw in the satellite photos, that Rabiya was a way-station for tanker trucks smuggling oil over the 380-mile long Syrian border. To call it a porous border would be a giant understatement. It was really no border at all.

It was another backdoor plan, with Colonel Abrams' troops attacking the smugglers from the east while Chuck and his men came in from the west and tried to find the head smuggler Omar Habibi. Chuck thought Abrams sounded strange when he talked about Habibi and even stranger when he told him to keep his eyes open for any contraband he could find. He supposed that was what the trucks were for, although Abrams had been cryptic about that too. Now the waiting began and Chuck's mind began to drift back to the conversations he had had with his father about the newly formed Iraqi government.

"The insurgents are diverse groups of Sunnis, Shiites, and Kurds, all with their own sub-groups, tribes, neighborhood militias, even criminals and kidnappers with no political agenda. There is no common strategy," he said, "and that's what makes them hard for the Iraqis to fight. There's no real high command or single leader to attack. So, there won't be one battle, but a hundred separate, disconnected battles to fight."

"But doesn't that mean they'll win," Chuck had said.

"They don't have to win. All they have to do is make the country ungovernable by denying the Iraqi people the security and basic needs they expect from their government. Then they'll be vulnerable to another strong man like Hussein."

"How could they ever go back to that?"

"When they're facing daily bombings and massive casualties they may opt for security over personal liberties."

If Don was right, Chuck realized that all the killing and dying the Mad Dogs had done would be for nothing, especially if another Saddam Hussein took over. *Or would it?* He still had the thought that young democracies all have to go through rocky times in the beginning and maybe Iraq was going through its own inevitable and inescapable growing pains."

Loud explosions from the east stirred him from his reverie and he said quietly, "Let's go." With night-vision goggles on and lights off, the jeep and trucks lurched into action and headed for the west side of Rabiya. Approaching a ramshackle building on the edge of town that intelligence said housed Omar Habibi, Chuck could see that only three guards stood at the entrance. Abruptly stopping 500 yards from the shack, two of the new men got out and set their sniper rifles up on short tripods on a small ridge. Three quick shots took the guards out and they jumped back in the jeep and drove to the building. Chuck was about to motion to the men that he would go in first and they should follow. But one of the new men surprised him with "Colonel Abrams wants us in first."

"Why?" Chuck whispered.

"Because we know their security system," was all he said.

With no time to argue about why he wasn't informed about the security, Chuck said simply, "Be my guest," and two of the men rushed into the shack carrying their big-barreled guns. Inside, there was nothing but a ladder going down into a hole. Each man pulled a strange-looking ball out of his pocket and threw it down into the opening. Instantaneously, machine guns started blasting from all sides of the tunnel underneath. It was outfitted with motion detectors that set off guns in every corner, shooting up every inch of the room below. The soldiers had set them off with Kevlar balls covered with a special ultra-springy rubber until the guns emptied their magazines. When the firing stopped, they motioned for the others to follow, carefully. *Definitely CIA spooks*, Chuck thought as he entered the building. The six men climbed down the ladder first and carefully picked their way through the underground, bullet-ridden room to a door at the other end. A simple padlock hung on the latch and they made quick work of it with their modified M-4s. The two with the strange guns then quickly aimed upward and fired a gooey substance at the ceiling. Whatever it was, it coated what looked like several large sprinklers on the ceiling.

"Nerve gas," one man said to Chuck.

"Masks?" Chuck asked, reaching for his gas mask.

"Mixed with acid," he finished, "This'll contain it for 10 minutes."

Real James Bond stuff, Chuck thought as he realized gas masks wouldn't protect them against the acid. The men blasted the door at the other end of the room and entered yet another rock-walled cave with wooden crates stacked on top of each other.

"Load 'em up," spook-one said.

"What about Habibi?" Chuck asked, realizing instantly that Omar Habibi was probably never the real target if he even existed.

"He's not here, so we take the contraband."

How do they know he's not here? But not wanting to argue, Chuck and his men began hauling the crates out to the entrance. Two of the spooks had driven the truck into the building and lowered a winch cable down into the hole to haul up the crates. One-by-one they loaded the trucks while a blazing firefight raged outside. Tanker trucks were exploding right and left as drones hit them with missiles while about 100 smugglers tried to defend their base.

"Two minutes," spook-one said and there were only two crates to go. Working feverishly, Chuck and Private Brian Malone tipped the last one up on the two-wheeler. With Malone in front steadying the crate and Chuck bringing up the rear, they started rolling it toward the door. All of a sudden, they heard a sort of yawning noise from above like metal scraping on metal. Looking up, Chuck saw a big steel door poking out of the ceiling and it appeared to be inching downward. Instinctively, he shoved Private Malone through the opening leaving himself and the crate on the other side. The big door slammed down in front of him, missing his foot by inches and he heard a loud, howling alarm go off. The door was probably supposed to come down when they first entered, but when they shot the other door to pieces something must have short-circuited and delayed its closing. The alarm was obviously meant to alert the smugglers that there was a break-in. But right now, they had their hands full fighting Colonel Abrams' forces, and the battle sounded like it was getting closer.

"One minute," spook-one said as the four dogs left in the outer room lunged for the door. Seeing it was securely shut, they backed up and began blasting it with their M-4s. The bullets ricocheted all over the room with one searing Greg Hanson's shoulder and they barely dented the eight inches of solid steel. Private Hawkins yelled "Get the Stinger!"

"There's no time," spook-two shouted as he hooked the cable to the last crate and it started its journey upward, "Besides, a missile will cause a cave-in and your lieutenant will be buried alive."

"30 seconds," spook-one said casually as he and his men followed the crate up through the opening. It was apparent that they didn't care if the Dogs came along or not because they got what they came for. Realizing they couldn't do their leader any good if they were dead and with furtive looks all around, they bolted out of the room and clamored up the ladder with Juan Rodriquez screaming, "Dog Two to Dog One," into his radio. The signal couldn't penetrate the rock walls and there was no response.

"Dog Two to Dog One!"

No response. Chuck couldn't hear him. Just as Malone emerged from the hole, the goo gave way and the acid and mustard gas sprayed all over the now-empty chamber. The Dogs all leaped into the big jeep with one of the CIA guys at the wheel, letting the other five men man the trucks when suddenly an enemy onslaught rushed their position.

"Dog Two to Dog One!"

Making their getaway in a hail of bullets, one CIA man in the passenger seat was shot to pieces just as two others sprayed the militants with the .50 caliber machine guns mounted in the rear of each truck. The Dogs joined in, killing what was left of the enemy with their M-4s. The drivers all gunned their vehicles away from the death-ridden scene, but Mike Sandstone jammed his foot down hard on the jeep's brake and jabbed his gun barrel into the driver's face.

* * *

Mark decided the key words he was using were too vague and came up with some new ones that were more specific. He typed in words like "*holocaust*" and "*genocide*." The computer immediately spit out words related to the Jewish holocaust. *Nothing new there*, he thought. But "*genocide*" gave him a few more interesting results. The word "*Africa*" came out, which made him think of the extremist groups on that continent. But after some extensive research, he realized that once again, *Prophecy* was predicting something that had already happened.

It was the blood-thirsty, sadistic slaughter in Rwanda. The Hutu tribe was the majority and they brutally butchered more than 800,000 of the minority Tootsies while the rest of the world stood by and did nothing. Ironically, back in colonial times, the two groups were the same people. They were all Roman Catholics. It was Germany and Belgium that divided them into Hutus and Tootsies by how many cows they owned. At any rate, no one did anything about the slaughter. The United States and Europe basically ignored it because Rwanda has no strategic value, let alone any oil. But many thought it was more racist than that because both sides were black.

The United Nations concentrated its efforts on Yugoslavia and its ethnic cleansing and many believe it was because most of its people were white. In fact, other countries sent tens-of-thousands of U.N. troops to Yugoslavia, but only 450 to Rwanda. At the time, Bill Clinton was the U.S. President and all he did was commission study after study of the situation. In the meantime, an entire race of people was nearly wiped out. Some said the powerful Catholic Church could have stopped it before it began by telling the Hutus that what they were planning was a mortal sin. But instead, it stayed silent figuring the majority should rule the country.

Then the computer pumped out "*repeat massacre*." He didn't get it until he stumbled upon the word "*Jonjaweed*." With further research, he realized that *Prophecy* was predicting another massive bloodbath in Africa. This one was in the Darfur region of Sudan. The Jonjaweed were a rag-tag bunch of disaffected Arab tribes who were killing thousands of black Africans with the approval of the Sudanese government. Incredibly, they believed they were the only true Africans and the indigenous blacks are not. They were cowardly and didn't take on their victims directly, but rather burned villages, stole cows, and raped women.

But once again, this massacre had already happened and there was no prediction for the future. Mark realized that the world and the U.N. would undoubtedly let another killing spree go by without doing anything about it, but he needed specifics on where and when. He also realized that much of the world considers most Africans to be ignorant black savages who will always kill each other no matter what we do. He knew instinctively that this idea was sinfully inhumane and that it completely ignores all the poverty and suffering of the victims of such a genocide. But as inhumane an atrocity the whole thing was, it was clearly not what his handlers were looking for and he knew he had to change the focus of his research.

Narrowing his search parameters even further, he now began looking for biological disasters. Having no luck finding any evidence of a nuclear or conventional arms crisis in the making, he changed tactics and began looking for an impending chemical or biological weapons attack. He found many references to plagues and widespread illnesses, but no biological attacks. Among the tens of thousands of terms that turned up was "*H5N1*." It reminded him of the ever elusive "*³He*" but it made no sense to him. Since it showed up only once, he thought it was unimportant or a mistake and went on to the next few thousand hits.

After narrowing down the list of clues to a few hundred, he began his research on the whole issue of mass epidemics and what he found surprised him. The first worldwide flu pandemic came from birds and hit in 1918. It spread like wildfire, primarily from soldiers returning from World War II and disappeared as fast as it came, but not before killing 20 million people. He found that similar pathogens had cropped up twice after that in 1957 with the Asian Flu and 1968's Hong Kong Flu. He read that scientists were now concerned that almost 40 years later, we are overdue for the next big one and a big one it would be. The 1918 flu killed only 3% of the people who caught it. A modern Avian Flu would be much stronger and spread much faster.

Nothing here, he thought. But then further research showed why scientists are so worried. The experts say it may be only a matter of time before some type of bird flu mutates and gets into human cells. If this happens they project that up to 35% of the human race would get sick and because of modern air travel, it would spread faster than anything we've ever seen. With people flying everywhere, every day, pathogens can travel from one continent to another in less than 24 hours. *Man, it would make 1918 look like the sniffles,* he thought. It was all very interesting and scary, but still no prediction of any kind of biological attack.

As all good scientists know, discovery is 1% inspiration and 99% perspiration, so he went back over his massive results one more time to see if there was anything he missed. His eyes strained as he read over the data repeatedly looking for something, anything that would give him a clue to some type of biological crisis. He found nothing. So, with a sigh of resignation, he started all over again, feeding key words into *Prophecy* and waiting for it to run its routines.

His next round of results produced words like "*smallpox*" and "*ebola*" and suddenly things got interesting. Research showed that there is a suspicion that the Russians are still working on developing a smallpox virus that could kill millions. There was also evidence that someone, somewhere might be working on the ebola virus. But massive programming of *Prophecy* turned up nothing more specific and Mark was again frustrated. Exhausted, he drifted off to a fitful sleep and randomly dreamed about some of the data swimming around in his brain. As in most dreams, it made little sense and especially the "*H5N1*." But suddenly it hit him like a lightning bolt out of the blue. It was as if a voice shouted and whispered two words to him at the same time. The words were "*pathogen*" and "*designation*."

"That's it!" he screamed himself awake, "H5N1 is the scientific designation for bird flu!" *But what does it mean?*

He went back to work and soon his question was partially answered as the computer began spitting out more data. This time the words "*death*," "*experiment*," and the letters "*CDC*" came out. Realizing that "*CDC*" had to mean the Center for Disease Control, he started researching the organization's handling of infectious diseases and immediately ran into a roadblock of classified government information.

Getting Bill's help, he broke through the classified barrier and found something that made him wince. In its own research into the Bird Flu threat, the CDC was mixing the 1918 flu virus with the current Bird Flu virus to see how it might spread. *Sounds dangerous*, he thought as he fed new words like "*flu*" and "*epidemic*" into *Prophecy*. What came out scared him even more. Words like "*theft*" and "*pandemic*" came back. He could only conclude that it was a prediction that someone might steal the flu mixture from the CDC and use it to spread another massive flu epidemic, this time around the globe in a world pandemic. "You gotta' be kiddin' me!" he bellowed.

But before he had time to contemplate the significance of this finding, Bill came in and anxiously asked if he was making any progress. He had heard his shout. Mark stared at him dumbly for a few seconds before he could muster, "Not really. All I've got is that *Prophecy* says we're probably in for a huge bird flu pandemic that will kill millions."

"That's it?" Bill said, clearly disappointed, "Bird flu?"

"I'm afraid so."

"Do you at least know when?"

"I have to do more research, but I would say in the next few years."

"Next few years!" Bill bellowed, "We could all be dead by then."

Seeing his frustration and hearing the desperation in his voice, Mark offered an olive branch. "Well, there is the CDC thing," he said.

"The what?"

"The CDC thing. It looks like they're working on a flu virus that someone might steal and spread around the world."

Bill was a bit dumbfounded at this one. "Now that might be something," he said pensively, "I'll tell the big boys about that and they can increase security at the CDC and make sure that doesn't happen."

"That's probably a good idea," Mark said as he began to mentally digest the gravity of the threat.

"But we desperately need the big one," Bill said excitedly, "The big terrorist attack."

Mark wondered how desperate the need really was.

* * *

"Where's the other entrance?" Mike Sandstone screamed as he shoved his gun into the CIA agent's cheek. Meanwhile, the Dogs' other unnofficial medic, Abdul Hameed, slapped a bandage on Greg Hanson's flesh wound.

"What the hell!" the agent yelled as Sandstone pushed the hot gun barrel into his jaw, "There *is* no other entrance you moron!" he spit out.

"Wrong answer asshole!" Mike yelled, grabbing him by his collar and slamming his head into the steering wheel, "Let me put it another way. Go there now or I blow your brains all over the road!" He figured that with all the intelligence the CIA guys had on this spot, they must know if there was another entrance.

With a blood-covered face and spitting out a couple of teeth, the agent spewed, "Our orders are to get outta' here once we got what we came for."

"You just got new orders," Mike barked, tightening his finger on the trigger. Now all the Dogs trained their guns on him and Dan Walker yelled, "Move now!"

"Five seconds," Jim Hawkins said, mocking the agent's countdown in the cave.

Looking at all the guns in his face and realizing he had no choice, the agent jammed the jeep into gear and turned back southeast.

"Eagle one," came a voice on the radio, "What're ya' doing?"

"Keep going," the agent said, "I'll be right behind you." Then, turning to Sandstone, he said, "When we get there, yer' on yer' own."

"Just get there," Mike said with outraged disgust.

Meanwhile, inside the dark cave, Chuck hoped his men were long gone as he looked for a control box that he might be able to jerry-rig and open the steel door.

With no luck, he started feeling around the walls and knocking on them with his gun stock to see if there might be yet another room behind them. It all sounded like solid rock until he suddenly got a hollow noise that sounded like he was knocking on fiberglass. Then his tactile senses told him that it was exactly that, a fake fiberglass wall made to look like rock. *Another way out?* he thought and realized at the same time that if it was, there might be guards on the other side.

Shining his flashlight everywhere he searched for something, anything he could use to cut through the fiberglass quietly. Then he saw it. In the corner sat a small barrel, the size of a pony beer keg, with a skull and crossbones on it. *Gotta' be acid.* Hoping it was the same acid that was supposed to come out of the ceiling in the other room, he put a scarf over his face and carefully pried open the lid. *Acid all right. Just hope it does the trick.* Looking further around the cave, he found an old metal can and carefully poured some of the acid into it. It hissed as it went into the can, slowly eating away it's metal. With no time to spare, he then painstakingly dripped a stream of the corrosive chemical in a circle on the fake wall and jumped back as it began to sear through the fiberglass.

When the sizzling stopped, he wrapped his backpack around his gun butt and began softly tapping around the inner edge of the circle. After several minutes of tapping, it started to give way and finally much of it fell in on the other side shooting sharp arrows of light into the dark cave. Quietly pushing through the rest of the circle, he crawled through the hole, careful not to touch the acid-coated edge. A strange sight awaited him. In a large, well-lit sterile room with stainless steel walls, the first thing that caught his eye was a large printing press along the far wall. Next to the press was a long series of shelves containing metal boxes. He walked over to one of them and lifted the lid to reveal an amazing sight. There in the box were neatly stacked bundles of American hundred-dollar bills. *A counterfeiting operation!*

He had heard a report that North Korea was counterfeiting billions of American dollars but he never heard of it in Iraq. The word was that North Korea printed incredibly high-quality U.S. money in the same place it printed its own money. Then, scouring the printing press inch-by-inch, he spotted what looked like very small Korean words on its underside. *If North Korea's crazy president is helping the jihadists we're in big trouble ... especially since they've got the bomb.* But whoever's money it was, if they flooded the American market with it, it could ruin the U.S. economy, not to mention make them very rich in the process.

Stunned by all the cash, he knew he had to find a way out and he started scanning the room for an exit. Then, as his eyes focused, he saw it. A small opening in the wall with a sheet draped over it. Pulling back the sheet, he saw a rail track with a cart on it. *They probably use it to send the funny money out.* Then he stopped dead in his tracks as he suddenly had an epiphany. *This was what Abrams wanted all along. There probably was no Omar Habibi. He just wanted the money.* With no time for disappointment in the man he had always considered a hero, he began stuffing stacks of cash into four plastic garbage bags he found in the corner while a vague idea of what to do with it began forming in his mind. Stuffing and thinking, a wisp of a thought about how greed rules the world drifted into his head and he reluctantly remembered a passage in *The Book* about money and politics.

We're All too Greedy

Communism is the domination of business by government and Fascism is the domination of government by business. In the U.S. we are supposed to walk that fine line between the two, not leaning too far either way. But with today's corporate-ization of America we are leaning too far toward Fascism. It's not a Republican or Democrat issue because everyone is guilty, especially us for letting it happen. We ignore the fact that there is too much money in politics. Even the best Republican of them all, Abraham Lincoln, said *"I've got the South in front of me and the bankers behind me. And for my country, I am more afraid of the bankers."* Then Franklin Roosevelt and Dwight Eisenhower warned us about big business unduly influencing government and apparently, we didn't listen because it's worse now than ever. But as long as Americans have food on the table and hope for the future, they don't care. I don't blame the administration and I don't blame Congress. I blame the American people for letting the system get broken and for their unwillingness to fix it.

CHAPTER 18

Up on the surface in Rabiya, with fierce fighting going on all around them, the big jeep pulled up to another building about 100 yards from the first one. "This is it," said the CIA man, "I'm outta' here."

"Not so fast," said Mike Sandstone, "Is there the same kinda' security here?"

"No ... no security ... just guards. I'd gas 'em."

That set an alarm off in Mike's head as he remembered that Chuck's backpack contained five gas canisters he had taken from Salif. "Thanks for nothing," he said as the Dogs watched him drive off into the desert. Grabbing Chuck's pack, he passed out the canisters to everyone and motioned for them to enter the building quietly. When they got inside, it was the same scene as the first building with a hole and ladder. Following his finger counting one-two-three, each man ripped the pin out of his canister and threw it down the rabbit hole.

There were six guards in the tunnel who had undoubtedly heard the battle going on above, but were probably ordered to stay put and stand-guard, no matter what was happening outside. Chances were they didn't even know what they were guarding.

"Gas!" one yelled and they reached for their gas masks while running down the tunnel. But the gas filled the passageway before they could all get their masks on and three passed out. The other three ran on to the counterfeit room. What they didn't know was that it was sealed off by another steel door so that they couldn't get to it. The gas also could not penetrate it.

One-by-one, the Dogs descended the ladder wearing their gas masks and flash-lit their way down the long, dark corridor. A fierce shootout ensued and ended in a stand-off. The three militants on one side and the Dogs on the other, all wearing gas masks. By this time, Chuck had wheeled himself on the cart to the sealed door at the other end of the small passageway and realized that it was impenetrable from his side. *I'm screwed!*

Shooting back and forth in the narrow tunnel on the other side of the door, neither side could make any headway. Then Jose Moreno decided to take some initiative and threw a percussion grenade at the three militants. The brilliant explosion blinded them long enough for the Dogs to move in and kill them. Everything went suddenly silent, except for one sound: rocks falling from the ceiling in front of them. The Dogs all stood very still waiting to see if there was going to be a cave-in. Only a few big rocks fell in their path and then the sound stopped. Breathing a sigh of relief, but realizing it may not be over, they quickly started making their way past the toppled rocks.

Chuck had heard the shooting and the explosion from the other side of the door and figured they were the enemy. He started rolling the handcart backward, thinking the hostiles would blast the door open to get to him. He made it all the way back to the counterfeit room and sat with his legs over the edge of the cart, regaining his breath. Then he heard it. Three taps, a pause, two taps, a pause, and then one tap. *It's my guys!* The pattern was a code the Dogs had worked out long ago for just such a situation. It meant three things. Three taps meant "We're here." Two taps meant "Get out of the way." A last single tap meant "Gas." Chuck put his gas mask back on and catapulted himself backward into the money room, waiting for the impending explosion.

On the other side of the wall, demolitions expert Butch O'Shaughnessy pounded hollow titanium stakes into the rock face at strategic points around the outside of the door and then carefully filled them with soft plastic C-4 explosives. Stringing the detonation wires from each stake back into the tunnel, they all backed up and waited for the explosion. He pushed the detonator button and the blast echoed off the cave walls, throwing rocks and dust in all directions. The door fell away causing a small cave-in and O'Shaughnessy crossed himself in gratitude. Clearing away the rocks, the Dogs all yelled "lieutenant!"

It took Chuck only a second to answer, "I'm here!" He had put four bags full of counterfeit cash on the cart and yelled, "Pull the cable." Luckily the C-4 had only dislodged part of the rail and the Dogs obediently pulled on the cable until the cart appeared in the tunnel with the bags. "Send the cart back," Chuck yelled and the Dogs once again obediently followed orders without question, pulling the return cable so that the cart made its way back to their leader. He hoisted three more bags of cash and himself onto it and shouted, "Pull!" Everyone pulled and all cheered when he emerged from the passageway with his last stash of loot.

"Let' get the hell outta' here!" said Sniper Steve as he ran for the exit.

"One more thing," said Chuck, "Butch, set a timer for three minutes."

It took O'Shaughnessy just thirty seconds to do as he was told. He handed the small, but powerful C-4 bomb, which could not be deactivated, to Chuck who placed it on the cart and carefully pulled the cable returning it to the room with the counterfeit printer.

"*Now* let's go," he said calmly and they all headed for the ladder.

Private Jim Hawkins was the first to peer out of the opening with the explosive sounds of heavy combat echoing all around him. But he immediately hurtled himself back down the hole and landed on Dan Walker, knocking him to the ground.

"What the hell!" Dan yelled and was answered by Private Hawkins screaming "Snipers," with no jokes this time. He had felt bullets whiz by his head and knew that ISIS snipers had located their position. They apparently intended to pick them off one-by-one as they emerged from the tunnel.

"Two minutes," Butch said nonchalantly.

"Shit," Chuck said just as calmly thinking *why didn't I tell him to set it for longer!* They had been in tougher spots before, although he couldn't remember when. "Is there any other way outta' here?"

"Nope," was the expected answer. They had checked.

His men wondered if he had finally gone off the deep end when he quickly grabbed the bags of money and threw them one-at-a-time out of the opening. Each was hit by bullets as they landed on the ground outside. "Snipers all right," was all he said.

"One minute!" This time Butch yelled the countdown.

"Give me yer' vest," Chuck ordered Private Walker who instantly obeyed. Quickly sliding on the bullet-proof vest, he climbed the ladder and said, "Don't think it hasn't been fun ... because it hasn't." He then stuck his gun out of the opening and started firing in all directions in a 360-degree radius. After completing the circle, he knew he couldn't avoid it any longer as he raised up out of the hole and randomly rapid-fired in the direction of the snipers. Fully expecting to be shot to pieces, he was amazed that he felt no bullets and no pain. Then off in the smoky haze he saw why. Jumping the rest of the way out of the hole he screamed, "C'mon, yer' clear." Thinking their lieutenant had somehow miraculously killed the snipers, the Dogs didn't have to be told twice. They all piled out of the opening and ran just in time to hear the C-4 underground explosion and feel the ground shake beneath them. Looking back, they saw smoke and dust shoot out of the hole they had just come out of and wondered how Chuck had done it.

"It was them," Chuck yelled sensing their thinking and pointing at a group of soldiers moving toward them from off in the haze.

"I'll be damned," laughed Sniper Steve as they all realized that Chuck probably had not hit even one sniper and that Colonel Abrams' troops had arrived in the nick of time.

"Rather be lucky than good," Chuck yelled as he picked himself up after being knocked down by the blast. He grabbed all seven bags of money and stuffed them back down the hole that was left by the explosion. *Lucky seven*, he thought as he turned to thank the approaching soldiers. "Your timing was impeccable men," he told them, "Now where can we get a truck." But before they could answer, Chuck's cell phone began to ring.

* * *

Three weeks of intense research hadn't turned up anything useful. Mark's research had taken him to some strange places over the last few weeks, but this one was the strangest. After feeding words like *"catastrophe," "global destruction,"* and once again, *"mass death,"* he found words in *Prophecy* that pieced together the story of a giant asteroid flying toward earth. He discovered that there are millions of asteroids hurtling through space at an incredible speed of around 45,000 miles an hour and scientists have identified about 100,000 of them. They originally formed when the solar system began four-and-a-half billion years ago and there are a surprising 700,000 of them between Mars and Jupiter alone. Most are tiny, even microscopic, but not all. Many are 5 to 500 miles in circumference.

100,000 asteroids will pass between the Earth and the Sun and 1000 of them are big enough at 1 mile in diameter to destroy life on Earth. But the most intriguing fact of all was that about 4000 asteroids are heading for the earth right now and the largest one is the size of Texas. These, however, are just the ones we know of and there are likely many thousands more out there that we don't know about. Oh, one more thing. One hits the earth every 100 years or so. *So, we're due*, Mark thought.

Then he found something intriguing and something that he had always wondered about. He discovered that many scientists believe a big asteroid hit the earth just off the Yucatan Peninsula about 65 million years ago releasing upwards of a billion times more energy than a nuclear bomb. It made a crater 110 miles in diameter and wiped out three-quarters of all life on earth. It was probably the one that killed all the dinosaurs. These scientists also believe that some of the few species that survived were little rodents that lived underground. With their predators gone, they came above ground and began the chain of evolutionary life.

But it wasn't the scientific theories he found captivating. Rather it was the story he found in *Prophecy* itself. It was a tale about a big asteroid exploding in the atmosphere above the earth in a blast equal to a 15-megaton nuclear bomb. But was it just a tale? Or was it a prediction that already come true? More research gave him the answer and what he found made him gasp. He discovered that back in 1908 an asteroid the size of an office building did indeed explode over a wilderness region in Russia, devastating the area. The implications of the prophecy were devastating and renewed Mark's flagging faith in his work.

Now feeding a wider variety of words into the program at a fast and furious pace, he found an actual prediction that an asteroid could hit the earth in the future. It looked like it could be in the year 2036 and that it could wipe out most of the life on the planet. Bouncing back and forth between *Prophecy* and his scientific research, he turned up several astronomical studies that said an asteroid will come very close to the earth in 2029 and that the planet's gravity will affect its orbit. The studies also said that same asteroid will return seven years later in 2036 and there is a small chance that it will hit the earth. Not a big chance, but a chance nonetheless. Mark noticed right away, however, that this prophecy was different than any he had found so far. Unlike the other short messages he had discovered, this one looked like it could actually be a long story. A rather graphic story of the predicted collision and the cataclysmic events that might follow.

But the story wasn't easy to piece together and he had to do it literally word-by-word. It was like a giant jigsaw puzzle and he found himself throwing out more words than he used. He knew this wasn't what his handlers were looking for, but he also knew this could be the major scientific discovery of the century. It might even be the Apocalypse. So, he went to work assembling bits and pieces of a devastating narrative that might just explain how it all will end. Sleeping just five hours a night and taking short catnaps during the day, he became obsessed with the storyline. It took 13 days with many interruptions and questions from Bill, but painstaking, methodical research eventually paid off. He finally had a disjointed chronicle of events that followed the asteroid's earthly collision. Translating the texts' ancient mathematical figures into modern day terms as well as using some of his own creative writing juices, he turned it into a somewhat cohesive story written in the present and future tense.

> *"The meteor approaching the Earth is called Apothis,"* it read,
> *"It is six miles across or roughly the size of Mt. Everest. Its massive*
> *size keeps it from slowing down or breaking apart. If it hits, it will*
> *hit with a force of 100 megatons of dynamite, which is equivalent*
> *to more than seven-and-a-half billion Hiroshima nuclear bombs. It*
> *will create a crater 165 miles wide and send out a ball of fire that*

will incinerate everything within a radius of 176 miles. A thousand miles away from the impact a superheated wind traveling at nearly 480 miles per hour will set fire to everything in its path. The wind is moving so fast that within hours the heat increases all over the planet cooking nearly every land creature."

Mark's research found that this was not an unlikely scenario. In fact, along with creating a Tsunami several hundred feet high that would race across oceans at incredibly high speeds, he found that the earth's crust would rise up all the way to the upper atmosphere and envelope it. This would cause a layer of fire to encircle the planet and the surface would spontaneously ignite into a worldwide firestorm. It would kill all vegetation and the sulfuric ash would drop the oceans' PH level to that of battery acid, making the earth uninhabitable. But it would be far from over there.

This sounds familiar, Mark thought as he reflected on the popular theory that an asteroid killed the dinosaurs. But he reminded himself that this was a modern-day account of events and besides, the story was so engrossing he couldn't tear himself away from it. It went on.

"Molten rock ejected by the initial explosion buries creatures in a radius of 200 miles around the point of impact. Populations would disappear in minutes. Some hardy creatures that survive will struggle to stay alive, but in the end nearly 70% of the Earth's species will be gone. The sun's warming rays are extinguished in a massive cloud of soot and dirt leaving the planet dark and desolate. An ice age envelopes the Earth."

All looked bleak as Mark leaned back in his chair and pondered what could be the end of all existence. He thought about how he would be in his forties when the big one hit if he lived that long. He then contemplated the end of his life and the lives of everyone he knew in one big explosion and it gave him some solace that his parents would probably be gone by then. He thought about what it must have been like for the people of Hiroshima when the bomb hit their city. But most of all, he thought about Julie. *I guess she escaped the big blast anyway.* Then thinking about Julie made him think about *Prophecy* and he had a stark realization. *It doesn't necessarily have to be this way.* Then he went back to work.

* * *

America Is Bankrupt

If a corporation operated like the U.S. government it would be bankrupt in a few months. That's because we spend about $779 billion more each year than we get in tax revenue. Then, there is our national debt, which is the money we owe other countries. It recently topped $22 trillion or about $65,000 for every man, woman, and child in America. The debt increased by 17% partially because of the recent tax cut for the rich. But the government doesn't have to worry about bankruptcy because it believes it has an unending line of credit. It doesn't, of course. No one does. But because of political expediency, it cruises along, ignoring reality and acts like there's an endless supply of money. America just keeps borrowing to keep its head above water and we hide our heads in the sand to ignore the growing debt. In fact, we borrow over a staggering $2 billion a day and pay over $900 million a day in interest on the national debt. That's $900 million every day that doesn't buy food, medicine, or shelter or anything else that would improve people's lives. It doesn't even buy bigger and better weapons that we could use to kill our enemies. It just pays the interest on money we never should have borrowed in the first place. And apparently, none of our leaders realize that someday, someone is going to have to pay that money back. Unfortunately, it will be our kids, grand-kids, and probably even our great grand-kids. Currently the U.S. Government owes an average of over $167,000 for each family in America and if we keep borrowing at this rate, it will be a lot more.

Maybe it was all that counterfeit money he had just found and its possible effects on the American economy that made Chuck think about this passage from *The Book* as his cell phone rang in the midst of the deafening gun battle going on around them. Maybe not. Who can explain the mysterious connections between our thoughts? It did occur to him, however, that with the part about the tax cut, this passage must have been written pretty recently.

He fleetingly remembered his father saying that the country had made a deal with the devil with all the borrowing and deficit spending because our financial institutions make billions of dollars off of it. "After all," he had said, "All the interest payments go through them and they get a piece of every dollar." One thing he did learn from his father was that Social Security, Medicare, and Medicaid make up over 40% of America's total federal spending and the country's number of elderly will double by 2030. That means that, as much as the conservatives hate to admit it, the only way to pay for these programs is through the dirtiest of dirty words, a *tax increase.*

"They would rather see older Americans lose their benefits than pay for them with a tax increase," his dad had said, which was an odd criticism because he was a conservative. In fact, many conservatives believed the costs were too high and that we should find ways to reduce them and maybe even cut some benefits rather than raise taxes to pay for them. Going in the exact opposite direction, Congress actually passed a big tax *cut* bill that decreased federal revenue and increased the national debt. Their reasoning was that in the long run, it would stimulate the economy and increase overall revenues down the road. A few months after that, America had to borrow three hundred billion dollars to pay on the national debt, increasing it even further. But this was all meaningless now in this life-and-death situation as the Dogs watched Chuck calmly answer his phone with thunderous gunshots and explosions ringing out all around them.

The voice at the other end said in a thick accent, "We trade your soldier for Yaman Habbash and Muhammad Shafiq tomorrow ten o'clock Sanbar Road eight miles north of Anbas. Come alone. Any tricks, he dies."

"Ana mowafiq," (*Agreed*) was all Chuck could barely get in before the voice hung up. He hoped they meant 10PM and not AM. The Dogs gawked at their leader with their mouths gaping open. "Wrong number," was all he said and laughed. They all knew something was going on, but all trusted him enough not to ask.

Jack Ryder had been suspicious of Chuck staying behind in Salif for good reason. Chuck didn't stay late only to grab the gas canisters as he said. He grabbed them all right, but he also wrote a note and pinned it to one of the dead bodies. The note read "Will trade your soldiers for ours" along with his cell phone number. Chuck hoped the jihadists holding Corporal Luis Salgado would take him up on his offer and they apparently did. Now all he had to do was sell it to Colonel Abrams and he thought he might have just the leverage to do it.

Chuck didn't like keeping his men in the dark on the way back to the base, but he had no choice. They were unknowingly involved in smuggling the bags of counterfeit currency he had fished out of the tunnel after the soldiers left. To involve them any more in his plans would implicate them further in a criminal enterprise than they needed to be. He took his leadership role seriously, knowing that his men would do anything he told them to do, and wanted to give them as much plausible deniability as possible.

"We trade Habbash and Shafiq for Salgado," he told Colonel Abrams the next morning.

"I don't even want to know how you set this up, but the fact is these guys have killed a lot of people and they're valuable assets."

"I know, but now they could be responsible for saving one of our own."

"Ya' know we don't negotiate with terrorists don't ya'?"

"Yes sir, I do, but that's the official story isn't it?"

By then it had come out that the U. S. had paid the Afghani warlords to help them fight ISIS and the very same Somalian warlords that killed American soldiers in Mogadishu to fight against their own Islamic extremists.

"That *official* story," Abrams said, "is what we're all about lieutenant."

Without a word, Chuck took his phone out of his pocket and handed it to the colonel. Abrams stared in amazement at the photo of the large printing press that printed counterfeit money in the tunnel in Rabiya. Showing no emotion whatsoever, he said, "What you want me to say is yeah, go ahead and spring these guys. Do it at 8:00 o'clock tonight. But I can't do that because the United States does not negotiate with terrorists."

Chuck got the not-so-subtle message and recruited Private Brian Malone to help him. He figured that if everything exploded, a private would have a more valid defense of following orders. They stashed a Humvee and staked out the brig from a lean-to about 50 yards away. It was 7:45 PM.

"What are we waiting for?" asked Malone innocently enough.

"Not sure," said Chuck, "But I think we'll know when it happens."

At 8:02 PM a lone guard hurried out of the brig's front door. Chuck suspected that Colonel Abrams would get him away from his post somehow and now figured he called or had someone else call and summon him. "Get the hummer," he said and Malone was off. Chuck then entered the brig carefully and, after adjusting his eyes to its dim light, started searching for Habbash and Shafiq. He didn't have far to go as they were the only prisoners currently being held.

"Put your mattresses up against the door and stand back," he said in perfect Arabic as he placed a small amount of C-4 explosive in the lock of their cell door and covered it with a mattress and several pillows on the other side. They did as they were told and he pushed the button for a muffled explosion. *Man, I hope no one heard that.* He entered the cell and slapped handcuffs on the prisoners and started to lead them out. It occurred to him that they didn't seem surprised at any of it. Heading for the front door, he was about to turn one last corner thinking it was all going too smoothly when a voice said, "Hey Jimbo, time for zoom-zoom."

Chuck stopped dead in his tracks and instantly pointed his not-standard-issue .45 caliber revolver at his prisoners and motioned for them to stand against the wall and stay quiet. He silently hoped the voice would go away, but he knew it wouldn't. Stepping around the corner and into the light he said, "Your friend had an emergency ... I'm taking his place."

Seeing he was a superior officer, the soldier snapped to attention and saluted as Chuck noticed him clutching something in his left hand. "What's zoom-zoom private?" he asked, already knowing the answer.

"It's a ... a card game we play, sir."

"Uh, huh. Where are the cards?"

"I forgot 'em sir."

"Uh, huh. And what's that in yer' hand?"

The soldier's face turned ruby red and beads of sweat began to form on his forehead and upper lip. "Nothing sir."

"Looks like something private. Let's have it."

Slowly, the soldier opened his shaking fist to reveal a zip-lock baggie full of marijuana. Chuck figured that this young private must smoke pot with the guard, probably to relieve the boredom of the monotonous prison job.

"It's not mine sir," the scared young man blurted out.

"Uh, huh," Chuck said, barely able to contain his urge to laugh out loud, "Looks like good stuff. Now get outta' here and this never happened."

Every muscle in the private's body seemed to shudder all at once and Chuck wondered if he might actually collapse with relief. "Yes sir," was all he said as he saluted and turned to leave.

"And private," Chuck said returning his salute, "We're here to kill, not to get high."

Another "Yes sir" and he was gone. Chuck went back for the prisoners and the timing proved to be perfect as Brian Malone pulled up in the Humvee just as they exited the brig.

"You're goin' home," Chuck said, again in perfect Arabic, "But you have to get down and stay under this blanket." They obediently laid down in the back of the hummer and he placed an army blanket over them. "Move over private," he said, "I'll drive." Private Malone thought that was a bit strange, but obeyed instantly as his lieutenant climbed behind the wheel and they were off. They saluted the guards as they drove through the gate and Chuck breathed a sigh of relief that phase one of his plan was over.

Once they were out of sight of the base, Chuck stopped the Humvee and said, "This is as far as you go private. Yer' gonna' have to walk back."

"Wha ... ?"

"Can't get you involved anymore. Just forget this ever happened and you'll be all right."

"I respectfully decline sir. I'm goin' with you."

"I appreciate the offer son, but no can do. Now get out."

"Can't do it sir."

"Well, let me put it another way private," Chuck said, now pointing his .45 at the young soldier, "Get out or I'll shoot you."

Malone had seen his lieutenant kill too many people without a second thought not to take him seriously. Reluctantly he climbed out of the Humvee. He figured Chuck had needed his help because it would look suspicious if he drove out of the gate alone since soldiers always travelled in pairs or more.

"Thanks for your help Brian," Chuck said as he shifted gears. Then he was off in a cloud of dust. It was 8:20PM and Anbas was seventy miles away. Chuck planned to get to the exchange point shortly before ten o'clock. *No sense in being there any longer than I have to.*

CHAPTER 19

Working at a frenzied pace, Mark began feeding phrases into *Prophecy* like "*asteroid solution*" and "*explosion prevention*" in many different combinations. His first four days of research turned up nothing. But on the fifth day he got a hit when the word "*rocket*" began repeating itself. After doing some research, he found that some scientists have suggested developing a special oversized rocket that could be fired at an approaching asteroid in an attempt to change its direction. Since no such rocket exists today, one would have to be developed and it looks like they may have about 30 years to do it.

He also kept seeing the word "*telescope*" and finally found one scientist's recommendation that we launch a $700 million infrared satellite into deep space toward Venus to keep track of these asteroids. He knew he had to warn the powers that be, but from past experience, he also knew they would probably do nothing.

Then he began to wonder if this was really how the Earth would end. He remembered that Jesus said the end of days would be violent and that the Old Testament's Zechariah 14:12 said something like, "*Their flesh shall rot while they stand upon their feet, and their eyes shall rot in their sockets, and their tongues shall rot in their mouths.*" He had always thought that described a nuclear holocaust, *but maybe it means an asteroid collision.* But then he found something else that gave him reason for a little optimism.

Suddenly words like "*gravity*" and "*gravitational tractor*" and "*gravity guide*" started pouring out of the computer. It was confusing, but as he had done before, he immediately began his own research into asteroids and gravity. Initially all he found were several hundred scientific articles on the fact that large asteroids produce their own gravity. Thinking this was a dead-end road, he was about to give up when he discovered an essay in an obscure scientific journal. The piece was entitled "Tractor Beam; Did Star Trek Have It Right?" An old Star Trek fan, he couldn't resist this one as he poured over the article.

The scientist who wrote it criticized the idea of shooting a rocket at an asteroid as useless and ridiculous. He said the only effective way to divert an asteroid's course is to send a space ship to fly right in front of it. The ship's own gravity will then slow the asteroid down so that it will reach the earth later than it originally would have. The earth will then be at a different stage of its orbit and the flying rock will hopefully miss it altogether. But, the author warned that we would have to get the ship to it very early to give it time to slow it down. *Not exactly a tractor beam, but it does make sense.*

Mark got busy feeding the computer again and this time he got back words like "*ship*" and terms like "*gravity pulls*" that made him think the Star Trek scientist may have been on the right track. But then some new words started coming in that confused him. Words like "*wondering planet*" and "*rogue sphere*" raised his curiosity enough to prompt him to do more research and what he found was even more disturbing. He discovered that there may be billions of planets roaming the universe that have been pulled out of their orbits by the gravitational tug-of-war of other planets. Many astronomers believe that four-and-a-half billion years ago, one of these planets hit the earth and the collision created the moon.

Some astronomers theorize that there may be twice as many of these planets wondering between the stars of the Milky Way Galaxy than there are stars themselves. They travel at about 72,000 miles per hour and many of them are undoubtedly larger than earth. If they collide with earth, it would be the end of our world. Then it hit Mark that no rocket or spaceship could prevent a collision like this. He immediately took his findings to his CIA handler.

"This isn't what we're looking for," was Bill's predictable reply.

"I know, but sometimes a search turns up something better than what you're actually looking for."

Bill looked at him with a suspicious glare, but then a slight scowl began to turn into an even slighter grin. "Okay," he said, "I guess it's better than nothing and I'll make a deal with you. I'll give this to the big boys if you'll narrow your search down even more to terrorist attacks and ignore all this other stuff."

"I'll do my best Bill, but remember, when these books were written there was no such thing as terrorism and there are mountains of translations to do."

"Do whatever it takes Mark, 'cause we're running out of time."

"I will, but I'm racking my brain trying to figure out how to speed this up."

"I know you are and I also know you can do it," Bill calmed down a bit, "Unfortunately, yer' gonna' have to keep at it 24/7 until we find something."

"I know it's urgent bill, but is there more to it? Is there something else going on that's got you so nervous?"

Bill stared at him for a few seconds, then looked at the floor, then at the computer, and then back up to Mark. "Well," he said slowly, "I didn't want to put more pressure on you than you already have, but the powers-that-be are saying if we don't come up with something concrete soon, they'll pull the plug."

"Really ... but it feels like we're getting close." Mark's reaction to this news surprised even himself. On the one hand, he didn't like what he was doing. But on the other, he found it exhilarating. "We'll find something," he said, determined to refocus his research to find something relevant to a terrorist attack.

"Well, don't find it if it's not there."

"Thanks for the pep talk Bill. It really put my mind at ease." Mark had a habit of sarcasm in tense situations like this, but no one seemed to mind because his was a great mind.

Mark could tell that, like many people, Bill probably had an inherent mistrust of scientists. He probably thought they all take a lot more time in their research than is really required to make sure they get it right. And he was right, but Mark fully understood what was at stake here and he was already accelerating things up to a dangerous level. *Maybe that's why I missed something ... I went too fast.* He knew that was a possibility and that he had to find a happy median point between going too slow and too fast. He also knew that when this was all over, he was going to do some serious research into "*H5N1.*" *One crisis at a time,* he kept reminding himself. But now, what he was doing wasn't working and he realized he had to come up with a new plan.

Just then, the computer began spewing out hundreds of strange words. Words like "*gamma*" and "*Sleipner*" now provided him with a brand-new mystery to solve. He knew what "*gamma*" meant and thought he remembered hearing the word "*Sleipner*" before, but he couldn't remember when or how. He figured that since Sleipner was capitalized it must be a proper name. So, looking around a bit defensively, he started a new round of research into the new confusing words. He knew that while everything he had found about global warming was devastating information, it still wasn't what he was looking for.

* * *

Jasnine knew that the implications of dinosaurs living in the Garden of Eden were mind-boggling. It could mean that evolution and the Biblical story of creation were both right. *Could Adam and Eve have lived at the same time as cavemen and dinosaurs? Were they caveman and cave woman?* It sounded crazy, but even Charles Darwin believed in both evolution and The Book of Genesis.

But she knew her job now was to first find out if these things were really dinosaur fossils. Archeologists spend a lot of time on their knees and as she stood up and looked around, she heard Hanif starting up the backhoe. Most of the digging had to be done by hand, but the backhoe came in handy for the bigger jobs. She knew that Hanif's job was to keep an eye on her for the Shiite government, but she didn't mind.

Stretching her arms and legs, she continued to survey the dirty brown land that looked like the moon if the moon had a desert. There were holes everywhere, left by looters looking for ancient artifacts, which they sold for ten or fifteen dollars each. The same artifacts often sold for thousands and even tens of thousands of dollars in the United States, Europe, and Japan. She had dug up the past in deserts before, but this one was somehow more brutal. Part of it was probably that she was all alone, except for Hanif and the armed guard standing nearby. Normally she worked alongside a gaggle of eager graduate students, but it was too dangerous for that here. How did she manage to avoid being kidnapped and held hostage by the jihadists? It didn't hurt that she was rumored to be a direct descendant of a famous Islamic Imam.

It was still now, but the slightest breeze could kick up the sand in an instant, stinging your eyes and getting into the very pores of your skin. As she brushed her coal-black hair away from a striking, soft-lined face, she remembered that this one was more than just an archeological dig. It was a look back at the possible origin of man and it could conceivably reconcile evolution and the Biblical story of creation. *Was there really an Adam and Eve or was it just a story that people would understand? Does it really matter if there was or wasn't?* She reflected back on her conversation a few years ago with a leading creationist, Father Raymond McGinnis.

"It really boils down to your estimation of the age of the earth," he had said.

"How so?" she asked, knowing what was coming.

"Well, most scientists estimate it at 6 billion years old."

"Give or take a billion."

"Yes, but that's based on the theory that the earth formed over billions of years at very slow stages of evolution."

"So?"

"So, the theory comes from analyzing many layers of dirt and rock and estimating their age."

"Again ... so?"

"Well, contemporary evolutionary theory says those layers are billions of years old, but maybe they're not. Maybe Noah's flood sped everything up and laid those layers down in about a thousandth of the time the evolutionists say it happened.

Maybe what looks like millions of years of rock strata and soil development actually only took a few thousand years or so."

"Not very scientific."

"Well how about this for science. Mountains form slowly today so everyone thinks they must've formed slowly in the past. But this completely discounts the flood, which could've formed them a lot faster."

"Okay, okay. So, what're you saying?" Jasnine had asked skeptically and almost mockingly.

"Just that the earth may be a lot younger than we think and that God may have, indeed, created it as it's described in Genesis. I mean maybe a Biblical day was really a thousand years or more." Father McGinnis was clearly willing to ignore over a hundred years of scientific research to reach his conclusion.

"What about the dinosaurs?" she asked with no notion of what she might get for an answer.

"Oh, they might've been there," he answered, "They may have existed at the same time as Jesus. Even the Bible describes them."

"C'mon!"

"Yeah, Genesis says all animals and man were both created on the 6th day of creation. That could include dinosaurs couldn't it?"

"Doubtful."

"Well, remember ... the Bible was translated into English a long time before the word *dinosaur* came about. But the word *dragon* appears 21 times in the Old Testament alone. Jeremiah 51:34 says, *'he has swallowed me up like a dragon,'* but there are lots more. Job talks about a 'behemoth' in one part and a 'leviathan' in another and it goes on and on."

"Okay, okay. But what about carbon dating?"

"There's a lot of evidence that it's inaccurate when it's used on animals."

"Oh, I wouldn't call it *a lot* of evidence."

"Well, some evidence. Carbon dating determined that one Allosaurus bone was about 16,000 years old, but scientists estimated its age at 140 million years."

"One mistake doesn't make a valid argument."

"Yes, however, there was more than one. But let's say I'm wrong about all this for a moment. How about the idea that in the days of creation, time hadn't been invented yet so it was meaningless. Couldn't that mean that God created man and it took millions of years to do it, but the Bible had to describe it as seven days so people would understand it?"

At that point, Jasnine realized the complete futility of arguing with any creationist and especially with one as well-informed as the good father. *A little knowl-*

edge, she thought, *nothing more dangerous.* But her thoughts were interrupted by Hanif. "They're coming," he said, slightly out of breath, "They'll be here in about 30 minutes."

* * *

Chuck turned onto Sanbar Road and headed north into the pitch-black, cold desert toward Anbas. *Funny,* he thought, *how it can be so hot during the day and so cold at night.* Exactly eight miles from where he turned, he saw blinking headlights up ahead. Blinking his own, he came to a stop on the side of the road. The two vehicles' headlights shined directly at each other, making it hard to see much of anything as Chuck heard a voice say in broken English, "Send them here."

In perfect Arabic Chuck answered, "I will when you send my man here."

Wearing night-vision goggles that were turned down to compensate for the headlights, Chuck could see two figures walking toward him from the other vehicle. He maneuvered the handcuffed Habbash and Shafiq out of the Humvee and put leg chains on them so they would have to walk slow. "Let's go," he said, nudging them forward with his M-4.

It was a surrealistic scene as the two men stumbled forward in a clumsy, dreamlike motion illuminated only by the night's flickering stars and the glow of the dueling headlights. As they walked, they could see the two people walking toward them coming into focus. When they met in the middle, Chuck quickly went over to Corporal Luis Salgado and threw a big leather coat over his shoulders. Only when he looked him straight in the face it wasn't Salgado. As he suspected, the jihadists' took Salgado to draw Chuck out and kill him for the reward. They would then sell Luis to the highest bidder.

The Arab man in Salgado's uniform drew his gun, but Chuck was too fast for him as he turned the gun around and shot him with it. The imposter crumpled to the ground as Chuck quickly leveled the gun at his two prisoners while pulling his M-4 out from under his coat and leveling it at them. At the same time, he raised a grenade high in the air and yelled in broken Arabic, "Send my man out now or these two get it and you guys eat the grenade."

He could hear men off in the darkness cock their rifles and there were a few tense moments when they tried to figure out if he had actually had time to pull the pin. They reasoned that he only had two hands, but then again, he was the head of the dreaded Mad Dogs and rumored to be a super-soldier and a killing machine.

"You die too," came a voice in English.

"But I die anyway, so I got nothin' to lose. Now it all depends on how many of you clowns wanna' go down with me." Chuck figured correctly that the voice would understand what he said and he meant every word of it. He knew this was the moment of truth and he knew something else: that he was truly ready to die. He suddenly understood exactly what *The Book* meant when it said, "You can't really live until you no longer fear death." He wasn't afraid to die and he was more than ready to take everyone with him. Then, nothing but silence. A silence only the desert can produce. Time seemed to stand still as he stood there in the glaring headlights ready to toss the grenade as soon as he heard a shot.

"He's coming out," the voice finally said, after what seemed like an eternity and through his night-vision goggles, Chuck saw a stooped figure get out of a car behind the headlights. *Better not be any more tricks or everyone gets it.*

An ISIS soldier pushed the shaking form toward Chuck with his rifle and as he came into focus he thought he could make out his man. When he got close enough, he examined his bruised and bloody face up close and saw that it was indeed a badly beaten Luis Salgado. Still holding up the grenade, he reached down and pulled the leather coat from the dead man's limp body and handed it to Salgado. "Button it," was all he said. He then shoved Habbash and Shafiq toward the other headlights. There was a tense moment when Shafiq stumbled and fell down, dragging Habbash with him, but it gave Chuck a second to turn Luis around and head him back toward the hummer.

Slowly he walked backwards nudging him, aiming his rifle at the figures in the darkness, and holding up the grenade, waiting for the shots that would inevitably come. He didn't have to wait long as the militants sprayed the two with machine gun fire from off in the distance. He instantly pulled Luis to the ground and said, "Stay down." He expected the jihadists to come after them and planned to shoot them from the ground in one final stand. But they never came and soon they heard several trucks drive off into the desert.

"Maybe they're afraid of you even when yer' dead," Salgado snickered faintly.

"I doubt that," Chuck said, "It was probably the grenade." But he wondered why they really pulled out because they easily could have killed him and gotten the reward.

As they stayed down to make sure the bad guys were really gone, Luis choked out a new rendition of an old tune. The original lyrics were "Jadda. Jadda. Jadda, Jadda, Jing, Jing, Jing," but his version went, "Kevlar. Kevlar. Better than a sloppy slut." It was a song of praise for the Kevlar bulletproof vest that saved so many soldiers' lives. The leather coat was filled with it as was the vest under Chuck's uniform.

"You never could sing," Chuck said as they lay there quietly laughing.

* * *

Greed and Power

Congress should raise the federal minimum wage. It would be good for the workforce and good for our country. The more workers make, the more they will pump back into the economy. But corporations take the short view instead of the long view and don't want to pay their employees any more than they have to. Consequently, millions of people get stuck earning about $10 to $14 an hour, not enough for a good, hot meal or to get you drunk on a Saturday night. For the last 19 years the lot of the working poor has been getting worse and worse. Median hourly wages, when adjusted for inflation, are lower today than they were in 2000. Median household income fell seven years in a row and pay inequality is at its highest level in 30 years. Businesses always argue that increasing the minimum wage will force them to lay off workers and reduce hiring, but it is a hollow argument. After the 1997 wage increase, the country had the strongest job recovery in 3 decades. And during the last 15 years, states with a high minimum wage have had better job creation than states with a low wage. As always, it all boils down to greed and power. Companies are greedy and the poor have no power. Greed and power caused the fall of the Roman Empire and it could cause our country to fall as well.

For no apparent reason, Chuck's thoughts drifted to this passage from *The Book* as he helped Salgado to his feet and into the Humvee. They drove off into the unforgiving desert night, both pondering their extremely good luck that none of the shots had hit them in the head. An exhausted Luis Salgado immediately slouched down in the seat and passed out, which gave Chuck time to remember how economic theories like this one sounded so much like his friend Tom Griffin. Tom had always stood up for the little guy and had defended many victims of bullying in high school. Now, as an adult, he fought a different kind of fight for a more equal distribution of the world's wealth and was an advocate for the poor and underprivileged. Even as a teen-ager, he held socialist-leaning economic theories and this was just like him. But Chuck had long ago ruled Tom out as *The Book's* writer and besides, his dad's friend, the philosophy professor was a rabid liberal and this also sounded a lot like him.

But then it was snap back to reality as he drove through the base gate to be greeted by four MP's with their rifles aimed straight at his head. "Quite a welcoming committee," he said as he gladly gave himself up to them, "Just one thing though … get Corporal Salgado some medical attention. I think he could use it." As they carried the shaky Salgado away on a stretcher, he managed a quasi-salute of thanks to his lieutenant and Chuck knew then and there that it was all worth it. Fully expecting to be immediately arrested and put in the brig, he was surprised to hear a sergeant say, "Sir I am to escort you to Colonel Singleton's office."

"Escort away," Chuck said as he followed the MP's and thought about the trump card he was about to play.

"What the hell were ya' thinkin' son?" Colonel Bernard Singleton said when he entered his office. He stared Chuck straight in the eye with a glare that could melt ice.

"Gettin' my man back sir."

"Well, gettin' yer' man back cost us two valuable assets and probably lost us a lot more men in the future."

"With all due respect sir, from what I can tell, you weren't gonna' get much outta' them anyway." Everyone knew that the information they got out of most of their ISIS prisoners was negligible. It was partially that they didn't talk, but mostly because as soon as they were captured, their comrades changed their location and strategies making whatever they had to say useless.

"You don't know that lieutenant," the colonel's volcanic voice slowly began to rise, "Besides, that's not for you to decide … it's none of your damn business!" The voice was seething with anger like lava boiling up through the earth's crust trying to find a way out. "No one's gonna' get you outta' this one! But you can make it easier on yourself and tell me who helped you!" The lava was now boiling to the top.

"No one helped sir," Chuck said, wanting to save Duke Abrams for another day.

"Bull Hockey! You couldn'tve done this alone!" It finally erupted in an explosive crescendo, spewing rage and obscenities all over the room.

"Permission to speak freely sir?" Chuck said, wanting to calm things down a bit.

"Permission granted." Colonel Singleton's voice had slightly less of an edge.

"I think I have a way out of this."

The Colonel got up from his chair and walked around the desk, all the while eyeing Chuck closely. They stared at each other like this for a tense 30 seconds. "I'm listening," he finally said.

"When I put leg chains on the prisoners I attached a small homing device to one of their shoes. I would bet that right now they're being debriefed by some major players and if we track the homer by satellite we could bag a bunch of ISIS big shots."

Colonel Singleton stared at Chuck incredulously. "And just where did you get the homer?"

"Does it matter sir?" Chuck asked innocently.

"I 'spose not. You must have a spook friend. Lord knows the place is crawlin' with 'em. I 'spose you think this is your get-out-of-jail-free card." He continued to eye Chuck suspiciously.

"Only if you approve," Chuck said with genuine respect and reverence for his commanding officer.

In an instant, the look on Colonel Singleton's face changed from suspicion and rage to trust and resolve. "Aw hell, let's get to the satellite truck and you can give 'em the coordinates," he said and they hurried out of the office, "But if you're wrong, we're both cooked."

Once Chuck gave the satellite crew the homing device's coordinates it was easy to track it to a suspected militant's safe house about 30 miles north of Baghdad. Colonel Singleton and Chuck watched as a big screen satellite picture honed in on a single building that looked like a large house sitting all by itself, away from other buildings. The Army Intelligence Office confirmed that it was indeed a likely location for some very big ISIS, and possibly, Al Qaeda leaders and Chuck thought he almost saw the beginning of a smile cross the colonel's face. Everyone knew that speed was now of the essence and the order was given. While on routine patrol 20,000 feet up, two F-16C's were ordered to bomb the building.

"Ten minutes to target," the radio operator said once the order was given and now the painful waiting began. Chuck knew his entire life rested on this one bombing run and he was a bundle of nerves inside. But to everyone in the satellite truck he looked almost serene and sleepy calm. When the radio operator said "One minute to target" and began counting down, Colonel Singleton threw a look Chuck's way that said *you'd better be right or we're both in trouble.*

Aiming its laser precisely at the house, one jet released its GBU-12 smart bomb, which has laser sensors in its nose. The sensors picked up the reflected laser pulses and guided it to the target. "First bomb away," the pilot's voice came over the radio, "Preparing second." The F-16C's made a sharp 180-degree turn to come back and drop another one to make sure they hit their target. 20 seconds later they heard, "Second bomb away" and 10 seconds after that, "Target achieved." Now it was really nerve-racking time as they all waited for U.S. soldiers to arrive on the scene to see who they had just killed. *Hopefully, not a bunch of women and children*, they all worried. Although the satellite truck was air-conditioned Chuck felt himself starting to sweat profusely. It made his shirt stick to him like wet paste, but *can't show it*, he thought. And he didn't.

Ninety grueling minutes later a lieutenant with a digital camera sent real-time video back to the base and they were startling. The two 500-pound bombs had pulverized the brick house, blasting a 40-foot wide crater, vaporizing its walls, and hurling concrete blocks 300 feet into the air. The pictures up on the satellite truck's big screen were devastating and everyone in the truck assumed that no one could have survived the bombing. Colonel Singleton looked at Chuck with a scowl on his face, but medics then began to carry bodies away from the crater and the Army cameraman went in for close-ups. Chuck wondered how any bodies could even survive the bombing, but figured they must have been leaving the house just as the bombs hit. *Just in the nick of time*, he thought, *five seconds later and we might've missed them.*

And there they were as the lieutenant went from body to body relaying the pictures through the satellite truck to Army Intelligence's Face Recognition Program for identification. Everyone in the truck watched in amazement as the pictures were freeze-framed long enough for thousands of photos of known militants to run by until each person was matched up and identified. The first three dead bodies were top Sunni militant leaders. But the bonus came with the fourth body when a medic shouted, "This one's alive." Someone had miraculously survived the blast, but just barely, and if he stayed that way, he might provide a wealth of intelligence. Colonel Singleton did an about-face and clapped his hands in joy. Then there was a top Al Qaeda leader named Abdullah Al-Sunnah. He was obviously dead, but the colonel pounded the table anyway just thinking about the great public relations this would give the Army. But the best was still yet to come.

All of a sudden, there he was. The long-sought ISIS leader Mohhamad Mehdi lying dead in a pool of blood. But more importantly, there up on the big screen, was a live feed of two of his top lieutenants and one of them appeared to be alive. "Two survivors!" Colonel Singleton yelled, "Looks like a home-run lieutenant."

"At least a triple," Chuck murmured as he looked from the Colonel to the screen. Though outwardly calm, he felt like he was about to collapse from the stress of the last two hours. But he always remembered his father's eloquent words, "You may be crapping yourself inside, but never let 'em see you sweat." At this moment, he realized that while his dad was reluctant to give advice, his words had gotten him through more than one tight situation. *Maybe the old man is smarter than I thought.*

"Wait for me outside," Colonel Singleton said, snapping him away from the hypnotic glare of the big screen, "We've got somethin' to talk about."

Chuck shot back a suspicious glance Singleton understood to mean that he had better not double cross him. But the Colonel had worse things than a double cross in mind for him.

CHAPTER 20

Free Will

How can there be free will if God knows everything that will happen in advance? The answer is simple. God is certainly capable of knowing everything in advance, but chooses not to. Rather, God knows every conceivable outcome of every life situation, but prefers to leave the actual final result up to us. That is "free will." There isn't just one future, but many possible futures and we determine by our actions which one will actually happen. Let us not be the "blind fools of fate and slaves of circumstance" Robert Service talks about in *The Spell of the Yukon*. Let us instead, control our own destiny as much as is humanly possible.

Chuck thought about this entry in *The Book* as he waited for Colonel Singleton outside of the satellite truck. *Am I a blind fool of fate and a slave of circumstance*, he asked himself, *am I just following the herd and not pursuing my own path?* But he didn't have time to answer that question as the Colonel came out and said, "If I'm gonna' swing this, you gotta' be invisible for a while and that means a classified mission that no one can talk about."

"What might the mission be sir," Chuck asked with both relief and respect. Relief that the Colonel apparently wasn't going to double cross him and respect for him for living up to their unspoken bargain. He realized that Singleton would take all the credit for killing Mehdi and that was okay with him. Considering his notoriety with the militants, the less attention he attracted, the better. But he also felt suspicion, which was confirmed with the next word out of his mouth.

"Afghanistan," the Colonel said.

"Afghanistan," Chuck repeated with resignation as his suspicions were confirmed. *Could this be a suicide mission?* He knew that many men who were sent back to Afghanistan these days never returned.

"Yeah, the Taliban are acting up again and we know where some of their main forces are. You and the Dogs will go in and work with the locals to kill a few and put a dent in their opium trade. It should only take a week or two."

"I thought we were negotiating with them."

"We are, but they wanna' negotiate from the strongest position possible."

"And we want 'em at the weakest position possible."

"Right you are lieutenant."

"But I thought we routed 'em."

"So did we. But they're back and bigger than ever in the south and east along the Pakistani border. They just broke 800 prisoners out of a prison in Kandahar and about 400 of them were Taliban soldiers."

"Oh shit!"

"Oh shit is right ... especially since the other 400 will undoubtedly join up."

"So, they're re-building their ranks."

"More or less, but it gets worse. They're operating out of the border mountains and Pakistan does nothing about it. Hell, they're even planning on forming their own government in the south."

"How could they do that?"

"Well, apparently we took the money we were 'sposed to spend on rebuilding their infrastructure and spent it on Iraq. We were 'specially supposed to rebuild their agricultural system so they wouldn't be so dependent on growing opium poppies. But we didn't do that and it left it vulnerable to the Taliban coming back in and getting a foothold. They even announced they're gonna' build Islamic schools there."

"Real schools or just schools for boys?"

"Both ... I think."

"I thought they didn't let their girls go to school."

A little taken aback by Chuck's cultural knowledge of the Taliban, Colonel Singleton responded, "They didn't, but now it looks like most Afghanis want both sexes to get an education and the Taliban might be listening."

"That's funny after they blew up about 200 schools in the first place."

"Yeah, but remember ... it's the Middle-East."

Where have I heard that before? "Well ... I guess politics will always upstage religion."

"I guess, but I don't really give a shit. You'll meet up with a local warlord and he'll show you where the enemy is holed up."

"With all due respect sir," Chuck said, "Are you sure you can trust this guy?" U.S. forces had worked with some of the warlords in the Afghanistan invasion. Some had been reliable and some not. Of course, Chuck knew that money would be involved and that they would side with whoever had the most of it.

As if he read his mind, Colonel Singleton replied, "No we aren't, but we are sure we can trust his greed and you're gonna' give him cash for his help."

"How much?"

"That's none of yer' concern soldier. You'll give his men the bag of money you're given and won't look inside."

"Of course, sir," Chuck said with a smart salute and half-smile.

"It's eight-hundred-thousand-dollars," Singleton said as if in an after-thought. Possibly he thought Chuck should know the amount in case the men tried to say they underpaid them. They both knew that the Afghanis on the other end would steal money out of it each step of the way before it got to the warlord and someone in the chain might try to say there was less than there actually was. But, it was a moot point as both men knew that Chuck would look inside the satchel anyway.

"Money talks 'ay?"

"Especially here." Singleton gave him a quizzical look on this one as he got up and walked to the rear of his office. Unlocking a door in the back he went to a safe in the corner of the room and spun the combination. He fished out a satchel of cash and handed it to Chuck. "This is your ticket to a successful mission lieutenant, protect it well. And this time, no beatin' up any Afghani perverts."

"Wouldn't think of it," Chuck said, not missing a beat.

"And leave the poppy fields alone."

Chuck shot him a glance, wondering how he knew about that. The pervert beating was common knowledge and almost legendary among the soldiers. In his last tour in Afghanistan a young boy had flagged him down as he left a village and through an interpreter told him that he had escaped from a prison. He seemed reluctant to say more than that, but after extensive interpreting by Abdul Hameed, it became clear that he had been held prisoner by the village commander in a harem of boy sex slaves. Chuck told his superiors, but to his amazement, they ordered him to keep quiet about it.

"Ever heard of bacha bazi?" his commanding officer had said.

"Is that like Bocce Ball?" Chuck answered.

"No, it literally means 'boy play' and it's the old tradition of keeping boys as sex slaves. The Taliban banned it back when they were in power."

"And now?"

"Now many of the militia commanders are bringing it back bigger and better than ever and molesting kids right and left."

"Ya' mean the commanders that we put in charge of the villages?"

"Yes, and other rich Afghanis and warlords. Poor families are selling them their boys to do what they want with them."

"And we let it happen."

"Yup. We ignore it to protect our *wonderful* relationship with the Afghan military."

"Well, is there anything we can do about it?"

"I suppose we could start by following our own laws but that isn't gonna' happen."

"What laws?"

"The Leahy Law for one. It says U.S. military aid money has to be cut off to any foreign military implicated in gross human rights violations and I'd say molesting kids is pretty gross."

"How do they get by the law?"

"A loophole as usual. It's called the notwithstanding clause."

"The not-with-what?"

"The notwithstanding clause. It says the Afghani military aid should be available *notwithstanding* any other provision of law."

"Figures."

"It does, doesn't it ... and in the meantime the abuse continues."

After that conversation, Chuck couldn't help himself as he paid a routine visit to the village commander and beat him to a bruised, puffy pulp. He then loaded all the boys up in a truck and drove them to a safe house being run by an informant he had worked with a year earlier. When he returned to base, the Afghanis had already complained to the base commander and he was immediately arrested.

"Why'd ya' do it lieutenant?" the colonel asked, "We told you to keep it quiet."

"I did keep it quiet sir and didn't tell anyone."

"That's not the point son and you know it. Ya' know you just ended yer' career don't ya'?"

"I suppose sir, but I didn't really have a choice."

In the end, however, they buried the incident and sent Chuck back to his unit to avoid any bad publicity. He heard later that they paid off the village commander to keep quiet about it.

The poppies were a different story and he still wondered how he had gotten away with setting fire to several opium poppy fields owned by Afghani warlords back then. He still remembered how angry he had been when he found out that the CIA made deals with them to help capture and kill the Taliban. In return, the U.S. forces looked the other way while the warlords grew three-quarters of the world's opium and the Taliban protected them in return for money they used to buy arms. Such was the contradictory nature of the Middle-East. The opium was shipped over the mountains into Iran and Pakistan to be refined into heroin. Because Chuck's brother had died of a heroin overdose, he couldn't bring himself to look the other way. He thought back to the night he crept out of camp with a flame-thrower on his back.

"Whatcha' doin'," Scott Sampson had drawled as he crossed paths with him coming back from the latrine. But he knew exactly what he was doing. He also knew about Chuck's brother.

"Nothing Tex, go back to bed," Chuck stuttered, looking around nervously.

"Looks like somethin' to me," Scott said, looking at the flame-thrower. "Wait a minute," he said as he turned toward their barracks. Then throwing a look back at his frozen lieutenant, "Trust me."

Chuck did and Scott returned with the rest of the dogs rubbing sleep out of their eyes and several more flame-throwers. "Let's go," was all Scott said.

"This is my party guys," Chuck said, "And yer' not invited."

"Well, we're crashin' the party and, besides ... somebody's gotta' kill those guards."

"Thought I'd do that."

"Let's go," Scott said again and they traipsed off to the poppy fields.

The Afghani whose fields they burned that night complained and it got Chuck and his men in hot water with the CIA and the State Department. But in the end, officials decided to cover it all up to avoid the media finding out about their collusion with the warlords. They were growing more opium than ever with large areas of the country outside of government control. Then there was the opium corruption that ran rampant through the ranks of the Afghan government and the Afghani police. The U.S. paid for some poppy eradication, but much of the money went into the pockets of corrupt government officials. However, the eradication program wasn't working anyway because it provided no help to farmers to plant alternative crops.

Most of the increase in poppy cultivation was occurring in southern Afghanistan, especially in Kandahar, Oruzgan, and Helmand. Coalition forces in Afghanistan had now increased to some 40,000 in the hope that they could stabilize it enough to allow non-opium development and better governance that would restore the Afghanis' faith in their government. Unfortunately, the government couldn't extend its authority much outside of the capital and coalition forces were little match for the Taliban's hit-and-run tactics. They were also not much of a match for the warlords and tribal leaders or the deep rivalries among ethnic groups. But most of all, they were having a tough time fighting against poppy growers and drug smugglers when it was their only way of making a living.

"This is for Mikey," Chuck said as he shot his flame-thrower at the poppy fields. Mike was his younger brother and best friend. They were inseparable growing up and Chuck was Mike's hero. He was a budding football star himself and everyone assumed a college football scholarship was in his future. That is until he severely broke his leg in a game and he discovered Oxycodone. After the surgery his doctors put him on it for the intense pain and he developed an addiction to it.

He refilled the prescription as many times as he could, but when it ran out, he started buying it from drug dealers. Finding that too expensive, he turned to heroin, which was a lot cheaper than Oxycodone. A year later he died of an overdose and it wasn't the heroin that killed him. It was the fentanyl, a drug 50 times stronger than heroin, that drug dealers mix with their product.

Chuck blamed himself for not being there when his brother needed him. He had suspected him of using some type of drug but when he suggested addiction counseling Mike joked, "Rehab is for quitters," and he said he didn't have a drug problem. He realized now that Mike probably heard that line from other addicts and that he should have known something was wrong.

He remembered his dad sitting in his study staring at the wall for three days straight, not saying anything to anyone. Although Mike was Claire's son from another marriage, Don loved him like he was his own. He always said Mike reminded him of another boy he had known, but never said who it was. Chuck thought then that he was being selfish in not sharing his grief with his mother, but he had noticed while growing up that Don didn't share his feelings with anyone. Then two days after the funeral, he announced that he was going to a journalism conference. Chuck remembered hearing the surprise in his mother's voice when he told her.

"Why now?" she said, "Why didn't you mention it before." Don's only answer was that he forgot. Then he said he needed something to take his mind off of Mike. Chuck thought it was strange but was too lost in his own grief to think much about it at the time. Two days later three local drug dealers died of drug overdoses on the same day and Chuck wished his dad was at least there to revel in the miserable justice of it all.

Snapping back to the present, Chuck heard himself say, "Yes sir," as he wondered again how Colonel Singleton knew about the poppy fields.

"This is strictly black-ops and yer' on yer' own lieutenant," said Singleton.

"Yes sir," he said again, knowing that if they were caught, the brass would deny everything.

But as he drove back to his barracks to brief his men about their upcoming mission, his suspicions started to grow about the money. He had never seen an Army officer with this much cash to throw around and he noticed when Singleton opened the safe that there was plenty more inside. He knew the CIA had a lot of cash and that massive amounts of money had been squandered in the early days of the war. In fact, he had heard rumors that millions of dollars had been brought in to buy Iraqis' loyalty and that much of it was still unaccounted for. According to one story, a truckload of cash was delivered to their base and no one ever heard of it again. Chuck had to wonder if the $800,000 was part of that load and if other officers had shared in the booty.

As for going back into Afghanistan, he had heard the stories. Militants were now launching more than 600 attacks a month on coalition troops. Not only was the Taliban making a comeback, but other Muslim extremists were going to Afghanistan to fight the infidels. The insurgents were operating from Pakistan, helped by corrupt Pakistani officials, some radical Islamic parties, Al Qaeda, and ISIS. They were loaded with recruits from Islamist seminaries in Pakistan and Afghanistan that offer both religious and combat training.

Intelligence reports said it looked like Al Qaeda and ISIS along with their allies were honing their combat tactics in Iraq and taking them into Afghanistan, which was symbolically significant. Significant because before September 11, the country was the hallowed ground of the jihad. It was the land where fighters from across the Muslim world beat the Soviet Union in the 1980's, fought alongside the Taliban in the 1990's, and filled terrorist training camps run by Al Qaeda after that. Most of the foreign fighters were Sunni, but they were increasingly fighting alongside the Taliban. Apparently, they preferred that to getting embroiled in the Sunni-Shiite fighting in Iraq. Some, however, were fighting for individual warlords against both sides, which was why Chuck was suspicious of teaming up with any of them.

At any rate, all this meant that fewer Muslim fighters were coming to Iraq and he thought he had noticed a slight downturn in the enemy numbers. In the years since the U.S. invaded Afghanistan, Iraq had attracted Saudis, Yemenis, and Syrians as the largest groups and Algerians, Tunisians, and other North Africans as the second largest. They learned their deadly trade in Iraq and took it with them to Afghanistan, complete with suicide bombings that were previously rare there. Out-gunned and out-manned, the Taliban turned to more terrorist tactics than ever before and that meant massive suicide bombings, not that it compared to the huge daily death toll in Iraq. Army intel said many Yemenis and Syrians were being trained as suicide bombers in Iraq. They then travelled through Iran to Ouetta, Pakistan and crossed the open border into Afghanistan.

All these jihadists were beefing up the ranks of the Taliban and emboldening them to launch fiercer and fiercer attacks. They were fighting the West and most of all, America, like they had fought the Soviets years earlier. To them, we were one more invader and it was their duty and destiny to fight us for God and country. But mostly for God. In the end, they, like the Iraqis, considered this another crusade against Islam.

The Taliban was growing stronger every day and gaining sympathy and support from their fellow Pashtuns in Pakistan who helped them gain power in Afghanistan in the first place. Reconstruction efforts had been exceedingly slow and often the Afghani people got more help from the Taliban than from the coalition forces.

Will Daniels had told the Mad Dogs about what was going on in Afghanistan, but they knew better than to think or talk about it too much. They also knew better than to wait outside the satellite truck for Chuck, although they had a sense of what was going on. So, they waited anxiously in their barracks and their patience paid off as he came strolling in like nothing had happened. They also knew better than to ask him any questions. All they had to know was that their leader had put his life on the line and rescued one of their own. Luis Salgado would get out of the hospital in a week or so.

"Officer on deck!" Private Brian Malone was the first to stand up and salute, followed by all the Mad Dogs as Chuck walked in.

"At ease," Chuck said and he meant it. He didn't want them to make a big deal out of what he had done. It was his job and that's all. Besides, their smiles and back slaps said it all. Then there was an awkward silence, broken only by Jim Hawkins, looking up in a sort of daze. "Ya' ever wonder why dogs tilt their heads when they hear a noise?" he said.

"Probably so they can hear better ... or maybe so they can see past their long snout," said Chuck without hesitation. Then it was down to business as he began briefing them on their Afghan mission. They were to leave tomorrow in the late afternoon. They all went to bed early that night to catch up on their sleep deprivation.

The next day Chuck was called to Colonel Singleton's office once again for a last-minute briefing. The Colonel told him that after using heavy equipment to pull the concrete slabs out of the building wreckage, body parts of several women and children were discovered. They had apparently been inside when the bombs hit. And once again Chuck asked himself the $64 million question, *is it worth the cost?*

Back at their barracks all of the Dogs pondered this question silently when they found out about the dead women and children and the mood was somber.

But in Iraq, emotions change with the hot, desert winds and right then Hawkins came dancing in wearing a plaid skirt, white blouse, red lipstick, and a 1950's blonde, bouffant wig. Flouncing about the room like a teen-age girl at a debutante ball, he sang the 1963 hit song "My Boyfriend's Back," but with the words:

"The Taliban's back and there's gonna' be trouble."
"Hey La, Hey La"
"The Taliban's back."

The performance was first greeted by a few seconds of astonished silence. This was beyond the pale, even for Hawkins. But then, instead of a gradual build-up of chuckles and chortles, the Dogs suddenly erupted into howls of convulsive laughter.

"Where'd you get that skirt?" Ron Jenkins asked, half-falling out of his chair.

"Screw the skirt," screamed John Borland, "Where'd ya' get a wig like that in Iraq?"

"Yeah, 'specially blonde!" sputtered Jenkins between belly-laughs.

"From yo' momma," Jim said as he pirouetted, "After I screwed yer' sister."

"Don't you mean his brother," howled Mike Sandstone. They were laughing so hard now they were turning blue from a lack of oxygen.

"Always knew you were a cross dresser," squealed Dan Walker.

"Don't ask, don't tell and that's enough guys. Let's get some shut-eye," Chuck choked out between his own snickers, putting an end to the hilarity.

But it wasn't enough for Jim Hawkins as he laid down on his cot to plan his next prank.

CHAPTER 21

Pouring down more coffee than anyone should ever drink, Mark tried to fight his way through his blurred vision and fend off sleep long enough to research the strange words he had found. "*Gamma*" was the most interesting of the group but "*Black Hole*" was right up there in the running. He knew gamma rays were radioactive and his hopes were raised when he thought it might somehow relate to an impending nuclear explosion. *This is more like it.* But what he found made him flinch.

He discovered that stars collapse every day shooting big gamma ray bursts out into space. The whole star falls into itself all at once, which causes huge nuclear reactions that spew out massive amounts of deadly radiation. It's the biggest explosion since the Big Bang itself and brighter than a million-trillion suns. *What is it with all this space stuff?*

And then there were the black holes. When a star that was millions of miles across compresses itself down to a single atom, it also creates a black hole with a massive gravitational pull that sucks everything in it. There are tens of thousands of them scattered across the universe and scientists used to think they were stationary. But recently, they discovered that there are wondering black holes right next to our own galaxy traveling thousands of miles an hour and devouring everything in their path. So far, none of them seem to be heading our way, but if one did hit us it would create tidal waves several miles high that would flood all the continents and kill billions. The possibility of a gamma ray burst, however, was a different story.

The closest star that could explode is 8000 light years away, but even at that distance, Mark found that a gamma ray burst headed toward earth would take out the ozone layer and boil off the entire top level of our atmosphere. Temperatures would soar, everyone would be blinded and get severely sunburned, and our cells would stop regenerating and reproducing. After one month, almost all life would be wiped out. It was all very unlikely, but not impossible.

Mark wondered why the gamma warning was in the data in the first place. *Does it mean that a gamma catastrophe already happened or that it will happen? Is it a warning so that we can figure out a way to avoid it?* Whatever it was, he was getting tired of all these dire predictions of disasters that might occur long after he was dead and longed for a terrorist plot more in the immediate future. *Damn, are we just plain doomed?* But he knew he didn't have time to answer that question as he could feel the sandman approaching and the computer began to spit out some more data. This time it contained an explanation of the ever-elusive word "*Sleipner*" and it gave him another reason for renewed optimism.

Eager to find anything less depressing than a world-wide disaster, he was slightly encouraged when he discovered that Sleipner with a capital "S" was the name of a Norwegian natural gas drilling site about 100 miles out to sea. However, his optimism quickly turned to pessimism as he realized that it involved more global warming information. *Man, I can't get away from this crap!* But needing a change of pace from the doom and gloom research he had been doing, he went on to read that Sleipner had figured out a way to avoid sending deadly CO_2 out into the atmosphere.

He found that Natural Gas rigs normally emit massive amounts of CO_2 into the atmosphere, but Sleipner had found a way to contain it. It captures all the greenhouse gas and pumps 3000 tons of it into huge underground reservoirs every day. Scientists aren't sure if it will eventually leak, but it, at least, gives them time to figure out how to plug it if it does. They theorize that all coal plants could be fitted with a CO_2 capturing system like Sleipner. *At least there's a little good news.* And Mark was about to find out that there was even more.

* * *

The next night, with lights off, the silent helicopters descended against strong headwinds in the coal-dark mountains near Helmand Province in Southern Afghanistan. Without touching down, the camouflage-wearing Mad Dogs lowered themselves to the ground on cables and scattered. When they all gathered in the rocks, Radioman Mike Sandstone sent out a signal that they had arrived to the local warlord's forces. Then, using the GPS satellite locator, they hiked to the prearranged meeting spot and there they were, down in a small valley, waiting. Four men standing guard raised their rifles as they approached, but Chuck gave them the password and they relaxed.

"Who's in charge?" he asked calmly.

"I am," said a tall Afghani with a slight accent, "Let's meet in private." He led the way around a large rock formation and stopped. "Got something for me?"

"Yes, I do," said Chuck as he pulled the packet of money out of his backpack and handed it to him.

The turbaned man opened the pack and looked closely at the cash inside. Chuck cringed as he shined a small flashlight on it in what was supposed to be a lights-out operation. But he figured the surrounding mountains would prevent anyone from seeing it and he waited as his new colleague did a quick count to make sure it was all there. He turned off the light and looked at Chuck and smiled as he stuck the money into his shoulder pack. "Wait here," he said, "My men will take you to the mission." 10 minutes later, six Afghani men came around the corner and the lead man motioned for him to follow them.

"Must be our escorts," Chuck said and they started marching east toward the Taliban stronghold in the city of Garmser. As they walked through the moonless night, sometimes tripping and almost falling on the rocky ground, Chuck remembered his briefing about Helmand. Colonel Singleton said that the main livelihood here was growing opium poppies and opium made up about 70% of the Taliban's income. They charged the warlord opium growers for protection and safe transportation of their product into Pakistan where it was made into heroin. Chuck remembered the Colonel saying the U.S. wanted to put a big dent in the poppy production, but couldn't because they had to team up against the Taliban with the very warlords who produced it.

But opium wasn't the only thing crossing the border and making the Taliban a lot of money. All kinds of contraband did that, and especially black-market cigarettes. The Taliban could be quite the entrepreneurs as they charged a duty on each pack of cigarettes that passed into Pakistan and the warlords had a piece of everything. Chuck remembered his dad saying once that war made everyone money. Everyone except the poor civilians.

After the Afghan invasion, the Taliban faded away for a while and waited for their chance to fight a guerilla war in rural areas like Helmand. Now they were back, launching hit-and-run attacks and paying poor farmers $4 for every rocket they fire at coalition and Afghani troops. British and American forces made up the largest part of the contingent in Afghanistan, but not large enough. And the new Afghan Army recruits were no help with absenteeism running at 40%. Compare that to several thousand Taliban soldiers and all the warlords' militias and you get a no-win situation. Then something his father had said when the U.S. first invaded Iraq popped into Chuck's head.

"If the British Army couldn't control the 84-mile flat-land border in Northern Ireland," Don had said, "How do you think we can control Afghanistan's 1500 miles of rough mountain border with Pakistan?"

Chuck had answered with, "Well they won't be alone. We'll be there and the rest of the coalition."

"You mean the coalition of whose-its and what's-its?"

"No, I mean NATO."

"Well, their hearts are in the right place, but there won't be enough of 'em to do anything because we'll be sending too many of our troops to Iraq."

How does he always know all this? It was amazing to Chuck how many of his father's predictions had come true over the years. He remembered hearing him say once that the only reason Osama Bin Laden got away when the Army had him trapped in Tora Bora was that America had already taken a lot of troops out of Afghanistan and sent them to Iraq, leaving them short-handed. Don had even predicted the current situation he found himself in.

"They'll be back," he said back then.

"Who?"

"The Taliban."

"Why do you say that?"

"Well, first of all, I seem to remember that our original intent in Afghanistan was not to destroy the Taliban as much as it was to get Al-Qaeda. When we couldn't do that, we said the primary goal had always been to get rid of the Taliban and it was declared a big success when they disappeared."

"Well wasn't it?"

"Hell no! Ya' gotta' look at history, which we never do. Whether it was the British in the 1830's or the Russians in the 1980's, when Afghanistan is attacked, they first leave Kabul and the cities and fade away into the mountains. They lay low for a few years, letting the invader establish itself in the cities and then they start their guerilla skirmishes in the rural areas. They escalate into real war with the guerillas melting back into the mountains after each battle where no one can get at them. Why do you think we didn't get Bin Laden back then?"

Chuck could well-understand how he got away as he now trudged over the jagged rocks and steep hills much like Bin Laden's escape path. But aside from his father's accurate predictions about the war, he wondered what he would think of him now teaming up with the warlords who grow the opium that killed his son.

After marching all night, the head Afghani motioned that they had arrived. Climbing up over a rock formation he pointed down into a valley with a small village at the bottom. "That's them," he said as his men began setting up mortars on their side of the rocks.

"What's the plan?" Chuck asked.

"We wait for dark and slip into the village before dawn while my men plaster it with mortars. Then we kill the enemy."

"Sounds good," Chuck said. Then came the customary question commonly asked of all collaborator forces, "How do we identify the enemy?"

He got a blank stare at this one. Either the Afghan leader didn't understand the question or didn't care and something told him it was probably a combination of both. An unaccustomed chill then swept over him in a wave of surprise. Looking around for distraction, he noticed that all the men were bedding down for the day, finding cover from the brutal sun under canvasses they pulled out of their knapsacks. They were the color of the sandy-brown rocks around them.

Chuck couldn't sleep, as usual, and the head man walked over to him and asked casually, "Where ya' from?"

"San Diego," he said instinctively, not surprised at the man's English.

"Rad dude ... Surf's up, rockin', smokin' hot, big tits and ass."

"Ya' do know that not all Californians talk that way, don't you?"

" Not all tits and ass? Really?"

"Really."

"That's disappointing 'cause that's how we poor, sexually frustrated Arab boys like to think it is."

"Educated in the states, huh?"

"Harvad," he answered in a mock Bostonian, aristocratic accent.

Chuck wondered if he really did go to Harvard, but whatever the truth, something about these guys made him uneasy. "What's yer' name Havad?"

"Bob."

"Bob, huh."

"Bob."

"What's your favorite movie Bob?" Chuck often asked the odd question to see how familiar someone was with American culture. Typically, he got answers like *Die Hard* or *The Avengers*. But not this time, and Bob's answer astounded him.

"That would be *Butch Cassidy and the Sundance Kid*," came his surprising reply, referring to an old cult classic about two bank robbers in the old west.

"Yer' shittin' me!" said Chuck amazed, "That's one of my favorites too!"

When two very different men from opposite ends of the earth have the same favorite old and obscure movie, it's a colossal coincidence. When those two men are sworn enemies and as different from each other as Chuck and Bob, it's a downright miracle. Whatever it was, however, it made Chuck even more curious and anxious about this man who he was about to risk his life with in a perilous battle. But now he wanted to get some sleep before the mission and he tried to get the mystery out of his head. Unfortunately, another bizarre thought took its place with his father's opinion of the Taliban that he was about to attack.

"They'll keep a guerilla war going and going like the Ever-Ready Battery bunny … attacking and retreating, attacking and retreating indefinitely," he had said.

"Well, they can't do it forever, can they?"

"Not forever, but close to it. They've got a lot of patience and are willing to carry this thing into the next generation if they have to."

Then, Chuck asked a question he immediately regretted. "Why didn't we know this going in?"

"Once again, we were too arrogant to bother researching the history. Or maybe we did and just ignored it."

"So, what're we supposed to do now?"

"The only thing we can do is flood them with money to rebuild their country so they see the advantages of no Taliban."

"Aren't we doing that?"

"Yeah, but we won't be able to sustain it because all our money will be going to Iraq. And that'll make it that much easier for the Taliban to make their comeback."

And again, dad's a prophet, Chuck mused as he finally drifted off to a fitful sleep.

"Wake up," the unusually soft and lyrical voice said as one of the Arab fighters rousted Chuck from his slumber, "Time to go." Rubbing the sleep from his eyes, Chuck looked around at the rugged, leathery, and creased faces of his new allies and realized that they looked like the rough land around them. With their dirty, weather-beaten skin and cold, dark eyes, they looked like they had spent their entire lives outside in the cruel elements, never knowing the comfort of any indoor warmth. In a sense, they *were* the land; harsh and fiercely independent.

* * *

The ragtag group reached Garmser just before dawn and one group of Afghani fighters split off to set up their mortars. It was an impoverished place set in a valley with jagged, rocky mountains all around, but it had one unique feature. Set up in an oval pattern around the inside perimeter of a Taliban neighborhood were seven tall, ornate minarets from which Islamic music blared and clerics called Muslims to daily prayer. The men divided up into groups of four with two Americans and two Afghanis each and moved around the outer limits of the area. The plan was for each pair to casually walk into the village and mix with the local populace who were probably just rising from bed. Then, when the mortar fire started, they would converge on the Taliban stronghold and blow the place to bits with C-4 explosives.

So far, so good as the men began their nonchalant stroll toward their target, gazing at the strange minarets, which could be seen from everywhere. Suddenly the morning quiet was shattered by mortar fire. Buildings exploded, people started running in all directions screaming, and the men broke into a hurried run. Most of them reached the ring of minarets when, all of a sudden, a barrage of machine gun fire erupted out of nowhere. Stunned, the men dove for cover as they realized where the fire was coming from. The minarets were actually camouflaged machine gun nests. They looked like World War II pill boxes in the sky. The machine guns were mounted on turrets that could be turned in all directions and the gunners were protected by thick steel. It was now painfully clear that they had been set up. Most likely, one of the Afghan fighters had sold them out to the Taliban and they had walked right into a trap. Chuck instantly wondered if they had heard about the bounty on his head and wanted the reward.

"Our first mission isn't going that well is it," Bob said to Chuck with a sly grin as he crouched behind half-a-wall that looked like it was once part of a small house.

"You could say that," Chuck casually answered, blindly firing his rifle over the top of the wall, hitting nothing.

"Must be one of my loyal men." And that was that. It was now time to try to figure a way out of all this.

Without missing a beat Chuck took stock of the situation and instantaneously figured out their only route of escape. Unfortunately, four minarets were directly in the way. Pulling out his radio, he said quietly, "Dan, time for the fast ball." On the other end, Private Dan Walker knew exactly what that meant as he reached into his backpack and pulled out a black ball that looked like it was made out of tar. Before the Army, Dan had been a pitcher in the minor leagues and he planned to go back to it if he lived through the war. Now he was throwing the pitch of his life as he wound up and threw the black ball at the tower holding the minaret nearest him. His new Afghani comrades stared dumbly at him as the pitch missed its mark. In broken English, one said, "You play baseball ... now?" one said.

While Dan was winding up for his next pitch, Chuck sent another radio message, this one to Sergeant John Borland. "John," he said calmly, "Time for cowboys and Indians." Just as cooly, the sergeant pulled several items out of his backpack and assembled them into a crossbow. He then methodically loaded it with a strange-looking arrow with a rubber ball on the end. Steel-nerved, he took rock-steady aim at the minaret tower nearest him and with one eye closed, let the innovative arrow fly in a slight arc. "Bull's eye," he whispered as the strange-looking shaft stuck smack-dab in between two girders in the tower. At the same time, Dan Walker's second pitch hit its mark.

About 100 yards to the west Chuck was in the middle of another radio trans-mission, this one even more peculiar than the last. "Chick football Ron," he said to Private Ron Jenkins, the Dog who could see in the dark. Ron had been an amateur soccer player before the service and his comrades often made fun of him for play-ing what they considered girls' football. Incredibly, he pulled a small, black soccer ball out of his backpack and set it on the ground just outside of his hiding place. "Go," he said into his radio and the rest of the Dogs started firing their machine guns at the minarets. Then, in one swift move, he darted out from behind a shack, took instantaneous aim, and kicked the ball into an arc as if he were making a free shot in a neighborhood soccer game. The ball hit the ground just in front of his minaret tower and softly rolled exactly underneath it. "Score!" he said as he jumped back behind his cover. Dan's ball, the arrow, and the soccer ball were all made of C-4 explosives.

Just then Chuck's walkie-talkie crackled to life. "The enemy is grouping on the south side," it said in a garbled radio voice, "The towers are gonna' keep you pinned down while they come in and pick you off."

Who is that? he thought, but figured he didn't have time to figure it out. Still, the distorted voice sounded vaguely familiar. At any rate, if the Taliban were com-ing in from the south, that meant he had to change his escape route or they would run right into them. "Get some C-4 under that tower," he said pointing north and not taking the time to be clever, "Just get as many balls under it as you can ... I'm gettin' this one."

With that, he pulled an odd-looking helmet out of his backpack and put it on his head, covering it with a woman's headscarf. He then pulled an equally strange-looking vest and pair of pants out of the pack and put them on. They were both bullet-proof. Then it was Arab women's clothes over the top of that as Bob stared on in disbelief. Finally, Chuck pulled a dismantled cane out of his pack and con-nected the pieces together. With no hesitation, he bent over slightly, leaned on the cane, and walked out from behind his cover with the scarf hiding his head and face. To anyone looking, he appeared to be an old Arab woman who was probably half-blind, going to market, or the Suk as they called it. No one paid any attention to him. That is, until he started limping toward a minaret tower.

While Chuck was waddling up the path, Dan Walker was on his fourth throw. The first three had either fallen just short of the minaret or landed past it and the sweat was now salting his eyes as he threw his last C-4 ball. "Home run!" he said to himself as it rolled precisely under the structure.

At first, no one noticed the old woman making her way down the path. But as she got closer to the tower, some voices yelled "Ta'aly ya mara walla nadrib belsilah"

(*Get back lady or we'll shoot.*) and "Gif walla adrib belsilah" (*Stop or I'll shoot.*). Chuck kept going as if he had heard nothing and hoping they might think he was deaf. The Taliban fighters yelled again and again until finally, the voices turned into machine gun fire. He picked up the pace at this point as he felt the ground exploding around him. The gunners were giving him one more chance by shooting at the ground. He was almost there and wondered when they would shoot him. But he didn't have to wonder long as their patience finally gave out and a short burst of bullets struck him knocking him to the ground unconscious.

The rest of the Dogs saw him go down and all prayed for the best. Three minutes later their prayers were answered as they saw him move his right hand slightly. He was subtly reaching for his own C-4 ball and the machine gunners didn't notice. As if on cue, the Dogs started firing at the tower nearest him while he rolled the C-4 ball under it. It stopped right where it needed to and once again, as if on cue, his men fired smoke canisters all around him. The thick smoke gave him the cover he needed to get up and escape. The bullet-proof helmet and the Kevlar vest and pants had added about 50 pounds to his backpack, but it was worth every ounce.

No sooner had he gotten back to Bob and his men, than he radioed, "Hit it." The Dogs followed orders and detonated all the C-4 bombs by radio wave. As if in slow motion, all five towers collapsed at once and they began their run north with their new allies. They got what they expected when the other two towers all turned their machine guns on them. But what they didn't expect were the snipers that lay in their path.

CHAPTER 22

The temperature was about 125 degrees with high humidity and Jasnine wasn't sweating a drop. Her glands had adapted over the years to too many hot and humid climates. Besides, as a native Arab, she was somewhat naturally acclimated to it. Sitting and gazing out at the lonely desert, she realized that it could be both ugly and beautiful at the same time. Ugly in its barren bleakness, beautiful in its infinite and endless horizon. But Jasnine's ponderings were interrupted by a slight movement off in the distance. Two black SUVs were approaching.

After a long and painstaking search, her assistant had found someone who knew someone who knew someone else who might have the alleged dinosaur bones and they were now at the gate to her dig-site. The guard let them enter and she watched them drive up the long, rough driveway. When they stopped, an armed man jumped out of the lead car and looked around furtively. Apparently seeing nothing, he walked around to the second vehicle and opened the rear door. Two long legs swung out of the SUV first, followed by six feet of a handsome man in a dark suit and sunglasses. She thought he looked a little like an Arab James Bond.

"I am so happy to finally meet you Dr. Ahmed," he said extending his hand.

"And you are?" she said, shaking his hand briefly.

"Dr. Yusef Mohammed at your service."

"Doctor of what?" she asked.

"I actually have two doctorates in Archeology and Anthropology," he said with no pride in his voice.

"Impressive," she said, wondering what universities they were from.

"Not nearly as impressive as the famous Jasnine Ahmed."

"That's the first time anyone has called me famous," Jasnine said with a wisp of a grin, "Infamous maybe."

"Beautiful *and* modest," Mohammed said, "But we should probably get going. I must apologize for this, but my assistant must search you and for your own safety, we must put a hood over your head on the way."

"What ... and mess up my beautiful hair?" she said laughing like she had been expecting both. Her hair was actually dirty and stringy from all the sand blowing around the dig-site.

The bodyguard gingerly ran his hand and a metal detector up and down Jasnine's body and around her head before putting on the hood. She got in the car and they drove off into the desert. *Famous huh*, she thought as they drove down the bumpy desert road.

She thought maybe Mohammed called her famous because of her discovery of the 2000-year-old astrological temple in northern Brazil. It was 120 tall stones placed in strategic positions to read the stars and planets. *Take that Stonehenge*, she silently joked at the time.

But 'infamous' was another story. Maybe it was her work on the half-dozen seven and eight-foot tall skeletons found in the rainforest on the border between Ecuador and Peru. She took a lot of heat from other archeologists for postulating that it proved the old legend that a race of giants once inhabited the region.

But as if that wasn't enough, shortly after South America, she was digging in another dicey territory in the Hukawung Valley in Myanmar. There, stuck in miniscule cracks of tree bark, Jasnine found an almost perfectly preserved female insect that looked like a miniature version of the thousands of descriptions of aliens from people who claim to have seen them. A triangular head sitting atop an elongated neck with a face showing nothing but big bug-eyes was almost exactly the way they described what they saw. The body, by comparison, was small and frail compared to the oversized head, which supposedly housed a larger-than-normal brain, possibly for telepathic communication.

But it wasn't Jasnine's estimate that the bug was at least 100 million years old that got her into hot water with her colleagues and peers. No, it was her casual conversation with a reporter who asked her why the insect's face looked so much like the hundreds of drawings of alien beings discovered over the years. She couldn't help herself as she joked, "Maybe it came here as an amoeba on a meteorite from Mars millions of years ago. You know hundreds of them hit the earth every day."

"What could that mean?" asked another reporter who seemed to be genuinely interested.

"Well, it could mean that the amoeba evolved into that insect you see before you and later into an alien race of people who inhabited the earth back before or during the dinosaur period." She was only half-joking.

"You mean the ones with the big eyes and flowing bodies we've seen in so many ancient drawings?" one particularly sharp reporter who worked for an archeological magazine asked.

"And in the sci-fi movies," said another, "Don't forget them."

An amazed and uncomfortable hush descended over the crowd of reporters as they chewed on Jasnine's statement and its possible implications. Anticipating the flurry of questions that had to be coming, Jasnine switched gears abruptly and said, "Or it could just be a mutated earth bug that got too close to some unknown radiation or ate too much pesticide."

"But what about the identical alien faces?" one curious reporter asked.

"Could be coincidence," was all she said.

It didn't help that the scientists present all said they had never seen anything like it and they gave it a new name, "Aethiocarenus burmanicus." They even created a whole new order for the bug, naming it "Aethiocarenodea." Also, of no help was the fact that the bug's head appeared to be able to turn a full 180 degrees, literally looking behind itself. That led to another joking statement from Jasnine that it reminded her of The Exorcist. She said it in an almost imperceptible low tone, but not low enough. That's all it took for the reporters to start picturing the headlines.

"I can see it now," one said, "Scientist believes demon was exorcised out of grasshopper."

"How 'bout scientists say there is nothing like it on our planet?"

"Well, let's not get away from the real reason we're here," another said, "How 'bout Myanmar discovery suggests those big-eyed aliens may be our ancestors?"

That brought a good laugh but it was short-lived as Jasnine recovered a bit and said, "I think I'd go with coincidence. You would be amazed at how many unlikely coincidences we scientists have seen in our work."

That seemed to placate the reporters for a while, until it started to sink into their heads that the odds against this type of coincidence were astronomical, especially since some of the pictures were estimated to have been drawn *before* the discovery of Aethiocarenus burmanicus and some after. Some were on cave walls and some on parchment.

Then came the inevitable question of if the drawings were of the bugs, why were they made to look like full-sized men? In fact, there could be any number of theories about that, but the reporters were more interested in the alien angle and that's what they went with.

It then wasn't long before words like *alien* and *evolution from space* began creeping into their stories. So, what began as an indiscrete little joke blossomed into a question sweeping the nation, *"Did we come from aliens? Did human life start on Mars?"*

Yes, it had started out as a joke, but what Jasnine never mentioned to anyone was that a part of her believed it might be true. Knowing, however, that if the public got ahold of it, she would lose what little credibility she had left, she decided to keep her real extraterrestrial feelings to herself. But in the end, it didn't matter because one of the reporters outed her as the source of the life-from-Mars theory. After that, she was sent to the far east to dig up some less controversial artifacts.

But even that didn't work as she immediately became embroiled in a local controversy involving the underwater city of Yonaguni in Japan. It was a giant, pyramid-shaped rock city that some thought looked like a big turtle. After doing some tests, Jasnine determined that it had sunk an estimated 10,000 years ago, a long time before the Egyptians built their pyramids. But therein lies the rub. Other archeologists believe that 10,000 years ago mankind was not capable of constructing such a complex. And to complicate things even further, some skeptics believe the rock complex was formed naturally by erosion and they accused Jasnine of falling for a sexy, but unscientific theory.

Fearing the bad public relations it was getting, her foundation sent her away to Ethiopia to decipher some ancient texts. A little-known fact about her was that in addition to being an archeologist, she was also a cryptographer and had a real talent for deciphering ancient texts. *Surely, she won't get into any trouble in Africa*, they thought. But they were wrong as she found something that cast doubt on the long-held belief that the Age of Enlightenment began with Rene Descarte's *Discourse on the Method* in 1637 and continued on with John Locke, Issac Newton, and other philosophers for the next 150 years.

In deciphering the writings of a 17th century Ethiopian philosopher named Zera Yacob, Jasnine discovered that he had come up with the Enlightenment's concepts of reason, science, secularism, skepticism, and human equality about 5 years before Descarte. Archeologists and cryptographers around the world immediately discounted her findings and accused her of using unscientific research methods and not being a real cryptographer. It could have been a case of scientific jealousy because scientists have been known to be jealous of each other's work. But Jasnine suspected it was more than that and that her critics' motivation was probably a little racist. She figured that it was simply difficult for many scientists to believe that an African, not a white European, could have conceived of the complex and revolutionary ideals of the European Enlightenment.

Now, however, none of that mattered as her thoughts were interrupted by their arrival at their destination. "We're here Ms. Ahmed," said Mohammed, "I am sorry, but we must leave the hood on until we get inside."

"No problem," came Jasnine's muffled voice. As they led her by the hand down a musty stairway into a tunnel that led to an underground room, Jasnine began to wonder if they knew that her unusual theories had lost her a lot of credibility in the archeological community and that no one wanted to hire her right now. *Maybe that's why they recruited me*, she thought. The bodyguard gently removed the hood and Jasnine rapidly blinked her eyes trying to adjust to the light. She found herself standing in a typical office with a desk, chairs, and a computer.

"This is my office Dr. Ahmed," Mohammed said, "The bones are in the next room along with the equipment you will need to analyze them."

"As you know," she said, "It will take at least 48 hours."

"Yes, and we have first class accommodations for you while you work. Your guards have been informed that you will be gone for a few days."

"Well then," she said, sounding a little uneasy, "Let's get to it." With that, Mohammed opened the door into a laboratory full of archeological diagnostic equipment and a table full of very large bones.

* * *

Just as the Mad Dogs and their new Afghani allies started to think they might actually have a chance of escape, it was suddenly like the fourth of July, only all the fireworks were pointed directly at them. "Snipers!" yelled Bob who had just caught up with Chuck. They had begun their run of escape when a half-moon full of snipers opened up from the rooftops, forcing them back into whatever little cover they could find. This was obviously the Taliban's Plan B and it was a good one. As the snipers kept them pinned down, reinforcements would come in from the south and close the vice.

Chuck immediately began firing his M-4 in the snipers' direction, but Bob pulled him back saying, "Don't waste yer' bullets ... they're in pillboxes up there." Peering more closely, he saw that his Afghani partner was right. The pillboxes contained narrow slits from which the snipers could shoot out of, but the Dogs had no chance of firing into, at least from their position. The only chance they had of getting a bullet into the slits was to charge them head-on and hope to get off a lucky shot or two.

For the first time, a look of hopelessness and resignation began to creep across Chuck's face. Looking around at his men and up at the Taliban soldiers, he casually began taking off the women's clothes and handing them to Bob who said, "No thanks, not a transvestite."

"Wait a minute," Chuck said through a strange half-smile, "You didn't see LeFors out there did ya," reciting Paul Newman's famous line from *Butch Cassidy and the Sundance Kid*.

"LeFors? No," answered Bob, instantly grasping the movie reference with his own odd smile while quoting Robert Redford.

"Oh good. For a moment there I thought we were in trouble."

The smiles turned into chuckles and then to full-bore belly laughs. Their men thought they had gone mad, but they knew that it was the entire situation that was really mad and absurdly funny at the same time. They were out of options and laughing seemed like the only thing left to do as they prepared to run straight into enemy fire and distract them long enough to give their men half a chance to get away. Of course, in the process, they would try to take as many Taliban with them to the afterlife as possible. In mid-laugh they jumped to their feet simultaneously and both screamed a war cry as they ran out shooting.

But their suicide-rush was abruptly cut short as suddenly they heard a familiar sound that stopped them dead in their tracks. Looking around furtively, everyone's eyes came to rest on two attack helicopters rising over the rooftops and heading for their position at full speed. With machine guns sticking out of their doors, they first strafed the rooftops heading west. That cowered the snipers. Then with a quick, gravity-defying U-turn, they turned back east and fired their missiles at the machine gun pill boxes. Back-and-forth, back-and-forth they went, strafing in one direction and firing missiles in the other. The scene made Chuck and Bob laugh even harder as they tried to collect themselves and make a hasty plan. Then came a somewhat familiar voice over Chuck's radio. "You're not out of it yet boy," it said, "Yer' gonna' have to paint 'em."

Chuck quickly grabbed his backpack and headed for the nearest minaret, realizing as he went that the voice had to be Jack. Shooting a glance back at Bob, he yelled, "Later dude." Bob nodded with a grin and maneuvered for a position he could fire from. Hoping the helicopters had taken the minaret gunners out, Chuck climbed the ladder up to the machine gun nest. When he got to the top, he saw two blood-spattered bodies lying in the prone position, one's hands still on the gun. Instinctively, he pulled what looked like a rifle scope out of his pack and looking through the lens, he aimed it at the nearest rooftop pillbox. It was a laser sight and it projected a small red dot on its target. No sooner had he painted the target than a Predator drone appeared out of nowhere and fired a missile at the laser dot, hitting it dead center and destroying the pillbox and half the roof it sat upon. The Predator's targeting system was tied directly to the laser. Wherever the laser dot was, that's where the drone fired. From his high vantage point, Chuck now had a clear view of all the pillboxes and he began targeting them one-by-one in quick succession as Predators came from everywhere and blew up everything in their sights.

"Nice shootin' Tex!" the radio screamed to life, "Now get outta' there!" Chuck didn't need to be told twice as he slid down the minaret ladder and ran to catch up with his men who were already sprinting north. He wondered how close the Taliban fighters were and soon got his answer. The helicopters returned and began a methodical extermination of the approaching troops with the Predators lending a hand. Firing as they ran, the Dogs and the Afghanis realized that in an unexpected way, they had just achieved their objective of killing as many Taliban soldiers as they could find. But they also realized that if it weren't for the helicopters and Predators, it would be their bodies lying back there.

As they approached the edge of town, they saw four American military trucks heading for them and they threw up a communal cheer as they piled in. As the smoking city of Garmser faded into the background, the men started to wonder who it was that had saved them. The only person who knew about their mission was Colonel Singleton, but he told Chuck he was on his own and he probably wouldn't have minded if he got killed in the process. That would be one less scandal he would have to deal with. And besides, they couldn't figure out how Singleton could know that one of Bob's men had betrayed them. *Oh well,* Chuck thought, *sometimes you don't want to ask too many questions.* At that moment, he noticed that Bob had made it into his truck and he threw him half-a-grin. "I love America," Bob yelled laughingly.

"And their big tits and ass!" Chuck smiled and both men laughed themselves hoarse as the trucks roared back into the mountains.

* * *

After a plethora of bad news about global warming, Mark was only now finding that there might be some light at the end of the tunnel. In addition to storing CO_2 underground, there were other ideas for keeping it out of the atmosphere. One involved a giant filter that will actually clean it out of the air. The filter stands 120 feet high and 60 feet wide and cleans the air as soon as it gets dirty. Experts are looking into the idea of outfitting all coal plants with the filter system.

Another was aimed at getting rid of carbon dioxide altogether and was much more revolutionary because it could replace the whole petro-chemical industry. Through chromosome manipulation, scientists are trying to create a bug that will eat CO_2 sunlight, and water and spew out liquid fuel for cars and trucks. The genetically engineered bacteria would be fermented in fermentation refineries, both big and small. Scientists envision companies, cities, and possibly even individuals having their own micro-refineries to make their own fuel. *I think the oil industry might have something to say about that,* Mark thought. Not only that, but these ideas sounded expensive and he wondered how the bill would be paid.

Then it hit him. *Profit.* One simple word. More sleepy research found that big corporations are looking into ways that cleaning up the environment could make them money. *Money*, he thought, *always the best motivation.* As long as there is a profit to be made, companies will come up with ingenious ways to clean up the environment and he stumbled onto yet another developing technology involving underground storage. Some American scientists are experimenting with using wind power to drive giant air compressors which will pump pressurized air into porous rock aquifers 3000 feet underground. When demand for power is high, valves will release the air to power turbines that produce electricity.

Another discovery that gave Mark reason for optimism was an underwater project he read about. It involved putting turbines underwater in rivers and oceans with their rotors propelled by tidal currents instead of wind. Researchers estimate that America's rivers and estuaries alone could provide about half of the yearly energy production of America's hydro-electric plants. But the ocean is the real story. There is so much energy sloshing around in ocean waves that, in theory, a fraction of it could power the world. Most of the ideas involved buoy-like structures tethered to the sea floor getting knocked around by waves with the movement producing energy.

But then the many sleepless hours of intense work crashed down on him all at once and he couldn't hold his eyes open any longer. The computer screen faded out of his blurry vision and his head dropped down on his chest. He was asleep at last, but not for long.

* * *

"I wanna' refund," Chuck said as he and Bob jumped off of the moving trucks and watched them disappear deep into the jagged mountains.

"Sorry, no refunds ... just store credit," Bob said.

"You really do know yer' American retail don't you," Chuck said as they hot-footed it into the brush.

With a smile curling around his face Bob said, "Money's gone anyway." When they figured they were safe, they made camp.

"Can we expect more of yer' faithful men to screw us?" Chuck asked Bob as they sat down for a well-deserved rest.

"I don't think so," Bob said as he motioned toward three of his men dragging a struggling Afghani militant into their midst. Chuck recognized them as the men who had stayed behind to fire mortars into Garmser. They proceeded to wire three long branches together into a tee-pee. They set it up over a pile of sticks and logs and hung the prisoner from its point by his hands. "Ana ma sawait heech! Ana ma sawait heech!" (*I didn't do it! I didn't do it!*) was all he could shriek as they doused the wood with gasoline and lit it. The flames licked his legs and started his clothes on fire as he screamed in agony.

"Must be the traitor," Chuck said casually, but inwardly repulsed. He had smelled burning flesh before and knew it to be a vile stench not easily gotten out of your nostrils or your mind."

"Probably," Bob said.

"Probably! Ya' mean you don't know for sure?"

"He was the only one missing from the raid, so it's probably him. But it doesn't really matter."

"How do ya' figure?"

"Well, whether it's him or not, the rest of these animals are gonna' think twice before betraying us now. It'll probably keep us all alive."

Tough land, tough life, Chuck thought. There were some more muffled screams and Chuck heard one of the Afghanis say "Mothalath el-mot" (*Tripod of death*) and then spit on the burning man. Another man joined him and they both inhaled the smoke coming from the now lifeless, smoldering husk.

"What the hell?" he turned back to Bob.

"Yeah, I wish I could say it was some sort of religious ritual where they absorb his strength, but it's not. They're just enjoying a rotten traitor's last few breaths of life."

As if he were punctuating Bob's observation, the smoking carcass half-screamed one final, "Rahmat Allah!" (*Mercy of Allah!*) through melting lips.

"Well, I hope yer' right. I don't wanna' repeat of Garmser."

"Don't worry, we won't. By the way, who were yer' friends?" Bob asked as they laid down to rest.

"I wish I knew. This whole mission was black ops."

"Well, you must have a guardian angel."

"I must," Chuck said dreamily, wondering how Jack had pulled it all off.

The Dogs and their new partners' next mission appeared to be a bit easier and less prone to betrayal. They were to march 20 miles to a rendezvous point deep in the mountains where they would pick up horses and ride the rest of the way to the target. It was a bridge on the Pakistan side of the border that spanned a wide gorge. It was the only bridge for many miles and was a main route for opium smugglers and Taliban forces. They would often cross it at night into coalition-held territory in Afghanistan and launch deathly raids, after which they escaped back across it into Pakistan. The mission was to blow the bridge and if there were enemy forces on it in the process, so much the better.

As the Dogs prepared for their rocky hike, Chuck noticed Bob handing out capsules to each of his men. Noticing his stare, he walked over and offered him one saying, "It's a tough hoof and my guys are dead tired. The meth will help."

"Great," Chuck spit out, "First we've got traitors, now we got strung out killers."

"Sometimes that's the best kind. Anyway, thought I'd offer."

While Chuck turned back to his pack to make sure everything was zipped up, he couldn't help but remember when the Army tested crystal methamphetamine on one of its own units. It was a reconnaissance outfit that had to go for days without sleep and to some brain trust in the Pentagon, speed seemed like a logical option. It worked too, except that 99% of the men suffered mild psychosis for days and weeks after they completed a no-sleep mission. They also showed very little conscience when killing innocent civilians in the line of fire. The Army junked the project in a hurry.

CHAPTER 23

The Dogs and their new partners were off on a long trek through a brutal landscape with sharp rocks and steep cliffs. They walked in silence for a while, trying to conserve their energy. But finally, it all got too boring for Chuck and he opened up a little to Bob.

"Why do you do it?" he asked him while slogging through the moonless and eerily quiet night.

"Why do I do what?"

"Fight for the bad guys."

"Excuse me ... who invaded who here?"

"Fair enough ... but still, why?"

"Why do you think?"

"For your country."

"For my country and Islam. Like it or not, I'm Afghan and more importantly, I'm Muslim and I'm tired of everyone sticking their noses into my country and trying to hijack my religion ... and that includes ISIS and Al Qaeda."

Surprised by his answer, all Chuck could say was, "But they're your people."

"Not mine. They're just another buncha' crazy fools."

"Then why are so many of yer' kinsmen joining 'em?"

"Do ya' really wanna' go there?"

"Why not? We've got the time."

"Okay. There are three reasons. First of all, a lot of 'em figure they would rather endure the jihadists' oppression than another ten years of fighting. They don't really like 'em, but they see them as the lesser of two evils ... kinda' like your presidential elections."

"You got that right," Chuck said, stumbling slightly on the rocky path.

"Secondly, everyone knows the Taliban honestly believes its own cold, heartless B.S. They believe their fanatical religious views are what makes a good Muslim and a lot of people are afraid they might be right."

"Yea, I get it," said Chuck, "My dad used to say many people probably believe in God because they're afraid not to. I guess the idea of goin' to hell or no afterlife at all is too scary for 'em."

"Something like that," said Bob, "But still, too many Muslims buy into their extremist bullshit and are true believers ... kinda' like your president and his followers."

"How do ya' make that connection?"

"Well, the jihadists aren't that different from the neo-con extremists in the White House. They both think theirs is the only true way and they'll go to great extremes to prove it."

"Yea, but the Taliban kills for it."

"And you don't?"

"We kill to give Iraqi's their freedom," Chuck said, doubting his own words before they even came out of his mouth.

"How? By putting the Shiites in power? They're just another buncha' tyrants and are oppressing the Sunnis just like they were oppressed under Hussein. Besides, it's your brand of freedom, which may not be right for them."

"Whatdya' mean ... *our* brand of freedom?"

"Well, your *free* democracy is based on the cooperation of the masses for the greater good. People have to cooperate with each other to make a democratic government work. My people are descended from fiercely independent nomads who are incapable of cooperating with anyone. It's in our genes."

"But wouldn't your people cooperate with each other if they saw that it would get them freedom of choice?"

"Do you really have freedom of choice or do you just think you do?"

"What the hell does that mean?"

"Could your idea of freedom be an illusion spoon-fed to you by your media? If you closely analyze many of the choices Americans make, you'll see that your biased and profit-driven media often brainwashes them into making them. For one thing, it has everyone convinced that they have to have all these non-essential things to be happy."

Where have I heard that before? Chuck thought. "Yeah, we are quite the consumer society."

"But it's more than that. You don't have to look much further than who you elected president. In the face of so much evidence to the contrary, Fox News convinced America that he was a good choice."

"Okay, okay. We're gettin' a little off-track here," Chuck said, feeling a little like he was talking to his father, "You said three reasons."

"Oh yeah. Most of all, it's probably the homeboy syndrome."

"The homeboy syndrome?"

"The homeboy syndrome. They're their homeboys. Any way you slice it, the ISIS idiots and Al Qaeda morons are their fellow Arabs and, as ruthless as they are, that makes 'em preferable to the white invaders who are on yet another crusade against them."

"Yea, that actually makes some sense."

"Don't sound so surprised Butch."

An eerie silence followed and as they wound their way around the twisting and turning trail Chuck looked long and hard at his new comrade in the moonlight. He was different than his men because the desert had not had time to burn its hard lines into him as it had in them. The harshness of this rough, desolate region had seared its way into their faces until you couldn't tell the difference between them and the land. The deep creases in their leather, craggy faces resembled the deep cracks in the dry, desert wadis. It was the desert gene that was deeply ingrained in all of them and growing in Bob.

Chuck broke the eerie silence with, "I probably shouldn't ask this but what do you think of our attempts to give the Iraqis democracy?"

"I guess I would say Americans are incredibly naïve if they think they can force a democracy on a people with a completely different set of values and world view."

"Yeah, I'm beginning to see that. But you gotta' admit, democracy is a hell of a lot better than what they had under Hussein."

"Maybe. Maybe not. But it's not a real democracy anyway."

"What does that mean?"

"Just that we Muslims can't trust any kind of democracy you Americans try to foist on us because the west's track record sucks."

"Huh?"

"Between the two world wars, the British and the French *allowed* us dumb Arabs to experiment with self-rule and our own democracy. But they always had a commission or some other body that let it go only so far. All of us, including the Iraqis, remember that and see Americans' democracy as a sham. You guys will always be calling the shots."

"Well, at least we got Hussein. You gotta' admit that was a good thing."

"Yes, it was, but you should've withdrawn once you got him and left the Iraqis to their own devices."

"It's funny ... that's what my old man says."

"Although, he *was* the only one strong enough to keep Iraq from the bloody civil war it's in now."

"Yeah, but how many did he kill in the process?"

"Not as many as your invasion," Bob said with one eye raised, "Who's the real terrorist ... the country defending itself from an outside invasion or the invader?"

"Oh, c'mon! You call us terrorists when Islamic extremists deliberately kill civilians."

"Many of us don't agree with that, but many also feel we have little choice because we don't have an organized military."

"Another one of dad's arguments. You sure we're not related?"

"Man, I hope not."

"Well, anyway, killing innocent women and children is pretty hard to justify any way you slice it."

"And you don't?"

"Well, not on purpose. We only go after military targets ... but there's always gonna' be collateral damage."

"Whatever the intent, the result is the same. Besides America lost its moral high ground when it started torturing prisoners."

"You mean water-boarding?"

"Yeah and sending them to other countries to do a lot worse."

"But don't you fight fire with fire and hasn't it prevented some attacks?"

"That's what your spooks tell us, but their business is lying. The problem is it makes you look like the bad guy and it's increasing your enemy's recruitment."

"That's what I hear." Chuck remembered his father saying the same thing.

"Well, it's kinda' hard to tell people you're fightin' for their human rights when you keep violating them ... and Guantanamo didn't help much either."

"What's that mean?"

"It means that you've got the wrong guys to begin with. In the beginning yer' country paid the militants ... especially my country's warlords ... a bounty to turn in *terrorists* and you paid more for leaders. So, they rounded up anyone they could find and sold them to the CIA who took 'em to Guantanamo."

"Who were they?"

"Some of 'em were young Pakistanis who crossed the border to fight and knew nothing about Al Qaeda's leadership. Many weren't fanatics when they went to Guantanamo, but they sure were when they got out. They were recruited to the cause inside because it was easy to see that the Americans were the bad guys."

"How do ya' know all this?"

"See that guy over there," Bob pointed to one of his men.

"Yeah."

"He was a simple opium farmer when a local warlord sold him to the spooks. By the time they let him go, he was a full-fledged recruit. But, what's the point of all this anyway?

"Whatdya' mean?"

"What're we doin' here with all this deep political discussion between two people who are accidental allies today and probably enemies tomorrow?"

"I dunno'. I guess it passes the time." Chuck was also surprised at how wide-ranging the conversation had gotten with this stranger, but he was intrigued even though it was making his already-serious doubts about the war much worse. But not wanting to dwell on those doubts, he went back to the root of his argument with, "All we ever wanted was to give you democracy."

"And that's the problem isn't it. You can't *give* a country a democracy. It has to develop one on its own ... or not. Besides, at what cost?"

"Whatdya' mean?"

"Your attempt to *give* us a democracy is basically ruining our next generation."

"How's that?"

"Well, the Iraqi Association of Psychologists says a third of the kids there have post-traumatic stress disorder and 92% of them show signs of learning impediments."

"You mean there actually is an Iraqi Association of Psychologists?"

"Oh yes ... we even have doctors and lawyers over here."

"Point well taken. But hey, we're trying to build 'em schools. The jihadists keep blowing 'em up."

"And who started the war? You did with the invasion. Besides, you can't give a country a democracy by invading it. If you want them to adopt democracy you have to set a democratic example and America hasn't exactly done that."

"We haven't?" Chuck regretted the question as soon as he asked it and again he felt like he was talking to his father.

"You know what I mean. Were you championing democracy when you overthrew the democratically-elected leader of Iran and installed the Shaw in his place? How'd that work out for ya'?"

"Okay, that's one example.

"Were you championing democracy when you forced Israel on us, giving us no say in the matter? And then, was it democracy that made you supply the Israelis with the weapons that kill thousands of Palestinians?"

"We were just trying to protect our security."

"Well, so are we. Besides, you were really just trying to steal our oil."

"Don't you mean buy it?"

"Buy ... steal ... what's the difference when you're filling the pockets of royal families and dictators who oppress their people. Besides, that oil belongs to the people, not the ruling families, but somehow the huge oil wealth never makes its way down to them."

"Okay, okay," Chuck said waving his hand in surrender. "I guess I just don't get why the Iraqi's don't see that a unified Iraq is in their best interest and try to get along."

"Because they're Arabs and this is the Middle-East."

"Now what the hell does that mean?"

"It means, my ethnocentric friend, just what it says. Ya' ever heard of the scorpion and the frog?"

"The what and the who?

"The scorpion and the frog. Well, the scorpion can't swim and he asks the frog for a ride across the river. The frog says no because the scorpion might sting him, to which the scorpion says 'I won't sting you because then we'll both drown.' So, the frog gives him a ride and halfway across, the scorpion stings him with its deadly poison. As they're sinking, the frog says 'Why did you do that ... now we're both gonna' die.' Ya' know what the scorpion says?"

"No, but I'm sure yer' gonna' tell me."

"The scorpion says simply 'This is the Middle-East.'"

"I thought he said it was in his nature.

"And I thought you never heard the story."

"I lied."

"Well he did say that, but I like the Middle-East better because it kinda' describes the nature of many Middle-Easterners and explains the unexplainable over here."

"Nice fairy tales you guys grow up with."

"Oh no, our fairy tales are a lot worse than that. Besides, this is one of yours ... adapted to our culture of course."

"So, what's the point ... that there's no hope for the Middle-East? That it will ultimately devour itself?"

"Maybe, but probably not. It's just that it's really none of your business. We will have to find our own way and it probably won't be the same as yours. And we need to do it without outside interference."

"So yer' fightin' ISIS today and it may be us tomorrow."

"Now you got it. My friend one day will be my enemy the next."

"And vice-versa."

"Right ... kinda' like how Iraq was your friend one day and your enemy the next."

At that moment, Bob broke off from the group and led them down a side path. Apparently nearing the end of their arduous journey, Chuck thought about how difficult it was to reconcile this articulate, highly educated, and logical man with the fierce and brutal warrior he had recently seen on the battlefield. Never had he seen such an instinctive fighting man. He clearly had a talent for killing, yet Chuck sensed that he had a disdain for doing it. His men, on the other hand, seemed to have no such compunction. He had noticed in Garmser that they killed without discretion. Women, children, dogs, cats, it didn't matter. If it moved, they shot it, making no distinction between them and their foes. But there was no more time for reflection as they saw a dim, flashing light up ahead.

* * *

Jasnine was finishing up her analysis of the bones when there was a knock at the door. She opened it to see Dr. Yusef Mohammed decked out in his standard dark suit and sunglasses. *Man, he's a good-looking terrorist*, she thought.

"I understand your work is almost complete," he said, "and I would like to talk to you about another matter."

"Sure thing," she answered, "just let me finish up here and I'll be right with you."

"I'll be in the office when you're ready."

When Jasnine entered the office Yusef was alone. "What can I do for you Dr. Mohammed?" she asked.

"Well, it's more what I can do for you. How would you like to make $150,000 to do what you do best?"

"And what's that?" she said skeptically.

"Appraise some ancient artifacts."

"$150,000 for appraisals huh. Sounds a little hinky."

"Nothing hinky. These are genuine artifacts, legally excavated from my country. They just need appraisal."

"Can I see some of them before I answer?"

"Absolutely ... as long as you don't mind going for another blindfolded drive."

"They're not here?"

"No, we have them stored in a more preservative environment and a more secure place."

"Well, what's their estimated value?"

"It ranges, but many are invaluable. After all, we are the cradle of civilization and have treasures from the Roman, Greek, Byzantine, and Islamic periods. There are 10,000 archeological digs in Iraq right now and we have the best of the best."

The Middle East is unique for its overlapping civilizations which left it with an array of sites and monuments ranging from prehistoric to modern Islamic times.

Jasnine knew better than to ask who the *we* was, but she had a pretty good idea. They were people who controlled a very large portion of the ancient antiquity trade in Iraq and Syria and they were making inroads in Libya. Estimates were that they controlled about 4,500 archeological sites and dealt in over 100,000 valuable artifacts. Illegal excavation of antiquities had been going on in the Mesopotamian area for decades, which is why many areas are full of spider holes. But these people took it to a whole new level.

Until recently, looting was carried out by various armed groups or individuals or even governments. Yusef's group consolidated the whole process into an industry. They buy their own excavation equipment and hire their own archeologists and digging teams. They even license local people to dig and charge them a 20% tax on anything they find. Of course, they keep the big stuff for themselves.

They use existing smuggling and criminal networks that have trafficked drugs, people, and other contraband for many years. The goods are transported along 1000-year-old smuggling routes and sometimes guns are brought back in over the same routes. The objects usually pass first through Turkey or Lebanon before being moved to Switzerland, Germany or Italy. They usually change hands several times along the way, creating a paper trail that is used to sell them to auction houses in London and New York. Many go to dealers and buyers in Vienna, Munich, London, New York, Tokyo, and Paris. Dealers use the legal trade in antiquities to move artifacts that have been looted for decades amid conflicts in Syria, Iraq, Yemen, Egypt, and Libya. The group has gotten so brazen in recent years that it sometimes sells its booty online or through established connections with private collectors. Interestingly, Pre-Islamic artifacts seem to go to Europe and the USA, while Islamic art often goes to countries on the Persian Gulf.

Estimates are that the group makes about 150 to 200 million dollars a year, although some estimates are much lower. But it still makes illicit antiquity sales its second highest revenue generator. Their biggest source of income is selling oil on the black market. They were ISIS and they could be ruthlessly cruel to anyone that gets in their way.

"Well Dr. Ahmed, what do you think," asked Mohammed, "Do you want to come work for us?"

"It depends on the artifacts, but if I like what I see ... throw in the dinosaur bones and we might have a deal."

"That has always been my plan. Shall we go?"

"Yes, let's," she said, knowing she would have to be extra-careful on this one.

* * *

Exhausted, the Dogs and the militants followed the flashing light to their final destination they breathed a sigh of relief. They had reached the horses that would take them to their next assignment and they had the whole day to rest and prepare for that night's journey. Their mission was to blow up a key bridge between Afghanistan and Pakistan and the convoy of trucks on it. The Taliban used the bridge to cross into Afghanistan to attack coalition forces and to smuggle heroin into Pakistan. Normally they would destroy it from the air with smart bombs, but there was a big problem with that. It had a radar station that would detect any incoming jets and give them time to clear the viaduct.

Besides that, technically, it was located a few hundred meters inside Pakistan, who was America's ally, and the military was worried about political fallout. They needed it to look like a rival warlord did it. It was also now a hotbed of Islamic militants and extremist training camps were springing up all over the place.

What made this caravan a particularly valuable target was the fact that for the first time ever, high-ranking leaders from ISIS, Al Qaeda, and the Taliban were purported to be in it. Informants said they would be coming from their first-ever meeting to explore ways their armies could work together and finance it with a pooled smuggling arrangement and this caravan was the first test case.

"A divided enemy we can handle," Colonel Singleton had said, "But a united one ... not so much."

As an added bonus, Intelligence said ISIS had a new chemist who had figured out a way to make more heroin out of the opium poppies more efficiently and an informant said he would be in the caravan.

To make matters more complicated, the Army wanted to blow up the convoy while it was crossing the bridge to make sure it got the leaders and the most opium possible to make a dramatic statement. The bridge was too big to hurl explosives at it the way they did at the minarets in Garmser and exact placement was crucial. That meant they would have to move in closer to the guards than they liked. It was a risky mission, but then *aren't they all?* The plan was to ride all night, conduct reconnaissance the next day, and hopefully plant the C-4 and blow the bridge the next night.

All the dogs were expert horsemen, but they had a few things to learn from their militia partners about riding through the rough, spikey mountains at night. The trails were narrow and one false step could send horse and rider tumbling over a 5000-foot cliff. The Dogs were amazed that even strung out on meth, the warlord's men expertly picked their way along the path as if they were one with the horses and the land. They also seemed to be natural warriors and Chuck wondered if they were so used to fighting that they forgot what they were fighting for. *Maybe it's just a way of life for them*, he thought.

They got to within a mile of the bridge just before daylight and Bob quickly led them to a small valley. "What?" said Chuck looking around and seeing nothing. Without answering, Bob and his men dismounted and started pulling some dead branches off of a mountainside. Chuck and the Dogs figured it out just as the last branch was tossed aside to reveal a cave cut into the mountain and they all silently led their horses into it.

"This is our home for the day," Bob said once they were inside, "We rest and then we recon the bridge. Did you bring enough night goggles and C-4 for us?"

This was a dicey question as Chuck knew how dangerous it was to give combat equipment to someone who might very well be your enemy in the future. So, he said, "You guys got us here and we need your help with the recon, but we'll plant the bombs tonight."

"Just sayin' if ya' got any extra, I'll give ya' 20,000 for it."

"Dollars?"

"No, rubles ... ya' moron. Yes, dollars."

Chuck was a bit taken aback that Bob would pay that much, let alone that he might be carrying that kind of money around with him. "Don't think so," was all he could muster.

"Can't blame a guy for trying," laughed Bob and they both shared a smile. Both knew that if he did loan them night vision goggles they would keep them and they would certainly skim off any C-4 they could get. Both also knew that the stuff might be used against Chuck and the Dogs in the future.

"Better get some sleep now and we'll take a look at the bridge later." Both men were used to going without sleep and catching catnaps here and there to make up for it.

Staring at the horses and ever the observant one, Jim Hawkins asked no one in particular, "How and why do horses sleep standing up?" No one paid any attention as they bedded down for a nap.

About mid-day Chuck roused his men and they began gathering sticks and scrub brush together from outside of the cave. They methodically wove them together with twine while the militia men laughed and made fun of them in Arabic.

"So, you wear women's clothes and you sew them too," cackled Bob, joining in with the laughter.

"Beats bein' seen through binoculars and gettin' yer' head blown off," Chuck said easily.

Bob said something to his men in Arabic and they all stopped laughing. "Can you show us?" he asked, suddenly serious. He and his men had never used camouflage and always felt like they simply blended in with the landscape, which they often did.

"That's the plan," Chuck smiled, "Turn around and I'll do your wardrobe." The Dogs had used this type of camouflage many times before, mostly on sniper missions where they had to lie on their bellies for hours, waiting for their target to appear in their long-range scopes.

"Turn around 'ay? I knew you were gay."

"About as gay as you and your sheep bangers."

"I resent that," Bob said with a sly grin, "We prefer goats."

"I thought you liked little boys. What's that old Arab saying? Oh yeah, women are for children, boys are for pleasure."

For the first time since they joined forces, Chuck thought he noticed Bob looking a bit uncomfortable, but he regained his composure quickly and said, "You mean like your Catholic priests?"

"Well, not exactly." Now it was Chuck's turn to feel uneasy.

Sensing it and wanting to get back to the ribbing word-play, Bob gave him an opening with, "Well, we do love our goats."

"And do you screw 'em before or after you slit their throats?" Chuck recouped.

"Depends on how good lookin' they are," Bob whipped back.

"Well, I've seen yer' women so I don't blame you."

Bob feigned insult and said, "Don't let the veil fool you, they're hot under that abaya."

"Yea, hot and sweaty in that get-up."

"The sweatier the better. It's the smell of animal lust."

"More like animal shit."

"Okay, okay. That's enough cultural sensitivity. Are ya' gonna' dress me or what?" Bob said without pause, turning his back to Chuck who now strapped a camouflage outfit around his neck and waist. He had to reach around his body to do it and Bob chortled "I knew it."

Ignoring him, Chuck said, "If you crawl on all fours..."

"Again, with the gay stuff."

"If you crawl on all fours," Chuck said again in an exaggerated voice, "yer' virtually invisible, even with long range binocs."

"Thanks ... even if you are a fairy."

"Yeah, well I'd rather be a live homo than a dead hetero."

"Me too," Bob said as he showed his laughing men how to put on the camouflage.

CHAPTER 24

When they finished all the camouflage suits, the Mad Dogs and Bob's men crept out of the cave one-by-one and moved toward their target, knowing the land around them was probably being scanned by guards with field glasses. They climbed up a slight incline and saw about ten men walking back and forth on the bridge and several stationed underneath it on each side of the gorge. It took all day, but using digital, long-range binoculars they located the spots underneath the viaduct where they would have to place the C-4 and pointed laser beams at them so they could see them in the dark. They then turned the beams off and slowly and carefully crawled back to the cave. All there was to do now was wait for nightfall.

Although they were supposed to be resting, Chuck couldn't and plopped down by Bob. "Well, one thing you gotta' admit is that the Qur'an is not really about peace and love. I mean, it says kill the infidel ... kill non-Muslims."

"Actually, that's an old misconception," Bob answered, a little surprised, "That's only in self-defense and as a last resort. It actually tells us that there is no compulsion in religion and to respect others' beliefs."

"I musta' missed that."

"Then there's the one that says, 'Oh prophet! Exhort them, your task is only to exhort; you cannot compel them to believe.'"

"Well, I've read it and what I come away with is a lot more anti-infidel than that."

"Each to his own, but what about your Bible?"

"What about it?"

"Doesn't Exodus 31:15 say, 'Anyone who does work on the Sabbath day shall be put to death?'"

"Maybe."

"And doesn't Deuteronomy 25:11 and 12 say if a guy is in a fight and his wife grabs the other guy's balls you should cut off her hand and show no pity?"

"Don't know about that one."

"Or how about Genesis 38:8 that tells a guy whose brother has died to screw the brother's wife and raise their offspring."

"That's the way they did things back then."

"Yeah, but this guy knew the offspring wouldn't be his and instead of buggerin' his sister-in-law, he jacked off on the ground and God killed him for it."

"Well, maybe that was just a parable."

"Maybe, but what kind of message does that send? I guess it justifies the dogmatic Catholic belief that spilling your seed outside of a woman's pussy is a sin, but killing the guy? Come on ... we'd have to kill everyone."

"Speak for yourself."

"Oh, so you never choked the chicken."

"Well, at least I never fucked a sheep."

"Remember," said Jim Hawkins, listening in on their conversation, "They prefer goats ... and the secret is stuffing their hind hooves into your boots so they can't get away."

Both men looked at Hawkins like he was from another planet as he once again, took a joke a little too far."

"Anyway," said Bob, "What about your Bible's obsession with cock and balls?"

"What the hell?"

"Yeah, Deuteronomy 23:1 says 'no one whose testicles are crushed or whose male organ is cut off shall enter the assembly of the Lord.'"

Chuck was amazed at Bob's Biblical knowledge and its specificity had him stymied.

"Okay, okay. So, you know your Bible," Chuck said in growing frustration.

"You mean, *your* Bible," Bob corrected.

"O. K. My Bible. But you can't take one or two verses and define the whole book by them."

"Kinda' like people do with the Qua'ran?"

"Fair enough."

"Well, are ya' surprised that an uncivilized Arab would know all this stuff?"

"I didn't mean that ... but I guess Americans can be a little holier-than-thou."

"Really ... ya' think."

"Yea, but that's just cuz' we're the superior race."

"I guess I walked into that one," Bob chuckled, "But you guys do think you're the center of the universe and better than everyone else."

"Maybe."

"Definitely. Ya' know how they call someone who speaks two languages bilingual and someone who speaks three languages trilingual?"

"Yeah, so what?"

"Well, you know what they call someone who speaks one language?"

"Ya' got me ... what?"

"American."

"Very funny. But I think they actually call someone who speaks three languages multilingual, not trilingual. In fact, I don't think trilingual is even a word."

"I rest my case. I guess you're just smarter than us."

Chuck regretted making the correction but he didn't want to go there. Night was approaching anyway and it was time to get ready.

The Dogs crept out of the cave and headed toward the bridge followed by Bob's men who would cover their retreat in case they were spotted. Dusk was a special time for black-ops soldiers because its twilight murkiness made it hard for the enemy to distinguish things on the landscape they surveyed. Chuck crawled up to the first laser pointer and waited for his men to get to the others. By the time the last man got to his laser it was pitch black on the mountainside and all the men put on their infra-red, night-vision goggles. He turned his laser light on and at one-minute intervals each man turned his on so that they wouldn't all go on at the same time. It probably wouldn't have mattered anyway because each had a tiny screen in front of the laser beam that prevented the jihadists from seeing it. But he preferred not taking any more chances than he had to. The plan was for the Dogs to place their explosives at the laser targets and for the warlord militiamen to detonate them by radio signal once the Taliban troops were on the bridge, hopefully after the Dogs had returned.

When the lasers were all on, Chuck began his methodical descent, carefully picking his way along, not wanting to knock any rocks loose that might roll down the mountainside and alert the guards. The next Dog began his crawl three minutes later, the next three minutes after that, and so on down the line. Each man crawled for exactly three minutes following the laser beam and stopped so that only one man moved at a time. When all were stopped Chuck started the process all over again. Even in the dark, one moving object was a lot harder to see than several moving at the same time. Besides, they couldn't be sure that the Taliban guards didn't have night-vision goggles themselves.

Two hours later, after a painstakingly slow crawl over steep and treacherous rocks, each man was within ten feet of his destination. Each knew what he had to do and he did it. With the same tediousness as the climb down the mountain, they slowly crawled to their targets to plant the explosives. Mike Sandstone had the most difficult job because his two laser targets were toward the middle of the bridge, which meant he had to climb out over the gorge to get to them. Normally Chuck would have taken on such a dangerous assignment himself, but Mike's gymnastics background made him more qualified. He also carried a potato gun, which would silently shoot a ball of C-4 covered with strong adhesive at the last laser target toward the middle of the bridge.

So far everything was going like clockwork. They planted their explosives and now awaited Mike's return from the middle of the bridge. But that worried Chuck. Every mission he had ever conducted had some problems. Some were minor and some major. Most, however, had occurred early enough in the mission to solve. It was the ones that cropped up late in the game that were the most deadly. *Maybe this will be the one with no problems*, he thought hopefully. He secretly hoped that Garmser had given them enough problems to last for a few missions.

But it was not to be. Mike Sandstone had successfully planted his first C-4 and shot his second at the girder out in the middle of the structure using the laser beam as a target. It had stuck and he was on his way back. But as ill luck would have it, just as he set foot on solid ground he slipped slightly on an unseen small pile of rocks sending some of them rolling down into the gorge with a slight "plunk." Chuck was still under the bridge and froze in position, hidden from view by a network of steel girders. Sergeant John Borland and Privates Hanson and Walker weren't so lucky as they had made it out from under it. They quickly laid down and went into the prone position. *All that way and now he slips*, Chuck thought more-than-anxiously.

A guard must have heard the noise because suddenly a bright spotlight went on and aimed in Private Sandstone's direction. Luckily, he had made it back under the bridge and was hidden by steel girders and cement supports. Borland, Hanson, and Walker felt grateful to Chuck for making everyone wear their camouflage suits, which now hid them from view. The light shined directly at all of them, but they looked like part of the landscape and after sweeping back and forth a few times it went dark.

Everyone breathed a heavy sigh of relief and then waited the obligatory 20 minutes before moving again. Chuck waved his hand slightly and they began their slow retreat. But Sandstone instantly knew something was wrong as he caught a slight movement out of the corner of his eye. He froze in position and waited. Then there it was again. Unmistakably it was an enemy soldier moving toward him. Mike rightly figured he must be double-checking the falling rocks they had heard earlier. Without a sound he bent down and laid on his stomach with the camouflage over him, desperately hoping the soldier wouldn't notice the out-of-place scrub brush on this rocky ground. Seeing Mike lay down, the rest of the Dogs stood still and waited. It was the moment of truth and several of them prayed.

Meanwhile, back up on the mountain, Jim Hawkins had a bead on the Taliban guard near Sandstone and each of the Dogs took his own aim at other guards up on the bridge. Unbeknownst to Chuck, his newfound partners had their own night-vision binoculars and night scopes on their guns, given to their warlord boss by the U.S. Military, and their guns were now trained on the rest of the guards.

Bob didn't want to shoot because he knew all hell would break loose and the Dogs would probably never get out of there alive. But on the other hand, if he did shoot, it might give them a head start on getting away before the bridge blew. It was a Catch 22 and all he could do was wait and hope that the guard walked on by Mike without noticing him. There was probably about a 30/70 chance of that, but it was better than nothing.

Back under the bridge, the guard investigating the noise walked slowly around the pylons trying to focus his vision in the eerie darkness. He heard a crunching sound underneath his foot and stopped abruptly. His brain told him that there shouldn't be any scrub brush in this area and very few sticks to make a sound like that, but it didn't actually register as a suspicion. He was about to take another step and go back up to the bridge when something strange caught his eye. It was a tiny red dot on one of the bridge supports and even this peasant soldier knew what it was. Quickly he grabbed for the whistle around his neck and raised it to his mouth. When Chuck saw his hand go up, he immediately raised his gun while silently cursing Bob for not turning the lasers off like he was supposed to do. But instead of a gunshot or a high-pitched whistle, there was only a thud and the sound of a collapsing body. Greg Hanson had thrown a knife and hit the guard dead-center in his heart, killing him instantly before he could blow his whistle.

The Dogs all took a collective breath, but just as they started to get up to make their slow retreat they heard a thunderous roar coming from the Afghanistan side of the gorge. *Gotta' be the Taliban*, realized Chuck, *they're early.* Now there was no time for a slow climb back up the mountain as he motioned for his men to stay put. He also signaled for them to get ready. As always, he waited until the very last second, when he heard the trucks driving onto the bridge overhead. Then, with a sudden jerk of his hand they all ran for the edge of the gorge at full speed while he tapped his belt radio three times.

Bob heard the pre-arranged radio signal and yelled "Etlaq el nar!" (*Open fire!*) while pushing the detonator-button on his radio transmitter. His men and the rest of the Dogs opened up in a fuselage of furious gunfire at the soldiers on both sides of the bridge as if they had been storing up a massive amount of killing just aching to get out. Of course, their expert sniper rifles had already registered the exact distance of each target and they had calibrated the precision of each kill before they pulled the first trigger. But that just made the killing more fun.

"Good luck Butch," Bob whispered as he joined in on the sniper massacre, distracted by the results of his time-delayed radio detonation. The huge explosions were surreal as parts of the bridge began breaking apart and falling down into the gorge in what seemed like slow-motion, taking trucks and men with it. Bob and his men saw the scene before they heard it and it was like watching an old silent movie. Giant slabs of concrete and big steel girders flew in all directions. It really was like a movie as they watched the Taliban convoy go down with the collapsing bridge.

Bob heard his men cheering between sniper shots as they saw a strange sight descending the gorge about 100 yards away. Chuck and his men had exercised their back-up plan of base jumping off the cliff in short range parachutes and if the militia hadn't provided cover fire they would have been sitting ducks for the Taliban riflemen. They would have shined their spotlights on them, but they had them trained on the hill, never dreaming anyone would be flying down the canyon.

"Yee Haw!" screamed Ron Jenkins as he steered his chute past Chuck, "This is better'n a tornado in a trailer park." All the Dogs were expert paratroopers and they used the gorge's updrafts to guide them away from the melee of exploding cement and girders and toward the pre-arranged meeting place. *I hope he gets there*, was all Chuck thought as he glanced back at the bridge and noticed that not all the trucks had made it onto the viaduct. Bob was supposed to wait until a maximum number of trucks and men were on the bridge to blow it. But now he glided down the canyon thankful that whatever happened, his men had given them cover fire to escape.

Meanwhile, back at the smoking gorge, they finished off the remaining Taliban soldiers and walked down to inspect their handiwork. After shooting a few stragglers, they walked over to the trucks that hadn't made it onto the bridge and checked their contents. "Voila," Bob said with a look of satisfaction. "Kamel, you and Mojo take the horses. The rest of you take the trucks home and we'll meet at camp." The remaining Mad Dogs then watched him walk over to where the bridge had once been and light up a cigarette. Inhaling his first puff deeply and letting it out slowly, he mumbled, "Not bad for a day's work. Boys ... let's get your horses."

The surviving trucks were full of raw opium that belonged to a rival warlord. Not only had he severely interrupted his rival's supply line, but he had nabbed several million dollars-worth of opium for himself. "Thanks Butch," he said as he flipped the cigarette over the cliff and walked toward the cave. He had to meet Chuck and his men about 10 miles down the gorge and he didn't want to be late.

* * *

"More caffeine!" Mark blurted out and with that, he returned to work with a vengeance.

Eight hours of research turned up some startling information that brought him to one undeniable conclusion. *I've been looking in the wrong place. Chemical factories are a bigger threat than nuclear power plants.*

He found that there are nearly 30 times more chemical factories than nuclear facilities around the world and they appear to be much more vulnerable to a terrorist attack. The 14,000 chemical companies in 90 countries produce 21,500 chemical products and many of them could be deadly if released into the atmosphere. The clincher is that there are no global standards for protection against attacks on the plants and most have inadequate security. Many of the factories and storage sites are located near large population centers making them perfect terrorist targets and some extremist groups apparently know it. Copies of U.S. chemical trade magazines were even found in one of Osama Bin Laden's hideouts. Then he read a disturbing report by the Chemical Manufacturers Association that said, "Put in the right place, bombs can deliver the equivalent destructive power of a weapon of mass destruction."

The lack of security shocked Mark at first, but further research explained why. The world runs on chemicals and the chemical industry wields a lot of power and has extensive influence with governments around the world. In the U.S. alone, the industry makes up about 2 percent of the gross domestic product and is the country's biggest exporter. It directly employs almost 1 million people and accounts for about five-and-a-half million more jobs in other areas. *Always the money*, Mark thought, *money trumps everything, even human life.*

He was right in a sense. Like any business, chemical companies want to make as much money as possible and cutting corners on security can help them do that. More profit makes everyone happy. The company CEO gets a big bonus, the stockholders get their dividends, and millions of people see their retirement accounts go up. Of course, that is if the factories have no big disasters resulting in billion-dollar lawsuits.

Immediately realizing that Europe and the United States would be the most likely targets, he decided to focus his research on both. He figured that his nuclear power research had been too broad and his chemical plant research needed to be more narrow and focused. He did see that Chechen rebels had planned to bomb a chemical plant in Russia at one time, but that seemed to be an isolated case. *If ISIS wants to make a big statement against western imperialism,* he thought, *this would be the way to do it.*

Mark's research turned up a number of past attacks on chemical factories and storage sites, but he knew he needed future, not past attacks, and he kept looking. One thing he did notice was that many of the places that were attacked were close to cities and towns and had loading docks, trains, trucks, and even ships loaded with chlorine, flammable liquid pesticides, acids, and liquefied petroleum gases. He found several past attacks, including one on an industrial gases plant near Lyon, France and another that ended with a foiled plan to blow up two 12-million-gallon liquid propane tanks about a mile from a residential area in Sacramento, California. Mark figured that there were probably a lot more that never got reported since chemical companies rarely report their security breaches.

More research found that cyber-attacks on industries around the world have increased dramatically over the last few years and chemical factories may be especially susceptible to them. They may be even more vulnerable than nuclear power plants because many of them have outdated safety and security systems, which makes them easier targets. A cyber-attack could shut down those systems and cause too much venting of dangerous fumes, a spill, or even an explosion.

Realizing what a major threat all this could be, he began looking into likely targets and what he found in the U.S. alone made him wince. Chorine gas, sulfur dioxide, and hydrogen fluoride appeared to be three of the biggest threats. A New Jersey chemical company's 180,000 pounds of chlorine or sulfur dioxide could form a cloud that could endanger 12-million people. At chemical plants in Michigan and California, a rupture of one of their 90-ton rail cars of chlorine could threaten 3 to 4 million people. The list went on and on and this was just in the U.S. There were many more in Europe.

Mark decided that the only way to narrow the huge list down to some likely targets was to use the same method he used for the nuclear power plants and feed each chemical facility into *Prophecy* individually. He knew it would take a long time and he desperately hoped that it would yield significant results. His research project, not to mention the lives of millions of people, could depend on it.

* * *

Maneuvering a parachute down a sometimes-narrow gorge in the dark took some real precision, even with night-vision goggles on. One slightly inexact tug on a guideline could send you crashing into a jagged cliff, so the Dogs tried to fly a straight and narrow path down the deep crevasse. All except Ron Jenkins that is, the most experienced skydiver of the bunch with more than 1000 jumps under his belt. That along with his 20/20 natural night-vision made him a little too cocky. He soared ahead of Chuck and the other Dogs and began literally flying back and forth, coming daringly close to the rock cliffs while singing the Lenny Kravitz song, "I want to Fly Away" gratingly off-key. Chuck often gave his men a lot of leeway to do crazy, daredevil things because he knew that the craziness was part of what made them great soldiers. Laughing in the face of death and always pushing the boundaries of safety might seem foolhardy to some, but it was what gave them an edge in tough situations. Here in this dangerous gorge, however, he knew his private was going too far, even if he was an expert jumpmaster. Then, suddenly the singing stopped.

A sudden updraft ricocheted Jenkins around the gorge like a shiny ball in a full-tilt pinball game. It blew him a little too close to a rock outcropping and he saw the small tree branch sticking out of it a second too late. The jagged branch barely caught the edge of his chute and it acted like a recoiling rubber band, slamming him into the side of the gorge with a sickening thud. It was like bungee jumping straight into a brick wall and it knocked him out cold.

Chuck was right behind him and knew he had to act instantaneously if he was going to help his crazy comrade. He steered his parachute directly at Jenkins whose limp body now hung from the rocks, blood streaming down his face. Guiding his chute with his left hand and pulling out his knife with his right, he knew he had only seconds and would get only one shot at it. If he made one wrong move, his canopy would probably lose air as well and they would both be lost. Slowing his chute down right before he reached Jenkins' limp, hanging figure, he locked his muscular legs around his torso while he sliced through his drooping nylon parachute lines. Because of the abrupt stop, his own chute was already starting to collapse and the two entwined bodies started to bounce down the rock wall. Trying to grab onto any foothold he could find, Chuck quickly realized it was futile to think he could hang onto the rocks. He quickly snapped a large clamp onto Jenkins' belt so that they were now strapped together and desperately jump-kicked away from the canyon wall, hoping to catch some unlikely air in his parachute.

But instead, they fell awkwardly with their communal chute catching sporadic puffs of air and slowing their descent in brief spurts. Chuck desperately yanked on the guide wires to maneuver the chute open. It was difficult as his legs were wrapped tightly around Jenkins in a death grip and they started to cramp. Still they dropped and Chuck knew it would soon be a moot point as they would be too low even if the chute did catch some air. He was afraid he had finally run out of his famous "Chuck Luck" as his men called it. *Maybe I did go too far this time,* he thought with his one big regret that he was taking one of his men with him. *Maybe I should have left Ron hanging on the rocks.* But then, that wouldn't have been Chuck.

"Lord," he gasped out loud, "I get you not saving me, but would you please save this dumb bastard?" Now Chuck began peeling off his parachute backpack. As they plunged downward, he clumsily tried to wrap its straps around Jenkins' shoulders, while at the same time unhooking the clamp that joined them together. He thought maybe without his weight, the parachute might somehow catch some air and he knew he had just seconds to see if he was right. He also knew he was asking for a miracle and he didn't miss the irony of asking for divine intervention on the one hand while committing suicide on the other. But he had no other options. *Better one of us live than both of us die.*

In a marvel of coordination as they plummeted in jerky motions, he got the backpack on Jenkins and with his cramped legs still wrapped tightly around him, started to unhook the clamp so he could freefall away from him the rest of the way to the bottom. Then he felt it. First it was only a slight breeze. But it quickly turned into a gust of cool air rushing up from below and he thought he was hallucinating. *Too late,* he thought, *we're too low!*

Nevertheless, he held on for a few more precious seconds and here it came with full force. He didn't know how or why, but a strong blast of air burst out of nowhere and suddenly inflated the parachute significantly slowing their descent. He quickly wrenched the toggles and then let up on them, maneuvering the chute to catch as much air as possible. Then another miracle happened. They actually started moving upward. A flicker of hope flashed in Chuck's eyes as they momentarily hung in mid-air limbo, his legs still wrapped around Jenkins and the clamp still holding them together. He now tried to guess which way the wind would blow and to steer the chute in that direction to take advantage of every gasp of air the updraft could spit out. It was difficult because the chute was now attached to Jenkins.

Looking up for the first time, he could see the dawn's first few shards of golden sunlight glinting off of something high above him. Then, to his astonishment, the two suspended bodies slowly started to resume their sail down the length of the canyon and *wait ... it can't be! We're going up!* They jerkily glided forward and upward for a good thirty seconds. *Impossible* was the only word he could think of.

But the glimmer of hope began to fade like the air that left his chute as the upwind suddenly died as fast as it had come and the canopy began to collapse once again. The impossibility of it all came crashing back in on him. It was now almost like the air was being sucked out of the gorge by a giant vacuum cleaner and the pre-dawn air became eerily still.

It was another spinning plunge and glancing down, Chuck thought he could barely make out the outline of the ground coming up fast. Their brief ascension had bought them a little time, but he knew it wouldn't be enough as he once again desperately tried to unhook the clamp so that Jenkins could fall by himself. He knew it was over for him, but hoped beyond reason for another miraculous updraft that might stall his comrade's fall.

Strangely, as he reached for the flailing clamp, he felt no fear whatsoever. All he felt was a sort of blissful acceptance of the inevitable. He had always wondered if he really was not afraid of death or if it had all been an act of bravado. Now he knew it was no act, but he still felt one deep regret: taking Ron Jenkins with him. All within a matter of seconds he fleetingly wondered if getting his man killed was just one more nail in the coffin of an overall failed war fought for all the wrong reasons. And what about the morality? *Is there any?* He guessed he would never know the answer to that question as he finally got a firm grip on the clamp.

CHAPTER 25

Chuck always wondered what imminent, certain death was like and now, as he again plummeted downward in jerks and starts with a flaring chute, he knew. He hesitated a few precious seconds in unclamping himself from the still-unconscious Jenkins and suddenly experienced what the Dogs called *slow time*. That's when everything around you slows down to a snail's pace and Chuck thought he could actually see the air slowly whooshing by his face. *No time for slow time*, he realized as he once again pushed in the clamp lever to unhook them while trying to unwrap his painfully cramped legs from around his comrade's torso.

No life flashed before his eyes as the airless parachute flailed in the still morning air, spinning faster and faster toward the hard-scratch canyon floor. There were no thoughts of mom. No thoughts of dad. No thoughts of his brother Mike or of past loves. No thoughts of anything. There was just a resigned acceptance of death and failure and a desperate desire to free himself from Jenkins' limp body. All this in barely a few seconds with the wind rushing by his ears and right through his body. He did have one fleeting thought about whether it had all been worth it, but he had no time to pursue it as yet another miracle seemed to be in the making.

Once again, just as the clamp and his legs were about to set Jenkins free, their descent seemed to slow down by a slight hair. He knew it couldn't be an updraft this low to the ground and besides, looking up, he saw that the parachute was still collapsed in a long stretch of nylon. It didn't register in his over-taxed brain that it was no longer flailing in the wind. Then, swiftly it was like being slammed into a brick wall as suddenly they came to an abrupt halt in mid-air with a bone-jarring jerk and then actually started to move upward. And then a familiar sound flooded his ears. *No way!*

But it was. A helicopter hovered overhead and somehow it had hooked his parachute with a big hook on the end of a heavy elastic cable, slowing and then stopping their plunge with a jerk that Chuck thought would shatter his bones. So hard was the jolt that it freed Jenkins' body from Chuck's frozen vice-grip legs. But luckily, he hadn't yet unhooked the clamp and his passenger's limp body hung in the air. A giant bungee jump cord had saved their lives as they hung between the death of the desert below and the lifeline above. The glimmer returned as Chuck felt himself going up instead of down. The chopper was pulling the cable up at the same time it climbed out of the gorge.

Using night-vision goggles, the helicopter crew had been monitoring the Mad Dogs' progress floating down the gorge when they saw Chuck's daring rescue of Jenkins. They were all daredevils and the pilot was the wildest of the bunch as he maneuvered the whirlybird down into the gorge while his men lowered the cable from an immense hydraulic spool to the falling men. The scene was surreal as it looked like an enormous fishing line the gods were using to fish from Mount Olympus. In spite of their Herculean efforts the helicopter crew knew it wouldn't likely reach them in time, but like Chuck, they prayed for an updraft. It came and when Chuck and Jenkins started their glide upwards, the chopper followed overhead chasing them with the hook dragging through the air. The updraft gave them the time they needed to get the cable into position to hook the chute when it began to collapse and fall the second time. They knew they had only one chance as they swung the hook into the parachute lines and hooked it like a 250-pound Marlin. They then watched the cable stretch to the end of its elasticity, terrifyingly close to the ground, and jerk to a stop with a wrenching thud.

"That was one-in-a-million Cap!" yelled one of the helicopter's crew as they began their gradual ascent.

"Wha...?" Ron Jenkins said, suddenly coming to life.

"Now he comes to," said Chuck, "Hold on."

"Did ya' get the name of that truck?" Jenkins said as they flew through the air.

"Ya' gotta' nasty concussion. Now shut up and hold on."

Unbelievably, with the rotor-blades beating out a faint beat, Ron started singing "I wanna' fly away," though this time with slurred words.

"One more word and I'm unclamping us!" Chuck said calmly as the ravine wall came into view.

Jenkins believed Chuck would do it and shut his mouth in mid-refrain just as they cleared the top of the gorge. The chopper flew over a flat area and lowered the cable gently to the ground. When they touched down, Chuck cut his chute away and waved to the pilot. Then he saw a small parachute come flying out of the chopper and watched it swish off into the morning haze about fifty yards away. He disconnected his groggy friend from his belt and laid him down on the ground. Walking over to the package, he picked it up and saw a note attached to a piece of wood. It said, "Mission scrubbed. Pick up at 0900 tomorrow at meeting spot. Scott OK."

Checking Jenkins over, he found that miraculously he hadn't broken any bones, although he had bruises everywhere. His head had taken most of the impact and he had sustained a severe concussion, but he was tough and after a few drinks of water he was ready to go. Making some shade with their backpacks and what was left of the parachute, Chuck told him to lay down and get some rest. "You're gonna' need yer' strength for the hike," he said.

They preferred hiking at night to avoid the intense desert heat, but knew they had no choice now if they wanted to reach the rendezvous point. All they had to do was get close because Chuck had a GPS satellite transmitter on his belt and Bob had a receiver. After 30 minutes of rest they started out and Chuck wondered what kind of mission would cut their Afghanistan operation short. Then a slight smile found its way onto his normally stoic face as he pulled the crumpled note from his pocket and looked at it. "*Scott*" and "*OK*" were two of the best words he had heard in a long time."

* * *

"I've got news," Mark told Bill, "But it isn't great."

"Let's have it," said Bill.

"I found 230 chemical plants that would make easy targets for an attack."

"230 is a lot," Bill said, "Can't you narrow it down to a few?"

"I could, but I would most likely miss a bunch."

"Well, it is something isn't it and I guess somethin' is better than nothin', which is what we've been getting. I'll take it to the boys upstairs and we'll see if it's enough to keep us going. Bill's dispassionate expression showed his lack of confidence in his own words.

What else can I do? Mark thought as he realized the standard scientific process was not working. Then he remembered Professor Goldschien's words, "When you hit a road-block, think outside the box and do the unconventional." With this recollection, he jumped up and went to work programming the computer with thousands of unrelated words. Thus far, he had cross-referenced only related words, assuming *Prophecy* was structured in a linear, related fashion. But that didn't work and he realized that he couldn't make that assumption. So, now it was time to think non-linearly and in a random, chaotic manner using unrelated words on the off-chance that it would uncover the kind of prediction he was looking for.

But why stop there, he thought as he also decided to select even the alphabetical letters in a completely random fashion, going backward and forward, instead of picking them in a linear order as he had been doing. He knew it was a long shot, but a long shot was all he had left.

He also knew that he was literally starting all over again and that worried him. But he had a glimmer of hope that his new random program would find the prophecy of doom he was searching for. He knew thousands and maybe millions of lives might depend on his success and he could feel the sweat coming out of his fingertips and onto the computer keys.

Mark was following something similar to the Chaos Theory, which says that some systems in the universe are not as predictable as others. It also holds that a very small occurrence can produce unpredictable and sometimes drastic results by triggering a series of increasingly significant events. It's the old Butterfly Effect where a butterfly flutters its wings in China, causing severe weather thousands of miles away in New York City. But he wasn't concerned with this element of the theory, just the random chaos part, and that's how he structured his computer program. It wasn't the orderly science he was used to, but it was his last hope.

Toiling for several days while taking short catnaps in-between, he feared overworking the mother of all computers and losing his mind at the same time. But he knew he had no choice. Then, finally, it started spitting out its first round of results.

His heart almost stopped when he saw that the long-sought-after word "*Ayles*" was among them. But his enthusiasm left as quickly as it came when his caffeine-saturated brain remembered that "*Ayles*" had been in the same group as the other global warming-related predictions. So, he now embarked on a whole new round of research and what he found made him cringe.

His previous research had shown that some serious effects of global warming were imminent twenty to thirty years from now. But a new U.S. Government report said that the earth is now heating up at higher temperatures than at any time in its history and those serious effects will be much more grave than previously thought. Searching further, he found new evidence that the threats are a lot more immediate and causing big and dramatic environmental problems here and now, not years into the future. The northern Canadian territories, for instance, used to see 10 months of winter and the 155,000 people living there used much of it to hunt caribou and walrus. Now the winters were down to six months and those people have much less time to hunt.

Then there is the sad case of the Polar Bear. The Polar Ice is melting so fast that it is causing Polar Bears to drown. They have to swim too far between ice shelves to hunt seals and end up drowning in the process. To make matters worse, the bear cubs' survival rate is going down. Some scientists estimate that at this rate, two-thirds of the Polar Bears in the Arctic will die by the middle of this century and if they disappear altogether, it will upset the delicate balance of nature and lead to other big environmental problems. So serious was the matter that the U.S. Interior Department declared the bears an endangered species and some scientists predicted their eventual extinction.

However, none of this was what Mark was looking for as he sat back in his chair in frustrated silence. But then the computer suddenly whirred to life and began droning out more results. He read the data hopefully, still looking for the ever-elusive "*Ayles*." "Bingo," he said out-loud as he saw it. But again, he had to couch his zeal as he read that "*Ayles*" was the name of a 41-square-mile floating shelf of ice that jutted into the Arctic Ocean from Canada's northernmost shore. He went on to read that scientists were amazed and alarmed to discover that it abruptly broke away and drifted out to sea. It was 100 feet thick and 3000 years old and it looked like global warming was to blame.

Scientists had expected climate change to melt ice shelves gradually over many years. But now it appears that it is happening much faster and right in front of our eyes. Ayles was one of six major ice shelves in Canada's Arctic and environmentalists were concerned that the others might be in the same danger, not to mention the rest of the ice shelves around the world. Greenland and West Antarctic, for instance, are melting faster than anyone thought and could be gone in a few decades.

Mark found that if the Greenland Ice Shelf melts, it would raise the sea level by 20 feet and if West Antarctic goes, it would raise it another 20. A rise of only 20 feet alone would kill millions of people and it would certainly flood all coastal countries. Many places like South Florida, Louisiana, Manhattan, and all of Bangladesh would be inundated and it would put 250 million people in China under water. Warming temperatures were also producing drought in some areas and more than half of the 4000 lakes in China's Qinghai Province are disappearing because of it. In Africa, one study said that if the famed snows of Kilimanjaro continue melting at their present rate, they could be completely gone by 2025. The situation was getting more and more urgent with discoveries like the remaining Canadian ice shelves are 90 percent smaller than when they were first discovered in 1906. But the truly frightening prediction was that the sea could rise as soon as the middle of this century.

The computer started humming again and what Mark read stopped him cold. There it was, the designation "*3He*" for helium 3 that never made any sense to him along with the words "*moon*" and "*rocks*." With a little research he discovered what *Prophecy* had been trying to tell him all along, strange as it was. Helium 3 was first found in moon rocks brought back from the Apollo missions. It comes from the constant solar winds produced by the sun. ^{3}He bounces off the earth's magnetic field, but the moon has no magnetic field and it has been soaking up the stuff for billions of years.

Mark found that if you could dig helium 3 up and put it into a fusion reactor you would have a giant source of clean, non-radioactive energy. And giant may be an understatement as it is estimated that a mere 40 tons of it would be enough to serve America's electrical needs for a year. Of course, no one had yet figured out how to mine helium 3 from the moon and get it back to earth, but it looked like *Prophecy* may be predicting that it would happen. *Certainly, valuable information for the future!* But that wasn't to be good enough as Bill walked in with the bad news.

* * *

As Chuck hiked across the sizzling desert, he felt numb. Many soldiers realize early on that anesthetizing themselves to the death and destruction going on around them is the only way to survive it, but this was different. This was more like a feeling of hopelessness. He hoped it was simple fatigue, but suspected it was something more. He feared that the same old doubts were creeping back into his head and he knew it was dangerous, especially in the middle of a mission. They reached the meeting spot by nightfall using their GPS satellite tracker. "Gotta' get me one of these," said Bob admiringly.

"This one's on me," answered Chuck, tossing the device to him. He had two more in his backpack.

"Glad you made it," Bob said sarcastically and sincerely at the same time.

"Both of us," Chuck said, relieved.

"Shall we get down to business?"

"About that. We have to go back tomorrow morning."

"Why?"

"New mission back home."

"That's too bad because our mission was to take out some Taliban big-shots that are meeting in Mula Qala."

"Yea," Chuck said, "I figured that when we brought along our sniper rifles."

"Well, that means less work for us and the boss got his money so I guess everybody's happy."

"I guess," Chuck said, a little disappointed.

After checking Jenkins over, Abdul Hameed said, "Other than a total lack of singing ability, he'll be okay. But he needs some rest to recover from the concussion."

Ron's predictable reply was simply, "I can rest when I'm dead."

"That might be sooner rather than later," Hameed said, "if you don't take care of yourself."

"Sorry Tyler, you don't get to use your numbers," Chuck told Tyler Adams. He was the best spotter in the business and was always right on the money when figuring out precisely where a bullet would go. He was an interesting soldier, having graduated from MIT with a Master's Degree in Physics. He joined the Army the next day. When anyone asked him why, he simply said, "numbers" and numbers were his specialty. He loved numbers and would sometimes get overly-excited about mathematical equations and metaphysical theories.

As a sniper spotter he used a high-power spotting scope to analyze the distance to the target, the wind speed and direction, the terrain, and the weather conditions to calculate the path of the bullet and told his sniper partner the numbers to dial into his gun. At long distances, bullets travel along a curved trajectory and the sniper has to compensate for that by aiming higher than the target to allow for the bullet to drop due to gravity. Tyler told his sniper partner what numbers to set his rifle to and his aim had to be within one centimeter of accuracy or the shot would miss. Often times they would hit their target from 500 yards away.

Contrary to what many people believe, snipers don't always put themselves in a high position over the target. Not only are they more visible that way, but shooting downhill requires special adjustments for the effects of gravity and the adjustments have to be perfectly precise. Consequently, most snipers try to shoot from a location that provides them with the most cover and from which a shot will go unnoticed. This often means getting into a position where the shot is fired close to a large object so that the crack of the bullet will sound as if it came from that object. The noise bounces off a building or a large tree and sounds as if it came from there. With a 20 millimeter or heavy .50 caliber rifle, snipers can even shoot the parts off of a jet fighter, a missile guidance system, or a radar detector. But usually the targets are human. It didn't matter to Tyler as he just liked the exactness of the numbers. When they pitched camp for the night, Bob's men sat around smoking opium, probably to take the edge off of the meth, and Chuck bedded down next to Tyler.

"I still don't really understand why someone with your intelligence would volunteer for this grunt outfit," he said as they laid back on their sleep-sacks.

"Probably for the same reason someone with your intelligence did, lieutenant."

"I doubt it. What was it really?"

He thought about the question for a few seconds and then gave the answer he always gave, "numbers."

"Numbers," Chuck answered in a curious tone, "Ya' mean like lucky number 7?"

"That's one of 'em. Christianity says there are seven vices and seven virtues. It says God created the earth in six days and rested on the seventh, but it's a lot more than that."

"I'm listenin'."

"Well, numbers are black and white ... there's no grey." Tyler was referring to the numbers in his spotter's scope, but was willing to let Chuck steer him into talking about the cosmic numbers of life.

"But most of life is grey Tyler ... and subject to interpretation." Chuck's response belied his recent uncertainties.

"That's exactly why I like numbers. They're unambiguous and there is no interpretation."

"Well then, what the hell are ya' doin' here ... the greyest of grey areas?"

"Wrong. Iraq and Afghanistan are the most black and white places in the world."

"How can you say that when the reasons we're here aren't that clear in the first place. And the enemy is even greyer. We don't really even know who they are."

"It doesn't matter who they are. They're bad people and they need killin'."

"Not all of 'em. Don't ya' think some of 'em are fighting us because we invaded their country and that makes us the bad guys?"

"There is that, isn't there." Although Tyler was usually stuck in his numbers and theories, Chuck occasionally enjoyed prompting him to cast a little doubt on his own opinions. *After all*, he mused, *why should I be the only one plagued by doubt?*

"Sure ... and Daniels says one man's terrorist is another man's freedom fighter."

"Yes, he does, although he didn't exactly make that one up," said Tyler pensively, "But Will looks into things too deeply. These guys are bad mothers and that's it. I don't care about the politics ... they kill innocent people and that's enough. If I started to see the jihadis' side of things, the grey would interfere with the good-versus-evil fight and I couldn't kill the evil bastards."

Chuck thought about this for a moment and decided to change the subject. "What was that crap you were telling Hawkins the other day about six numbers making up the universe?" As weird as he was, Jim Hawkins was the only one in the outfit who seemed to relate to this mathematician, although Chuck understood much more of his theories than he let on.

"Oh, nothing much. Just that the whole universe is governed by just six numbers and they were set at the beginning in the Big Bang."

"Okay. You got me. What the hell does that mean?"

"Just that mathematical laws determine our very existence and just six numbers underpin atoms, outer space, and you and me."

"What are they?"

"That's the $64,000 question, if you'll excuse the pun. But that can't be answered easily. Ya' sure you wanna' go there?"

"Why not? It's not like I've got anything better to do."

"How flattering," Tyler said and continued, "Well, the first is the cosmic number Omega and it measures the amount of material in the universe. It kinda' tells us the relative importance of gravity and the expansion of the ever-expanding universe. "

"Okay, I vaguely get that."

"Epsilon is another. It explains how all the atoms on the earth were made. It also defines how firmly atomic nuclei bind together."

Just then Jim Hawkins interrupted with, "Hey math dude ... I gotta' question for you. Whatever happened to the number-one pencil?"

"That's about as dumb as asking why is there a white crayon?" Tyler often enjoyed playing verbal volleyball with Jim and could give as good as he got.

But, not to be outdone, Hawkins shot back, "Well if yer' so smart, tell me why hot dogs come ten to a pack but hot dog *buns* come in packages of eight?"

"Why do I even try?" said Adams. Then turning back to Chuck and without missing a beat, he said, "Anyway, there's L for antigravity. It controls the expansion of the universe."

"I thought gravity controls the expansion."

"It does, but along with anti-gravity. Then there's Q, the ratio of two fundamental energies."

"Dare I ask what they are?"

"Probably better if you don't. But the last is something you will get. It's D, the number of dimensions in our world."

"Three?"

"Three ... that we can *see*. The String Theory says there are nine spatial dimensions, which means there are more that we can't see. Some theorize that life in these other dimensions is going on right in front of our faces, simultaneously with ours, but we can't see it."

"Wow," said Chuck, feeling like he had read this somewhere before.

"Yeah, and there are those who believe that some people's brains are specifically tuned into the electromagnetic waves of those dimensions. Kinda' like a radio receiver ... and that they see people in those dimensions, only they think they're seein' ghosts."

"Don't some people actually see ghosts though? Haven't there been some documented cases?"

"Absolutely, and I think the spirits of the dead do walk among us. I even think we each may have our own guardian angel, but I think they exist in another dimension."

"So, both might be true."

"Yes. There may be life in other dimensions going on around us and some of them might have dead people from this dimension in them."

It was all too much for Chuck to think about when he was this tired and he regretted asking the question in the first place. "Let's hit the hay," he said and Tyler seemed relieved.

But it wasn't meant to be, as suddenly a light appeared and they heard the sound of several guns being cocked.

"Hands up!" a rough voice shouted from behind the light. It was the man Chuck had given the money to.

"What's goin' on?" asked Bob as the Dogs raised their hands.

"The money he gave us was fake," he said in broken English.

"You gave him counterfeit money?" Bob turned to Chuck in amazement.

"No, I gave him the money my Colonel gave me," Chuck lied.

"Now you die," said the Afghani and turning to Bob, "The boss wants you to do it."

A look of surprise and disgust came over Bob's face. Then it turned to one of resignation and that worried Chuck as he started to gingerly move his hand slightly toward his knife.

"No problem," Bob said as he and his men swung their AK-47s toward Chuck and the Dogs. But then, all in one sudden motion and in unison, they turned them back on the Afghanis and shot them to pieces. When the shooting stopped Bob said laughingly, "You're welcome Butch."

"Didn't say thank you," said Chuck, surprised and relieved.

"I'm sure you were thinkin' it," Bob said, "Now let's all get some shut-eye while we can."

"I'll go for that," said Chuck, relieved that his new comrade didn't ask any questions.

But in the early morning darkness Bob came over to him and whispered, "What's the deal with the money?"

Chuck looked at him with a wide grin spreading across his face and said, "I'll tell you that when you tell me your real name and who you really are."

After a long pause and a grin of his own, Bob started to say something but stopped short as they heard two helicopters approaching in the darkness. "Another time then," he said curtly.

"Another time," said Chuck as he got up and roused his men.

The two warriors looked at each other with genuine, but reluctant affection that neither would admit to, as the helicopters landed nearby. "Hopefully not," said Bob, "For both our sakes."

The Dogs climbed aboard the choppers and they took off with Chuck and Bob still sharing a long stare. On the way back to Iraq Chuck smiled, thinking about the note that said, "Scott OK." Then a look of satisfaction came over his face when he thought about how he had switched the money Colonel Singleton gave him with the counterfeit money he got from Rabiya and paid a world-renowned neurosurgeon cash to fly to Iraq and operate on Scott.

CHAPTER 26

A corporal met the helicopters as they landed back at the base and told Chuck that Captain Johnson wanted to see him immediately.

"Must be a big one," Mike Sandstone said as they jumped to the ground.

"Aren't they all," Chuck said, his calm voice belying his very real alarm, "You guys hit the mess hall and I'll see you back at barracks."

On his way to Johnson's office all he could think about was whether the captain had already heard about the counterfeit money. He doubted it, but he didn't know how close he was to the warlord. *Maybe he already called him.*

"You wanted to see me sir," Chuck said as he anxiously entered the office, trying to hide his apprehension.

Johnson looked up from his desk and stared at Chuck for what seemed like an eternity, as if he was trying to decide what to say. After several anxious seconds he finally said, "Sit down lieutenant, I've got a weird one for you."

Breathing a deep sigh of relief, Chuck sat down. If Captain Johnson noticed his heavy exhale, he didn't let on, as he explained the mission.

"This will have to be a surgical strike with a delicate touch," he said, "ISIS kidnapped an archeologist and is holding him for ransom."

"All due respect sir, but why do we care."

"Well, for one thing, he's well-connected. We got calls from the top brass saying gettin' him out is a priority mission."

"You mean gettin' him out *alive*, right?"

"Funny, but they didn't use that word."

That really got Chuck's curiosity going, but he figured he had better leave it alone. "Where are they keepin' him sir?" he asked.

"Intel says it's an underground facility 50 clicks south of Mosul."

"Underground?"

"Apparently there are a buncha' ancient artifacts stored there and the brass wants us to liberate them."

Not this again, Chuck thought. "More artifacts sir?" he said.

"I know. Yer' probably thinkin' what is it with all these artifacts."

"That's kinda' what I was thinking sir."

"Me too. But apparently, they're hugely important to the Iraqis and that means it's important to our fearless leaders ... so important, in fact, that they said if we rescue the archeologist at the same time, so much the better."

"So, the artifacts are the primary mission and the archeologist is the secondary?"

"Kinda' looks that way doesn't it. But the official mission is to rescue the archeologist."

"And pick up a few statues along the way if we can."

"Now yer' gettin' the idea."

"You're not kiddin' about the *delicate*," Chuck said, wondering why the good captain didn't say this in the beginning, "When do we go?"

"Well, that's the tough part ... at zero-2200."

"Sir, the men haven't slept in days. Why the urgency?"

"Intel says the bad guys may've been tipped off that we're comin' by our Iraqi comrades."

"Yeah, their spies probably saw us land and figure somethin's up."

"That's the concern ... and if they know we're comin', they might move the stuff and the archeologist."

"What's the security?"

Pulling several satellite photos out of his desk drawer, Captain Johnson said, "We think the artifacts are being stored underground here with four .50 cal gun trucks patrolling the surrounding area and 12 or so guards walking the perimeter."

"Man, they must be valuable!"

"Yeah, but the big problem is that when the kidnappers contacted us about the ransom, they gave us their standard threat that if we tried a rescue, they would kill the archeologist immediately."

"Surprise ... surprise. How 'bout back-up?"

"It'll be there if you need it."

Chuck thought that was a bit cryptic, but didn't have time to ask about it because Johnson handed him a small black box that looked like a GPS locator. "Here," he said, "You might need this."

Taking the box sparked a key question. "If you don't mind me asking Captain, how did intel find the location?"

"That's the weird part. Apparently, ISIS was paying this archeologist to appraise their stolen artifacts so they could sell them for big bucks."

"So?"

"So, he apparently had a tracking device on him that led us there."

And that led to another obvious question, "Why would an archeologist have a tracking device on him?"

"I'm afraid that's above my pay grade lieutenant."

Chuck always noticed that superior officers never missed a chance to call him by his rank to remind him of his subordinate position.

Staring at the floor and thinking about it for a few moments, he finally said, "Wouldn't they have searched him?"

"Maybe they did, but it signaled the location before they found it."

"But wouldn't that make them wonder why an archeologist would have a homing device on him?" This was getting stranger by the minute.

"You'd think ... but again ... above both our pay grades."

"Maybe they didn't find it," Chuck said.

"Maybe not."

"But that would mean..."

"Yup," Johnson interrupted, "But let's get down to the mission."

Chuck knew what he meant. The archeologist must have had the device implanted in his body and, since a metal detector apparently didn't find it, it must be a new prototype made of all-plastic. Chuck had heard that they avoid metal detection. This could only mean one thing. He was CIA.

Just then Chuck's thoughts were interrupted by the corporal knocking on the office door. "We just got the other photos sir," he said as he entered the room and handed Johnson a large envelope. Pulling several photographs out of the envelope, he stopped and stared at one in-particular.

"Better have a look at your target lieutenant," he said handing the picture to Chuck.

"You gotta' be kiddin' me," was all he could muster as he stared in disbelief at the photo of a very pretty, dark-haired woman holding what appeared to be an ancient statuette. Once again, the intelligence was a little off and the archeologist was a woman.

* * *

Bill's bad news could have been worse, but it sure could have been a lot better as he told Mark, "The boys upstairs say you've got three days to come up with a real impending terrorist plot or you're done."

"But what about the chemical plants?" Mark asked in disbelief. He guessed he should have seen it coming, but he hoped it wouldn't.

"Too broad," said Bill, "And besides, we would never have time to analyze all of them. We need something more narrow and specific and we need it now.

Mark knew it was now or never and that he had to zero-in on terrorism only without the distractions of other threats to the world. So, he got down to it and the first thing he found was that some 40,000 ISIS and Al Qaeda members are operating in 102 countries with most of them active in the Middle-East, Africa, Asia, and Europe. They will continue to mount most of their attacks in places like Iraq, Afghanistan, Yemen, Libya, Tunisia, Algeria, Egypt, East and West Africa, the Western Balkans, and Caucasus. But their supporters are expected to increase their strikes in the United States and Europe. He also found a call by Osama bin Laden's son, Hamza, and others, for more attacks on the West. These calls increased after President Trump named Jerusalem as Israel's capital. But he knew this was too general so he narrowed his focus.

Next he came across a report on Trump's call for a draw-down of troops from Afghanistan from 14,000 to 7,000. *Nothing new about that*, he thought. But then, he read that Afghanistan was becoming the new epicenter of regional and global terrorism with both ISIS and Al Qaeda moving fighters there. From 2017 to 2018, about 69 ISIS leaders and 200 to 300 jihadist soldiers from Iraq and Syria relocated to Afghanistan and it looks like that will continue into 2019.

That made him realize that drawing down U.S. troops in Afghanistan will encourage the growth of ISIS and Al Qaeda there and it could cause a big problem for the negotiations with the Taliban. They are based on their guarantee of preventing ISIS and Al Qaeda from using Afghanistan as a launchpad for terrorist attacks. But now he didn't know what to do about it. If he told Bill, it would be seen as too general and wouldn't stop the clock on his deadline. So, he looked further. Then, he stumbled onto the prediction of a new kind of terrorism: cyber war.

He discovered that terrorists are becoming increasingly more sophisticated in their computer skills and are focusing more of their efforts on cyber, rather than physical attacks on the West. He read that the satellite communications used by the military and by ships, planes, and other means of transportation are vulnerable to cyber-attack. In the worst-case scenario, hackers could turn satellite antennas into weapons which could disable the computer networks in cities and even countries.

Recently a major international communications company reported that in 2017, it saw an average of one cyber-attack per month and expected it to continue into 2019. It said someone in China even hacked an American defense contractor's satellite. That made Mark remember how easy it was for him to hack into the Israeli Defense Network, searching for information about the country's nuclear weapons program. But the same company also reported that someone had hacked the satellite communications of Southeast Asia telecom companies involved in mapping and imaging.

But none of this predicts any future attacks, he thought as he continued his search. After two-and-a-half days of non-stop research, he still had only general information to give to Bill and he was worried that his project of a lifetime might be coming to an end.

* * *

Chuck looked up as he trudged through the pitch-dark desert with the clear, bright moon, on his way to the target. As always, he was amazed at the clarity of the bright crystal canopy of stars above. With no city lights to interfere with the view, they looked like brilliantly twinkling diamonds from other worlds and he wondered if there was life on any of them. It triggered a memory of an article he had read once about the Hubble telescope discovering 16 new planets deep in the Milky Way. It made many scientists conclude that there are probably about 6 billion Jupiter-sized planets out there in the galaxy and there is a likelihood that many of them are like earth. He then remembered reading somewhere that of the 100 billion stars in our Milky Way Galaxy, some NASA astronomers estimate that 1 in 5 has an earth-sized planet with a potential for life. Of course, that would mean that there are hundreds-of-thousands of planets out there with possible life like ours, although astronomers couldn't explain why we are not getting massive radio signals from them through our radio telescopes.

As usual, Chuck was more conservative in his thinking as he remembered reading in *The Book* that scientists have identified 21 planets that could definitely support human life, although he had no idea where that number came from. He also remembered reading somewhere that NASA had found evidence of water on Mars and even a suggestion of microscopic life forms. Far-sighted astronomers foresaw crops being grown in its soil and minerals being mined from its mountains. But the big article he couldn't get out of his mind was the one about some astronomer who claims that there are several planets out there that are even *more* lush and fertile than earth.

But there was no time to contemplate the cosmos as he looked back at his men. On the way, the Dogs' four marksmen were joined by thirteen other snipers from other units. When they got close to the target they set up in a circle around it 300 yards away.

At daylight, four of the snipers trained their sites on two vents sticking out of the underground complex. They were 12 inches in diameter and the snipers' more-than-difficult task was to fire gas canisters into them, either knocking out anyone underground or forcing them to come above ground. At the same time, the rest of the snipers prepared to pick off the guards and any moving vehicles they could hit.

The plan was for the Dogs and the other men to attack in five gun trucks from five different directions under sniper cover and it was almost time. The snipers were in place, the trucks were parked a half-mile away in five different spots, and day was just starting to break. As soon as the sun's rays painted the horizon, Chuck gave the signal and the thirteen snipers started peppering the guards and the gun trucks while the other four put a bead on the two vents and fired their gas canisters. The first two shots missed their mark by a few inches and things took an unexpected turn when the escaping gas swirled around the vents, blocking the snipers' view. The Dogs rammed their trucks into the fray, driving back-and-forth, shooting the ISIS trucks with their .50 caliber guns in a motorized joust.

The four snipers anxiously waited for the gas clouds to dissipate so they could take another shot. But their wait was interrupted by the violent sound of crushing metal as two trucks crashed into each other in a violent collision throwing the Dogs out of theirs. They each instinctively rolled to a stop and four Dogs jumped up with blood streaming over their faces and shot the occupants of the other truck as they staggered from the wreck. The gas cleared and the four snipers started firing their gas canisters again until they hit dead-center into each vent. "Bull's eye!" one of them yelled. "About time," they heard another one say.

But the celebration would have to wait as Abdul Hameed shouted into the radio, "Here come the reinforcements." Everyone turned around to see six more gun trucks driving toward them from six different directions. The snipers tried to pick them off but they were moving too fast. "Give 'em all ya' got!" Chuck said calmly and the Dogs turned their guns on the approaching trucks and did just that. One of the trucks suddenly exploded and then another and another.

Has to be the back-up, Chuck thought as he looked up to see several drones above them firing hellfire missiles at the trucks. "Yay!" the men yelled and at the same time, Chuck thought he heard something beeping from his pocket. He couldn't figure out what it was until he remembered the GPS locator Captain Johnson had given him. He pulled it out and saw that a blinking red light was moving away from the battlefield. Looking in the direction the GPS said it was heading, he could see nothing but empty desert. *What the hell?* Then it dawned on him. The archeologist's tracking device must have started signaling again and she was moving underground, probably in a tunnel.

Instantly, Chuck took off at a sprint in the direction of the signal.

As he ran over sand dunes, he could tell he was catching up with it until he was literally right on top of it. He slowed down to keep pace with whoever was down there until he saw what looked like an opening up ahead. When he was about 30 yards away, he saw a head pop out of a hole in the ground. Instantly, he hit the dirt behind a small sand dune. Peeking up over the edge, he saw a man in a suit climb out of the hole pulling a woman up with him. She had blood on her face and dirt on her clothes and her wrists were in handcuffs. It was the archeologist and even through the blood and dirt, Chuck could sense her beauty.

Wondering how his men were doing, he turned around just in time to see the remaining enemy trucks blow up from drone fire. *The cavalry*, he thought. "Bring in the troops," he said into his radio and turning back around, he noticed a jeep approaching. Sticking his gun up over the edge of the dune, he took careful aim and fired. The fourth and fifth shots hit the driver and it gradually slowed to a stop. Seeing where the shots came from, Yusef Mohammed started firing his handgun in Chuck's direction as he dragged Jasnine toward the jeep, but the bullets fell short. Jumping out from behind the dune, Chuck started a slow trot toward them when Mohammed yelled, "Don't come any closer or I'll blow her brains out," and he pointed his pistol at Jasnine's head.

"You got nowhere to run pal ... yer' guys are all dead and that's what you'll be in about 5 seconds," Chuck yelled calmly.

"I mean it ... let me get to the jeep or she's dead," Mohammed answered shakily.

"If ya' think I give a shit about her, yer' wrong. We're here for what's down there." And he pointed at the ground.

"About that," said Mohammed with a deadly smile and holding up his hand, "This is a detonator for the many bombs down there."

"Why don't I just shoot you where ya' stand?"

"Oh, I don't know ... maybe because it's a dead-man's switch and if my thumb goes off the button, poof goes all that money."

Out of nowhere, Jasnine elbowed Mohammed hard in the jaw and kneed him in the groin at the same time, bending him over in pain with his hand loosening on the detonator. Instantly, she clamped her hand down over his and deftly replaced his thumb with hers. Then in one quick motion, she grabbed his gun and pistol-whipped him to his knees.

Chuck was stunned and impressed at the same time. "Man, you don't look like any archeologist I've ever known," he said, walking toward her.

"And how many have you known?" she said, whirling around to reveal a stunning face framed by bloody, but beautiful hair cascading around her slight shoulders.

"None, now that ya' mention it."

"Well, you should'nt have stuck your nose in here because I had everything under control."

"Yeah, it looked like you did when he had his gun on you."

"That was just for show. Besides, I let him capture me so he would take me to his real headquarters. But you blew all that with your cowboy act."

"Excuse me, but I think my *cowboy act* just saved your life."

"Keep tellin' yourself that soldier boy. Now how 'bout coming over here and gettin' me outta' these cuffs?"

"Really? You can't do it by yourself?"

"I could, but I'd prefer that you do it since I dislocated my wrist when I popped ole' Yusef here. You know how hard it is to punch someone when yer' in hand-cuffs ... or maybe you don't."

Chuck said simply, "Yes ma'am," as he walked over to Jasnine, admiring her spunk. When they looked into each other's eyes, her beauty triggered a catalyst to his rugged good looks and something stirred in both of them."

Probably just the heat of the moment, they each thought as Mohammed wobbly tried to stagger to his feet. Suddenly, two shots rang out of nowhere crumpling him back to the ground in a heap.

Chuck instinctively grabbed Jasnine and drug her behind the jeep as two more shots struck its door.

"Sniper!" he yelled.

"Ya' think?" Jasnine said, calmly and sarcastically.

Ignoring the slight, Chuck peeked around the edge of the jeep's door and looked up at a small sand dune a football field away. Spotting the glint of a rifle bar-rel he said, "He's too far away," just as two more bullets ricocheted off the jeep two inches from his face.

Suddenly two more shots resounded but they didn't come from the sniper. Instead, they were fired *at* him and he died instantly. Chuck figured that either Sniper Steve or Abdul Hameed had done it again.

All of a sudden, the desert floor near the combat zone swelled upward and started to wrinkle like water ripples. At first, Chuck thought it was an earthquake which would be unusual in this area. But, Jasnine knew better. "He had his own deadman's switch," she said with a peculiar grin. The sniper had done what Mohammed couldn't. When the Mad Dog sniper shot him, his thumb slipped off the deto-nator switch blowing up the artifact storehouse under their feet.

Feeling the ground reverberating under their tires, the Dogs beat a swift retreat just as it collapsed into a giant sinkhole. The battle was over anyway and they had won. "Here he is," shouted Jim Hawkins as he saw Chuck and Jasnine walking toward them, "And he's got himself a girlfriend." The Dogs all laughed in relief and drove toward them to pick them up.

"Why do you suppose they killed their own guy?" Chuck asked Jasnine.

"Because he knows too much and they didn't want him spilling his guts to your guys," she answered back.

"About what?" he asked suspiciously.

"The artifact black market."

"Yeah, sorry about all those valuable relics. It must be quite a blow to people in your profession."

"It is," she said, again with the wry smile, "But I'll live through it."

She felt much worse about the lost dinosaur bones than about the artifacts. Now she would never get to make that discovery of a lifetime. But then, that wasn't her real mission anyway.

What she didn't tell him was that one night before Mohammed took her prisoner, she snuck into the big warehouse and discovered that most of the artifacts were fake and the ones that were real were fairly worthless. She correctly figured they were decoys ISIS wanted the Americans to find, so that they would think they had gotten the real ones and give up the hunt for them. Now it appeared that the Mad Dogs had inadvertently helped ISIS accomplish that goal.

"Here's our ride," said Chuck and he helped her up into the truck.

"Glad to see you made it," said Sniper Steve, "And this must be the lovely archeologist."

"Yup," said Chuck, "And I'm glad to see you haven't lost yer' touch. I assume the sniper was your handiwork?"

"I wish," said Steve, "But that honor goes to dead-eye Dick Hameed."

"Thanks Abdul," Chuck said as they drove off, "That was a one-in-a-million shot." Ever the modest one, Abdul Hameed looked at his feet with a slight smile on his face.

CHAPTER 27

As they pulled into the base, a corporal ran up to their truck and said, "Captain Johnson has ordered your men back to their barracks and me to escort you to his office."

Probably pissed about the artifacts, Chuck thought, *not exactly the surgical strike he had in mind. Or maybe he found out about the funny money.* Either way, he figured he was in trouble.

As he entered Johnson's outer office, Chuck saw the captain sitting at his assistant's desk with a strange look on his face. "Hello lieutenant," he said, "Guess you lost the loot huh?"

"Yes sir," was all Chuck could say. He was exhausted.

"Well, no matter," Johnson said, "Because I've got a new mission for you and it's another weird one."

"Weirder than the last one sir?" Chuck asked, relieved.

"Much weirder. Come with me," he said as he got up from the desk and led him into his inner office.

As he walked through the door, Chuck saw two people sitting on folding chairs and one standing up. He looked from man-to-man, as he often did, to size-up the situation. He had to focus his eyes to make out who they were.

The first face he saw was Jack the spook, as he had grown fond of calling him. *Why in the hell is he here,* he thought. The second, he didn't recognize, but the third almost took his breath away.

"Hi lieutenant. How goes the war?" the big one said. It was Scott Sampson and he held onto a cane.

"Whaa," was all Chuck could utter as he walked over to Scott and gave him a big bearhug.

"Watch it," Scott said, "Not quite all the way healed yet."

"Oh sorry," Chuck said trying to recover himself, "But you look great."

"Nice of you to lie lieutenant, but I will be good-as-new after a few more months of hard-core physical therapy."

"Well, you look a helluva' lot better than the last time I saw you."

"Thanks to you Chuck," Scott said uncharacteristically using his first name. Chuck threw a quick glance at Captain Johnson to see if he reacted, but, as usual, his stony stare betrayed no feeling or emotion whatsoever.

Then the back door to Johnson's office creaked open and the last person Chuck expected to see entered the room saying, "No hug for yer' old man?"

Again, it was, "Whaa?"

"Yeah, it's me," his father said, "I figured someone oughta' bail you outta' this one and it might as well be me."

Chuck stared at his dad in bewilderment. "Bail me out of what?" he stumbled, instantly worried that he was caught on the funny money scam.

"You're burned over here son. Remember that Wanted Poster your guys found a while back with your picture on it?"

"Yeah," said Chuck, uneasily relieved that it might not be about the money after all, "What about it?"

"Well, now the bad guys have gone digital and spread it all over the Internet! Yer' blown my boy and it's not safe for you to be here anymore."

"When was it ever safe to be here?" Chuck asked, bristled at the word *boy*, "How is it not safe now?"

"Well, for one, the reward got jacked up to $250,000."

"So?"

"So, every jihadi within a hundred miles is gonna' be after you to get it."

"Not to mention the bounty hunters that'll come out of the woodwork to get you," added Jack.

"I think I can handle that," said Chuck with a little trepidation in his voice.

"It's not you we're worried about," said Don, "It's your men. When they come after you, they're gonna' get the Dogs in the process."

Chuck had always worried that his daredevil tactics might endanger his men's lives and now it looked like that worry might have been justified. He could risk his own life, but he knew he couldn't risk theirs. "One thing," he said, "Why didn't they kill me and collect the reward when they had me?"

"Could be several things. They might not've known it was you or maybe they did and the big boys ordered them to stand down."

"Why would they do that?'

"To get the reward higher and collect it later themselves."

"Alright," Chuck said, "What's the deal?"

"The deal is," Don answered, "That we get you the hell out of Dodge to protect you and your men."

"And do what?"

"Well, we've been tasked with a big mission to rid the world of evil and the army has agreed to lend you to us to do it."

"Am I hallucinating or did you just say 'rid the world of evil'?"

"Yeah, sorry about that. I couldn't resist it. A very rich man assembled this team to do what the government can't. We won't be hamstrung by any ridiculous rules of engagement and will be free to carry out more efficient missions that might actually accomplish something."

"What kind of missions dad?" Chuck asked, still a little dazed.

"We'll get to that. But rest assured that we'll be doing more surgical strikes than all-out attacks."

"And I'm gonna' work strategy and planning," Scott said, "Until I'm fully recovered ... then I'm back out in the field with you."

"But first," Jack said, "Meet Mark Jacobs, the computer nerd who brought us the rich guy. No offense son."

"None taken," Mark said, intimidated by everyone in the room, "But let me correct you on one thing ... our benefactor brought me to you, not the other way around."

"And we're delighted to have you," Don jumped in with a hint of sarcasm, "Anyway, Mark has a great computer program that finds big problems around the world and the bad guys who're causing 'em."

"What's so great about that?"

"Well, it can supposedly predict the problems *before* they happen."

"That does sound great, but does it work?"

"Hopefully ... or we wouldn't be here. But the best part about it is its name. Guess what it's called."

"No clue."

"C'mon ... just guess."

"O. K. Fortune Teller."

"Nope. It's called Prophecy," Don said, with a strange, faraway look on his face. It was as if he was wistfully reminiscing about something from his distant past.

Seeing his father's dreamy expression made Chuck think that the word 'Prophecy' might have some special significance for him. But as Don's face slowly began to change, the word suddenly hit him like a hard slap in the face. *Prophecy and Redemption* was the original title of *The Book* and that made him start to re-think whether or not his dad really did write it. It also occurred to him that he must have been the one who wrote "Is this the prophecy I've been waiting for?" across the top of the old email he found. *So, he knew about the program way back then*, he thought, *but why would he be waiting for it?* From the wry half-grin sneaking onto Don's face, Chuck guessed he was thinking the same thing and he looked like he was waiting for a reaction. But, without betraying his thoughts by his own facial expression, he simply said, "Why Prophecy?"

"That's the cool part," Don said, going back to his usual stony stare, "Because it looks for code language that predicts the future in all the big religious books."

"You mean like the Bible and the Qur'an?"

"Among others."

"O. K. If it's so great, why isn't the CIA all over it?"

"They are," said Jack, "Or were ... until they decided Mark wasn't predicting enough terrorist attacks and cut him loose."

"Unfortunately," Don chimed in, "He was workin' with a buncha' suits who were fixated only on terrorism and nothing else. But like I always told you son, there're a lot worse bad guys out there than just the terrorists."

"Like who?" Chuck asked, knowing the answer that was coming.

"Like the rich bastards who finance them, for one," Don said.

"And most of them are richer than God," Jack chuckled.

"True enough. The terrorists are just a symptom," added Don, "With Jacobs' help, we're gonna' go after the disease. But all that in due time son. Right now, I wanna' introduce you to the latest member of our little group, someone you may remember."

Tom Griffin then entered the room and said, "Hi Chuck. Seems like I just saw you."

"This is too weird for words," Chuck mumbled dumbfounded.

Then something swiftly clicked in his head and he said, "Don't tell me. You're the wild ninja of Syria."

"Afraid so," Tom said, "But I think it's *white* ninja of Syria ... and I'm not proud of it. I just wanted to give 'em something to think about the next time they want to attack an aid convoy."

Still looking befuddled, Chuck looked from Tom to his father and said, "Dad ... can I talk to you alone a minute?"

"Use my outer office," said Captain Johnson.

When they closed the door behind them Chuck said, "If I'd wanted to go mercenary I would've joined Black Water."

"Oh, you don't wanna' go with those crazy mothers. They're all about war for profit, not about right and wrong."

"And how are you different?"

"Simple. We're non-profit and apolitical. Like I always told you, whenever money is involved, yer' not fightin' for what's right, only for what's profitable."

"Okay, but why would I give up the backing of the U.S. government for some hair-brained billionaire's idea of what's right and wrong?"

"First of all, he's a trillionaire. But secondly, you wouldn't be givin' up anything because we'll be workin' with the CIA ... just unofficially."

"Off-book?"

"Yup. We'll have access to their intelligence but there won't be any official record of it."

"So, like they say in Mission Impossible, if we're caught or killed, the secretary will disavow any knowledge of our existence."

"Right," Don said with a grin, "But there's an advantage to that, namely that we don't have to work with the official government types."

"Why is that an advantage?"

"You know why. Because the government is too heavily influenced by money and politics to know what's right and wrong. With those as priorities, you get constantly shifting alliances and strategies that do nothing more than fill the pockets of the rich and get guys like you and the Dogs killed in the process."

"How about some specifics." This was something Chuck had suspected for a long time, but couldn't quite figure out.

Sensing that his son was looking for a concrete example, Don said, "Well, didn't you find it a little strange that you didn't run into more ISIS fighters when you went into Raqqa?"

"Maybe," Chuck said with suspicion in his voice and remembering the Dogs' surprise at the slim enemy numbers.

"It was because we let about 4000 of 'em go before we invaded."

"Why would we do that?" Chuck was astounded.

"So, they could fight Assad's troops in the northwest and southwest. With Russia's help, he's regained control of a lot of the territory he lost to ISIS. Now he wants the rest of it back and especially the oil fields and we don't want him to have it."

Chuck had to think about that one for a moment. It was hard for him to understand any justification for letting a vicious and brutal enemy like ISIS go free just when they had them in their cross-hairs.

Don read his mind and said, "That's what happens when politics are involved, not to mention profits and greed."

"Back to the oil, I suppose."

"Always."

"And no oil with this rich guy?"

"Oh, I imagine he owns his share of oil stocks but at 85 I don't think he gives a crap. Anyway, I hear he's more into alternative energy now than anything else."

"And how long will it be before we're all killing each other over that?"

"Not long ... but for now we just fight the good fight in our little corner of the globe as we see fit. No governments, countries, or corporations to manipulate us."

"Unfettered by big government and politics, 'ay?" Chuck said referring to their conversation from months earlier.

"Hopefully," Don answered.

"But, what about ISIS?" Chuck asked.

"Well, you took their 'capital' and beat 'em back to Baghuz and now they're on the run," Don answered and it was true that about 15,000 to 20,000 ISIS soldiers had retreated to the Iraqi border with Syria and into Syria itself. Estimates were that 3500 to 5500 were left stuck in several towns on the Euphrates River and a swath of desert along the border. But that's not to mention the thousands in Yemen, Afghanistan, Libya, and West Africa.

"Ya' think they're finished or will they be back?"

"Not as ISIS, but probably with another name or names."

"Whatdya' mean?"

"Well, 60 or so Shiite militias fought along-side us against ISIS because their religious leaders said it was their spiritual duty. Now Iraq is telling them to disarm and join back into a secular society. But they want jobs, not secularism. And they know if they do disarm, they lose any leverage they might have to get those jobs and keep their religion. The only problem is that there are no jobs to give 'em, so where does that leave 'em? Most likely they'll continue fighting, probably in splinter groups, but this time it'll be against the Iraqi government."

"I guess we should tell that to the Iraqis since they declared December 10 a national holiday to celebrate their victory over ISIS and terrorism."

"Yeah, I think the government was just glad it finally had some good news to tell people, but it'll never last. Before long they'll be back at their tribal and religious wars. They don't know any other way."

"You don't think the big part's over?"

"The big part, yes. But a lot of smaller parts are comin' and they'll go on forever. Only this time, it'll be a guerilla war of insurgency and that's not a war you wanna' fight. For our forces it'll be more like an occupation than a war. You've done yer' job here son ... now it's time to move onto more productive things."

"Like what?"

"Like stopping the big, bad guys from killin' thousands, maybe millions of people."

"I 'spose that means a little killing of our own."

"Only if there are no other options and if it's absolutely necessary. We'll try blackmailing 'em first by appealing to their greed and lust for power. But if that doesn't work ... well, how many ways can I say it? Some guys just need killin."

Chuck thought about this for a few moments and finally said, "I don't think I'm ready for all this."

"That's OK," Don said, "Because you don't have to be."

"What does that mean?" Chuck asked after as few tense seconds.

"We don't plan to throw you into our messy world of espionage right away."

"What's yer' plan?"

"Well, you always said you wanted to be an FBI agent. Now you get the next best thing."

"CIA undercover?"

"Yes, but first you go through your training at The Farm."

"And after that?"

"After that, you're a CIA operative and a liaison between us and the agency."

"So, I'll be CIA and working with your little group at the same time."

"You got it."

"Which gives you an inside man." Chuck always knew his father to have a plan-behind-the-plan.

"You could put it that way. But let's not get ahead of ourselves. First comes The Farm and I think the gradual adjustment will be a good thing because I know you've been struggling with doubts about this so-called war."

"I never said that."

"You didn't have to ... it's written all over your face. Besides, if anyone gets it, it's me. You don't think I have my own demons?"

"Your demons? Ya' mean from your service?"

"You might say that ... among other things. The company wasn't always right when they had me kill people and I will have to live with that the rest of my life. But this is our chance for redemption."

And there it was. It was like his father had wrapped up all his fears and feelings into one word. *He must know I've killed a lot of people who probably didn't deserve to die,* Chuck thought. He desperately tried to poke holes in Don's argument, but the more he tried, the more he recognized that he could be right. Finally, his conscious-inner voice confirmed what his sub-conscious had already concluded: that he was right. *Redemption,* he suddenly realized, *that's what I need.*

"It's what we both want isn't it?" Don said, almost as if he read Chuck's mind, "To redeem ourselves from our past sins and we can only do that by sparing the innocent and killing only the really bad guys who need to be killed to save other lives in the future."

"I take it you weren't really on the back-lines back then were you?"

"Not exactly."

"And Jack?"

"You might say we were ghosts over here back then."

"And that's how Jack got the helicopter in Garmser?"

"What's a Garmser and what helicopter?" said Don with an uncharacteristic grin.

Suddenly, without knowing why, Chuck's mind flashed back to the sign he had found with the familiar name on it and it hit him. *Al-Haj Hussein* was the same name as on the napkin he found in his parents' garage that was part of *The Book*. "So, you and Jack were spooks together over here," he said, trying to piece together the realization that Don must have written *The Book*, "Did ya' ever eat at a restaurant in Raqqa?"

"As a matter of fact, we did," Don said, again with a wry half-smile, as they returned to Captain Johnson's office, "Why dya' ask?"

"What was the name of it?" Chuck persisted.

"Jack, what was the name of that place we used to eat at in Raqqa?" Don yelled across the room.

"Al-Haj Hussein," Jack answered casually.

"So, you crossed the border and went all the way over to Syria just to eat."

"That and a few other things," Jack said, "But it wasn't much of a border then. A good four-wheeler would get you where you wanted to go."

"Were those *other things* informants by chance?"

"Many of 'em ... yes," Jack answered, "Most of 'em were pretty unreliable, but every now and then we'd get one who actually knew somethin' and it led to some serious carnage."

"Yeah," said Don, "One of 'em actually tipped us off to the chlorine barrel bombs Assad was using on his own people. Of course that had more PR value than anything."

"Well, it sounds like you had a lot better snitches than we have."

"Sometimes, but not all the time. But why do you want to know about that son?" Don asked with a knowing smirk.

"I saw what was left of the place when I was there."

"Figures that we would bomb the crap out of the one and only joint with decent food in that hell-hole," Don said, not wanting to push it, "We told 'em to stay away from it and that the intel we got there was a lot more valuable than a bombed-out building."

"Just admit it man! You can't live with the thought of never eating their shawarma again," Jack chided Don.

"You got that right. Screw the informants ... but oh, that shawarma. It was heavenly," he wailed, licking his lips and staring off into space.

"And the Fatah," Jack said, rolling his eyes and rubbing his stomach.

"But how did you know we ate there?" asked Don, again with the smile.

"I found an old placemat from the place in our garage and it had some strange writing on it. Then seeing the sign on the ground in Raqqa, it didn't take much to put two and two together."

"Good detective work my boy," Don said with irony in his voice.

"So, all those times you were on your journalism assignments when I was growing up," Chuck said, not wanting to bring up *The Book* in front of everyone, "You were really *on assignment*?"

"You could say that," Don answered.

"Did mom know?"

"She had an inkling but she knew I couldn't talk about it."

Then Jack piped in with, "Yeah, when I came back, your dad asked me to look out for you while you were over here."

Now it all made sense. His chance meeting with Jack and all the times he had missed getting killed by inches.

"But wait," Jack said, "There's another member of our little group that you must meet," as Jasnine Ahmed walked into the room. She had showered and cleaned up and looked gorgeous even with a few bandages on her face.

"Archeologist huh," Chuck said, looking her up and down.

"Oh, I am that," she answered, "But I also have a side job."

"Does your side job happen to have three initials in it?"

"Maybe," she said, glancing over at Jack.

"Dinosaur bones ay?" said Don, "Interesting cover."

"Who says it was a cover," said Jasnine, tossing back her glistening, black hair and smiling.

"Were they real?" Don asked.

"And can I ask where you put the homing device?" asked Chuck.

"Both good questions," Jasnine said with a laugh, "But they're mysteries best left unsolved."

At that moment, Chuck saw a glance between his father and Jasnine that told a story he didn't think he wanted to hear. *Something went on there*, he thought.

"Not to beat a dead horse," Chuck said, turning to Jack and his father, "But are we completely done with ISIS?"

"Not by a long-shot," said Don, "ISIS offshoots have cropped up all over in places like Egypt, Libya, Somalia, and The Philippines, not to mention Afghanistan. Hell, last year ISIS told its followers in other countries to stay home and launch terrorist attacks there instead of joining them over here. Believe me, they'll be keepin' their guerrilla campaigns going around the world."

"Yeah," said Jack, "And that's not including the thousands who've trained at terrorist training camps over here and then gone home to do the attacking. We figure that they've gone back to about 33 of their home countries.

"On top of that," said Don, "The FBI and NSA have over a thousand investigations of domestic terrorists going on right now in the United States alone and they can't do 'em all themselves."

"That's where we might come in," said Jack, "But we also might help in some of the other countries."

"That's about it son. Now all that's left is for you to make up your mind."

The minutes clicked by with Chuck looking from face-to-face and then gazing down at the floor. Everyone in the room understood his apprehension and patiently awaited his answer.

Finally, always a man of few words, he said simply, "I'm in."

"Good choice," Don said as they all breathed a sigh of relief.

"Take care of yer' old man," said Captain Johnson as he shook Chuck's hand and looked at his father, "And you, keep this one outta' trouble ... if you know what I mean."

"I do ... and you got it Sam," said Don as they all filed out of the office and headed for the tarmac where a helicopter was waiting to take them to Balad Air Force Base.

As they lifted off, Chuck looked down to see all of the Dogs below standing at attention and saluting him. *Figures*, he thought, *that they wouldn't obey orders*. He knew he would miss his band of brothers and hoped they would all survive the war without him instead of in spite of him. The chopper flew them to Balad where a private jet awaited them.

When they got settled in on the plane, Chuck looked at his father and asked, "Why dad?"

"It's simple son. When I lost yer' mom I lost everything that meant anything to me ... except you. Life was meaningless and I'm sorry I couldn't do anything for you back then. But, when Jack called and offered me a chance to spend some quality time with my boy and do something good in the process, I thought maybe I could make up for some of that."

"Don't call me boy dad."

"Oh yeah, sorry lieutenant sir. But the question you gotta' ask yourself is do I wanna' be a blind fool of fate and a slave of circumstance or do I want to forge my own destiny?"

That did it. Now Chuck knew for certain who wrote *The Book.* "It was you wasn't it," he said with a sense of certainty in his voice.

"What was me?"

"You wrote this stuff," he said, pulling a sheet of paper from his rucksack and handing it to him.

Don looked at it with no surprise on his face. "What gave me away?" he asked.

"Who else would quote *The Spell of the Yukon?*"

"Ya' got me. I knew you found it. Why did it take ya' so long to bring it up?"

"Because I wasn't sure until now that you wrote it. A lot of it doesn't sound like you."

"There's a lot you don't know about me."

"But did you really write that happiness is a warm, fluffy towel?"

"I'm afraid I did, but that was a long time ago. Nowadays, my only happiness is the absence of pain."

"Now *that* sounds more like you. So, you must've written that Prophecy might be the program you were waiting for. How did ya' know about it way back then?"

With the faraway look returning to Don's face, he stared off into space and said dreamily, "Someone told me it was comin' a long ago and I guess it's here now." Then, it was back to the cold glare and he said, "But enough of the twenty questions. We'll have plenty of time later to walk down memory lane."

"Okay. But one more thing," Chuck said with memory connections now flooding his brain, "Did you have anything to do with Mike's drug dealers dying back then?"

Don's eyes narrowed to a deadpan glare at the painful memory as he said, "Well ... if I did ... it probably saved quite a few lives even though we couldn't save your brother."

"So, is that a yes?" Chuck asked thinking he saw a tear forming in his father's eye.

"Not sayin' that. But whoever it was, did the world a favor."

Seeing that he wasn't going to get an answer on that one and wanting to change the subject anyway, Chuck blurted out slowly, "Okay, dad, but you and Tom ... really?"

"War makes strange bedfellows son. But once you get past all his cosmic crap, he's better than any special forces soldier I ever worked with. He may just have a little too much of a moral conscience. But that's enough of the pop quiz for now. We can talk more about our personal stuff later. Right now, I'm just damn glad to see ya' son."

"Me too dad," said Chuck as he sat back in his seat contemplating his new team and his new mission, whatever it was. All he got from his father was that they were going after the real bad guys and he hoped he was right. *It's so hard to know who they are and who they're not*, he thought.

Again, as if he read his mind, Don said, "I know what yer' thinkin' son. How do we know who the real bad guys are?"

"That's exactly what I was thinking," said Chuck.

"That's where the computer geek comes in. Basically, the real bad guys are the ones controlling and financing the lower-level guys you've been fighting and Jacobs is gonna' find 'em for us. You can fight these little guys all day long and not make any difference."

"Who are these big, bad guys anyway?"

"Well, our trillionaire patron for one ... at least he used to be, until he got religion, that is. Now he wants to make up for his past sins by fighting the good fight with his information on these guys and we're his army."

"Who're the rest of 'em?"

"They're the ones who start wars and disasters like famines and disease epidemics for profit. Probably a buncha' rich ass-holes who're tryin' to get more power and wealth for themselves. That's all they know and when you get to their level, that's all you got left."

"The conspiracy theory about the seven men who run the world?"

"Apparently, it's not that simple. For one thing, there're a lot more than seven and for another, they don't all work together."

"What do they do then?"

"Don't really know, but it looks like some of 'em kind of compete with each other to see who can get the most power."

"How're we gonna' find 'em?"

"That's what Prophecy is supposed to tell us. Remember, it predicts the future and when Jacobs finds some big injustice being done to the masses, he traces it back to whoever caused it and we go to work to stop them."

"Sounds like science-fiction."

"It does. But if it works … it works."

"So, he's gonna' help us find 'em?"

"That's the plan. They usually stay in the background, but you can't get that rich without leaving some kind of paper trail. Catching them, though, is not that easy because these clowns are a whole different breed of cat."

"How so?"

"They believe they're above the law and they don't play by the same rules as us. That makes 'em hard to take down."

"And that's our job, right?"

"Yup, and hopefully we save some lives and help some people in the process. Then we get what we both want."

"Redemption?"

"Redemption."

"What do you need so much redemption for?"

"Probably same as you, but with a few twists."

"Like?"

"Like I killed a lot of bad people to save a lot of kids, but they may not all deserved to die."

"You just said they were bad."

"Yeah, but were they bad enough to die or should I have tried something other than murder. Besides, was it really my decision whether they should live or die?"

"I suppose only you can answer that one."

"Well, in the end it didn't matter anyway because I got caught and they offered me two options; go to prison or work for the CIA. I chose the latter as it seemed like the safer of the two."

"Was your name Dan or Don Forester back then?"

"Why would you ask that?"

"Because I found an old ID with your papers with your picture and the name Don or Dan Forester, I couldn't tell which."

"It was Dan … That used to be my name in another life. But I think some questions go better unanswered."

"Oh come on! You gotta' give me a little more than that."

"Well, I'll give you one tid-bit now and the rest later. Your dad was a good friend of mine and I knew you when you were just a tot."

"You never told me that!" Chuck said in complete amazement."

"You never asked," Don said coolly as he thought about how his ex-wife Jan had adopted Chuck after his dad, Jack, had died and then later died herself, which led to him adopting him.

"I guess I never thought about it."

Seeing that going nowhere, Chuck switched gears to Jack. How does ole' Jack feel about redemption?"

"He doesn't think he needs it. Or maybe he thinks he's beyond it ... I don't know. But, apparently, it's what our benefactor wants too."

"I guess it's what everyone wants," said Chuck, a little dejectedly. Staring out of the airplane window, he dreamily wondered what Don's other life was all about and pondered the next chapter of his own life at The Farm and beyond. As the big jet flew off into the puffy clouds, he could only imagine what was coming. But, whatever it was, he hoped his father was right and that his future wouldn't be a repeat of his past.

The End